RUMOURS OF RAGE AND REVENGE

CELIA RALK

Editor: Cat Jay PA & Authors Services
Proofreader: Messenger's Memos - Fiction Editing Service

First published in 2025 by Celia Ralk
ISBN 978-1-7635903-6-6 (paperback)
ISBN 978-1-7635903-5-9 (ebook)

CONTENT WARNING

Rumours of Rage and Revenge is an adult fantasy novel, the third instalment in the ***Crooked Crowns*** series and some content may be triggering for some readers.

This book contains

- Blood
- Violence
- Death (including the death of a minor)
- Funerals
- Explicit sexual content
- Somnophilia
- Voyeurism
- Manhandling
- Physical abuse
- Degradation/name calling
- Slapping
- Spitting
- Breath play
- Multiple partners
- Rituals involving cutting and blood sharing
- Homophobia
- Drug addiction and relapse
- And as always, coarse language

This book is intended for mature audiences.

If you are feeling distressed or need to talk, please reach out to your local services and supports.
Your mental health and wellbeing is important.

Rumours of Rage and Revenge has been written using the Australian English dictionary, so readers familiar with American English may find inconsistencies within the grammatical language. I, as the author, am Australian, so take that as you will.

Crooked Crowns is an LGBTQI+ friendly and inclusive (on page) series.

*For those of you who wanted a happy ending,
and for those of you who wanted devastation.
This book didn't heal me, but it set me on a
healing path. That doesn't come without a lot of
heartbreak and tears.*

Welcome to the end xo

RUMOURS OF RAGE AND REVENGE

GLOSSARY AND PRONOUNCIATION GUIDE

Elanist - El-ah-nist - The centre-most continent, home to Vequil fae.

Tirenas - *Ti*-reh-nas - The largest eastern continent, surrounded by few islands. Tirenas is home to predominantly Darsmun fae.

Morrin - More-in - The largest western continent, home to Resmigian fae.

Vequil - Ve-kwil – Those with an affinity for elemental magic. These fae reside in courts inspired and powered by one of the following elements; fire, water, earth, air or spirit.

Vequil Inalis - Ve-kwil In-*ah*-lis - These fae come from a dwindling heritage able to channel and draw power from each element, effectively being able to manipulate *all* elements. They are unable, however, to draw from the additional power a Vequil fae might have, specific to their court.

Darsmun - Darz-mun/mon - Fae with an affinity for solar magic. They reside in one of the two solar courts (day or night) and their affinities usually correlate to their home court. Those belonging to the night court tend to channel a gentler version, though both the Obsidian and Cerulean courts magic wielders have the ability to manipulate the mind and sight.

Resmigian - Res-*mee*-jan - Fae with an affinity for seasonal magic. They reside in one of the four seasonal courts (summer, autumn, winter, spring) and their affinities correlate to their home court. The magic of the Resmigian fae is predominantly passive. Traits specific to the Resmigian fae include slanted, upturned eyes and what one dwelling outside Morrin might consider abnormal height. For those with mixed heritage, carry-over identifiers include elongated fingers, longer necks or torsos, etc.

Soliqe - *So*-leek – Shifter fae who once had the ability to transform into any number of animals, people, objects, etc. depending on their origin both familiarly and geographically. Some bloodlines have diluted over the centuries, with majority of the shifter fae in Tirenas bearing wings and remaining in a state of partial shift where their wings are always there, though they cannot shift further in either direction. Telltale signs of a Soliqe fae are the longer, more sharply pointed ears than other fae. They hail from northern isles that no longer exist, and now the majority take up residency in Tirenas to work for the king. A Soliqe fae will also have increased hearing and sense of smell.

Daemdrana - Daym-drana - A dragon like creature bearing feathers as well as scales and who's wide, feathered tail can also spark flame, albeit less powerfully than their mouth.

Phoenix - A creature with the ability to be reborn after death.

Death's Daughters - Beings created for the sole purpose of maintaining the worlds karmic balance. They are not born, instead brought into the world via neutral magic, and are replaced when their bodies or minds are no longer fit for the task. Death's Daughters are the product of banshees and the three-headed goddess. With no moral compass of their own, they monitor the multitude of actions and choices, and their immediate and long term consequence to ensure within the battle between good and evil–the powerful and powerless–outcomes regress towards neutrality. No side shall eternally overpower the other, and no creature shall be allowed to overpower the deities.

A BRIEF GUIDE TO THE VEQUIL FAE

All Vequil fae, the race of fae native to the continent of Elanist, belong to one of the five courts. Once, Elanist was governed by the Golden Kingdom. While that is no longer the case, the land is still divided geographically by the court borders and continues to follow the naming conventions begun aeons ago.

Any Vequil fae whose powers have manifested are identifiable by the markings found on specific parts of their bodies, in tribute to the magic they possess. The court of a Vequil fae who has not yet manifested can be identified by their skin colouring.

COURT OF WAVE

Court of the water fae. These fae possess the ability to manipulate water in any form, along with the ability to heal. Water fae generally have wide eyes, round features, and a fair complexion. Many water fae have varying shades of blue undertones to their skin, or simply patches of skin that shimmer blue. All Vequil fae are marked by the power of their house, though universally among the courts those markings are the colour of ash. The water fae hold their intricate swirls along their throats, over their collarbones and under their chins, surging up like rolling waves. Water fae are the most placid and docile of all the Vequil fae, and are normally the first to attempt to defuse any unpleasant situation or hostile conversation.

COURT OF FLAME

Court of the fire fae. These fae control and wield flames at whim, along with the elements of fire. This might include bringing water quickly to the boil, conjuring a flame, burning someone without touching them, or even warming the surrounding air. Those belonging to the Court of Flame generally have hair that ranges from auburn to copper and the most common eye colouring is shades of brown and hazel. Their skin tone appears in shades of copper, rose gold, and rust. Fire fae are marked by raging tongues of ash-coloured flame, dancing around the sternum and ribs, and sometimes extending downward. Fire fae are the most antagonistic and easily offended of all the Vequil fae.

COURT OF SOIL

Court of the earth fae. These fae are able to manipulate the earth, be it the dirt, the trees, a flower, or a single leaf. Some have the ability to speak to animals or to shapeshift. However, the process is taxing and the occurrence of these abilities has dwindled throughout the ages. They are typically the shortest of the Vequil fae, though this is beneficial for those who can shift into an animal form as it makes the shift an easier process. Their skin tends towards various shades of brown or green. Those belonging to the Court of Soil have marks that run up their spines, shaped like vines or branches, or like the roots in the earth. Earth fae are the most excitable of the Vequil fae and absolutely abhor footwear.

COURT OF BREATH

Court of the air fae. These fae have the ability to manipulate the air to their will, whether to provide or remove. These fae are lethal, perhaps more so than any other Vequil fae, though they are also the most light-hearted and easy-going. Telltale signs of an air fae are the sharp facial features such as a pointed nose or high, angular cheekbones, and the silver tinge to their skin, eyes, or hair. Air fae bear marks along their hips and below their navels, with some even extending to wrap around to their spine. Like gusts of wind drawn by an abstract artist, some form tight coils and others flow like a soft breeze, the tendrils billowing gently around the skin. The Court of Breath is where the artists and visionists dwell. Air fae are the fastest of the Vequil fae.

COURT OF CANDOR

Court of the spirit fae. Their magic is connected to the spirituality of the individual as well as their surroundings, the ether. The Court of Candor was once a repository of the knowledge and history of the Vequil fae. The Court of Candor disappeared not long after the Golden Kingdom fell. Maps no longer mark the locations of the temples, libraries, or any of the spirit court. Instead, they show empty land. Fae from the Court of Candor don't typically have any obvious outward signs aside from the lack of other courts' traits and characteristics, and a slight violet shimmer to their skin. They have the ability to speak mind to mind, and to see the future in varying degrees of clarity or accuracy through waking visions, dreams, or nightmares. The Court of Candor's history is shrouded in shadows, though it is rumoured their charcoal markings climb from the nape of their necks and circle their scalp, fashioned almost like a scrolling ancient language. Spirit fae are generally the quietest, and most reserved of the Vequil fae, though have always held themselves with a sense of surety.

THE VEQUIL INALIS

Directly translated means *the original vequil*, meaning the very first of its kind. Something new. These fae have the unique ability to harness all elemental power, rather than being limited to only one. However, a Vequil Inalis may not draw on the additional strengths and attributes of a single-element fae. Where an air fae possesses increased speed, or the water fae are able to heal, a Vequil Inalis does not possess such power. They may only pull from the water, fire, earth and air, with the exception of intuition and other Candor related power. An Inalis can be identified by their multiple markings, though they bear no other telltale signs of heritage. The Vequil Inalis fae originated in royal blood, and while they are not limited to such bloodlines now, a royal Inalis will be far more powerful than their non-royal counterparts. Royal Inalises are uniquely identified by markings made not of charcoal, but gold.

CHAPTER ONE
CLARA

Clara woke from another restless sleep, trembling at the echo of fear. Her dreams overwhelmed her with dread and suffocated her lungs in a thick smoke, which taunted her all night. It had been occurring for weeks, seemingly at random. Some nights they were bright, leaving her eager to wake; to see the fae and Phoenix who danced with her subconscious mind in the flesh. To bask in the sunlight.

But some mornings she woke with lethargy as the intangible visions fled like fiends, feeling such frustration that she couldn't keep hold of them. Those nights were unpleasant, and on the days that followed Clara felt as though the universe dragged her about while she watched on.

Today, her chest felt tight and painful. Her eyes burned as they opened, her muscles aching in kind.

Clara let out a long, slow breath before she turned to her left. Isobel lay sound asleep on her belly, with the comforter barely covering her ass. Her petite body sprawled across her section of the mattress, her knee drawn up and pressed to Clara's thigh. One arm hung behind her, likely dangling off the edge of the bed, while the other was bent with her hand nestled under her porcelain cheek. Oh, how Clara loved waking to find herself tangled up in Isobel. It took away some of the dread and discomfort of the night before.

Clara gently eased stray locks of bright-pink hair away from Isobel's face. She was angelic, like the most reverent painting. With a barely there touch, Clara trailed her finger along Isobel's soft skin, over her shoulder and down the lines on her back. Along the charcoal-shaded marks that labelled her a wielder of Soil magic. She traced over the pointed and jagged lines, then moved to the other darker tattoos Isobel had inked into her skin. The mermaid with its tail that mimicked an opening flower bud, its elbows extended into thorn-like barbs, only bigger, more dangerous and far more deadly. Mermaids were vicious creatures with a penchant for dramatics and murder. Clara hoped she never got on the wrong side of the merfolk.

As Clara tried—and failed—to read the old language that was scrawled along various sections of Isobel's back, she also noticed the defined grooves and planes of muscle. Strength and power radiated from Isobel. Clara knew Isobel had worked hard, for stars knew how long, to hone her body into just as much of a weapon as her magic. Clara's mind wandered to thoughts of Isobel training. Of her gleaming with sweat and the beautiful, confident smile Isobel gave right before she bested her opponent. Clara couldn't help but smile, too, even as her stomach dipped, and a horde of butterflies flew rampant in the deepest parts of her.

Isobel stirred slightly and wriggled further into her pillow, so Clara let her hand rest on her stomach and turned her head to the other side. To Beau, where he remained asleep and oblivious.

Well, perhaps not entirely oblivious. Clara hadn't exactly been subtle of late. She noticed he often contemplated his words or held information back. Noticed his omissions and secrets. Since she'd gone to see Ora, something in the air had shifted. He knew something, and every day, he kept it from her.

But Clara was keeping secrets from him, too, so she let him have his. Let him wallow and worry; he would tell her when he was ready.

In her attempts to allow him space, Clara found she gave more of her time and attention to Isobel. She caught Beau's attention in doing so, but he kept his mouth shut on that front as well.

The early morning sun peaked through the half-drawn curtains, and Clara sighed. She knew she would not get any more sleep, and it took everything in her not to grumble out loud. Instead, she carefully slunk from the bed and silently dressed. Before slipping out of the bedroom, she scrawled a note and left it on her pillow.

I'm heading down to the bay. I'm sure someone will be there when I arrive. See you soon x

Sure enough, within a handful of paces from her house, Ryland fell into step beside her. He didn't say anything at first, only nodded in acknowledgement as he monitored their surroundings. She hadn't seen him since Elisabeth's funeral. A strange feeling burst in her stomach at the realisation, something akin to regret or perhaps guilt.

"How are you?" Clara asked tentatively, sparing him only a brief glance before she looked away.

"I'm fine," he answered quickly, though it wasn't short or snappy. "Thank you for asking."

Clara nodded, not entirely sure what to say next. Ryland had been friends with Elisabeth, possibly for longer than Clara had even existed. What could she say? Nothing helpful, not really, so she squeezed his hand briefly, then they continued their walk in silence.

Even though it was early, heat radiated from the rising sun. Summer was well on its way.

"Summer is coming . . ."

The voice trailed off in Clara's mind, as the vision from months ago haunted her. Fear prickled Clara's skin upon recalling the ethereal tone. Why couldn't she have exciting visions, or prophecies of good, hopeful things?

"Clara." Ryland pulled her from her uncomfortable memories. "As much as I enjoy your company, I am not here on a social visit."

"I'm not surprised." Clara offered a smile, and to her surprise, Ryland responded in kind.

"We need to discuss your coronation."

"Must we?"

"We must."

Before she could roll her eyes, whine, or attempt to get out of this conversation she did not wish to have, two familiar faces whirled past them.

"Holy smokes!" Oren called as he spun and smirked, then continued to walk backwards. "You're up early! Feeling okay, dear?"

Without missing a beat, Aleska smacked her brother's shoulder and hissed, "If you comment on it, she'll revert. Leave the woman be!"

Oren chuckled while Aleska winked at her, then she followed as her brother began setting up for the morning's training session.

"Clara," Ryland repeated. "This is important." Clara remained silent, but he continued anyway. "There isn't all that much fanfare, I assure you. We should go now, get it done, and you'll be home in time for lunch."

Ryland offered his hand, but Clara planted hers firmly on her hips and shook her head.

"Absolutely not," she said vehemently. "If I am not here when Beau and Isobel arrive, not only will I send them into a panic, but they'll murder me for it. We wait. There is no rush."

"Clara, your kingdom is currently without a ruler. It makes for a dangerous situation." The earlier patience left his tone with every word, though as always, he remained polite. Pushy, but polite.

"Why? Because someone might steal the throne?" Clara couldn't keep the exasperation out of her voice. Maybe it was the poor sleep, or her disinterest in the coronation itself. Either way, when Ryland answered, she immediately rolled her eyes.

"Yes, actually."

"Ryland, the vast majority of Elanist is unaware we even have a throne left. No one will claim it between now and sunset."

"You can only put it off for so long—"

"I do not regret to inform you, my friend, that I can put it off for as long as I like." Then with a sigh, she added, "But yes."

"So you'll do it today?" Pushy, indeed.

"Yes," Clara repeated, as Ryland nodded earnestly.

His shoulders dropped ever so slightly, and the lines around his eyebrows lessened. Some of his very noticeable anxiety seemed to ease.

"How's your training coming along anyway?"

"It's good." Clara nodded as she watched Oren and Aleska cover the refreshment table with bottled water and trays of fruit. Then Oren dumped a bag at his sister's feet and pulled out far more weapons than Clara would've expected. "I'm much more aware of myself when I move, and I'm closer to beating my opponents, I think. Though I don't know whether they're just letting me out of pity or to keep me motivated."

"She bit off my ear, so I tapped out for fear of what else she might bite off," Finch called as he brushed past us, offering a wave over his shoulder before he took an orange slice and stuffed it into his mouth—rind and all.

"I swallowed some of it too," Clara whispered with a shudder. But when Ryland chuckled, Clara easily followed suit.

"Come." Ryland gestured for her to follow him as he walked towards the water. "Show me how close you are."

Ryland rolled up his sleeves. His face was now expressionless—not negatively, simply blank and waiting, observant. Clara's palms were suddenly clammy, and butterflies danced under her ribs. She took a deep breath, shook out her arms and rolled her shoulders, then moved into position—feet shoulder width apart, stance open and diagonal for balance.

Ryland stood similarly, but more naturally. He'd been training far longer than she had, after all. It was to be expected; this was second nature to him. Still, she swallowed her sigh of envy.

Bouncing on her toes a few times, Clara quirked her mouth into a slight smile. Mere weeks ago, bouncing on her toes while preparing to strike, plus considering defensive manoeuvres and trying to stay ahead of an opponent would've had her rolling her ankle at the very least. Now, she stayed balanced.

Bracing her core and breathing steadily, Clara stayed upright. Pride flushed the back of her neck and warmed the butterflies still swarming in her chest.

Before she could move, Ryland darted forward. He almost caught her off-guard, but she hadn't stepped into the ring with him expecting a slow dance, nor an easy win. She'd expected him to use her naivety against her, or her slow reaction time.

For quite a while, Clara held him at bay. She even landed a kick to his thigh, which he responded to with a smirk. But then he grabbed her leg and spun her until she fell to the ground.

Immediately pushing back to her feet, Clara noticed how much longer it was taking for her to grow winded. Another twitch of her lips crossed her face.

But then Ryland feinted left, and Clara realised too late that his dart to the right was also misleading. He was quickly behind her, and even though she whipped around, his arm shot forward with his practice blade poised. Clara dodged, but his leg had slid between her own, hooking around her knee and swinging out to the side.

Clara collapsed in a heap of sweat and frustration.

"Not so close after all, I suppose," she huffed as she took Ryland's extended hand.

"Don't fret, Clara." His tone was much more relaxed than earlier. It soothed Clara's bruised ego, if only a fraction. "I've been doing this for many, many years. You'll need a bit more practice to beat me, I'm afraid." He clapped a hand on her shoulder. "But I am impressed."

Clara gave him an appreciative smile before they moved to the refreshments table. Sometime between when she started sparring with Ryland and now, Isobel and Beau had arrived and were now training as well.

Isobel flitted around Aleska, a dizzying kaleidoscope of pink, blue, and black. They met each other's strikes with such ease, both their faces beaming. More than anything, she looked at ease, happy to be sparring. It came to her so naturally. Like she was a dancer made of the most violent beauty.

Not to mention the charged energy circling her, haloing her being. It was hot and heavy, even from this distance. Clara couldn't take her eyes off Isobel. The butterflies in her chest settled, but a frenzy grew lower, in the deepest parts of her core.

Isobel was unapologetic and fierce. She was sleek and sharp, like Death's messenger.

The thought had Clara clamping her lips together, so she didn't let loose any lustful noises or charge over there and pull the female to her lips.

There was a conversation to be had with Beau before any of that could happen. One that absolutely terrified her.

What if he said no? And shut down the idea of including Isobel in their relationship more than he already had?

But what if he said yes? What if he was okay with expanding what they had together? With allowing Clara to explore her feelings for Isobel?

Clara didn't know how she would react to either answer, so she simply did not ask.

Fear was not something Clara succumbed to often, but when it sank its claws into her, she struggled to shake them free.

As if her thoughts of him summoned the Phoenix, Clara felt his gaze piercing her from where he'd paused his training with Oren. As she turned to face him, she watched as Oren swiped Beau's legs out and he fell flat on his back. It was almost comical how similar their losses had been.

She stared only long enough to watch Oren help Beau back to his feet, turning away as they began circling one another again and Isobel's victory laughter filled the bay. Clara couldn't help her adoring smile as her attention shifted back to Isobel.

Ryland spoke softly beside her. "Do you know what those tattoos say?" Clara shook her head, and within the next breath Ryland was speaking again, though she didn't take her eyes from Isobel. "The top one loosely translates to 'born from hell' or 'forged by hell.' The lower one directly translates to 'pain is power.'"

Clara looked towards him now, her brows drawn. "Are you fluent in the old language?" After finding out he was not, in fact, a scrawny little child, she'd never really thought about how old he was, but perhaps he could've been around when the old language was spoken.

"No, actually." The faintest hint of a scoff followed Ryland's answer. "I can read it well enough, but I cannot speak it as easily. I know what they say because I asked her."

"Was that all?" Clara sighed.

"You should ask her about them."

"For someone who constantly has fun facts to share, that was entirely unhelpful," Clara muttered as she dug her toes into the mismatched stones.

"I can't be perfect all the time, Clara." Ryland laughed, then drank from his bottle. But he didn't say anything more.

CHAPTER TWO
CLARA

Isobel stayed quiet while Clara explained their change in plans, but Beau asked more questions than Clara had answers to. Thankfully, Ryland was his informative self and provided the information she could not.

"If it's such a quick ceremony, why bother going back to the palace?"

"Because traditions must be upheld, and certain elements of the ceremony require it to be on royal grounds."

"Like what?" Beau folded his arms as he huffed.

Clara couldn't help rolling her eyes, nor the slight smirk of approval at how his biceps bulged. There may have been tension between them, but that was no reason for Clara to stop admiring him. He was stunning after all.

"Like an ancient silken scroll that will wrap around her wrists and bind her to her throne. It is as old as the Golden Kingdom itself. The names of every king and queen who have come before her are branded in the threads. It cannot leave the castle grounds, and Clara cannot be coronated without it."

Despite his usual patience wearing thin, Ryland kept a cool tone. His jaw was clenched, but otherwise he appeared calm.

Clara interrupted Beau's next question, sure Ryland would appreciate something slightly less accusatory. "Who is involved?" Clara patted Beau's thigh softly as his eyes flew to hers, her touch a silent request to let it go.

Whatever pent-up frustration he'd been letting out in this conversation seemed to dissipate. His face and shoulders relaxed, though his pursed lips remained. Clara left her hand on his thigh, and he shuffled ever so slightly towards her. The warmth radiating from him was a welcome sensation, despite the glaring sun above them signalling summer's impending arrival.

Clara only vaguely heard Ryland's response before another vision pulled her out of the present.

Striking blue eyes with swirls of teal fragments. So similar to the island seas.

Trinkets and beads weave through her fair hair, tinkling in the subtle breeze. They also decorate her body, wrapping around her fingers and toes, her wrists, and her ankles. They hang over her delicate collarbone and between full, golden breasts.

The female does not speak, her thin lips frozen. Words echo around her, chilling and damning all the same.

Solstice.

Strength.

Power.

Peak.

The Lady of Summer is coming.

"Clara," Ryland said, his voice stern and eyes full of concern. "Were you even listening?"

"No." She shook her head softly, not meeting his eyes. "Sorry."

"What did you see?" Beau asked, worry flooding his gaze as he searched her face.

"Something is coming on the summer solstice." Clara winced as she spoke, immediately realising this was bigger than a simple *something*. "Rather, someone. The 'Lady of Summer.'" She pulled her top lip back and scrunched her nose, unable to stop herself. "I fear it will not be beach bonfires and toasted treats under the stars this year. Her visit brings violence."

"Fucking fabulous," Beau said with a sigh, while Isobel took a slow, strained inhale.

"We can deal with it later," Clara added in a hushed tone.

Equally quiet, but far more urgently, Beau hissed back, "The solstice is in six weeks! Later is running out." The concern in his eyes spread to a muscle feathering in his jaw and drew his eyebrows closer together. Even his hands were stiff by his sides. But Clara had already turned her attention to Ryland.

"You need two representatives. One professional and one personal. No," Ryland paused and gave Beau a pointed look. "It cannot be Beau or Isobel." As he focused on Clara again, his expression softened, and his tone grew less exasperated. "Nor can it be your mother or brothers. Who would you like to choose?"

"You," she answered immediately. "You can be my professional representative, correct?" Ryland nodded, so Clara continued. "Can Maja be my personal representative? Granted, I've only met with the woman a handful of times, but I—"

Ryland smiled softly and held his hand up to halt her. "Yes," he said with a slight chuckle. "Maja will be fine. I'll have Samara prepare her to be ready on our return."

"Which will be when, exactly?" Isobel asked, her voice so gentle and entirely at odds with her earlier violence. The contrast was striking.

Beau had the same contrast. Some of the words to leave his mouth were the most tender words ever spoken to Clara, but he would then immediately follow them with the most brutal acts. He'd tell her something romantic while pulling another male's heart from his chest, she was sure.

With his nose turned up, Ryland muttered, "As soon as you lot have bathed."

Despite the heaviness in the air as it circled her and the prickling sensation along the soles of her feet, which she knew only meant trouble ahead, Clara laughed. Isobel's radiant smile sparked, as did Beau's trademark cocky grin. Ryland rolled his eyes, but the corners of his mouth rose as well.

Their arrival in the Golden Kingdom's throne room felt somewhat anticlimactic. Clara had expected a stronger wave of emotion to roll through her. Something to acknowledge the sister she'd never wanted, then finally warmed to, and subsequently killed. Or perhaps some feeling for the biological parents she knew stood here, likely many times. At the significance of what was about to transpire, how her life would undeniably change, and the responsibility that was about to be thrust onto her shoulders.

Instead, Clara felt next to nothing.

No fear, as evidenced by the quiet wind barely swaying the trees outside. The leaves rustled ever so slightly beyond the floor-to-ceiling windows set behind the dais. Nothing tickled her neck or pricked at her palms.

She felt no anger about the choice she did not get to make or the kingdom that was almost hers—not to mention the sheer number of folk who were to be her responsibility. But there was no excitement either, for all the possibilities that lay at her fingertips. She knew great things could come from ruling a kingdom, a continent. With Jude by her side, magnificent things were on the way. She felt it deep in her bones, certain in her soul. Wondrous things for both continents would happen under their rule, now only mere moments away from certainty.

Clara slowly walked towards the dais, taking in the pristine throne room and bright kingdom beyond with apathetic eyes. Today felt like any other day. It lacked any feeling at all.

She took a deep breath as she traced her fingers along the arm of the lone throne. Deep mahogany upholstered in cream velvet fabric, studded and lined with gold thread. The spiked back was so high, Isobel could sit on her shoulders and her head still wouldn't clear the top. How tall had the regents been who sat here before her?

Before she could ponder much else, footsteps echoed down the hall. Ryland entered, followed by a short female whose hair shone silver in the sun. She was slim, with slitted brown eyes and a round, rosy nose. For every step Ryland took, the female shuffled thrice to keep up.

Behind them were Isobel, Beau, and Maja. The latter smiled with what looked like pride, and a mixture of appreciation and relief. Clara's smile was genuine in return, and she dipped her chin in acknowledgement. Maja squeezed Isobel's hand and patted Beau's before they separated and she came to stand beside Clara. Beau and Isobel remained near the dais, but far enough to the side that she could not hear their whispered conversation. Although she'd not felt much at being in the throne room, or at her impending coronation, Clara's heart fluttered watching those two converse and behave like friends.

The female introduced herself as Pia, the officiant for the coronation. She first spoke a verse in the old language, offering a new soul to the throne and promising it would be sat upon with care. Clara was then prompted to acknowledge those who claimed the role before her and vowed—within the best of her abilities—to keep her kingdom safe and her subjects cared for. Then she sat on the throne for the first time for the binding.

Pia wrapped the sash around Clara's wrists three times—once around her dominant hand and twice circling her non-dominant. She murmured something about it being symbolic, that Clara was aware enough to know when to take strength from external sources. Truthfully, she heard little else after that point.

At first, the silk was cool to the touch, a pleasant contrast to the warmth outside, which poured through the windows at her back. Yet as the minutes ticked by, and with every word from Pia's mouth, the fabric heated until it neared uncomfortable. It took all her concentration not to grimace.

Clara ignored what Pia asked of Ryland or Maja, and their responses. Instead, all she could focus on was where the silk seared along her skin. Just when she thought it might be too much, and she was a second shy of pulling the damn thing off her wrists, Pia closed her eyes and laid her hands over Clara's.

Another zap of heat and power struck through Clara's bound joints and then the sensation dissipated entirely. Again, the fabric was cool against her skin, which she was certain was now burned. Looking down, Clara noticed writing on the silk that hadn't been visible before. Lines and lines of scrawled names, some in cursive and others printed, some even in the symbolic lettering of the old tongue.

Clarenna Afron Hayes was the last name visible, and for a second, Clara's eyes stung. She wasn't sure a royal had been in a position such as hers before, adopted yet somehow managing to find their way back to the throne. But seeing both of her names on the fabric filled her entire being with pride and a sense of comfort she hadn't realised she'd needed.

Directly above hers, she'd expected to see her biological mother's name, *Lenore Hayes*. But staring back at her was only the male Elisabeth had said was her grandfather, *Vaughn Hayes*, and beside him, *Cressida*, who Clara assumed was his wife.

"She'd be so proud of you, you know." Maja spoke softly as Pia unwound the cloth from Clara's hands before gently folding it again. It was as if she could read Clara's thoughts. "Your mother."

Clara looked to Maja, wanting to nod or make a noncommittal noise of agreement.

But before she could, Maja shook her head and smiled, somewhat sadly. "Lenore, I mean."

"I hope so," Clara muttered, and found as the words left her lips, she meant them more than she'd anticipated.

"Congratulations, Queen." Pia spoke with her head lowered and gave a subtle curtsy before excusing herself.

"Congratulations indeed, darling girl." Maja paused, almost contemplative, before she added, "Spoken with your father lately? Fintan?" Clara's brows pulled together as she shook her head. "No? Oh, no matter, I'm sure he'll have something to say eventually."

As seemed to be the theme of late, Ryland appeared beside her before she could respond.

"Right, to the first order of business," he said, just as Beau and Isobel joined them. The former gave a mockery of a bow, while Isobel smiled with subtle pride and dipped her chin. "You need your own personal guard, a protective unit, or whatever you want to call them. Your security needs to be solidified. I'll have contracts brought up from—"

"No, that won't be necessary." Clara cut him off both verbally and with a definitive gesture.

"Clara—"

"No, of course a queen requires security," she interrupted him a second time. "What I meant was, the soldiers will remain in their current positions. Those who were on Elisabeth's detail will maintain their employment. There are to be no changes." She paused, then added, "However, I will request that an additional unit report directly to you."

"Oh?" Ryland's brows rose, but his expression suggested he wasn't surprised at all.

"Oren, Aleska, Finch, Mikhail, and Keyne."

"Clara." His tone was immediately cautious. "None of these individuals are qualified for the role."

"And how would you know?" Clara countered. "You've exchanged fewer words with them than I have fingers."

"None of them have military background or training. This is important."

"No, this is my decision." Clara planted her hands firmly on her hips. "Each of them is more than capable, and more importantly, I trust them. See to it that any additional training they require is provided." She raised a single brow in challenge, but Ryland shrugged and conceded.

"As you wish, Queen."

A smug grin threatened to bloom, though it turned into a half-assed scowl when she looked to Beau and found him trying to cover his amusement. Trying and failing. Instead of acknowledging him, she turned back to Ryland.

"When you consider our first conversation however many months ago," Clara said, as she looped her hand around Ryland's elbow and they left the throne room, "did you expect this? I mean, you all but told me you suck dick and that my impressive rack didn't do it for you."

"Clara!" Isobel gasped, the sound so pure Clara couldn't hold back her chuckle.

"Must you be so crude?" Ryland winced, but Clara didn't miss the smile that followed.

"I must," she replied with a shrug.

Ryland sighed and shook his head. "Yes, well, I stand by my statements."

Later that night, the sound of the crashing waves lulled Clara to sleep, but it soon morphed into choked sobs. By morning, the only thing she remembered was a woman crying, barely able to breathe. She woke shivering, covered in a layer of sweat, but grateful that the moonlight allowed her to see the rise and fall of Isobel and Beau's chests beside her. Her sigh of relief had never felt so heavy.

CHAPTER THREE
CLARA

Only half awake, Clara rolled onto her side. Stretching her arm out, she expected to feel a warm, toned body, but instead, her hand fell onto cool sheets. Panic lanced through her, and she shot upright, blinking furiously at the light. The cries from her nightmares echoed painfully in her ears but eased into a dull background noise as her eyes settled on the winged figure at the end of her bed.

Sunlight reflected off his golden wings so beautifully that for a second she forgot why she was worried at all.

"What are you doing?" she whispered, her tone still slurred from sleep.

"Dressing?" Beau slipped his second leg into his trousers, pulled on boots, then sat to lace and buckle them. He looked at her and raised an eyebrow, to which she rolled her eyes.

"I gathered that much, thank you, sir."

A devilish smirk danced across his face as his gaze raked over her. From her wild hair to her exposed breasts, and then further despite the comforter gathered around her waist. Beau winked, then refocused on his shoes.

"Why are you dressing so early? Where are you going?" Clara pressed.

"I'm heading down to the bay," he answered as he stood. "But I did not want to wake you."

Isobel stirred beside Clara as Beau walked towards her quietly, then lowered to kiss her forehead. The action sent a flurry of butterflies throughout her entire torso.

"I'll be training until lunch."

Clara nodded as Isobel yawned and pressed up onto her elbows.

Beau looked like he wanted to say something more. He even opened his mouth twice before thinking better of it. Instead, he gave Clara a mocking salute, his expression as coy as ever, before he nodded in acknowledgement towards Isobel. She gave a pathetic excuse for a wave in return, and then he was gone.

"And what's on for you today?" Clara asked Isobel, though she knew she wouldn't get a proper answer.

Isobel mumbled an incoherent response, stretched, attempted to answer a second time, then finally sat up. She rubbed her eyes with her fists. It was easily one of the most adorable things Clara had ever seen her do. She took a deep breath and muttered her reply. "Poppy—Samara—witch hunting."

Clara couldn't help the laughter that burst from her.

"You're continuing your search for the witches, you mean?"

Isobel hummed in agreement. "That's what I said."

"Are they coming here?" Clara asked as she stood from the bed and shuffled towards the wardrobe.

Again, Isobel hummed a response. Neither Clara nor Isobel were morning folk. But where Clara was grumpy and unapproachable if woken, Isobel was simply incoherent, and quite frankly, not awake for a while after she rose. So, the fewer questions, the better.

"I'm working this morning and then catching up with Seren afterwards, so I won't be of any help." Clara slipped into a simple dress, turning to find Isobel's jaw slack and her eyes glued to Clara's body. She smirked as she reached for the cardigan on her side table as she continued. "Otherwise, I'd have offered to help. Don't forget, they're in Morrin—where, I'm unsure, but there nonetheless."

Isobel nodded, and Clara reached down to cup her chin, warmth tugging at her chest. One day, she'd reach over, grab Isobel's face and kiss her with the heat of a thousand suns and the intensity of as many moons. But today, she simply sighed, smiled, and left.

Clara flipped the old wooden sign on the door of the bakery, signalling it was closed. Walking back inside, she found Mikhail staring out the window—at what, Clara was unsure. She thought nothing of it and continued her duties.

In the middle of wiping one of the display windows, a thud followed by a groan startled her. She whipped around to see Mikhail with his hand to his forehead and a wince clouding his face.

"Are you alright?" Clara asked, but the normally cheerful male barely gave her a smile in return.

He sighed, rubbed his head, then jerked his chin towards the window.

This time when Clara looked out, she saw Seren on the other side of the road. She smiled at passersby, but otherwise appeared to just be waiting for Clara.

"She makes me nervous," Mikhail muttered. Clara burst into laughter, her gaze flicking between her two friends.

As her laughter subsided, Clara couldn't decide whether to be mocking or sincere. "I don't think I have a retort for that, honestly."

"Mother, she's beautiful," he whispered, though Clara couldn't determine if he was speaking to her or himself.

"My brother certainly thinks so," Clara said and folded her arms across her chest.

An odd feeling spread through her, something unfamiliar. Hot, but not like her usual warmth of passion or fire of rage. Mikhail had a kind soul and a gentle heart. He was not so hard to look at either. He was strong, powerful, and considerate, always upbeat and approachable.

He deserved someone who could appreciate all the wonderful things about him and love him as much as he would certainly love them. Someone who he made nervous, and who blushed and walked into walls because they simply couldn't look away.

Except that someone wasn't standing across the street. It was not her brother's partner. Perhaps in a different time, if she weren't involved with Evian. But she was, so Seren was off limits.

Mikhail cleared his throat, nodded, and turned away.

The heat in Clara's chest turned to stone and plummeted through her body. Guilt ate at her, and thinking about it was giving her a headache.

"Mikhail!" she called with a sigh. When he wandered slowly back out front, she gave him a soft smile. "You buckle for no one, you hear me? I don't care how pretty they are, or how sweet. Know your worth, then find someone who believes it to be double that."

"It is a crush, Clara." Mikhail rolled his eyes as he closed the gap between them and wrapped her in a sideways hug. "Allow me my nerves, will you?"

"Only for today," Clara conceded. "As consolation for smacking that enormous head of yours into the wall."

He laughed, and some of the rottenness dissipated from her body.

"Go," he said, as he all but shoved her towards the door. "I'll finish up."

"I don't mind staying, truly."

Mikhail shook his head and shooed her again.

"I'll find you someone to deal with that crush of yours," Clara whispered, pointing a finger at him as she hung in the doorway. "As a thank you for all the dishes I haven't done. Bye!"

As she flitted out, his only response was a chuckle that was smothered by the closing door.

Clara jogged across the road to where Seren stood with eyebrows raised.

"Is that what you wore to work? Surely it's a health and safety concern." She folded her arms and shook her head but couldn't quite force the smile from her lips.

"I was on the counter today," Clara replied as she shrugged a shoulder. "No actual baking."

Seren smirked and looped her arm through Clara's, using it to drag her along the footpath towards the dining quarter. After a short stroll and a lengthy pause outside a flower shop, they sat under the patio of a tea shop. Come sundown it would turn into a bar, but for now it was the perfect spot for an afternoon catch-up under the gentle sun.

"Are you excited for Evian to come home tomorrow?" Clara asked as she sipped her water and briefly scanned the menu.

"Do you really need to ask?" Seren countered in an exaggerated tone. "I can't wait. I know it's only been a few weeks, but it feels like forever since I've seen the oaf."

Clara cackled, grateful she'd already swallowed her drink.

"So ladylike," Seren chided with a snort.

"Likewise."

They spoke for hours—laughed and reconnected for the first real time in over a year. Since before she'd met Beau and Neven, been taken to Tirenas. Before everything changed. As if Clara's thoughts of her Phoenix had cast him into Seren's mind, she cleared her throat and sat forward, leaning on her elbows.

"So," she drawled. "How is Beau?"

"You know, his smarmy, charming self. As always." Clara sighed and sipped her tea.

"Go on," Seren pressed.

"I love him with my entire heart," Clara started, but paused, contemplating how exactly to phrase what she wanted to say. "I love him . . . but I don't think I love *only* him."

Patiently, Seren sat in silence while Clara took her time explaining her current dynamic. She stared into Beau's eyes and found a powerful love and adoration staring back at her. Beau felt like home and adventure wrapped up in a devilishly handsome package.

But also, when she turned around to see Isobel standing beside her, suddenly she felt seen and heard and understood in a way that was so peaceful, turning away felt criminal. Felt like it shouldn't be an option.

She felt her heart and soul break at the thought of having to choose only one of them. There was no right answer and no good outcome. The idea sent chills down her spine, ice to the very bone. Left her nauseous and in pain.

Yet truthfully, if a blade was held to her throat, she knew who she would choose. But oh, how it would shatter her to.

She explained how Beau held her heart so fiercely, and he was so delicate and protective with it. Her heart was his—entirely. But her soul belonged to Isobel. They were entwined, and looped, and bound in the most magical of ways.

There wasn't a doubt in her mind that Isobel was her tetherbond, and the thought both thrilled and terrified Clara.

At the end of her ramblings, Clara groaned and dropped her head to the table.

"Oh yes, quite the pickle you've found yourself in, dear." Seren scoffed, though it was a light-hearted sound. "You've managed to find the other half of your soul and the keeper of your heart in the one lifetime. Poor you."

"But what do I do if they do not wish to share this lifetime with each other? With me, sure, but Isobel fancies women, and Beau is not fond of sharing. Showing me off, perhaps, but not sharing. I'm frightened to even bring up the discussion with either of them, in case I end up losing them both."

"The fates would not have brought the three of you together just so you could part ways. Do you know how rare it is to receive both? Your stars-determined soulmate and your consciously decided love?"

"The fates could very well take them away from me. The universe is not kind by default, nor does it care for anyone's success. We both know the world is harsh and unforgiving." Clara let out a rough, frustrated breath as she untied her hair and ran her hands through the wild mess. "Seren, what am I to do?"

"You know," she replied, and leant back in her seat. "Your brother begged me for what felt like an eternity just for a date. I fought myself for months, making myself sick with worry about how you might feel. What you would say, and how you would react.

"One night I got drunk, stumbled to your house, and apparently agreed to go to dinner with him. I don't even remember the conversation, just his teasing the next morning about me 'finally listening to my heart' and how it led me to him. Your brother is far too confident for his own good." She raised her brows and pointed a finger at Clara, who levelled a flat stare in return. Clara needed no reminder.

"I'm luckier for it though, that drunken night. Evian treats me well, and he makes me happy. He makes me feel special, like I'm the only one in the world who matters. He's everything I've ever wanted and more. Perhaps you should just drink yourself silly and see whose arms you stumble into?"

Peals of laughter floated between them, and Clara felt lighter. She'd missed this.

"The last time I got drunk and stumbled into someone's arms, Beau found me, scared Tomas away, and threatened to spank me if I asked him nicely."

Seren gasped as her hand flew to cover her open mouth.

"Oh, poor Tomas." Then her expression turned far more challenging. "Did you?"

Clara winked, and with a coy smile replied, "No." Her smile faded as she realised how much had changed since then. How much closer they'd grown, but were now separated again by secrets. "He's been keeping something from me."

Seren gave a contemplative look before she answered. "But do you trust him? Even a little?"

"With my life," Clara answered immediately. She exhaled slowly and looked away, then added, "Now, anyway . . ." A barely there chuckle escaped her, though at this point she wasn't entirely sure why.

"Then let him tell you when he's ready." Seren shrugged before taking a sip from her cup.

"Is that what you would do?"

"Of course, I trust your brother entirely."

Clara's brows shot up as she shook her head. "You put a lot of faith in a male who frequently puts his trousers on incorrectly in the morning."

"Eh," Seren said lazily and shrugged. "So he's not a morning person. Neither are you, princess." Seren winked and grinned.

Clara was hit with a wave of discomfort, perhaps even distrust, which was not a pleasant emotion. Ryland hadn't told her she *couldn't* mention the coronation or the Golden Kingdom, but Clara knew it wasn't for general conversation. A very annoying, very uncomfortable voice in the back of her mind reminded her of the reason she'd not seen her best friend in so long. It was because Clara hadn't trusted her.

So Clara didn't tell her she was in fact now a queen. Didn't tell the woman she'd grown up with and played pretend princess games with since before she could remember that it was now a reality for her.

She didn't tell Seren anything.

All she did was shrug, then gave a convincingly casual smile and drawled, "Family, what can I say?"

CHAPTER FOUR
EVIAN

Evian paused at the gates of the Cerulean Castle, inhaled a deep breath and clenched and released his fists. The last he'd seen of their queen, she'd been thanking Seren and her brother for their participation in Princess Solaris' funeral. No one had expected such a gesture, but Eveline knocked so forcefully on their door and then spoke so gently all anyone could do was stare and nod.

Now, he stood in her kingdom, soon to be entirely at her mercy.

Fear ricocheted along his spine, his collar felt too tight, and his shirt too thick. He wanted to make a good impression, and for this trip to be a success. He *needed* this to go well.

Without even noticing, Evian's legs moved forward, and before he knew it, he stood at the throne room doors. Though many fae noticed him, some stared with expressions of concern or apprehension. Others skirted closer to him and followed as he wandered through the halls. Only one stopped to ask where he was headed, and thankfully, was kind enough to point him in the right direction. Evian doubted he'd experience much more of that on Tirenas soil.

With a shaking hand, he knocked three times. The sound surprisingly echoed in the already busy corridor, bouncing off the tiles, the marble walls, even the breastplates of armoured guards. A second later, a winged male in a soldier's uniform opened the door and dragged his charcoal gaze over him with a raised eyebrow.

"My name is Evian Afron. I'd like to request an audience with your queen."

The soldier huffed a laugh, then stepped aside to allow Evian entry.

"Afron, you said?" She spoke in a voice as smooth as crystal. Her dark hair glowed in the morning sun, hazel eyes captivating him even from this distance. Evian was entranced, so much so he almost forgot to answer.

He cleared his throat. "Yes, ma'am. Evian Afron."

"How is your sister?"

Evian didn't miss the slight upturn of her lip at the mention of Clara. "Well, thank you for asking." He also couldn't help the casual grin that spread over his face, having such a normal and almost natural conversation with the queen.

She huffed and turned back to the documents in her lap.

"Majesty?" Evian called as he stepped closer to the dais where she sat. She looked up then, a delicate brow arched, her rosy lips pressed together. "I'd like to inquire about joining your ranks."

"And what is it you would like to inquire about exactly?" Eveline stood then, and took a slow, calculated step down from the dais towards him.

"How one might go about such a thing," he said, then immediately felt stupid. He couldn't help it. The midnight beauty made him nervous in the most invigorating sort of way. Both exciting and alluring.

The corners of her lips twitched, though she said nothing further.

"I would like to become a soldier. One of yours specifically."

Eveline hummed in contemplation as her head cocked slightly, and for a moment that felt like eternity, she simply stared at him. Though there was nothing simple about the way she gazed into the deepest part of him, all the way into his soul.

"Yldes," she called as she clicked her fingers, eyes never leaving Evian. "Take him to the barracks. Sort out a bunk and a uniform, consider him your fledgling. You have two weeks, Afron. Make it through that, and I'll consider your application."

Once she turned away, Evian could breathe again. He smiled to himself, because it was clear no one else cared. Evian muttered his thanks, and gripping the strap of his duffel bag a little tighter, he scrambled to follow Yldes who had already begun walking out the door.

His first day of training went smoothly. Although truth be told, there was no actual training involved. First, Yldes took him to a storeroom to find a uniform. It included thin cotton attire with reinforced elbows, knees, and crotch areas, which Evian assumed were for sparring and practice sessions. Then there was a full set of leather-and-wool clothing, much more difficult to get into but definitely secure. He was told that this would be his standard attire while on probation. Finally, he was given armour plates and weaponry holsters, dented and marred from previous use. Yldes had said he wouldn't need his own yet, so the items that mostly fit him would suffice for now. If he made it past the fortnight, he'd be measured and his personal wardrobe would be provided.

Then he'd had a tour of the barracks and castle grounds and been introduced to his bunkmate, those sharing his dorm, his chain of command, and those to contact if for some reason he couldn't get a hold of his chain. Privates, corporals, sergeants. Officers and captains had been named, but no in-person meetings had taken place.

After what felt like a million handshakes later, and almost the entire day, Yldes finally took him to the mess for dinner. Evian wasn't sure if the male liked his company all that much, but he was grateful for the silence he offered. In between rules, orders, and explanations anyway.

Yldes didn't join Evian, instead leaving to get some training in before bed. Evian didn't mind; actually, he preferred it.

This way, he was able to take his tray of food—piled with a double serve—out of the mess, across the lawn, and into the castle. By some miracle, he remembered the way to Eveline's suite on the first try. He knocked on her door but didn't wait for her to answer. Pushing the door open gently, Evian announced himself and waltzed on in, a lazily confident grin spread across his face.

"Excuse you!" Eveline hissed as she stood, her hands crossed immediately.

Evian shrugged a shoulder. "I was raised by feeders and healers, Majesty. It's so deeply ingrained in me, I simply could not help myself."

The queen scoffed, then stepped to the side to reveal the table she'd been seated at prior to Evian's arrival. It was covered in papers and inkpots, as well as a much fancier silver tray than his own, which was already empty. A cloth napkin was draped over most of it, but he still saw the cleared plate with very few crumbs and neatly placed cutlery.

Evian sighed, shrugged again, and moved towards the table. He carefully shuffled some of the documents around, placing the queen's tray on the floor at his feet, then his own tray on the table. Taking the open seat, he smirked up at her. "Ah well, I am famished."

After a few moments of Evian devouring a far more enjoyable meal than he'd anticipated, he felt Eveline's glare continue to burn down on him. The documents in her hand rustled as she planted both fists on her hips.

"If you cannot consume your meal with the proper etiquette and decorum of someone in the presence of a queen, perhaps you ought to find dining arrangements elsewhere."

Slowly, Evian finished his mouthful, maintaining his casual and cocky composure.

"Would you like me to leave?" he asked, and dabbed at his lower lip with a napkin.

For a moment she looked like she might rescind her suggestion. Truthfully, Evian had expected to be asked to leave much sooner than now. Her face went lax before she huffed, then ever so slightly shook her head and looked away.

Eveline returned to a frustratingly neutral expression, then shooed him out of the seat and towards the door.

Just before she could close it behind him, he turned to face her and whispered, "Next time, perhaps."

The next time he saw the queen, Evian was on his way to the mess. He, Yldes, and a few other soldiers had partnered up for rounds after sparring on the mats, finally calling it a night well after the moon had risen. The soldiers all bowed to their queen, as did Evian, though they were quick to carry on as she waved a dismissive hand towards them.

"Have you eaten this evening, Afron?" she asked, her words far less sharp than the last time she'd spoken to him. Evian assumed it was exhaustion on her part, especially considering the late hour. The slight sheen in her alluring hazel eyes only added to his assumptions.

"Not yet," Evian answered with a shrug and then clasped his hands behind his back.

"Perfect," Eveline drawled. "I have just the thing for you. Follow." She spun on her heel as she snapped her fingers. He followed her without hesitation.

The queen led him slowly down hallways and up staircases, her hips swishing and swaying her emerald-and-brown gown with every step. Evian was entranced. Before he knew it, Evian stood at the end of a four-poster bed. The cream-and-ivory-coloured linen was thrown hastily atop, and lace and frills sat in every direction.

Eveline stood before him, her dress now dropped to pool at her feet, her entire body naked. She stood so close he could smell the lavender in her hair, even as she pulled it over her shoulder and exposed her back to him. The sight robbed him of breath, so that for a moment he stood gaping like a fish, unsure of what to do or where to look.

Along her spine and down the backs of her thighs were patches of darker skin. Much like the colour of her father's, Evian had seen in portraits sporadically since arriving. It was such a beautiful contrast—rich umber to fair ivory. Truly magical.

Eveline turned around, raked her eyes over him so tantalisingly slowly, then smirked as she lay back upon the mattress. More dark skin spread across her hips, nearly symmetrical.

"Good thing you don't need to speak while feasting," she said, her tone low and sultry. The hairs all over Evian's body stood, his cock already aching at the sound and sight of her.

"My kind are coloured like that," he said when he finally found his voice. It came out husky and breathless as he closed the space between them and traced the outlines along her skin. "But it's because of their magic. You're coloured by the purest form of natural beauty, and I fear I cannot tear my eyes away."

Eveline parted her legs and arched her breasts up to him. A moan escaped his throat as she continued to spread her legs until she was fully bared to him. Evian knelt and dragged his hands up her thighs . . .

The violent burst of a horn woke him. Evian sat upright, his chest tight, his breaths coming fast. The ocean lapped at the side of the boat, and water sprayed up onto his window.

Relief washed over him as he realised he'd been asleep, and as he saw the shoreline of the Court of Flame on the horizon. Yet disappointment crept up his spine and flared behind his ribs as he remembered his dream.

Since that wasn't how his final interaction with the Queen of Tirenas had actually occurred. She'd bared herself to him, and while he had been captivated by her beauty and confidence, he'd turned her down.

Instead of dragging his hands along any part of her skin, he'd reached down for her dress and covered her with it. Evian apologised for the confusion and told her he was spoken for, and that he had no interest in climbing her ranks by any means other than his worth and honour.

Immediately, Eveline apologised, laughing hysterically while explaining she'd had a few too many wines. She told him his probation was over after only a week and a strictly professional position in her personal guard was his—if he still wanted it. He told her he would be honoured, dipped his chin, and left.

But every step he'd taken away from the queen was heavier than the last. The distance between them felt uncomfortable, and even though he tried to distract himself, his thoughts were consumed by her, despite having only sat with her twice. He was captivated, so completely and intensely enamoured that he didn't want to leave.

Somehow in the span of a week, his heart had attached itself to the daughter of a monster, and he didn't want to pry it away. Perhaps seeking her out wasn't totally about work.

In any case, he was indeed involved with Seren, and she had a right to know his feelings had shifted. He owed her that much.

Nerves bubbled and built until Evian was unable to sit still. The last moments of his journey home, both over water and on land, grew more and more painful as he closed the gap between a blissfully unaware lover and a broken-hearted female he'd never wished to hurt.

Evian dropped his bags in his room, then departed his quiet home. No one was there, and for some reason it left a heavy feeling in his gut. With a long sigh, he trudged down to his property line and continued towards Seren's house.

The sun had not set over Iloura as he wandered the cobblestone streets, so Evian had expected to see more folk along the way, yet no one passed him. He couldn't help but take that as a bad omen.

The curtains in the front sitting room of Seren's house rustled as he approached the door, and before he could even knock, she threw it open and flew towards him. Her small hands pressed firmly against his back, her arms encircling him tight.

She smelt the same, like saltwater and pine. It was a scent that had wrapped him in comfort and joy for the longest time, but now it only made the burn in his throat worse. Evian savoured it for a moment longer, breathing her in. He likely wouldn't get to again.

As he pulled away and Seren looked up, her face dropped, and fear filled her wide blue eyes. She took a step back and dropped her hands. He led her into the front sitting room, the bright sun dulled somewhat by the curtains. Silently, Evian gestured for Seren to sit, and she did so without question. Nerves coated her every expression and slightest movement. Evian was sure they dripped from him as well, but still he took a deep breath and told her he was ending their relationship.

He tried to be gentle. She deserved so much he could no longer give her, but kindness was something he would always extend. But no matter how tender he tried to be, hurt and rage contorted her face, tensing her body.

"Please don't be angry," he pleaded.

"I have every right to be angry!" Seren hissed as she stood, her arms flailing by her sides.

"I'm trying to do the right thing—"

"No, you're not," she interrupted with a scoff. "Certainly not very hard. I'm standing here feeling like my entire body is going to explode, and you did that. You took a part of me. I willingly gave part of myself to you, and you've shattered it with your selfishness." Her pointed finger did not touch him, but he felt the jab nonetheless. "One day we're proclaiming our love, and the next thing I know, you tell me you're leaving?"

"Please listen, let me just—"

"I don't want to listen." Her voice was soft, but not tender; it was cold and quiet. "I don't want to listen to your voice or how it might break when you tell me everything. I don't want to watch your face tell me something different from your words as you try to cover your emotions or figure out which parts of the story are necessary for me to know."

Evian's chest caved at the chill of her tone. He'd never heard her speak in such a way, and he hated that he'd been the one to bring this side out of her.

"I didn't plan for this," he murmured. "Seren, I did not intend it. I went to join their guard, and I saw her and I just—"

"Do not insult me by sharing your lustful thoughts and pining for *her*!"

"I'm sorry, this is not going how I wanted it to." Evian sighed as he shook his head and lowered his gaze.

"What did you want, Evian, for me to thank you? For me to congratulate you?" Seren let out a growl of frustration, then added much more quietly, "Please just go."

She was right. There was nothing left to say. Nothing more for him to do to fix this disaster.

He stood and walked towards the door. Evian moved to touch her hand, but she wrapped her arms around herself before he could reach her.

"I truly am sorry, Seren. And I did love you."

Walking away was painful, especially when he heard her cries. He knew she did not want him here, so as much as he wanted to comfort her, it wasn't his place anymore. Truthfully, he'd only make things worse.

Guilt spread like wildfire through his veins as excitement burst in his chest after he crossed the threshold into the street. He truly cared for Seren, and she would always hold a special place in his heart. Then a second wave of guilt washed over him as he realised it was not only excitement he felt, but relief.

Despite what she may think of him, he would never insult her by being unfaithful. It was a despicable act one simply should never do to someone they claimed to love. But now that his relationship with Seren was over, he was free to try for the queen's hand. What a queen might want with a water fae turned soldier, he wouldn't try to guess, but he was looking forward to finding out.

CHAPTER FIVE
CLARA

All thoughts of curling up on the settee after a gruelling shift evaporated once Clara entered the living room and found Evian sitting at the dining table. He stood as soon as he saw her and beamed, an expression she reciprocated.

"I didn't hear you come in," Clara said as he pulled her in for a tight embrace.

"You were asleep, sister." Evian kissed her temple and then released his hold. "Besides, I needed time to myself."

Clara only hummed in response, with high brows as she spun to pour herself a glass of water.

"She told you then," he muttered as he looked at his hands.

"Of course she did." Clara scoffed before taking a sip. "She was waiting outside the bakery when I arrived for work this morning. I'm disappointed I had to hear from her, though not entirely surprised."

Indeed, Seren had been standing by the door, her eyes red-rimmed and arms pulled tightly around her midsection. Clara hadn't felt entirely bad for Seren as she recounted the conversation she'd had with Evian the day before, though her heart ached to watch her friend in pain.

"I feel terrible."

"Because you think you made a mistake or because you hurt her?"

"The latter." Evian sighed loudly.

"Then do not feel bad, Evian. I've no doubt she'll have suitors lined up by the day's end." Clara placed the glass in the sink, then turned back to her brother. She couldn't help smirking as he scrunched his face in discomfort.

"That does not help."

"Is Eveline worth it, brother? Has she truly stolen your heart?"

"I didn't believe I could love anyone like I did Seren. With such intensity." He shook his head slowly, his eyes faraway, reliving the past. "Then I walked away from Eveline, and my heart broke in my chest."

Clara sighed before her tone grew serious. "If she hurts you, Evian, I will have another dead royal on my hands."

"You will do no such thing," he hissed, though there was no bite. "But you may offer some assistance."

Her eyebrows shot up, then drew together at the possibilities that swirled in her mind. "Oh?"

"I want to give her something—hold on." He gestured for her to wait, then bounded down the corridor to his room. After a moment of rustling, he strolled back to the table and handed Clara a long, narrow box.

Evian jerked his chin with an excited grin, so Clara opened the blue velvet box and found an ornate diamond necklace. It was simple and subtle, the opposite of what she would have expected him to give the queen.

"Where did you even get such a thing? You've only been home—"

Clara stands in the corner of the library, watching without being able to interact. Her voice makes no sound and her legs do not move. Evian hands a long blue velvet box to the queen of Tirenas. Smiles bloom on both their faces as she takes it eagerly. Before she can open it, the bookshelves rattle, and without enough time to do anything, the floor shakes so violently that Eveline falls. Clara is frozen, unable to help as the shelves collapse on the queen. Then the walls and ceiling cave, crashing over her brother.

In a blink, the stone, wood, and piles of rubble rise to reveal the queen, now dead, gift box still in hand.

Clara's heart rate spiked as she returned to the present. Her eyes darted between the necklace and her brother.

"Evian, do not give this to her," Clara warned and hoped it was enough. If he listened, she might prevent the scene from unfolding. Surely it would be enough.

"Is it so bad?" Evian asked, staring down at the glinting jewellery.

"It's beautiful, but please don't."

Her brother slouched, but his manner was far too nonchalant for the vision she had seen.

"I bought it for her, I can't—"

"Fucking stars, Evian! I'll give it to her if I must." Clara threw her hands up in frustration. Of all the times her brother could've been a stubborn twat, it had to be now, when something threatened them. She repeated, more sternly this time, "You must not hand this to the queen."

"No one is going to die if I give her a necklace, Clara." Evian rolled his eyes and ran a hand lazily through his hair.

"She will," Clara insisted. "And likely so will you."

Evian let out a long breath, searching Clara's eyes before turning away.

"No, Evian!" Clara said firmly. She slammed the velvet box to his chest before she continued, "You know what I can do, what I've *seen*. Please don't make me spell it out for you."

Her brother only held the jewellery box and waited in silence, his eyebrows raised. Clara groaned, then conceded.

"I do not know how or who will be involved beyond you and the queen, but if you hand Eveline this necklace, you will both suffer. I saw her die before she ever got to open the box. The walls and furniture collapsed, the ground shook, ensuring death and chaos. Do you hear me?"

"Okay," Evian said slowly. "What if I hand it to her outside?"

"This is not the time for your stupid jokes, Evian!" Clara snatched the jewellery box back. "Stars, you're infuriating! I'm trying to keep you both alive, so fucking *listen to me*. You must not give her that necklace. Anywhere or anytime. No."

"Okay," he repeated. "I'll return it. I'm sorry." Evian wrapped his arms around Clara. Part of her worried he might find some loophole, but her chest settled hearing him agree.

"Don't be sorry, brother," Clara whispered as she hugged him back. "Just stay alive."

That afternoon, Clara trained until sweat blinded her and every muscle screamed. She and Beau avoided eye contact, but truthfully, she was glad he was here. He trained with Oren as usual, while Finch partnered with Clara. If the earth fae noticed she was distracted, he said nothing.

Isobel was still in Morrin, and Clara expected her to remain there for a few days. The seasonal continent was vast, with each court eternally wrapped in its namesake season. Navigating the terrain was not something that could be done overnight. Though the logic did not quell the ache in Clara's chest or the itch along her fingertips. She longed for Isobel to return and wondered endlessly whether Isobel felt the same.

As the session wrapped up and they made to leave, Finch jerked his head over Clara's shoulder. "Expecting anyone?" he asked, before downing half his bottle in a matter of seconds, save for the few drops spilled down his chin.

Clara spun to find a group of six figures walking towards the bay. It was only as they drew closer, stopping a handful of paces away, that she recognised one—at least a little.

It felt like looking in a mirror, albeit a slightly warped one. His red hair was a shade darker than Clara's, his eyebrows and eyelashes a touch fairer. He had skin the same porcelain as her own, the same button nose, and high cheekbones. His eyes were so green they nearly glowed, ringed in brown.

Here stood an older male version of Clara.

Her heart sank, her stomach flipped, and her hands balled of their own accord. The stranger's smile was bright and wide. Perhaps it was sincere, but all the gesture did was rake uncomfortable furrows down Clara's spine. Beau's tense body was a welcome heat by her side.

"Got room for a few more on those mats?" the male asked as he rubbed his hands together. He had some nerve to show up unannounced, bearing such a blasé attitude.

Clara fought to keep her expression neutral.

"I'm sorry," she answered, her voice calm and as sweet as she could muster. "This private session has now ended. If you're interested in self-defence training, you'll have to speak with Keyne." Clara turned slightly, pointing to the instructor, all while keeping the male in sight.

Whether he came with good intentions, Clara did not know, but she certainly did not trust him.

"Self-defence is not why I'm here, daughter." His tone darkened, only by a fraction, but Clara did not miss the change. Nor how the casual, light-hearted glint in his eyes disappeared, and how his smile was now much less enthusiastic.

"Fintan," Clara replied flatly.

At the mention of his name, her biological father beamed.

"Ah, so you've heard of me," he said with a chuckle. "Excellent."

Fintan stepped forward with outstretched arms but paused when Clara moved back. Beau shifted to block his path, his arms deceptively casual and hands in his pockets. Clara had the sense that all eyes were focused on the three of them, but she didn't take hers from Fintan to check.

He seemed bothered only for a second before his expression relaxed into a neutral smile. "Right, let me introduce my companions."

Fintan gestured towards the members of his group one by one, the youngest of the bunch first. A boy—surely no older than fifteen—named Darius, with cheeks full of baby fat and wide hazel eyes. Dark-brown hair sat in choppy waves around his face.

The female beside him had the same fair skin and sharp bone structure, but aggression and disdain rolled off her. She stood close to the young boy, which made sense when Fintan introduced Brontë as Darius' older sister. Darius didn't have such anger yet; perhaps he'd be lucky and never meet such fiery emotions.

Terran and Hugo brought significant height to their group and acknowledged their introductions, but Reid was the only one to smile when Clara nodded at their name.

Clara did not introduce herself, nor anyone else. Not that Fintan spared any time for such pleasantries.

"Now, where's your sister?"

"Dead."

Perhaps she could've been more delicate when she delivered such news, but if their father had been present, he wouldn't have missed such a significant event. So Clara didn't have the patience, nor the care, to mince her words or coddle the male.

Shock flashed across his face, then a seemingly sincere wave of hurt. Of pain and distress. A small twinge of guilt niggled at Clara, though it didn't stop the next words from spilling icily from her lips.

"Yes, see, while you were out doing only stars know what . . . gathering folk who honestly don't even all want to be here"—Clara paused and gestured to Fintan's band of misfits—"your eldest daughter died, and I'm next in line. You're too late. Excuse me."

Brontë scoffed, but otherwise only silence followed Clara as she pushed past her biological father. Her arm brushed against Hugo's as she made to leave the bay, and a vision pierced through her mind as his sharp grey eyes fell to hers.

Shades of blue and green water thrash, circling her. She cannot tell up from down, nor left from right. Can hardly see her hands splaying out in front of her.

Reid's face flashes in and out of focus, their smile bright and striking. Their hand takes hold of Clara's, and in a blink, they're standing atop a hill.

As far as she can see, smoke billows and distorts the horizon. There is no noise, only an expansive silence, which feeds the empty, dreadful weight in Clara's gut.

She looks down, and the silence shatters as a scream so powerful and raw rips through her. The trees shudder in the distance. Reid shimmers in and out of focus, but Clara isn't paying them any attention.

Clara stands, not on a hill, but on a mountain made of bodies. Faces she recognises, and those she does not.

They are all dead, and their blood stains her hands.

CHAPTER SIX
EVIAN

The first three days Evian spent in Tirenas were with a female soldier named Dalia Rion. She hardly ever smiled and used his name even less. She referred to him only as "Hatch" and pointed at him aggressively. It took him almost thirty-six hours to pry the meaning behind the nickname from her, where she explained with a sneer it was short for hatchling, or baby bird. Rion considered herself rather funny and glared furiously when Evian did not share in her humour.

Her voice droned as she explained various sections of the handbook, then expected him to complete the sections. It was easily four hundred pages, outlining the rules and expectations of a soldier. Sometimes he answered successfully, though there was no praise for a correct response—only abuse at a wrong one. Evian always carried his handbook with him, jotting notes in the margins.

Nights were spent heavy in sleep, exhaustion devouring him as soon as his body fell onto his mattress. Never mind that it felt as if it was filled with straw and stones.

On the fourth morning, Evian was woken when Rion kicked in his door before the sun had risen and quizzed him on the protocol for dealing with an intruder. She then dumped a new uniform at the end of his bed while his roommates glared at them both.

That afternoon, he saw the queen for the first time since he'd returned to her kingdom. She glided down a hallway towards him, her hair and skirts floating out behind her. Evian couldn't help staring, which earned him a smack to the back of the head from Rion. He didn't miss the slight quirk of Eveline's lips as she noticed before she cast her eyes away and continued. Rion crossed her arms and stormed towards the sparring mats without another word, and Evian joined her but enjoyed the silence.

The dream he'd had during his journey home last time played on repeat in his mind all afternoon. By the time his training had ended, he'd decided to visit the queen's rooms and attempt to dine with her again. This time when he arrived at her door, there was a soldier stationed guard.

"Meal services are not required of you, soldier." The guard was older than Evian, with salt-and-pepper hair and fine lines present around his eyes. His voice was deep and stern, though polite enough.

"I have an urgent message for Her Majesty," Evian replied with a subtle dip of his chin. "I figured I ought not show up empty-handed."

The soldier raised his brow but did not comment further. Nor did he alert the queen of Evian's presence, so Evian gave him a casual smile and announced himself.

"Majesty!" he called, inching closer to the door. "I come bearing news and the finest dining experience I could gather from the mess!"

The soldier rolled his eyes but otherwise didn't stop Evian.

Eveline pulled the door open and rested her other hand on her hip. "Afron," she said in a tone he couldn't quite decipher.

"In the flesh," he crooned.

"This is not what you are employed to do." Eveline folded her arms and pursed her lips.

"That isn't what you suggested the last we spoke on the matter."

Evian failed to hide his smirk as the queen's body jolted with shock. Her arms flailed as she hurried to shoo the other guard away, her eyes wide and tone urgent.

"We shall not speak of that matter any further!" she hissed as the soldier rounded a corner. "It isn't in your contract and, frankly, it isn't proper. End of discussion."

"So add an employment clause." Evian shuffled the tray of food into one hand and plucked a grape with the other. "You're the queen."

Eveline scoffed, then her face hardened. "End of discussion, Afron."

Evian chewed his grape slowly, a smirk dancing along his lips before he answered her. "If you say so, Majesty." But before popping another grape in his mouth, he added, "I would like it on the record, however, that I am no longer spoken for."

The queen did not acknowledge his statement, though confusion and surprise swirled in her beautiful hazel eyes. She stepped backwards into her suite, and with a flick of her delicate wrist she gestured for Evian to leave.

"You're dismissed. Eat, study, go to bed—I do not care. But I do not wish to see you out and about and roaming my castle for at least a week. Do you hear me?"

Evian took a step closer to her, enough that she had to raise her stare to maintain eye contact. Her eyes narrowed, but there was no anger behind the expression. Evian grinned as he leant against the doorframe.

"Loud and clear," he whispered, then winked. He prayed she enjoyed his confidence as much as he believed she did, else his employment would end before it had truly begun.

Eveline laughed, and the sound healed something in him he hadn't realised was broken. It was a truly magical cadence, which was over far sooner than he would've liked.

She tried to sound casual, perhaps even aloof, but Evian didn't miss the fast rise and fall of her chest, nor the subtle blush across her collar. Nor did he miss how well her dress sculpted to her frame and complemented her breasts.

"You certainly are confident—I'll give you that much." Her smile was captivating, and her hand on his chest as she gently patted him sent sparks down his spine. "Goodnight, Afron."

Then she took a final step back and closed the door. Evian couldn't shake his smile, not even as he lay on his uncomfortable bunk and drifted into another dreamless sleep.

"Where are the three closest exits, Hatch?" Rion demanded as she halted abruptly outside the throne room.

Evian answered with a speed he was rather proud of— after all, he'd only been on the job five days.

"Southern exit, which is at the end of this corridor, just past the ground floor library. The front castle entrance is through the main entrance to the throne room. The third closest exit is down the hall we just turned out of, towards the stables."

"And what is the fastest route to Her Majesty's suite?"

"Right at the end of the corridor, up the stairs, turn right again. Halfway down the next hall, there's a landing with two flights of stairs. The left leads to the queen's previous suite from when she was the crown princess. At the end of the hallway past the landing is the queen's current residence."

"And why do you need to memorise both?" Rion pressed.

Evian refrained from mentioning just how well he'd memorised those locations.

"Because Her Majesty frequents both and could be in either suite."

Rion huffed in response. The rest of their walk to the outpost tower was silent, save for her quizzing Evian on passing soldiers' ranks. He got most of them right, and Rion did not hide her snicker when he ranked the officer incorrectly.

They relieved two winged soldiers, and for the next six hours, Evian would be stuck with only Dalia Rion's company. Half of him hoped she'd maintain her silence the whole time, though he knew better.

Within only a few moments, Evian's stomach gurgled loudly. He winced as Rion glared at him. Midnight could not come soon enough.

By the end of his shift, Evian's insides had turned on him. His throat burned after hours without water. He'd forgotten his flask, and Rion scolded him for it rather than sharing her own. Pain traced along his temples and speared down his nape, as aggressive as the rolling nausea in his gut. He'd not eaten since early that morning, having not been granted time for lunch. Now, he was parched, famished, and grumpy.

The mess had closed not long after he arrived at the watchtower, so his only other option was the royal kitchen. Though if he were caught there, Rion would take pleasure in his misstep.

With no other option, Evian loosened the buttons at his neck and rolled his sleeves to his elbows. He'd done well to memorise the layout of the castle and found the kitchens with ease. Soft footsteps sounded from inside as he swung the old wooden door open.

As Evian continued through the doorway, he spied a lithe body and a lazy grin spread across his face. After opening and closing two more cabinets and remaining empty-handed, she turned, and her beautiful stare landed on him.

"I thought I told you I didn't want you roaming," Eveline chastised, though there was a hint of something light in her tone.

Evian shrugged. "You told me you did not wish to *see* me roaming. Close your eyes and all our problems shall be solved."

Eveline only raised a single thin brow and planted her hands on her hips. Then she sighed and shook her head, turning away from him to resume her search of the cupboards.

"How was I to know you'd be awake at this hour?" Evian continued and sauntered closer to her. "Let alone fetching yourself something. You ought to have a peasant boy do that for you."

"Got any recommendations?" she asked, her tone now dripping with heat. Her eyes bore into his, save for the few times they flicked to his parted lips.

"I could think of someone," Evian whispered, as he leant nearer still, so close he could feel her quickening breaths on his skin.

Her gaze flew more frantically from his eyes to the unbuttoned collar of his shirt. Eveline's lips parted and her tongue darted out, and Evian struggled to look at anything other than her. More so, he struggled to understand how anyone might ever want to.

"Mother, help me." His voice was barely audible, but Eveline heard the words he hadn't meant to utter aloud.

"You wish to think of your mother while ogling me in such a state of undress?" She was quiet too. Softer spoken than he'd ever heard. Though every word was laced with desire, which Evian did not miss.

"I'm pleading with the goddess to help me stop thinking of you—wearing so little and tempting me so much." He dropped closer to her, breathed in her intoxicating cherry scent, then absently plucked a glass from the overhead cabinet she'd abandoned. "To stop thinking of all the truly wanton things I wish to do to you."

Fuck, she was beautiful. Almost as tall as he was, she didn't have to lift her chin to maintain eye contact. Her fair skin almost shimmered in the moonlight. It made him think of the dark patches on her back, the magical sections decorated in shadow.

When the queen smirked devilishly at Evian and bit her lower lip, desire unfurled violently within him. He clenched his jaw so he might restrain the growls and pleas already dancing on his tongue. He wanted to reach out and grab her, to drag her to him, pressed against him while he devoured her. While he worshipped his queen.

Instead, he brought his balled fist to his mouth and bit down on his knuckles. Something flared in her hazel eyes, which were yet to leave Evian's face. His ego told him it was Eveline's own need for him. Her lust-filled thoughts and wants she, too, was fighting to keep restrained.

Then she reached her hand up to cup his cheek. It was smooth as tranquil waters and felt equally like home.

"Perhaps," she whispered, low and seductive, "you should think of all the things you'd like for me to do to you. Do not forget who is in charge here, hmm?" Eveline chuckled sultrily as she tapped her hand against his face.

Evian hadn't thought he could be any more aroused until then. When the roles of sexual power switched and he was suddenly at her mercy. His cock twitched at the thought.

"Perhaps, my Queen," was all he could manage to utter.

CHAPTER SEVEN
BEAU

Beau didn't recognise the empty, fog-filled dreamscape. Not until an eery voice crawled along his skin. A voice he recognised with a sense of dread.

"Beauregard," Lorelai hissed.

He couldn't see her, though he wasn't entirely sure he would. Only puffs of darker smoke were visible in the distance, billowing in and out of focus.

"Apparently," he muttered. "Why am I here again?"

"I am here with a warning."

"Great." Beau rolled his eyes subconsciously, then silently hoped the deity hadn't seen. She didn't take well to his attitude.

"In only a few weeks, you will be taken. You will not recognise your assailants, but you will go with them. Clarenna will learn of your absence and attempt to save you. It is currently unclear to us whether she will succeed." Lorelai's tone was dull, bordering on apathetic.

Beau clenched his jaw, eager for her to get to the point.

"If she does not find you in time, there will be no need for my sisters and I to seek her out. However, if she reaches you, it will not be long until we arrive."

"You know, I'm glad you brought that up," Beau said. "I feel like I've been given a rather poor deal, if I'm being honest."

"You said you would do anything to keep her alive, did you not? Have you reconsidered?"

"No," he answered quickly. "I spoke the truth and stand by what I said. But why must I die for the *threat to be neutralised*? And when she inevitably destroys you and your sisters, won't your replacements take her life as payment anyway?"

"How dare you question me!" she hissed far more menacingly, and her voice shook Beau to his core.

"I'm as good as dead anyway." Beau shrugged. "I'd say now's as good a time as any to question you. If you're done with this life, yet so powerful, why can you not end it yourself?"

"My sisters are power hungry, and we are a trio. Fates and deities come and go as the centuries pass, some longer than others. My sisters and I have reigned longer than any of our kind, but we cannot survive without the others. And if not by another's hand, we simply will never end."

"You're not answering my questions."

"I'm not giving you the answer you want, Beauregard, because life is unfair. Yours shall not last much longer, and then you'll cease to worry on such matters."

"When you die, will others come for her life as payment?" Beau pressed.

"No," she answered flatly. "We will come with an army. Before stepping in ourselves, we are required to exhaust all options.

"One of the soldiers will release you from this world and send Clarenna into a fury yet unseen. I expect her rage will simply take over, and she will eliminate anything in her path. It will be considered an outcome of battle, rather than the assassination of a deity. Without your or her tetherbond's death, there is nothing powerful enough to send her into such a spiral. No emotion is devastating enough for her magic to explode. Would you rather we take the fae?"

Beau didn't answer. He didn't need to because Lorelai knew he'd rather it be him.

"Once this is done, she will be safe."

"You've yet to inform me how your kind can be killed, you know."

"I do," she answered, her tone far gentler than he'd heard it before. "But I cannot simply share that information with you. It is self-destructive—"

"Oh, heavens forbid we be self-destructive," Beau muttered as he rolled his eyes.

"I'm beginning to regret seeking you out, boy. Be quiet and listen. I cannot tell you outright, though there are beings who walk between worlds and lurk beyond Death's doors who can fill in the blanks.

"An eye for an eye, payment in kind, only she will bring the information you wish to find.

"I cannot say anything more. I have given you everything I can."

"I'd ask for your word, but you'll be dead."

"That is the hope, Beauregard."

Beau woke the next morning to an empty bed, Clara's side of the mattress cold and the blanket thrown back. His breath caught in his chest until he heard a clang from outside the room followed by swearing. Chuckling, he slid from the bed and dressed before exiting the bedroom.

He found her bustling about an otherwise empty kitchen, save for the half-dozen bowls and utensils covering the benchtop. Flour dusted her jaw, and various smudged handprints lined her apron. She smiled when she saw him, her shoulders relaxed, and Beau couldn't help but feel more at ease himself. Ringing burst through the pleasant silence, causing Clara to hurry towards the stove.

"Did you know," she said, stirring whatever was over the heat, "if you heat the lemon juice first, it enhances the flavour of the frosting?"

"Why, for the love of the stars, are you making lemon-flavoured frosting?" Beau closed the gap between them and wrapped his arms around her. Her cinnamon scent filled him with so much emotion, then the tart lemon overpowered it. He was glad she faced away, so his grimace went unnoticed. The yellow liquid swirled rapidly even as Clara stilled, then sunk into Beau's touch.

"Isobel's birthday is in a few days," was all she said, her voice serene.

"Right." Beau stiffened and dropped his hands to his side. Now was as good a time as any, he supposed. "That is something I wanted to discuss with you, actually."

"Oh?" She turned to face him then, her brows higher than normal and eyes wide with so much emotion—nerves, hope, uncertainty. Beau's gut rolled violently.

He needed to ask her—for so many reasons—but fear threatened to seize him. Weeks had gone by since Clara had begun to distance herself. Why, he did not know. But he was certain it had something to do with Isobel.

Every night he fell asleep wondering if he'd wake to a note telling him she'd gone. Left him to be with the other woman. His heart bulged with all the love in the world for Clara, then broke with twice as much force every time he followed her line of sight and landed on the fae.

Fear was not a comfortable emotion for Beau. It was not one he was familiar with or knew how to navigate. He clenched his fists so he might keep them occupied, for he did not know what to do with them otherwise. His heart thundered in his chest, echoing in his throat and his ears. He swallowed and nodded.

"I see the way you look at her," he said, trying to keep his voice calm. Clara's face softened into something far too close to pity for Beau's liking. "How your body leans towards her when she's around. For weeks now, you've been favouring her. I know it sounds petulant and childish, but I cannot understand why you've suddenly cast me aside. You are my everything, and I thought that was reciprocated, but now I'm not so sure."

Clara turned the heat off the stove before she answered, each second dragging out painfully. The words were out now, and Beau had no idea what would come next.

"Beau, you have my whole heart . . ." She paused for too long, and Beau's skin heated. Vulnerability was not easy.

"But?" he snapped, regretting the way his face scrunched and arms flailed, but he couldn't help it.

"Don't you take that tone with me—it's not so simple." She shook her head and sighed.

"Then explain it to me!" His heart felt like it might explode. His hands rose, then slammed onto the bench beside him. Clara jumped, startled by the noise, and a wave of guilt flooded him.

"For starters," she said flatly, her face and body hardening, "I'm not the only one who's been distant. You've been keeping something from me since we went to see Ora."

She was right, but he couldn't tell her why. Apparently, he'd not been as sly or covert as he thought.

"Oh, since you went to the whorehouse without an explanation and we had to search for you." He wasn't sure whether the bitterness of his words was intentional—to hide his secrets and avoid the conversation—or perhaps from the discomfort of finding her on stage, performing half naked for strangers.

"Stop it," she hissed and rolled her eyes. She jabbed a porcelain finger towards him. "Since that night, you've had secrets. I let you keep them because I trust you and believed you'd tell me when you were ready. Why can you not grant me the same courtesy?"

"Because I'm watching the love of my life fall for someone else! It is not the same thing." His words drifted into a whisper. Her face fell, and Beau's heart lurched into his throat. All the anger and frustration left his body; now only defeat lay heavy in his gut.

"When you come clean about whatever you're hiding, then we shall see." Clara folded her arms, but there was more than defiance in her eyes as she locked them on him.

Beau felt a growing numbness as he realised where this conversation was leading. "All I hear is that you are not denying you're falling in love with her."

Her eyes widened, but Beau wasn't surprised. Not really.

He'd seen it develop over weeks. If he was being honest with himself, he'd known for some time the females shared a connection. Something greater than friendship, more than the fact that Isobel had worked for her sister. Sometimes Clara looked at Isobel the way she'd looked at Beau, though such expressions were waning of late. He offered her a dejected smile, then turned to leave.

"Do not walk away from me, Beau!" Clara cried out, her silken hand gripped tightly around his wrist. "Please at least finish the discussion you started." Her eyes darted frantically between his when he faced her.

"I don't think there's anything left to discuss, Clara," Beau whispered as he softly cupped her cheek. He wasn't angry, not really. If she was happy, then he could be happy for her. It was all he wanted, even if she was not with him.

"Beau . . ."

His name on her lips was something he relished, something he craved so desperately. But when she pleaded like this, her voice near breaking and her grip on him so tight her nails pressed marks into his skin, his heart cracked.

"Is this it then?" he asked gently.

"Please," she whispered as she squeezed her eyes closed. "Do not make me choose."

"Why? Because you'll choose her?"

"No," she said, barely audible. A lone tear fell down her cheek as she reopened her eyes to stare up at Beau. "Because I choose you."

CHAPTER EIGHT
ISOBEL

The last thing Isobel wanted to do was question Clara's abilities or intuition; she had visions for a reason. Yet after what felt like an eternity combing through Morrin in search of Era and Tindal, they had come up empty-handed. They'd hopped from snowcapped mountains to forests with frozen leaves, to dying and empty plains. Beaches covered in autumn leaves, shorelines pelted with rain and hail. Caves that held more heat and moisture than they should, and ones so cold they had to huddle during their search.

Nothing.

No hideaways or hidden chambers.

The witches were nowhere to be found.

Poppy, Samara, and Isobel were equally exhausted and so decided to leave Morrin temporarily. At the very least, Isobel needed to speak with Clara. Perhaps there was a detail she'd missed that could point them in the right direction. Wandering around almost aimlessly had done them no good.

The twins bid farewell before transporting themselves back to the palace in Candor, while Isobel opted for a more scenic route to Clara's home. Isobel was beyond excited to see Clara again, and she wasn't even all that disappointed to see the bird boy. He'd grown on her a little in a strange sort of way. One particular shoreline in the Spring Court had a thousand fallen leaves. Two leaves had stuck together out on the water—one strikingly green, the other amber. It felt symbolic, almost, of how they'd grown together over the past few weeks. Isobel finally felt like she was a part of them, a true part of Clara's heart instead of just a guest.

She also stopped by the grocers, who stocked Clara's favourite pomegranate tea, purchasing a box and a bag of honeyed almonds for Beau. He shovelled handfuls of the nuts when he thought no one was watching. After her emotional epiphany along the beach in Bloom, she figured it'd be a nice offering.

Just as she was barely out the door, a gratingly familiar voice called out, and her shoulders rose instinctively. She turned and fought to keep her expression neutral.

"Isobel, how unexpected to see you again!" Fintan held his arms out to her, as if he might embrace her. Her lips pulled back, teeth bared.

A young male and female stood beside him, similar enough Isobel could only assume they were related. Her arms were folded tightly over her chest, and her already fair knuckles turned white around her biceps.

Isobel had only met Fintan once before, when he'd stopped at the palace to update Elisabeth on his ventures. About how he'd found two Vequil Inalis fae in Flame after years of searching, that he was finally making headway. Elisabeth tried to tell him about the kingdom he'd left her to run, but he brushed her off and hardly even looked at her. He spoke only of himself and his efforts, then left without so much as pretending to care how his eldest daughter was faring.

Elisabeth was pregnant when her father visited, but given the circumstances, she had kept it secret. Isobel hadn't always liked Elisabeth, but to be excited to share the news with her father only to be met with indifference was not what she deserved. No one deserved to be so blatantly discarded.

Isobel had no respect for this male after his behaviour.

"Hello, Fintan." Her words were forced through gritted teeth. "Please excuse me."

"Where are you off to in such a rush?" he called after her, but Isobel did not turn around.

"Why do you care?"

"I'd like to see my daughter, Isobel."

She spun with such velocity her bag smacked into her thighs and her hair whipped her face.

"Where is she?"

"I wouldn't tell you even if I knew for certain. She likes to wander; I suppose she gets that from you." Raking her narrowed eyes over the male, Isobel snarled. "You abandoned her for years. What makes you think she'd want to see you?"

"I'm her father—"

Isobel scoffed, the sound cutting him off. "No, she had a father. He raised her well, and he loved every second he got to spend with his daughter. You were traipsing across the continents searching for Vequil Inalis. Meanwhile, you don't know the first thing about Clara and left your eldest daughter to pick up the pieces of your kingdom. You're a selfish male with an ill-conceived idea of what it means to consider someone else."

"Can we leave yet?" the female growled at Fintan. She paid Isobel no mind. Fintan's hand waved dismissively over his shoulder, and the female rolled her eyes.

The boy murmured too quietly for Isobel to hear, but she could hazard a guess at what he said when the female spun to him and cupped his face.

"No, we're going home. We do not need to be here, despite what *he* insists."

Fury built in Isobel and swelled in the air surrounding them. She couldn't help that her voice rose, nor could she quieten the violent songs the breeze sang to her.

"You're collecting," she spat and looked down her nose at Fintan. "Just like Urian. Stars, this one's begging to leave and you're still trying to force her and a child to stay? What for?"

"To help—"

"In the war? No, Fintan, children do not serve in wars. Conscription is illegal. Leave them be, and while you're at it, leave Clara alone as well."

"Mother, you're awful." Fintan turned his nose up at Isobel. "What a disgusting attitude. If you let me get a stars-forsaken word in, Isobel Jeffreys, you might learn something of value. No one was forced into anything. No one was bound or coerced. I'm trying to keep my daughter alive!"

His words meant nothing to Isobel.

"And what of your other daughter?" she demanded. "Lenore did not have any world-altering visions of her, so what, Elisabeth wasn't important enough to protect? You forced her to run a kingdom she was never supposed to rule and now she's dead."

"That's enough, young lady," Fintan hissed as he took a menacing step towards her.

He might've been born to a royal family, but he bore no such markings. He was no king, merely a king's offspring. Fintan was delusional to think he'd have an effect on Isobel.

All she saw before her was a desperate male, picking which of his toys to show off.

"Quite right. I hope you have the day you deserve, Fintan."

As soon as she opened the door, the smell of citrus hit Isobel. Tension ebbed from her stiff shoulders and tight muscles almost immediately. She smiled to herself as she strode down the hallway, towards where she heard Clara and Beau. She'd barely cleared the threshold when their words became clear.

"No," Clara whispered, and a tear fell from her wild eyes as she stared at Beau frantically. Neither had noticed Isobel enter the room. "Because I choose you."

The tea and almonds fell from Isobel's frozen hands, and both the fae and Phoenix jumped at the sound. They had certainly noticed her now.

"Shit," Clara hissed, her face contorted by an emotion Isobel didn't want to decipher.

Clara called after her as she stumbled to the bedroom, but all Isobel could hear was the violent thump of her heartbeat in her ears and the sound of her footsteps pounding down the hall.

Her own. Clara's, maybe even Beau's—she didn't know. Didn't care.

Nausea flooded her body and dizziness danced in her mind. Pain lanced her heart and clogged her throat, while tears stung behind her tightly closed lids. She leant against the back of the bedroom door as Clara begged on the other side. Incoherent pleas Isobel didn't have the capacity to focus on as her entire world shattered.

I choose you.

Yet if the tables were turned, Isobel would have chosen Clara. There was never a question.

Fury surged along her skin as she considered the conversation she'd walked in on. Had Beau asked Clara to choose? Where in this stars-damned world did he find the audacity to dictate Clara's love life? If it were up to Isobel, he'd be thrown out with the rotten scraps and dirty rags. Though she would not have asked in the first place.

As fiercely as her heart beat for Clara, she was certain Clara's heart also beat for Beau, at least in part. She was not blind, nor was she stupid. Their connection was clear, and all Isobel wanted was for Clara to be happy.

Even if it meant sharing her with a *male*.

Why could he not consider doing the same?

Isobel stepped away from the door and began collecting her belongings to stuff into her already full bag. Clara burst through the door a moment later, tears streaked on her cheeks and her brows furrowed. Beau stood behind her in the hall, his hands in his pockets and his gaze averted. Isobel spared him little time or attention.

"What are you doing?" Clara demanded as she slammed the bedroom door closed.

"Leaving," Isobel whispered, sure her voice would break if she spoke any louder.

Clara balked. "But where are you going?"

"Anywhere else."

"Why?"

The question was hardly more than a sob, and Isobel couldn't for the life of her understand why Clara was so upset. She'd made her choice, and with a handful of words destroyed Isobel's entire world, leaving her soul shredded. Isobel was the one who should be crying.

But she wouldn't because she knew Clara felt something for her at least, and the last thing Isobel wanted was to make the situation worse for any of them. She would leave, then Clara would not have to choose after all.

"You know, I would never ask such a question of you." She stopped with a shirt crumpled in her hand and locked her eyes on Clara's, her heart and her mind at war over what to do next.

"Isobel, please," Clara took a step closer so only the bed stood between them, simultaneously too much space and not enough. "Don't go. Let me explain. What did you hear?"

She could hardly stop the scoff. Shaking her head, Isobel crammed the shirt into her already overfilled bag and then took a deep breath.

"That you would choose him. I won't lie to you, Clara, a part of me wants to strangle him with his own damned feathers. Rip them from him and tie them into a vicious gold rope. *Something*, I don't know." She shook her head again, as if it might rid her of the murderous thoughts painfully freezing her skin or the heartbreak climbing her throat. Then she added in a much softer tone, "But all I want for you is love and laughter and health and happiness. I care not for Beau, but I trust him enough to give you that at least. So I won't ask, and I won't make you choose."

Clara raced around the bed so quickly that Isobel did not realise what had happened until the space between them had vanished entirely. Her soft, shaking hand was pressed to Isobel's cheek tenderly, and the other brought warmth to Isobel's hip.

Then Clara's lips crashed into hers, melding so perfectly it was like they were created for one another. Stars, if she wasn't the most delicious thing Isobel was lucky enough to taste.

CHAPTER NINE
CLARA

She tasted delicious, like summer berries dipped in honey. Her lips were velvet and cool to the touch, balancing the heat radiating from Clara's skin. She stood so small, yet pressed against Clara's body as if she couldn't get close enough.

And they couldn't.

Isobel was perfect. So entirely and completely perfect it might drive Clara mad. It would definitely drive Beau to insanity, but he would have to learn to share, as he promised he could.

Clara could hardly breathe, yet somehow felt the most refreshed and invigorated she ever had. The air swelling around her simmered as the heat faded away.

"You beautiful fool," she murmured against Isobel's lips.

Isobel pulled away, her bright-blue eyes darting quickly between Clara's. Her brows pulled together as confusion covered her face.

"I don't understand—"

"I told Beau I would choose him because the love I have for him is the one I understand. It's a connection that's been through hell, that we had to work to gain. I also told him choosing him would break a part of me, one he would never be able to mend. You walked away before you could hear the rest."

Clara smiled at Isobel, but her confusion didn't ease. Perhaps it even turned to irritation as Isobel stepped back and wriggled from Clara's grasp and her smile fell.

"Was that all?" Isobel asked. Not looking at Clara, she fiddled with the strap of her bag where it sat on the bed.

"Mostly . . ." Clara mumbled, sensing nothing she said would make this situation better.

"I've wanted to kiss you from the second I laid eyes on you. Did you know that?" Isobel asked. "I've always had trouble focusing, even before the drugs. Truthfully, my whole life my head has been one chaotic mess—it's always so loud. But as soon as I saw you, I felt like I could focus again.

"The continual loops of noise and thoughts and images racing through my mind paused. They slowed, and everything was quiet. No more loud distractions, only you. You somehow managed to turn down the volume and give me peace.

"But hearing you choose him? It wasn't just quiet, and it certainly wasn't calm. Everything inside me turned silent and then shattered. Hearing that *hurt*."

Clara's heart broke. A lump formed in her throat, burning and solid. "Hurting you is the last thing I ever wanted to do," she whispered, unable to look Isobel in the eye. Guilt dragged heavy claws down her spine. "Fuck, I'm sorry." Her gaze flickered to Isobel, fleeting and brief, but Isobel wasn't looking at her anyway.

Clara sighed, then taking a slow, deep breath, Clara moved to kneel in front of Isobel. Despite the pain in her throat and the overwhelming fear threatening to seize her whole, Clara kept going.

"Almost everything about this has gone wrong, but kissing you felt like the most *right* thing in the world. So natural, like breathing. You don't calm me, Isobel—you frighten the living shit out of me. Every time I say goodbye, or you stand further away from me than normal. When you smile at someone else. You glare at Beau, or you look at us interacting for a moment too long before you sigh and look away. You scare me so much I can hardly breathe, but then you fill me with all the life of the universe, and everything is okay."

There was a long moment where neither female said anything, just stared at one another in a strange silence. Clara could hear Isobel's every breath and watched every twitch and movement of her body. She could feel a headache forming from all her wild and tangled thoughts, anticipating how Isobel might respond. Fear spiked through her at the thought that Isobel might not respond at all.

"I told him I wouldn't choose," Clara's voice dropped to a shaky whisper as she added, "Please don't go."

Isobel sighed, but her dainty fingers brushed the hair from Clara's face, and her palm rested on her cheek. "You stole my heart, my soul, captured my attention and every breath since. I love you more than words could ever possibly convey. All I can offer you is acceptance of the bird boy and an honest attempt at less glaring. I hope that means as much to you as you mean to me."

"Thank the fucking stars," Clara breathed as the tension left her body. She grabbed hold of Isobel's wrist with her free hand and pulled.

The sweetest squawk burst from Isobel's lips, but it quickly shifted to soft laughter as she landed in Clara's lap.

Clara's arms tightened around Isobel's petite body, and she squeezed so hard she worried the woman might struggle to breathe, but Clara couldn't let her go.

Not now, not ever.

"I don't think I can ever truly express how much you mean to me. How much I love you." Clara kissed her again—desperate and obsessive—but after mere seconds, Isobel pulled away.

"Is he still waiting in the hall?"

"Yes." Beau's voice travelled calmly through the door.

Isobel smirked. "You can come in now."

Not a second later, Beau strode inside.

"So how does this work?" Isobel asked. "I don't share your love of feathers."

Beau scoffed, but Clara only smiled, bright and calm as he said, "I figured we could do a week on, week off schedule. You know, like separated parents do with their offspring."

"Did you just call me a child, Hawthorne?" Clara shot at him with a raised brow.

"Not my favourite term of endearment," he muttered as a coy grin spread across his face. "But in the spirit of love and whatnot, I'll let it go."

Clara rolled her eyes as he sat beside them. "I don't know how this will go," Clara admitted as she rested a hand on Beau's knee. "I just know how I feel about each of you and that I'm selfish enough to ask you both to stay. Beau has promised he'll learn to share." She spared her Phoenix a pointed look, to which he huffed, but his body softened.

Isobel pressed a gentle kiss to Clara's jaw, and Beau's teeth clenched. When Isobel pulled away, her smug expression stared back at Beau.

"You do not possess enough testosterone for this to turn into a pissing match, Isobel Jeffreys. But I assure you, I would win either way."

Though his tone was strong, none of Beau's words held any bite. Perhaps this was how it would be from now on, meaningless jabs and shit-talking. Clara could get on board with that. Truthfully, she looked forward to it; light-hearted barbs, and a banter-filled friendship.

Maybe Isobel and Beau would grow to love one another. It wouldn't look like the love she shared with either of them, but love regardless. The start of a beautiful family.

Velvet blue peeks from a crisp white pocket. The wearer walks with purpose along a bright, boring hallway.

Clara blinked, and she was back in her bedroom. Beau laughed flatly at whatever Isobel had said, but Clara wasn't listening. She could hardly hear them over the echo in her head warning her to get ready. It repeated the word *"soon"* over and over, each time a little louder.

Evian takes a deep breath, smoothing his shirt before pushing open the heavy double doors, engraved in swirls and sunrays. A midnight-haired queen, crown poised atop her head, stares out over her kingdom from the floor-to-ceiling window. The smell of old books surrounds him, as does the gentle melody playing in the background.

Nausea violently roiled in Clara's gut, her skin clammy. Isobel was no longer in her lap; instead, she knelt in front of Clara with Beau close by her side. They wore twin expressions of confusion and concern.

Now . . .

The voice was a whisper, harsh and cold.

She opened her mouth to explain, but no words came out.

Now!

The blaring word echoed in her skull.

A small brown pouch flies through the shadows and lands silently on the topmost shelf. Bookshelves crash like dominoes, too fast for either of them to notice. They don't see it coming, don't have time to move. Eveline is crushed first, oblivious, with a beaming smile still on her face. The blue velvet box in hand. In another moment, Evian is submerged under too many books and heavy shelves.

The voice screamed, ear-splitting and painful. Unable to be ignored.

NOW!

Clara and Isobel landed in the Tirenas palace library, exactly where she'd stood in her first vision. The one she'd had when Evian had first shown Clara the necklace.
He had not arrived, so she frantically searched for the queen.

Clara watched as Eveline took slow, casual steps towards the window, just as the heavy doors groaned. Shit.

The tension threatened to suffocate her. Music played faintly in the background, but her heartbeat in her ears drowned out the sound. Her eyes were drawn to the shelf she knew was about to topple. Nothing had landed atop it yet, though a sense of foreboding ravaged her body. She had seconds to come up with a plan.

Without thinking, Clara threw out her hands. One created a solid wall of air, a wall of protection around her brother and the queen. The other produced a powerful gust of wind, so forceful that books flew from tables, chairs flipped, and fae cried out.

Eveline looked towards the sounds of concern, but Evian's eyes flew straight to Clara, as if he could sense her arrival. Isobel stayed silent, but placed one hand on her shoulder and lifted her other in assistance. With Isobel's help, Clara's surge of air homed in and focused. The fae calmed as the furniture and books settled.

Then the pouch exploded.

Clara hadn't seen where it had come from, only the bursts of light and smoke, then the fragments of fabric floating about the room.

Only when the last scraps fell to the floor did Clara ease her magic back to where it cooled the sweat beading along her skin.

Isobel's hand came away and entwined with Clara's own.

She offered Isobel an appreciative smile, and the pair approached the now furious queen.

"What in Helmos' name are you doing here?" Eveline hissed, her eyes wide and nostrils flared.

Instead, Clara flung her ire at her brother. "I told you not to give that to her!" Clara narrowed her eyes and furiously pointed at the velvet box in the queen's hands, and he averted his gaze and rubbed at the back of his neck.

Eveline's hostility all but evaporated, shock quickly overcoming her face, then she scoffed. "If your brother wishes to gift me things, you will not stand in his way." She tilted her chin upwards and had the gall to look down her nose, as if Clara had not just saved the ungrateful royal's life. "Let the male be happy."

Clara didn't miss how she spared a fleeting, soft glance at Evian. Nor how she clutched the jewellery box a fraction tighter.

"Respectfully, Your Majesty, you are insufferable sometimes." Clara sighed and pinched the bridge of her nose. "You're welcome, by the way, for saving both of your lives. Next time I'll let you suffer a little longer."

"Clara," Evian scolded.

"No, brother, you do not get to reprimand me. I told you what would happen, but you did not listen. Next time you deserve to suffer a fraction, and maybe then you'll learn."

"Told him what?" Eveline demanded, her tone one only a queen could master. Hard and sharp as stone.

"I told him you would die if he gave you that necklace. I saw it happen." Clara shrugged, but Eveline's shoulders shot back as her eyes narrowed on Evian.

His hands flew up defensively, then he plucked the blue box from Eveline's slim fingers. "I swapped it for a bracelet, thank you very much."

He opened the box to show Clara. Instead of the dainty gold chain she'd seen before, a thicker silver chain lay along the plush velvet interior. In place of the diamond pendant, dozens of emeralds and brown garnets were encrusted in the chain. It was just as beautiful, and just as deadly.

"Oh my," Eveline gasped, her hand splayed at her chest. An unfamiliar expression flooded her eyes as they clung to Evian. Then she cleared her throat and turned to Clara.

"Thank you, Clara. Now get out, I'm busy."

She nodded towards Isobel before physically shuffling them to the door and shooing them away.

"I expect a proper show of gratitude to come, Eveline. I'll return when I've thought of something." Clara winked, and Isobel poorly hid her chuckle.

Eveline ignored them both. She barely even nodded as she gestured once more for them to scurry along.

Then she looked back at Evian, who was still far too close for any soldier to stand.

A slender hand, adorned with silver and earth-toned jewels, clings to the hand of a strong, gentle soldier. Their fingers are bound tight, illuminated by the golden string tethering them together. It wraps around them and glows like sunlight, emanating love and warmth. An unbreakable connection.

Clara knows this hand well. It is one that helped feed and raise her since she was a babe.

This queen and another queen's brother.

Tetherbonds.

Clara blinked, back in the library. Evian waved goodbye as Eveline made to close the door. Two familiar hands poised on the other side of the threshold.

She struggled to compose her face, but lost the battle to the grin that bloomed. Truthfully, Clara could only feel happiness for Evian at having found his tether, whether they knew it yet or not. Clara did not say anything; it wasn't her news to share.

CHAPTER TEN
CLARA

"Are you going to tell me what your smirk was for?" Isobel asked, her elbow jutting playfully into Clara's ribs.

Finally back home, Clara was eager to curl up between Isobel and Beau. To soak up the goodness the universe had thrown her way over the past few hours—stars, over the last however many months. Sure, they didn't care for each other, but Clara didn't doubt their feelings for her. Feelings strong enough that they would put up with the other *for her*, for as long as they all lived. Pride bloomed hot and heavy in her chest, as did her gratitude.

Clara chuckled as Isobel slumped onto the settee. Beau poked his head around the corner, his shoulders relaxed as he gazed over them.

"I don't know if it's my place," Clara murmured and shook her head.

"Don't know if what is your place?" Beau asked as he stuffed himself behind Clara, between her and the arm of the chair, and placed his warm hand on her thigh. She leant back into him while Isobel answered for her.

"We arrived at the castle with plenty of time to save the queen and an admirer of hers. You remember Evian, don't you?" Her eyebrows waggled as her mouth inched upwards.

Beau's body stiffened for half a second before laughter burst from him. "Really?"

Isobel grinned as she nodded. "But Clara had a devious revelation as we were leaving. She smirked, and I asked why, but she's remaining tight-lipped."

"Clara . . . tight-lipped?" Beau scoffed. "She hardly knows the meaning of the phrase."

Even as Clara whirled around, her jaw open in feigned outrage, Beau continued to laugh.

"Fuck you, Hawthorne." Clara stuck out her tongue, but Beau seized it before she could close her mouth.

"I've told you not to tempt me, sweetheart." His voice was low and sultry, his fingers rough and firm. Butterflies erupted in her belly.

Clara hadn't considered what sexual relations, even sexual conversations, might be like when the three of them were together. Certainly not so soon. Nerves floated alongside the butterflies. Thankfully, Isobel took it well.

She clamped her hands over her ears, her voice slightly louder as she exaggerated a gag.

"I beg of you, don't make me ill."

The cocky grin on Beau's face morphed into a somewhat apologetic expression. But only somewhat, while his eyes told Clara she'd best behave, else he'd do more than grab her tongue later.

Secretly, she wanted to push their boundaries. She wanted to fluster Isobel and tease Beau. The excitement almost made her giggle.

Instead, Beau let go of her tongue, and it throbbed without the pressure. Clara cleared her throat and turned back to face Isobel.

"They're tetherbonds." She was genuinely happy to announce it. For her brother and Eveline, who after what she'd experienced from her father and after losing her sister, deserved to be happy. "I don't think they're aware yet, however."

An odd expression came over Isobel's face. A mix of happiness, but also something else that almost looked like longing.

"Shit." Beau sighed. "I was not expecting that."

"Do you think one half of a tetherbond knows before the other?" Isobel asked, her eyes darting between Beau and Clara before she looked away.

"No," Beau and Clara answered simultaneously, and the corners of her mouth twitched upward.

"It's not a thing for my kind," Beau continued. "At its foundation, sure, another soul made entirely for you. A connection beyond anything else. But this doesn't exist for Phoenixes, so I may be speaking out of turn."

Isobel seemed eager to hear his perspective for a change, which warmed Clara's heart all over again.

Beau stood before he said anything else. Gentle heat and a thrum of energy radiated down Clara's arm as his hand rested on her shoulder.

"I'm not blind, and neither are you two." He looked earnestly at Isobel. "She knows, and so do you. She's just nervous." Then he turned back to Clara, the promise of love and acceptance swirling in his amber eyes. "But she needn't be. We're all here together in this unexpected little throuple. Now, I'm going to be here, but elsewhere, so you two can have a very needed conversation. I love you." His thumb and forefinger grazed over Clara's chin before Beau left the sitting room.

It was unusual for Beau to respond so openly with Isobel around. Much less for him to have accepted what Clara had suspected for a while, but didn't have the nerve to voice. He was more mature than she gave him credit for, and perhaps she ought to mention that every so often. To thank him.

A few moments passed in a charged but not uncomfortable silence once Beau left the room. Isobel stared as she tapped the pads of her fingers to the tips of her thumbs while her hands rested in her lap. Clara couldn't look away from her. Beau wandered back out with a duffel bag slung over his shoulder and a dagger at his hip.

"If that bedroom reeks of sex when I get home, I'm burning the sheets." He winked and then continued down the hallway to the front door.

"Hypocrite!" Isobel called after him.

"Use protection!" His jovial voice boomed back and ricocheted off the walls.

Clara pinched the bridge of her nose—at least her mother wasn't home—but she couldn't quite rid herself of her grin.

Isobel rolled her eyes, though it was light-hearted.

"I know," Clara murmured as she placed her hand over Isobel's. "I've suspected for some time, actually, but the brute is right—I have been nervous."

Isobel's gaze flew to Clara's, the swirling blue and gold filled with hope. "I was worried maybe you didn't."

Clara shook her head. "It feels like a burning rope wrapped around my body, lodged into my bones. It squeezes my heart every time I'm close to you and grows barbs every time we part."

"That was rather poetic," Isobel whispered, then flipped her hand and entwined her fingers in Clara's.

"I'm struggling to express just how painful it is, and you think I'm poetic?" Clara barked a laugh.

"I think you're as beautiful as any painting or poem. Stars, since the night we met, I've been trying to recreate the feeling I get when I look into your eyes, but my brushes are ill-equipped and my paint is far too dull."

"Who's the poet now?" Clara jested with a smirk. Then, as every fibre of her being burned and froze at once, her breath lodged in her throat and she leant forward. She prayed Isobel kept her eyes fixed on hers, so she might miss the tremble of her hands as she reached out and tucked a stray pink lock behind Isobel's ear.

Isobel gasped, and Clara couldn't help but be pleased the female seemed just as nervous. Slowly, Isobel leant in close enough for their noses to touch. Clara's gaze fixed on Isobel's lips, then she struggled to look anywhere else.

The rope tugged and tugged—golden and bright—as fiery as it had ever been. It branded Clara's heart, and there was no going back. Not that she wanted to.

This was the moment.

And oh, how she'd dreamt of this. Of pushing her face into Isobel's, of tasting her lips and her tongue and everywhere else. Now she would finally know what it was like. To finally merge with this woman as it was intended. As was destined by the stars and the fates.

The anticipation and excitement were dizzying. To hell with waiting a second longer.

Isobel tasted like moonshine and birdsong and power. Like a thousand different things that all but overwhelmed Clara's senses. Isobel breathed life into Clara, a part she hadn't realised she'd been missing. It was as if she were awake for the first time, while simultaneously never wanting to be roused from the purest, most blissful dream.

Kissing Beau was rough, intense, and dangerously addictive, but kissing Isobel felt like peace and serenity. It was opposite and just as perfect.

Isobel let out a soft mewl as Clara's hands traced her velvet skin, sliding up her arms and along her back. She pressed Isobel as close to her body as possible. So close, Clara could feel Isobel's heart thumping wildly against her own chest. Clara's own raced alongside it as Isobel's hands sent sparks up her sides from where they rested on her hips.

Then she was on her back, Isobel straddling her, fingers clutched in her hair. Yet Clara couldn't think past Isobel's tongue on her lips and in her mouth, or the now violent tugging in her chest. She gasped, and Isobel pulled back, though she didn't go far. Tender kisses trailed past her jaw, down her neck, and over every section of bare skin.

"How do we make this official?" Clara whispered, entirely out of breath and giddy with need.

"The bond?" Isobel murmured, her mouth achingly close to Clara's ear.

All she could do was nod in response.

"There's a ritual." Isobel kissed the sensitive spot below Clara's ear, then again a fraction lower. "A few words." Her tongue travelled from Clara's erratic pulse to the tip of her ear. "Then we consummate our relationship."

"What do we need"—Clara's voice hitched—"for the ritual?"

"A blade." Isobel shrugged before she nibbled at Clara's ear, which drew out Clara's moan. Isobel mirrored the sound before she pulled away completely. "We break the skin and essentially combine our blood. There are a few words to be shared, then I've been told it feels as though your body is on fire or dumped under freezing waters. My parents are tethers, but my father is dramatic."

Clara chuckled, tucking loose hair behind Isobel's ear before she cupped her cheek. "Then let us find a knife. I like a little pain with my pleasure." She smirked, and as Isobel let out a peal of laughter, the sound soothed something deep in Clara's soul.

When Isobel stood and stepped away, Clara felt uncomfortably empty. But once she held out her hand and their skin met again, Clara felt relief.

In seconds they stood before the kitchen sink, the cutlery drawer open, and Isobel sliced her palm first.

"Repeat after me. Prick my skin and you shall bleed," she said softly.

Clara hardly noticed the sting of the blade as she cut her own flesh. "Prick my skin and you shall bleed."

"This life to share, I vow to thee." Isobel's eyes locked with Clara's, both hardly blinking. Clara repeated each statement slowly, with more certainty than she'd felt before. "For pain and purpose, the pleasure is mine." Isobel held her hand up, palm facing Clara. Crimson beaded and shone in the sunlight. Clara lifted her own palm to meet Isobel's. "'Til skies run red, and blood runs dry."

As soon as the words left Clara's lips, the faucet burst on and water sprayed violently into the sink, over the benchtop and covering the women before it. Clara smiled and closed her eyes as Isobel's hand pressed firmly to hers.

Pain lanced through her, from her crown to her soles, to the very tips of her fingers and toes. It was more than burning or frozen waters. It was the heat of a thousand suns exploding. The very blood running through her veins turned solid and prickled. Air came too fast, and yet not at all. Clara's soul vibrated and pulsed, pushing at every corner of her being. She gasped and cried out as Isobel groaned somewhere before or behind her. Unable to open her eyes, the sound of her tether's groan encircled

Clara, coming from every direction and inside her mind at the same time.

The most ferocious pain she'd ever experienced tore through Clara, and then it disappeared. Leaving only a carnal hunger and vicious need for the woman who stood before her. The one with the oceans and the skies dancing in her eyes and the heady scent of desire emanating from her perfect, petite form.

"Now we consummate." Clara left no room for argument, though Isobel didn't look at all interested in providing one. They didn't even bother to turn off the tap still spewing water into the sink.

Clara closed her arms around Isobel's waist and lifted her quickly. Isobel eagerly wrapped her legs around Clara's body, ankles locked, and clasped her hands behind Clara's neck as she walked them to the bedroom.

CHAPTER ELEVEN
ISOBEL

Isobel had never allowed herself to dream of consummating their tetherbond. She'd thought about it endlessly, had finally committed to her stars-given love—her soulmate—but had never really allowed herself to hope. Not with Elisabeth looming over her, or with Clara's undoubted love for the Phoenix.

But this felt like the purest high she'd ever experienced. The most powerful thrill, and the most unimaginable dream. And yet, as Clara held her close and carried her towards the bedroom—her hands tangled in Clara's hair while her legs were wrapped around Clara's waist—it was suddenly becoming a reality.

Isobel was overwhelmed by her emotions. Hell, mere hours ago she was packing to leave, but now that decision felt foolish.

Her body was alive in every sense, like she'd been woken from a haze and could now see clearly. Clara tasted of fruit and pastries as her tongue swirled in Isobel's mouth. Her hair smelled divine, and her skin was softer than anything Isobel had ever touched.

A small voice in the back of Isobel's mind repeated the words she'd tried so hard to push away.

You aren't good enough for her.

Elisabeth had snarled them at Isobel in a time of stress and anger, but she'd said them nonetheless. And she'd meant every word.

She's a queen. You're nothing.

Yet when Clara laid her in the middle of the mattress, then stood tall and raked her luminous jade eyes over her slowly with such approval, Isobel could ignore Elisabeth's voice as it all but disappeared when Clara looked at her like that. Like she wanted to devour Isobel or maybe devote herself to her. Pleasure lit her eyes and hitched up the corners of her rosy lips.

Isobel could hardly breathe as Clara pulled her shirt over her head, then dropped it to the floor, her gaze never slipping. Isobel couldn't have looked away even if she had tried, transfixed on the goddess in front of her.

A knock on the doorway made Isobel jump, while Clara only gasped. The Phoenix casually leant against the frame, his smirk wide.

"Are you aware that *all* the faucets in the house are blasting water?" He asked, his eyebrows raised.

Clara groaned quietly, but Isobel had no intention of answering. She certainly had no interest in entertaining the male while Clara stood there half naked. She was not his to dote on tonight, nor was she his to covet. Isobel narrowed her eyes slightly, then called to her uncharacteristically quiet air magic. For once, it sang not of murder but sighed contentedly. Without a word, Isobel sent a small gust of wind to close the door with the Phoenix on the other side. He chuckled softly and announced he'd be gone for a few days as his footsteps receded down the hall.

Isobel reached for Clara's hand, tugging her towards the bed. She giggled as she fell on top of Isobel, but then her smile faltered.

"What?" Isobel asked, her nerves skyrocketing as that annoying little voice started humming again.

"I think the taps are on because of me," Clara whispered, and slowly lowered her gaze from Isobel's eyes to her lips. Isobel's tongue darted out subconsciously, but the sound Clara made as a result had her wanting to do it again as warmth coiled and built at her core.

"I think we can worry about water wastage another time, love." She replied softly as she cupped her hand to Clara's cheek. "For now . . ." her voice trailed off as Isobel lowered her hand, her fingers barely tracing Clara's jaw and collarbone until her hand was at Clara's ribs.

Then Clara's mouth was on hers again and stars erupted behind her eyes, in her chest, and down to her fingertips and toes. Explosions and bursts of energy that set her body alight.

Clara planted one hand on the mattress beside Isobel's head. The other pressed to Isobel's jaw in a way that enraged the heat at her core and sent it spiralling lower, and she clamped her thighs together in response. Clara licked and sucked at her bottom lip, then her knee nudged Isobel's legs apart, causing her to moan into Clara's mouth.

Her body pushed against Isobel's, their breasts pressed together, Clara's pelvis tilted tight to Isobel's thigh. Isobel's hips bucked upwards as sounds of pleasure rolled from one tongue to another. The symphony was seductive, full of need, and absolute perfection.

In a heartbeat, Isobel's shirt was gone, and Clara was standing again. Her trousers were next, and then Isobel's were torn from her body. She inhaled sharply, but Clara only winked before she crawled back over Isobel, planting intoxicatingly delicate kisses along her naked torso.

Reaching halfway up her arms, Clara pushed upwards and smirked down at Isobel. "So hot," she murmured, then dragged her index finger up Isobel's arm and then down towards her navel. Then her finger dragged lower, past her already desperate pussy, only to send teasing zaps of power along her inner thighs. Isobel mewled, and her eyelids fluttered as her head dipped back into the mattress.

She could barely move while Clara toyed with her; heat and wetness building at her core as electric shocks pulsed so close to where she needed Clara to touch her.

As if she could read Isobel's mind, Clara stopped teasing and slowly circled Isobel's clit with her warm fingertip. "I can't wait to fucking taste you."

"Don't let me stop you," Isobel replied on a breath.

Clara chuckled low and sultry before she brought her finger to her mouth and sucked it dry. Decadent sounds rolled from Clara's tongue, while desire blazed in her eyes as she stared at Isobel.

Her eyes locked on Isobel's as she thrust open Isobel's thighs and lowered herself down the bed. Kneeling just past the mattress, Clara tugged Isobel to the edge, and then she feasted with slow, languid movements.

Warmth and passion. Isobel couldn't form a cohesive thought, let alone say a word. All she could manage were moans that made Clara press her tongue more firmly to Isobel's clit. She rolled her hips upward, and before long they moved as one. In rhythm, and loving every second.

Isobel buried one hand in Clara's hair, while the other cupped her own breast, and her lover moaned in approval. She gasped, arching her back when Clara inserted two fingers inside her and stroked at her inner walls. The overwhelming sensation radiated through her, a coiling feeling that built and built, ebbing and flowing, sliding her oh so dangerously close to the edge.

Isobel hadn't been with anyone before, knowing she wanted to wait for her tether. She'd known someone was out there for her, and wanted to give them all of herself. Isobel had expected to feel nervous, or more unsure, but she melded with Clara's body naturally. This was who the stars had made entirely for her, the soul splintered from her own until they met again. Clara was her other half, and there was no need to be nervous.

Everything was exactly as it was supposed to be. As Clara worshipped every inch of Isobel, she embraced the most blissful, exhilarating release. It soared through her with a power like nothing she'd ever known.

Breathless and flushed, her skin dampened with sweat, Isobel chuckled.

Clara lay beside her, and her hand ran tenderly along Isobel's bare skin, causing goosebumps to rise over every inch.

Isobel turned her head and kissed Clara fiercely.

"I love you," she whispered, entirely captured in those jewel-like eyes.

"I love you too."

Two days later, and they still hadn't left the bedroom. Felicity had knocked twice and left refreshments by the door, but otherwise Isobel and Clara had been in a sex-filled haze. They'd licked, flicked, and tortured every inch of one another—multiple times.

When another knock landed on the door, Isobel could only laugh as Clara hobbled to collect their tray. She tutted as she sprang past Clara, opening the door only a fraction.

But Felicity did not stand on the other side, rather, it was the Phoenix. Though even he couldn't dull Isobel's smile. She quickly threw a hand over Clara's mouth and held her behind the door.

"Yes?" she asked him politely.

"Have you seen Clara lately?" Beau asked, his tone full of jest and entirely too knowing.

"Seen Clara?" Isobel mused while she made a show of thinking. Rubbing her free hand over her chin was probably a tad much, but she'd been riding a high for the past three days. She'd be damned if he was going to bring her back down to reality, not yet anyway.

Beau rolled his eyes, though it was light-hearted.

"Yes, Isobel. I need to speak with her."

"Right, well, I'll let her know you stopped by. She's currently indisposed and not taking visitors."

To her surprise, Beau laughed. "It absolutely does reek of sex in there, by the way." Before he turned to leave, he called out, "It's not urgent, but it is time-sensitive, sweetheart. So come out soon, will you?"

Isobel narrowed her eyes slightly, then closed the door.

Clara burst out laughing as soon as Isobel removed her hand from Clara's mouth. She grabbed it, then kissed both sides. "As much as I would love to stay wrapped up in this sex-reeking room for eternity with you, I also have things I need to do."

Isobel groaned but didn't protest further. With a sigh, Isobel handed Clara her shirt from a few nights ago. It hadn't moved from its spot on the floor since Clara took it off, much like everything else besides the females and bedspread.

Just as Clara lowered the shirt over her head, a cloud of charcoal smoke erupted in the corner, and a familiarly daunting figure emerged.

"Apologies," Ryn muttered, sounding mostly sincere. "I didn't mean to intrude, but I have some pressing matters to discuss with you, Clara. Get dressed."

"Take a number."

"Why?" Isobel and Clara spoke simultaneously.

"I need help to acquire some information, and time is not on my side." She spoke almost dismissively, and doused in black and shadows, Ryn looked like a messenger of Death. Perhaps even Death's right-hand woman.

A shiver raked down Isobel's spine at the thought of a Reaper in Clara's bedroom.

"Where are we going?" Clara asked calmly, as she stepped into her trousers.

"Tirenas."

Such a way with words. Isobel fought not to roll her eyes.

"Must you? Right this second?" She asked, unable to keep the annoyance from her tone.

Ryn's depthless eyes landed on Isobel and seemed to soften slightly. "Congratulations to you both on the bond. I do sincerely apologise for ruining your post-bond haze, but I'm running out of time." Ryn sounded genuine, but as she reached for Clara's hand, a near-irrational anger clouded Isobel's vision and all she saw was red. She hadn't meant to snarl, and Ryn pulled away from Clara immediately.

"You know as well as I do that to transport someone else, one must touch. Is this going to be a problem?" She waited impatiently for Isobel to respond, her foot tapping the carpet.

Isobel huffed. "If she comes back with so much as a hair out of place, I will hold you personally responsible, and that will not be pleasant for you."

Ryn smiled at the threat, then dipped her chin in acknowledgement. Perhaps also in promise, but that was yet to be seen.

Clara strolled to Isobel and planted a firm kiss on her lips, then a gentler one on her temple before pulling away.

"I won't be long," she said. "Please let Beau know. I love you both."

And then Death's mistress and the light of Isobel's life evaporated in a cloud of darkness.

CHAPTER TWELVE
CLARA

Clara's heart thrashed and screamed in her chest as Ryn pulled her through the shadow-portal, but strangely enough, it wasn't painful. Not like when Isobel had walked away the night they'd met, nor any other time they'd been separated.

This felt like too much distance had been forced between them, or perhaps something essential to her had been taken, yet she was sure of its return, and calm enough to push past the discomfort.

Clara hated being away from Isobel. It wasn't natural and was a thousand times worse since they'd solidified their bond. Though she had no doubt they'd be together again soon, which helped keep her level and composed.

"Tethered life suits you, Majesty."

"Oh, please don't. I may have the title, but I've not yet worn the crown, so I don't think it counts." She tried to hide her blush with her hair, dipping her chin so it might cover her face.

Ryn chuckled, a short and deep sound. "You cannot shy away for long."

Clara inhaled deeply but didn't respond.

"Are you aware your father is in town?"

"My biological father?"

Ryn nodded, a low hum reverberating in her throat.

Clara remained silent. She was aware he was in Wave, of course, likely still in Iloura, though past that she didn't know what to think, let alone voice. How long had he been there? Why had he come in the first place? And why exactly was Ryn aware of his presence?

Clara hadn't wanted a bar of him when they'd met briefly, but was he still determined to see her? What did she want the answer to be? Did he know about the coronation? Her betrothal?

So many questions stormed Clara's mind and burned along her skin that she unwillingly grew lost in them until Ryn cleared her throat.

"Have you seen Ora recently?"

"Yes," Clara mumbled, still not entirely focused on the grim female.

"And you learnt a thing or two while in her company?" Ryn pressed, her face unreadable but her tone slightly more persistent. More firm, almost desperate.

"Are you engaging in idle chitchat, Ryn, or is there something specific you would like to know?" The words fell from her tongue with an exhaustion Clara didn't recognise. As if suddenly the weight of a thousand worlds lay on her shoulders.

"I do not *chitchat*, Highness." Ryn narrowed her eyes but composed her face quickly. "I merely wished to gauge what you know before sharing any further information. I need your help, so it would be more than foolish of me to frighten or upset you."

Clara hummed in agreement before she responded. "Yes, I spoke with Ora. She told me about Death's Daughters and Beau's secrets. It wasn't my favourite reading."

"Do you remember what I said to you the last we spoke?" she asked as she urged Clara up a familiar set of stairs, though she couldn't remember where they led.

"'*They're all going to die*' stuck with me, yes."

Ryn nodded. "You might be pleased to hear the future has shifted."

Clara halted abruptly, her eyes wide and hands frantically grabbing at Ryn's forearm.

"They're going to live?" she asked, with hope held dangerously close to her heart. But then she remembered that not everyone was alive even now.

"Not necessarily," Ryn quickly continued as she gestured for Clara to keep walking. "Their fate was certain when I arrived at your castle those months ago. Now, they could as easily survive."

The sliver of hope all but shattered in her chest. No one was safe, and Clara couldn't figure out a damn thing to change fate. Fifty-fifty wasn't good enough.

"Fret not." Ryn's voice was lighter than a second ago. "There is a boy who could help sway chance in your favour. Now, I do not usually dwell on future outcomes. However, I know with damn near certainty that with him on your side of the battlefield, you raise your chances—"

"Who?" Clara demanded before Ryn had even finished speaking.

"His name is Darius. He's only fourteen years old, but his power is—"

"No." Cutting her off again, Clara waved her arms for emphasis. "No children."

Ryn shrugged. "It's your call, Majesty. But I assure you, he'll sway the tide. If I were your adviser, I would strongly advise you to encourage him to stay. Only you can change his course. Speak to him at least, feel the abilities rolling off him."

The female looked hungry at the mention of this kid's power, and for the first time, Clara considered how well she truly knew Ryn.

Not well at all, she concluded.

No wind picked up at her nape, and her soles were void of any tingling. Her magic remained calm around Ryn, even though her body told her to be wary.

They turned four corners before Ryn spoke again.

"I need to ask a favour. The male I showed you a small portrait of when we met previously is dangerous and was scheduled for death in another realm. Somehow he escaped execution, and it has thrown off the balance of his universe. We do not know how or where he landed. The Tirenas library has thousands of ancient texts and may provide the answers I seek. Help me access it, and I will owe you a favour, Queen of Elanist, to call in at any time. I am out of options. However, between two level-headed queens, I'm certain you'll come to an agreement."

Ryn smirked, but before Clara could respond to her sarcasm or even ask what a photograph was, Ryn threw open heavy wooden doors. Beyond them stood Eveline with her back to Clara and two guards. One she would recognise anywhere—Evian. The other had short hair, dark wings, and a face full of outrage when she noticed Clara and Ryn and stormed over.

Evian quickly noticed and bowled past the feathered female to embrace Clara tightly. He smelled of home, although it was different, more like a memory that she had outgrown. Now, Isobel smelled like home to her, and so did Beau.

"Any other day and I might curse you for yet again wandering onto my lands without so much as a warning, but today, I'm glad you're here." Eveline sighed as she all but floated towards Clara, her thin fingers folded together.

It was the last thing Clara had expected to come from the queen's mouth, and yet looking at her worn face and untidy hair, Clara could see something was weighing on Eveline.

She felt for the queen, though she couldn't say she was entirely disappointed to find Eveline in such a state. After all, if she was pleased with Clara's presence, their discussion would surely go more smoothly.

"Care to enlighten me, Majesty, on this sudden change of heart?" Clara asked, watching as concern laced the edges of Evian's eyes and stiffened the unknown female's face.

Eveline sighed again, then she dismissed the female with a flick of her wrist. The queen's head cocked to the side as her attention landed on Evian, though with a subtle, resigned shake of her head, she allowed him to stay. Silently, she ushered them further into the grand hallway towards an alcove and another set of doors. Ryn stayed by the entrance, silent and stoic, and entirely imposing.

"I don't know where they're coming from or why, but I'm tired, Clara."

Sweeping open one of the doors before them, Eveline revealed what had once been an outdoor dining space, or perhaps a tranquil landing. The balcony had white marble pillars and stone flooring, and planters hung from a beam above the table and twin chairs. Even now, the view beyond was breathtaking, as soft clouds rolled over a lavender sky far in the distance.

But now all that remained of the planters were the few leaves and petals that clung to whatever shattered surfaces were left. Only one of the two chairs remained whole; the other lay broken and charred. Half of the floor had caved in, leaving a large, jagged hole where one might stand to watch the sunset.

"This attempt their timing was a fraction off. Perhaps they are watching me, or maybe they are amateurs playing assassin. The damned floor blew up just as I stepped back inside."

Smoke still rose in near-invisible tendrils, though the smell was not so faint. It wafted, almost as a cruel joke on her senses, and as it blew away another scent touched Clara's nostrils. It was not unlike when she'd murdered the king, though she would not voice that particular memory.

"Do you have many enemies?" Clara asked, before she could consider the question.

"My father was a terrible male. Brutal and violent and cruel." Eveline raised a brow, and the corner of her mouth twitched upwards in a bitter smirk. "I was his favourite daughter. What do you think?"

Clara couldn't help but grimace in response.

"Lighten up, Clara." Eveline waved her off, then continued as she pulled the balcony door closed. "I am not my father, but you cannot be so naïve as to believe I did not inherit more than his kingdom."

She scoffed, though Clara was surprised to find it was not as filled with disdain as it might've once been. "You said you're pleased to see me. Why?"

"I thought you said she was intelligent," Eveline muttered to Evian.

He shrugged, and his signature cocky grin spread across his face. Clara's heart swelled watching her brother, so at ease and comfortable here. She was happy for him, truly, but stars, she missed him.

"She's one of the smartest females I know," Evian replied, then without missing a beat added, "Smart mouthed too." He winked as Clara rolled her eyes.

"I need your help, Clara." Eveline turned from Evian, ignoring him as she poured out what felt like every ounce of her anguish.

Clara fought not to fidget under the queen's gaze. "How?"

"If I knew what I needed, Clara, I would not be turning to an amateur with less than a year's elemental wielding under her belt."

"Keep that tone up, Eveline, and I'll take my brother home and leave you to your foes." Clara narrowed her eyes. Then she and the queen both sighed—level-headed, indeed. "Truthfully, I don't know what help I'll be, but I will try."

Relief washed over the queen. She must've truly been desperate to be counting on Clara's assistance. Sure, they'd moved on from their hatred of the past, but for her to have hoped for Clara's help, perhaps she was more fearful than she had let on.

"However," Clara continued before Eveline could reply, "I need something from you in return."

"You may *request* whatever you like," Eveline responded quickly. Though Clara didn't miss the slight emphasis in her tone.

"Ryn needs access to some texts stored in your library. Provide her with these texts, and I will attempt to help you with your problem."

Clara gestured over her shoulder for Ryn to come closer, which she did almost eagerly. For a few moments, they discussed the information she needed, and which tomes and scrolls she would search. She did not allude to what she needed them for, though Clara supposed that wasn't Eveline's concern.

Then Ryn pulled a dagger from a pocket and held it to Eveline.

"What the fuck, Ryn?" Clara screeched. "What is that for?"

Ryn raised a single brow, confusion pulling at her lip and shoulders. "For the bargain," she answered, looking between Eveline and Clara as if they should've already known. "You might trust her enough to keep her word, but I do not. I hardly trust you enough to keep yours, Clara. We agree to the bargain and seal it in blood. As your fae ancestors did before you.”

“We haven’t practiced bargains in centuries.” Insult dripped from Eveline’s shrill tone.

“Why must we seal it in blood, Ryn?” Clara asked. “What else is there?”

An unfamiliar and unnatural smile contorted Ryn’s lips. It looked gruesome on her otherwise attractive face.

“Intelligent indeed, Clarenna.”

“You’ve never called me that before . . .”

An uneasy feeling skittered over Clara’s shoulders and down her spine.

CHAPTER THIRTEEN
EVELINE

"Clarenna Hayes, what kind of creature did you bring into my castle?" Eveline shrieked as the female's hair smoked and an acrid smell filled the room.

Evian gagged beside her. Charming. If he was going to prove useless in dire situations, she'd have to fire him from the guard. Perhaps still keep him as a consort, but she'd consider that later.

"I don't know!" Clara fired back, her eyes wild. "And for the record, she brought me."

"That is entirely not the point!" Eveline hissed, then turned her attention back towards the female whose eyes were now swirling black. "What are you?"

"Perhaps she's not the only intelligent one in the room." Her voice sounded serpentine, and there was something almost familiar about it, but Eveline couldn't put her finger on what.

"She's a Reaper," Clara whispered, her eyes locked on the female whose head snapped to Clara when she spoke.

"Fuck." Evian bit out the curse, then sprang into action. He raced from the room, and thankfully, the Reaper paid him no mind.

Eveline's father had told her relentlessly what would happen if the Reapers came, whether it was in the dead of night or middle of the day.

If they came, darkness would unravel.

He'd warned both his girls that Reapers were not to be trusted. They were bloodthirsty and cruel. Vile creatures who had no place in his castle.

He'd alluded to having wards placed to ensure they'd be kept out. Or at least be made to show themselves if they somehow made it inside.

Eveline supposed that's what was happening now. The swirling black eyes and burning hair, the animalistic expressions on the Reaper's face. Yet she'd seemed no more than a standard fae when she'd first arrived. Civil enough, and uninterested in conversation.

But something felt not quite right as she watched the female twitch before her. It was in the unnatural grin and snap of her neck, how her knees locked and bounced, wrists jerking and twisting repeatedly.

"Does she normally act like this?" Eveline asked Clara, her tone hushed but urgent.

"No," Clara responded quickly. "I've never seen this behaviour before."

Before she could say anything else, Evian burst into the room with one of the palace librarians in tow. She held a thin, linen-bound book to her chest, fear shadowing her face.

"Majesty," she squeaked as Eveline took the book from her. Now was not the time for pleasantries.

Most of the pages were empty, except for the last two. Second to last was a note, signed Luellena, her mother. Eveline had hardly known the woman, but her heart lurched at the sight of her handwriting and name all the same.

The last page contained only three lines.

Remove the wall.

Let power fall.

Vekna'avol.

Eveline didn't know what the last word even meant, but she read it aloud anyway.

Immediately the Reaper relaxed. So did Clara, as evidenced by how she clutched at the Reaper's shaking arms.

"Ryn?" she asked. "Are you alright?"

"Superb," Ryn drawled, then turned on Eveline with narrowed eyes. "Why, pray tell, are there curses under your roof for my kind?"

"Actually, I can answer that." Evian chimed in before any words could escape Eveline's open mouth. "As part of my initial training, I was made aware of any threats known to the guard. One of the first I was told of was an ancient being who came bearing gifts in exchange for respite and a witch capable of portal magic. He was said to have arrived millennia ago in the dead of night, wearing clothing and jewels so bright the moon disappeared.

"The being gave the king dozens of vials filled with all manner of powders and stones and liquids. He told him how to use them and their purpose." He turned to his sister, who stood silent. "That's how he got the threshnic stones and the uortna powder."

Clara visibly paled, and her nostrils flared as she swallowed hard.

"Why don't I know what either of those things are?" Eveline asked, unsure why she knew the least in her own damned castle.

"Threshnic stones can soundproof a location, in either a closed or open environment. A single ring will shield the outside world from whatever happens inside, even if it's painful, bloody murder." As she answered, Clara wore an expression Eveline couldn't name. "I'm going out on a limb and assuming the powder negates healing abilities. One dose will reduce a fae's ability to heal herself by half. Also fucking painful, I would gather." She folded her arms, now more than done and unwilling to talk again. Jerking her chin forward, she gestured for her brother to continue speaking.

Ryn hadn't moved, still as a statue, though her countenance had changed slightly. She seemed more interested than infuriated now.

"He also told the king about the danger of the Reapers. How aggressive and quick to judge one might be if they found out how powerful he was." Evian rolled his eyes, then sighed and continued. "His Majesty adored his ego being stroked, so believed the being without question. He enlisted the help of a few witches to create a protective spell over the grounds in case one of your kind ever came to visit."

Evian winced slightly, clearly uncomfortable with what he was going to say next, and Eveline couldn't blame him. As eager as she was to hear what Evian had to say, Ryn looked like she might pluck his life force straight through his lush mouth if she didn't like what she heard. Her father had said they were capable of such feats. That they could pull a soul from the gap in one's teeth, through their navel, or from under a fingernail. She's been raised on horrifying nightmares like them sucking eyeballs from sockets and swallowing them whole or flaying someone's skin to use as their own. Eveline tried not to shudder at the memories of frightful bedtime tales and warnings to behave, else the Reapers would snatch her before the sun rose.

"Essentially, the spell inhibits your morality and reverts you into your most beast-like form, which after prolonged exposure turns you on yourself. The end goal is suicide."

Ryn's left eye twitched, then her nostrils flared. Her lips thinned to only a line on her face, then she nodded once and turned to the librarian and barked, "You will hand over any and all information on this otherworldly being. About his encounter with your previous king and everything on the magic he brought. Do you understand?"

A small squeak came from the librarian, who did not make eye contact with anyone. Her owlish gaze jumped to each of them before it landed back at her feet.

"I don't care what you agree to in exchange for this information, Clara, but I have no doubt this is the male I've been searching for." Ryn locked eyes with Clara for a long moment, then nodded, her shoulders slumping slightly.

Ryn turned to Eveline, a sinister expression tugging at the corner of her mouth. "I'm sure you've heard all the bedtime stories, Majesty. Trust there is some truth behind every tale."

The Reaper winked, then ushered the librarian out of the room. The poor female was so tense that with a strong enough nudge, she might crumble.

"Well, that was intense," Evian said, his tone far more casual than a moment ago, but his hand rubbed at the back of his neck, betraying his nerves.

"And look at you," Clara drawled as she walked over to her brother. "The big tough soldier, come to save the day." The siblings chuckled as they embraced, and an odd sensation clung to Eveline's ribcage.

"Do not mock me, sister. I saved the queen."

While Evian puffed his chest, Clara simply rolled her eyes and turned back to Eveline. "I'll help you, bargain or not."

Eveline let out a long breath. "Thank the heavens."

Clara nodded earnestly. "What was that you read earlier . . . a counterspell?"

Eveline shrugged. "I assume so. It was in my mother's handwriting. Stars only know what she had to put up with from my father—I wouldn't be surprised to find a hundred other notes scrawled about the castle so I can fix where he's meddled."

"Perhaps you didn't inherit as much from him as you think," Clara murmured. "Genetics are fickle, a friend told me once. The gods decide what we need. I'd bet there's a decent amount of your mother in you, though I don't know how good that will prove to be."

"Clarenna Hayes, are you being friendly or are you simply daft and insulting?" Eveline spoke light-heartedly, though she already knew the answer. Clara's words struck a little deeper than the playful exchange she'd meant. Instead, they sank into the well of hope she'd thought had all but run dry after decades without her mother. Without a light to counter her father's dark effect.

She'd given up hope of being anything like her mother many, many moons ago. With every day that passed, Eveline grew further and further from her memory.

Yet perhaps there was more of her mother in her than she'd allowed herself to dream. Perhaps now she could carry her mother and Solaris within her, and be the light they could've become. Maybe the fiery redhead who murdered her father would help Eveline in more ways than she expected, and truthfully, she was excited to find out. Hope felt raw and painful, but for the first time in too long, she felt alive again.

CHAPTER FOURTEEN
CLARA

When Clara approached Ryn, who was immersed in her search of the Tirenas library, she showed no inclination to leave. Instead, the Reaper scrutinised her for a few long seconds, then flicked her wrist, causing a dark swirling portal to open beside Clara. Immediately, Ryn turned back to her book, skimming and flipping the pages greedily. She wondered who this male was that the Reaper was so insistent on finding.

Clara turned to inspect the vortex more closely. A strange hum came from the depthless centre, where the shades of grey and black were the darkest. Clouds of charcoal and lighter greys spun so fast Clara was dizzy watching, then suddenly they stilled. Nerves bubbled in her chest, though Clara knew it was due to fear of the unknown.

"I thought I needed you to touch me to go through the portal," Clara said, eyeing the swirling shadows sceptically.

"And forgive me for stating the obvious, but that you needed to go through it as well."

Ryn mumbled a noncommittal sound but did not look up from the text. Then in less than a moment, Ryn spoke again. "Take her home."

Heavy clicks sounded from Clara's right, and she whipped around so fast a muscle spasmed in her neck. Another Reaper—she had to assume—now stood before the portal. She dressed similarly to Ryn, though where Ryn's clothing was sleek and dark, this female's clothes looked as though they were made of moss and fawn pelts. Half of her wanted to reach out and touch the outfit, though thankfully her common sense prevailed and Clara kept her hands to herself. Reapers may not be the violent and vicious creatures Urian portrayed them to be, but they certainly weren't friendly.

The Reaper stretched a pale arm towards Clara. It was decorated with long nails and chains with miniature daggers hanging at seemingly random points. Not a bracelet, but jewellery all the same.

Clara took her icy hand and muttered goodbye to Ryn before she was dragged through the portal. How this stranger knew where she was going was anyone's guess. Being spat out in her living room was honestly not what Clara was expecting, despite mostly trusting the Reapers. She drew in a deep, relief-filled breath and rolled her shoulders.

"You're a fucking cheater," Beau grumbled as he slammed a handful of cards onto the floor.

"And you're a sore loser," Isobel responded, her tone light and melodic.

Beau stuck his tongue out, only proving her to be right, then made to stand when he noticed Clara.

"Oh, how I love it when the children get along." She sighed with a smile as Beau leant down and planted a short but sweet kiss on her lips.

"Woman, make up your mind," Beau drawled. "Am I old and grey under the moonlight or am I a child?"

"I see no moonlight yet," Isobel muttered. "Perhaps you could be both?"

To Clara's surprise, Beau laughed. An unfiltered, damn near cackle. Perhaps they truly were getting along. He'd voluntarily left them only a few nights ago, well aware of how they'd be spending their time. He'd even made jokes.

Seeing it happening before her eyes was a gentle thrill she hadn't expected, and at the very least, not so soon. Beau was not the kind to share, and Isobel had reacted rather strongly the last time someone else attempted to touch Clara. This was going to be interesting indeed, but Clara was more than excited to watch their trio evolve and grow together.

Maybe Beau might finally feel confident enough to spill his secrets. Clara didn't hope too hard for that, though. In stubbornness, he was her match.

"How was Her Majesty?" Beau asked, with an odd flourish to his voice that Clara didn't recognise. She raised a brow at him, though he only smirked and shrugged.

"She's got folk trying to kill her. Two failed attempts so far that I know of. She has no idea who they are or what their plan is, and she is getting desperate enough to even ask for my help."

"I'm all for helping the needy, but if she puts you in a dangerous position—a deadly position—she's going to have another threat to worry about." Isobel's face was hard, and she spoke with such a calmness it left Clara pitying whoever ended up on her bad side. Then her gentle lips curved into a menacing smile as she added, "And I don't fail."

"For such a bright and cheery individual, Isobel, you frighten me sometimes." Beau ran a hand over the back of his neck, his eyes widening comically.

Isobel only smiled more genuinely and patted his chest. She raised up on her tiptoes and whispered right into his ear, "Good."

He shuddered, and Clara couldn't help laughing.

It was short-lived, however, as Ryland appeared in the corner of the room.

"Is everything all right?" Isobel asked.

He nodded. "Peter has arrived at the palace and is ready to discuss plans for Christopher."

"Who the fuck is Peter?" Clara blurted.

Isobel tried to hide her chuckle with a cough but was unsuccessful. She cleared her throat before answering.

"Diedre's clan leader. I mentioned Elisabeth's request to her at the ball in Morrin, and she agreed to set up a meeting with him. I suppose that meeting is now."

"Yes." Ryland paused with a nod, then gestured for Clara to follow him. "He'd be doing us a favour, and we should not keep him waiting."

"Ryland, I don't even know what Elisabeth wanted with the wolves. I don't know what she was worried about. I barely even know Christopher, I—"

Clouds of black smoke and blinding bursts of light blind Clara. She tries to blink it all away, but it is of no use. Flashes of her nephew dart across her limited vision.

A hallway, bright and airy, filled with portraits of a small boy turned young man. No black clouds, only the long corridor, decorated and full of life.

Further down the hall, frames still cover the walls, but they are now empty.

The portraits are gone. Ripped away from some and torn beyond recognition in others. But the last frame, at the end of the hall, has never been filled.

As if Christopher simply does not exist.

Somehow, Clara knew this was not the vision her sister had received. Not only because their magic worked differently, but because empty frames would not have her searching for myths and legends or hiding away her only child. She also knew that while in the vision Christopher no longer existed in the portraits, it foretold that in that future he simply ceased to exist at all.

A hollow pit formed in her gut, uncomfortable and unwelcome. Visions like these reminded her why she'd cursed the Mother and decided she'd never existed in the first place. Why would a deity so full of love for her children create a reality in which a three-year-old had to suffer?

"Why can't they ever be good visions?" Clara muttered. "Something filled with love and light and—"

Isobel stares towards the performer, who sings a tune of two lovers, born at different times in different places, each bearing half of the same soul. She stands far enough away that she has to squint to see them, though she isn't paying them much attention. Her gaze reaches further, seeing nothing but searching everything. Flickers of gold tease her skin, and she worries about the dizziness and near-floating feeling scrambling down her arms. Too quickly, she decides she's breathing in second-hand recreational smoke. She's right to prioritise her sobriety, but she doesn't know the truth.

Beau wanders the outskirts of town, close enough to hear the thrumming, lively music and feel the bonfire's warmth. Yet far enough away that he's covered by the shadows of trees and dwindling residences. He's never been to a festival in Elanist before. A tug pulls him towards the flames, and he contemplates investigating, even steps towards the town before his chest constricts and he takes that feeling as a bad omen. He doesn't understand, so he leaves.

Clara's chest filled with an almost unbearable warmth as she blinked and found both lovers staring back at her. With a smile so wide it hurt and a single tear falling from each eye, she cupped a hand to each of their faces.

"Thank you, universe," she whispered, then pulled away from Beau and Isobel. "I appreciate the balance."

"Care to explain what the fuck that was?" Beau asked, his voice hushed.

"We were all at the New Moon festival in Breath four years ago," Clara said calmly, though her heart felt giddy. "You wandered along one side of the bonfire while I sat on the other." She turned to Isobel. "And you watched the male perform the song about tethers, just as I did. I felt someone watching me. You weren't—I doubt you even saw me that day, but I felt you."

Isobel blushed, a subtle rose colouring the bridge of her nose and the centre of her cheeks, and somehow she became even more adorable. The love Clara felt for both her and Beau was overwhelming. It filled her with such pride and desire and greed that all she wanted was for Ryland to leave so she could show them both exactly how much she cared.

But duty called, and Clara had to answer.

"When will you meet with him?" Ryland asked.

Clara sighed. "Honestly, I don't know. Can't you bring him here?"

Ryland gasped, then shook his head. "That is entirely improper, Clara."

"Yes, but is it unachievable? I am the queen, am I not?" She planted her hands on her hips and didn't wait for Ryland to answer before she pressed him a little harder. "Does that not allow me to do what I want?"

He sighed heavily as he contemplated a suitable response.

Again, Clara filled the silence. "Excellent, it's settled then. Bring him here at his earliest convenience, and I'll discuss what to do with my nephew moving forward. Tomorrow is Isobel's birthday, and tonight I just want to sleep. Do not bring him here within the next forty-eight hours."

"So much for *his earliest convenience*," Ryland muttered.

"Oh, shush." Clara gave him a pat on the shoulder and a kiss on his cheek before she started down the hallway towards her room.

She did not check whether Beau and Isobel followed her. She knew they would at some point. Despite it not yet being time for bed, all she wanted to do was curl up under the covers between her loves.

Unfortunately for them, they didn't get a choice in the matter.

CHAPTER FIFTEEN
BEAU

When he'd left a few days ago, Beau was dizzy with the thrill of Clara's reciprocated feelings. That she wanted him, that she'd announced clear as day she would choose him. It astounded him every time the words replayed in his mind, despite how many times he'd heard them since. He was pathetically drunk on love and willing to give her whatever she needed.

The longer he'd thought about it, the more he realised it was something he would need to continue—allowing the females their time alone. He didn't hate the idea and knew perfectly well how they would spend their time together. It still riled him a little, but he'd promised to learn how to share Clara. It would not be easy, though nothing with Clara ever was.

Beau didn't necessarily *want* Isobel fucking the love of his life—the first good thing to happen to him in a long time— but he also knew that while he was one of Clara's loves, he wasn't the only one. The time away had allowed him to process his thoughts. It gave him free rein to get pissed off and frustrated and grumpy, without saying something he would quickly regret.

Beau also considered how Isobel must feel, knowing the soul she'd expected to be entirely hers was attached to another. It wasn't exactly something she'd expected—something they had in common. He was smugly proud of himself for considering her in such a way, and for his somewhat uncharacteristic maturity. Perhaps the females had rubbed off on him.

Fuck, he'd even allowed Clara's winged friend, Mikhail, to carry him like a limp stars-damned doll across to Tirenas so he could see Diandra and Merrick. All to collect a birthday gift for the other woman. Beau chuckled silently to himself at the insane thought that he was buying presents for Clara's mistress. He knew she was more than that, but the thought was humorous nonetheless. Mikhail would hopefully be back in Iloura tomorrow with the gifts, and he could offer those as a token of his intentions for their future.

Phoenixes were inherently good at giving gifts, with a desire to shower their loved ones with trinkets and affection. His mother had explained to him as a young boy not to judge a gift by its material value, but to shower loved ones with acts of kindness instead. To dote on and provide for the ones he loved. Typically, a soulmate, but others as well, like friends and relatives, just not to the same extent. For Beau, that *one* was Clara, but for her it was Isobel *and* Beau. So, to show his love for Clara, he'd shower Isobel as well.

Beau hadn't expected to return home and find Isobel by herself. She'd been frazzled and skittish, while also focused on the empty fireplace. Honestly, it made Beau a little nervous. Not to mention, the closer he'd stepped towards her, the cooler the air had grown—no doubt her doing.

In contrast, as Clara sauntered down the hallway, the air grew warm and humid. Beau watched Isobel melt as she stared behind Clara. Fuck, she was a tease. She had both of them standing there, jaws slack and desperate to follow. Clara hadn't even said goodbye to Ryland before she'd turned away and left the room.

Turning back to Ryland for a very brief clap on the shoulder, Beau eagerly waited for the male to leave. Perhaps the urgency shone in his eyes because Ryland gave a coy grin and disappeared without a word.

Beau and Isobel were in the hallway before he could register that his legs had moved. His dick twitched, already wanting to escape the linen prison of his pants. When he entered the bedroom, the feeling only intensified.

Clara lay casually on her side, face propped on her hand. Completely naked and stunningly captivating, with all her divine curves on show.

"Fuck," he breathed.

Isobel moved like a wraith—fast and fluid—across the room until she was on the bed. She crawled to Clara, then whispered, "May I?" as her fingertips hovered over Clara's skin, skimming her full breasts and mouth, trailing dangerously close to Clara's rosy lips.

He expected to hate seeing Isobel so close, but there was a charged, heady energy in the room. Beau knew without a doubt how much Clara was going to enjoy being the centre of their attention. His cock hardened imagining the sounds coming from her and the expressions on her face. Without thought, his palm pressed to his crotch, and he did not miss the quick glance Clara spared him nor the slight hitch of her breath.

"Please," Clara replied, her voice a heavy plea. Fuck, she was going to torture them.

"She takes orders pretty well, too, you know." Beau palmed his growing cock again as his eyes locked with Clara's.

Something playful stared back from her jade eyes, and something devilish.

Beau saw Isobel's face scrunch as she shook her head. "I don't want to give her orders."

He turned to Isobel, his hand still pressed firmly to his aching bulge. "Do you want to take orders instead?"

Isobel pondered for a moment before she asked, "From you?" She turned her nose up slightly at the suggestion. "Or from her?" Isobel's face softened slightly as her eyes fell to Clara, her voice wistful.

Beau shrugged. "She is very bossy, but—" Beau closed the space between him and Clara, leant over, and pressed his fingers to her jaw. "Open up," he demanded.

Clara obeyed immediately.

Beau smirked before he spat into her mouth. "She can't speak very well with her mouth full."

A subtle pink tinge flushed Isobel's chest and cheeks. She looked away, then said quietly, "I'm not sure."

Something about the way she responded smacked Beau in the face. Her vulnerability, perhaps even inexperience. She seemed smaller suddenly, and a strange desire to protect her slammed into Beau's ribs. His voice softened as he asked, "Would you like to try?"

Clara was quiet, and her smirk had dropped. She watched Beau and Isobel intently, uncharacteristically still. Isobel nodded slowly, and Clara's eyes lit up—such a mischievous woman. But her excitement only made his cock harden further, and it begged to be touched.

"You say no, and I stop. Okay?"

Isobel nodded again, and Beau found he, too, was excited to see how this might play out.

"Clothes off." His voice was stronger now, far more authoritative as he locked eyes with Isobel.

She hesitated for a second, her eye twitching, and Beau thought she might flat out refuse.

She would have been well within her rights to do so. If she refused, asked him to stop, or gave him any sign she was no longer interested, he would stop. Orders were not for everyone, and just because Clara enjoyed it didn't mean Isobel was going to fit into that scenario. If Isobel changed her mind, they'd simply have to find a new game that included her, not the other way around.

But then Isobel stood and slowly removed her clothes. She was a petite thing, though Beau could see the muscles lining her shoulders and thighs. Not his ideal female, though Isobel wasn't for him; she was Clara's.

That's what all of this was for—Clara. Her happiness. Everything was for her.

"Open your mouth."

Slowly she did as he asked, though her eyes were clouded with trepidation and uncertainty, but her shoulders remained relaxed and her mouth stayed open. Beau was impressed, and surprisingly relieved she was still on board.

They'd go slow today. Small commands, just a taste of what their sex life might be like together. Beau couldn't help his coy grin as he considered he might end up with two females to command, and just what he might be able to order them to do. Images of Isobel pleasuring Clara, while Clara pleasured Beau, played in his mind.

"Well done," Beau said, low and husky. "Now share."

Clara leant in close to Isobel and pushed her tongue out of her mouth. Spit dripped off her tongue and onto Isobel's, and Beau couldn't help his moan. Fuck, it was torture. Clara then held Isobel's jaw as she kissed her hard. He watched their tongues dart back and forth as Clara's back arched and she pressed her breasts to Isobel's.

Isobel's hands roamed Clara's skin, leaving subtle pink lines as she pressed her nails in, trying to control her desire.

Beau groaned again, stroking his now fully erect cock through his pants. Oh, how he wanted to rip them off, to be rid of the confines. While he was seconds away from giving in, he wanted to give Isobel some time before his dick entered the game. While this moment was between them *all*, he knew Isobel had the most to come to terms with, and she had not been shy about her lack of interest in the male anatomy. Isobel needed the biggest allowances made, and Beau genuinely wanted to give that to her.

"Stars," he moaned. "I could get used to this."

Clara pulled away from Isobel and scoffed. "You're fucking full of yourself."

"You love it." Beau winked.

"I'd love it more if I was full of you, but you're happy playing with yourself." Clara's voice was so damn seductive, and she knew exactly what the sound of it did to him. Then she threw her head back and let Isobel trail kisses down her neck and collarbone.

Fuck.

"You want this cock, sweetheart?" Beau growled, his hand uncovering his rock-hard bulge.

Clara smirked and waggled her eyebrows.

"Come and fucking take it then, like the greedy slut you are. Take what you want. We're yours."

Surprisingly, Isobel moaned softly, her lips still pressed against Clara's skin, almost in agreement. She nudged Clara towards Beau, then watched as Clara walked the short distance to him.

Clara stopped, facing him, and slid one hand up his chest, pausing at his nape. Then she dragged him by his collar until the mattress stopped her from going any further. Without breaking eye contact, Clara unbuttoned his shirt slowly, allowing Beau to shimmy out of it as she moved to his pants. *Fuck,* she took her time.

Once again, he found himself damn near out of willpower and desperate to throw her onto the bed and fuck her raw. He wanted to ravage her and leave her screaming. Leave her bruised and tear-streaked. Meanwhile, Isobel also knelt beside them, silently watching.

Finally, once they were both naked, Clara lay on her back, pulling Beau on top of her. With one hand she stroked his throbbing cock, and the feel of her silken skin felt fucking divine. Her other hand flew to the back of his neck before she pulled his face to hers.

It'd been far too long since he'd felt her lips on his, since he'd tasted her tongue. Beau craved Clara so violently, he vowed he'd never let so much time pass between moments like this again. Stars, she was everything. His heart thundered behind his ribs, and his cock twitched as she ran her tongue along his lips. A burst of pain erupted as she bit him hard enough to draw blood, but it quickly fizzled into zaps of pleasure.

Clara pouted as he pulled away, but the expression was fleeting.

"You," he said to Isobel, barely able to form a sentence. "Sit."

"Where?"

"On my face, you beautiful, pure soul." Clara's tone as she spoke was dangerously low, filled with lust and need. Yet when she laughed, it was as if angels had offered them a private performance. Beau would never tire of the sound.

Isobel quickly moved to straddle Clara's face, then her body shuddered as Clara's tongue teased her.

"Careful," Beau growled, taking his cock in his own hand so Clara's were free to roam Isobel's thighs. "I'm going to fuck her now, and she bites."

Clara flipped him off, but he hardly noticed. Slowly at first, inch by inch, Beau slid his cock inside Clara. A little more each time until her hands dug into Isobel and her lower back arched off the mattress. Beau grabbed Clara's hips and held her steady as he buried himself fully, taking a moment to revel in her glorious, wet cunt before he began to pound into her.

While he wasn't thrilled that Clara's eyes were elsewhere, Beau supposed sacrifices would need to be made.

Every time Isobel ground against Clara's face, and with every aroused sound from the pink-haired female, Clara's cunt tightened around Beau. He could feel exactly how turned on Clara was, and he'd be lying if he said it wasn't some of the best sex they'd had so far. Her pussy walls gripped him tightly, and Beau fought not to fuck her harder.

Isobel leant forward and took one of Clara's nipples in her fingertips, twisting it lightly, and Beau couldn't help the rough moan that left him. Clara swore, though the sound was muffled by Isobel's pussy. Isobel shuddered over Clara, her face contorted with pleasure. Her hips rocked faster over Clara's face, jerky and losing their rhythm until she gasped sharply. She moaned Clara's name as she came undone.

Shakily, Isobel climbed off Clara and crawled closer. She knelt beside Clara, who was now propped up on her elbows and staring passionately at Beau. Her fingers moved and traced circles over Clara's swollen clit, and Clara looked like she could hardly breathe. She moaned and panted harder and harder the longer Isobel rubbed her. Isobel barely touched her, yet Clara was on fire. Watching her come so close to her climax was enough to send Beau racing towards his own completion.

But not yet.

He slowed his thrusts just a fraction, and Clara growled at him. Beau smirked but maintained his slower rhythm, though he kept his thrusts just as hard, just as deep.

Now that Isobel had moved off her face, he could see the tears welling in the corners of Clara's eyes, and the flushed, rosy complexion that left her freckles looking faded. The green of her irises stood out when she blushed, so stark and radiant—

and when she fucking looked at him like that, he was nearly ready to explode.

The pleading and desperation in her eyes was divine.

"Beau . . ." she moaned, her breaths hard and hands clutching his forearms.

"Fuck yes, sweetheart."

From the corner of his eye, Beau watched Isobel smirk. Then he felt a cool breeze despite the door and window being closed. It circled the room and rustled between some of his feathers.

Then Clara screamed.

"Isobel! Fuck!"

As she came, Clara's pussy clenched tighter and tighter until he couldn't hold on any longer. Pleasure exploded through him, and he thrust through his release as his cock erupted and filled Clara, leaving them both panting and sweaty.

Isobel sat back on her heels, her smirk still bright and proud on her fair face. Beau couldn't even be mad. Well fucking played, Jeffreys.

CHAPTER SIXTEEN
EVELINE

The hallway stood empty as Eveline strolled from the boardroom to her quarters, and each footstep echoed loudly against the walls. Normally, she'd be pleased by the solitude, but that was less the case since Solaris had died. Instead she preferred to be surrounded by the many fae that wandered the palace halls and attended to her needs. Even the streets filled with random fae were preferable.

Today, the emptiness felt bigger and more foreboding. She felt lonely, possibly for the first time. The silence was louder and the hallways much longer than yesterday.

Eveline was relieved Ryn had left, despite her now almost-normal presence. She'd been quiet and respectful, even civil up until the curse had sunk its claws in and she'd shifted. Once it'd lifted, she'd returned to her original visage, and the only sign of her true form was the freakish grin she'd given Eveline before heading to the library.

She was nothing like her father had described. All his stories of the Reapers had involved so much blood and gore and horror. Yet the only time Ryn had come close to resembling such a foul, beast-like creature was when the curse *he* placed over their home took effect.

Was she generally frightening to be around? Did she make Eveline uncomfortable? Were her eyes somehow too full and simultaneously empty every time they raked over Eveline? Yes. But Clara had genuinely worried about the Reaper and had come here with her willingly. They even seemed to have some sort of history. As little as Eveline knew about Clara Afron, she knew the female had no time for trouble or meddlesome folk.

Had her father known of the Reapers' true nature? Was it truly what Eveline had seen, or was Ryn an exception?

Questions, accusations, and betrayal swarmed her mind. She didn't know who to believe. While she didn't know enough about the Reapers to make an informed decision, she knew fae could not lie, though they could meld and warp the truth to their advantage. There were always loopholes.

Whether her father had used those to brainwash his daughters into believing his own version of reality, Eveline would never know. Even if she could ask him, he'd likely evade her questions. Was anything he said more than rumours of rage and revenge, of chaos and his own warped reality? The thought sat heavy in her mind and burned her throat.

Before she realised it, her fist was pounding on a small wooden door. It swung open to reveal a tall soldier, with ashy-blue wings and eyes so dark they reminded Eveline of Ryn. She tried not to grimace.

"Afron," was all she said.

Evian was at the door in seconds, then he rushed to don a shirt and attempted to tuck it into his waistband. She did not miss the sculpted torso, regardless of it only being shown for a heartbeat. Nor did Evian miss when she tracked her eyes upwards to meet his, and he met her gaze with a cocky expression tilting his lips.

Eveline let out a sharp, frustrated breath and signalled for him to follow. Without a word, she spun and stormed away.

"Someone's cranky," Evian jested as he fell in step beside her.

"Wouldn't you be?" she snapped back. When she turned her head to face him, her eyes already narrowed, she found his palms up in submission. "I looked a right fool earlier. I had no idea of my own father's history! Powders and stones and visits from beings of other worlds. I knew nothing, and so now I appear the idiot."

"You're far from an idiot," Evian murmured, but despite his soft tone and her heart skipping a beat, Eveline could not appreciate the sentiment.

"I fired my advisory council." The words fell from her tongue before she could consider them properly. Should she even be telling a soldier this? No, probably not. It certainly wasn't his business, and his rank did not allow him access to such information.

Yet when he asked why, so carefully and without judgement, Eveline answered. She did not care about his rank, only appreciated his presence and willingness to listen.

"I did not trust them." She shrugged, as if that was all that was necessary, but still continued. Talking to Evian was a comfort—almost as if she weren't so alone. "If I cannot trust those hand-selected by the royalty that came before me to advise and counsel me on both personal and political matters, then they must go. Those seats should be held by fae I trust implicitly, without hesitation or question. I knew hardly any of them. Was it hasty and not thought through? Yes, but I could count on one hand how many fae I currently trust, and none of those crones or decrepit old bastards are on the list. They were selected by my father, and I do not know if I even trusted him. I think it's high time I choose my own advisory council. If I keep this damned crown, that is."

"Do you not want your crown, Majesty?" Evian's voice had dropped much quieter despite there being no one close. They once again wandered the empty halls, slowly approaching her rooms.

However, such a question was treasonous. If the wrong ears caught her professing such a thing, she'd have more to worry about than unsuccessful assassins.

So Eveline did not answer; instead, she asked for his help.

"Why me?" he replied with a flat chuckle.

"Because, for some unknown reason, you are on the list of folk I trust. Do not ask why, as I cannot say—it is simply a gut feeling." Eveline paused and took a deep breath before admitting the next part. "My father used to call gut feelings 'fear for the weak and inept.' He figured you were confident and capable, or you were not. But one of the few things I remember about my mother was that she trusted her gut feelings."

Evian wrapped a large hand around her wrist and pulled Eveline to a stop outside her doors. She turned to face him, not expecting such a serious expression to be staring back.

"Eveline, I would fall on bended knee for you. Hell, I'd fall into an early grave for you. I left my family and my home for you. Simply tell me what you need, and it is done."

His thumb stroked the back of her forearm gingerly. It sent electric pulses up her arm and straight to her lungs, where it made her heart thunder.

"Evian, I tried to execute your sister." Eveline attempted a light-hearted tone, perhaps to lessen the intensity of his confession, or maybe to avoid acknowledging the truth behind his words. Either way, it fell flat, and Eveline was left near breathless as something bright glimmered in his eyes.

"Look, that isn't my favourite fact about you," Evian said coyly, a grin spreading over his face. "But my feelings remain unaltered. I believe everything happened as it was meant to. The Mother set things in motion so that this very moment could occur. Perhaps a little less death would've been preferable, but who am I to judge Her? Whatever you need from me, it will be done."

Eveline had to turn away from him to take a breath, for her lungs seized more and more the longer she looked at him. The longer she looked, the more she saw the earnestness in his face and pride in his eyes.

As she pushed the door open, she drawled low in the hopes he wouldn't hear the shakiness in her voice. "I'll use that against you later."

His breath was hot on her ear, and his voice sent shivers down her spine when he answered immediately. "Why wait?"

She could almost feel his hands on her waist, but knew he wasn't touching her, not here out in the open. A staff member could walk by at any minute, and while she and her heart didn't seem to mind, his rank would cause a stir. Eveline shouldn't be letting Evian into her room at all. But this conversation needed to be had in private.

Once Evian had closed the door behind him, and the lock was securely latched, Eveline began her pacing.

"First step," she said and began counting off her fingers. "Secure new counsel. Second step, figure out who the fuck is trying to kill me. Third—"

"I was thinking about that, actually." Evian cut her off, and surprisingly, she was filled with something that felt a lot like appreciation rather than annoyance. "What kind of motive, aside from the crown, would someone have to murder you?"

"I don't know!" Eveline hissed and threw her arms out dramatically.

Evian stifled his laughter—barely. "Well, let's go back to basics then. What kind of magic do you possess? Could it be related to that?"

All the air vanished from Eveline's lungs. Her limbs fell cold, and her eyes dropped to the floor. She shook her head slowly, but she couldn't be sure if Evian noticed. He stayed silent, waiting patiently for her to answer.

"I don't," she said at last, with a long and unsteady exhale. "I was my father's favourite daughter." A cruel smile tugged at the corner of Eveline's lips, and an almost laugh fluttered from her tongue. It held no warmth and was far too familiar to her father's for Eveline's liking. "Solaris was his spare. The one he cared very little for, though heavens know why. She was beautiful, a truly angelic creature, but for whatever reason, the gods did not bless her with any magic. Everyone believes she had magic of the Night Court running through her veins, and I worked very hard to make sure that was the case."

Eveline steadied her breathing before she continued, her eyes glued to the empty portrait frame on the opposite side of her room. At some point, it had held a family painting. Her mother and father with Eveline and Solaris as babes. She'd removed the painting after returning home from Elanist. With her twin sister dead, and her being unsure how she felt about her father, looking at it had been painful and confusing.

"In reality, I was gifted with both courts' magics. The ability to sever a mind from its body, and mind-manipulation, though some folk call it mind play. Severance comes from the Night Court—brutal but efficient and accurate. Lethal. Mind play is of the Day Court, like my father, built on tricksters and liars and manipulation.

"My father was not pleased that both of his daughters did not possess impressive magic. He screamed at our mother for months, blaming her and demanding that she fix it. But she couldn't, of course, as it was not her gift to bestow. It was not her *mistake* to rectify. So he took his blame out on my sister. She was the truest, purest being—all she ever gave the world was goodness and gentility—but he made it his mission to break her. Every day, sometimes multiple times. I tried to help her. And though my abilities were strong, they were never enough to overpower his.

"He would beat her. The back of his hand met her face more than anyone else's. He'd whip her and then manipulate her into forgetting. Or worse, he would force his cruel mind torture on her, and when she confronted him about it, he'd tell her she was being foolish. Then he'd demand to know why she was questioning him and offer to punish her so she might know the difference between the nonsense she spoke and genuine pain. Once he threw her into a rosebush, recently pruned of its petals but with thorns still strong. For weeks after, whenever he saw Solaris, he'd use his mind to convince her she was bathing in saltwater and the cuts would sting so much she cried. Then he'd just laugh. He could be the vilest creature, my father.

"So one day, when she came to me crying and begging for a way out, I gave her one. I gave her everything—every ounce of my magic. I have nothing left. When she died, my magic died with her, and I am glad."

"Eveline," Evian said quietly as he placed his hand on her cheek. He cupped it so tenderly in his warm palm. "I'm so sorry."

"You have nothing to apologise for," she answered quickly. Though she tried to hide her sniffles, she was unable to shield the few tears as they spilled. Evian wiped them silently, pressed a fleeting kiss to her forehead, and then placed his own forehead to hers.

Eveline didn't know how long they stood there like that. Her, in and out of bouts of hiccups and ragged breathing, and him, offering her more comfort than she'd ever known and more safety than she ever could've expected.

"Third step," Eveline whispered and took a deep breath. "Find something useful for your sister so that she doesn't hold the fact she saved our lives over my head forever. She's awfully cocky."

"She gets that from me."

Surprisingly, a peal of laughter burst from Eveline. It was the lightest sound she'd made in decades.

"Do not think for a second I had not noticed, soldier."

CHAPTER SEVENTEEN
CLARA

The next morning, Clara woke from a blissful sleep. Beau's arm lay across her, heavy and warm, and Isobel's fingers were interlaced with her own, her leg propped on Clara's. It was a perfect way to wake.

Though it was quickly ruined by the persistent knocking at her door.

"Yes?" she croaked, her mind elsewhere as Beau's body stirred behind her.

Isobel grumbled and rolled over, always full of disdain for mornings. Beau's hands wandered, but Clara tried to swat them away as they roamed higher, his fingers pressing along the sensitive part of her neck just below her jaw. His breath caressed her bare shoulder, and for a second, she forgot about the knocking altogether.

"You have visitors, Clara," her mother announced through the door, before her footsteps scurried away.

With a groan, Clara sat upright, sighing again before she slunk from the bed.

"Want company?" Beau asked as he propped himself up on an elbow and raked his golden gaze over her naked body.

Clara smiled but shook her head, intentionally bending far more slowly than was necessary to collect a shirt from the floor.

When Beau groaned and cursed, butterflies erupted in her belly. He excited her. It was a stark difference to the waves of calm that washed over her when Isobel was near.

She pulled clean trousers from the drawer, dragged them on quickly and tried not to stomp on her way down the hall.

In the living room, she was met by two familiar faces and one she did not recognise but could gather who it was easily. Ryland stood with Diedre, unfamiliar markings lining her forehead and nose, though they were in the same chalk-white she'd worn at the ball in Morrin.

A male stood between them, who Clara assumed was Peter, the leader of Diedre's clan, Claw. Hopefully, he'd come to speak about taking guardianship of her nephew.

Though he was not supposed to be here until tomorrow, at the earliest. Clara had been very specific, and though Ryland hadn't approved, she thought he'd agreed at least.

"Ryland." Clara nodded to her second-in-command, then to the female wolf. "Diedre." Both nodded back; a small smile graced Diedre's face, while Ryland remained neutral.

"And you must be Peter, I presume?" Clara asked politely, extending her hand to him. Peter nodded and clasped her hand tightly with both of his, then kissed her knuckles before he spoke.

"I apologise for the rush, Majesty, truly. While I understand you have personal matters to attend to today, unfortunately, I face the same issue. Returning to the mountain will take several days. I did not wish to leave before speaking with you; however, we need to leave within a matter of hours if we are to make a decent distance by sunset."

Clara nodded and smiled. She remained pleasant and tried her best not to let it show that she'd only just woken.

"Shall we sit?" Clara offered a chair at the dining table behind them.

Peter's eyes and his own chalk marks wrinkled as he smiled and accepted her offer, seemingly pleased with her response. He didn't come across as a male who would flaunt his own superiority in front of a queen, but he also didn't seem to be someone who would mince words or fall in line for the sake of a title. He held one, too, after all. From what she knew of the wolves—information mostly passed on from Ryland in fleeting moments—they were not governed by the fae. Rather, they were their own community, with their own sovereignty, and Peter was close to their king.

Only three of the five clans still existed—Claw, Tail, and Snout—with Claw the last to reside on Elanist soil. He was the leader and was fiercely protective of his kin.

"Ryland," Clara said sweetly, before he lowered himself into his chair beside her. "Would you ask my mother for some tea, please?"

Ryland nodded, bowed slightly, and then disappeared into the hallway in search of Felicity.

"Majesty," Peter started, but Clara waved him off.

"Please, just Clara."

He smiled, though his expression was tighter than before. "Clara. Let's get to the point, shall we? I know you're not one to beat around the bush and dabble in theatrical weavings."

"Please," she repeated and gestured for him to go on.

"You requested I take your infant nephew into the mountains, to raise and care for him indefinitely. All because of his mother's bad dream? Come now."

Clara narrowed her eyes at his scoff but willed her voice to remain calm as she answered.

"Not so much a bad dream as a forewarning of a devastating future. Now, let me be brutally honest with you, Peter, because even if I could lie, something tells me you aren't interested in theatrics either. I've had my own vision of Christopher's future. I have not made much sense of it yet, but I know for certain it is bleak. His mother is dead, and anyone else who looks after him is in danger purely because of their association with me. If he stays here, I risk my line and the continent's crown. I cannot look after a child, not amidst an impending war I currently have no way of stopping or winning. So I am asking for your help."

"You're asking for a business transaction," Peter replied, his tone neutral.

Being unable to read him infuriated Clara. She balled her fists below the table and hoped her face did not give her feelings away.

"Were we to take the boy, we would be compensated, yes?"

Clara only nodded.

Peter deliberated silently for a moment, then stood. "Clara, I'm sorry. I don't see how we can help. If the boy is in danger, you will bring that to my doorstep. Surely there is someone else capable and willing to raise the child for some coin. I have worked too hard to keep my kin safe. I won't throw that away for a crown who didn't care about us until we were useful to them."

She shot out of her seat, unsure whether what she said next would come out accusatory or rash. Whether it would shoot down any hope she had of changing his mind. "If we are to move forward, surely you understand both parties must be on board with change. I am not my royal predecessors."

His face softened. "Of course, Majesty. But this, I fear, is not something I can be on board for."

"Were you ever interested in hearing me out, or were you always going to say no?" She couldn't stop the accusation from crossing her lips, not that it mattered now that Peter had decided. Christopher would stay in Elanist, in danger, and the future of the Golden Kingdom was even shakier than before.

Peter let out a deep breath. "Truthfully—no, I was never interested in taking the boy. I was interested in hearing you out and meeting you. If this war does not take your life and this meeting hasn't solidified in you the feelings of your ancestors, I would like to meet you again, Clara. Please accept my sincere thanks for your assistance in getting Diedre home."

Clara nodded but spoke through clenched teeth. "I wish you safe travels, Peter."

It was the only truth Clara could offer him. She wasn't pleased to have met the male, nor was she interested in meeting him again. His reasoning was justified, sure, but it was cowardly. Clara did not, however, feel that it was appropriate to share these thoughts out loud.

"Diedre." Clara nodded towards the female again, who stayed quiet as she rose from her seat. She avoided eye contact, but the way her shoulders drooped suggested she likely hadn't known the outcome of this meeting.

In the space of a few moments, Clara's hope of getting Christopher to safety had been ruined. She had absolutely no idea what to do with him now.

Clara pulled the cake from the fridge quietly, though truthfully, she needn't have worried. Isobel was focused on the game she played with Beau on the floor of the sitting room.

Beau had tried to teach them both how to play, but for the life of her, Clara couldn't master it. After four rounds of being beaten, she'd given up and settled on watching Beau and Isobel go head-to-head. She understood the rules of the game well enough, which tiles went where, and how certain coloured pairings accrued certain points. She was now also very aware of which tile placements left her up shit creek without a paddle, and which gave her opponents a more advantageous move.

Isobel had lost two of the four games, and she was adamant it would not happen again. Clara caught Beau's subtle smirks, the twitches in his eyebrows and crinkled lines by his eyes every few moves. He was dragging this out, whether to let her win or simply extend the game, Clara didn't know.

She figured now was as good a time as any to acknowledge Isobel's birthday officially. Well wishes had been offered as soon as Ryland left, but Clara wanted to celebrate properly.

"I saw that!" Isobel shrieked. Clara's gaze shot over to find Beau chuckling, and Isobel had risen to her knees, pointing furiously. "Put it back, asshole."

"Put what back?" Beau teased.

"The tile up your sleeve! Put it back!"

"How about we take a break for a moment?" Clara called out, her voice warm and her heart full.

Isobel's face whipped around to Clara, and all fury left her expression. Her mouth hung slightly agape as her brows soared. She rose to her feet and rushed to Clara, her wide crystal-blue eyes darting between Clara and the pastel-yellow cake.

"What is . . ." her voice trailed off, but Clara answered anyway.

"Happy birthday!" She couldn't tame her beaming smile even if she tried. "I'm not very good at the whole gift-giving thing, I'm afraid, but I'm an excellent baker."

"Clara . . ." She could've sworn tears welled in Isobel's eyes.

Isobel took the cake from Clara's grasp and placed it on the bench, then she wrapped Clara in the tightest hug, one hand pressed to Clara's nape and the other firmly at her back.

"Thank you," she whispered.

"Not to ruin your moment," Beau chimed in, standing behind Isobel with one hand at the back of his neck. He looked almost nervous. "But I happen to be great with gifts. I hope you don't mind."

He handed Isobel a small brown bag overflowing with wrapping tissue. Where he pulled it from, Clara couldn't guess. Despite summer being around the corner, rain began pelting at the window above the sink. The sound of her heart beating violently in her ears rivalled the sudden downpour.

Isobel smiled genuinely at Beau before she pulled a stunning trio of paintbrushes from the bag. The handles were all various shades of pearl and decorated with intricate swirled engravings. Next, she removed a leather pouch, wrapped and bound with twine. Isobel set it on the counter to unwind it and revealed a dozen small transparent tubes of paint, each with handwritten colour labels. All in deep, rich, and vibrant earthy tones. Half were various shades of green, the others were browns and blues, and there was even a citrine yellow.

"Beau, these are beautiful. Thank you." Isobel traced a finger over the tubes and along her brushes. Her shock morphed into appreciation. "Now all I need is something to paint on."

"Shit, I almost forgot!"

Beau sprinted from the kitchen, his wings a blur of amber and gold behind him. Clara couldn't help but chuckle while Isobel's mouth dropped again.

"There's more?" she whispered.

Clara gave a lopsided grin and shrugged.

Before she could say anything further, Beau came back into the kitchen, a square canvas in his hand.

"This one has already been painted on, but you could paint over it if you wanted."

"Stars above, what did you get painted this time?" Clara asked jovially, but Beau levelled her with a flat stare. He handed the constellation painting to Isobel.

"This one is a good painting, thank you very much. At least for her." He jerked his chin towards Isobel. "It was the night you two met. I'm moving away from the worst night of the year and focusing on the happy memories instead."

"Thank fuck. It *was* morose."

"How do you know when we met?" Isobel asked, her eyes still roaming the painting.

"I'm pretty good at remembering faces, and considering I've been stuck staring at yours for weeks now, I was finally able to piece together where I'd seen you before you showed up to cockblock me in Breath. I watched you tip your drinks into a potted plant at the feast day last year in Tirenas. You looked so different that I had to ask Ryland to confirm it was you. Once he did, I set off to get this commissioned. Mikhail dropped it off early this morning while you two were still asleep."

Isobel gently placed the canvas on the bench, then whirled around and wrapped Beau in a hug. At first, the Phoenix didn't know what to do with her. His shoulders stiffened, and his eyes all but bugged out of his face. Then his body relaxed, and his hands pressed to Isobel's back, hugging her in return.

Clara's heart felt like it might explode. The faucet behind her erupted so violently that the spout loosened from the sink. The water poured so quickly it splashed out of the sides.

"This feels like a weird sibling moment of appreciation," Isobel muttered, her face still pressed against Beau's chest.

"I don't know about your kind, but siblings don't tend to share a female where I'm from."

Isobel quickly jumped away from Beau, her face aghast, and all Clara could do was laugh.

CHAPTER EIGHTEEN
CLARA

Two days later, Clara left Beau and Isobel asleep while she quietly readied for work. Did she want to leave the comfort of her bed or her lovers? No, not even a little. But Nerrida had been kind enough to coordinate her shifts around Clara's even more hectic schedule. So when Clara was told of this week's shifts just the night before, she said nothing. Grumbled under her breath but said nothing. Truthfully, she was excited to work at the bakery. She only wished it were not instead of spending time wrapped between firm muscles and petite hands.

After scrawling a note and leaving it on the dining table, Clara kissed her mother goodbye and headed to the door. To her surprise, when she opened it, Clara was met with a tall, slim fae male, so tall she had to crane her neck to meet his eyes. His hand was raised, ready to knock.

"Can I help you?" Clara asked, trying to keep the shock from her voice. It made her feel better to notice the fast rise and fall of the male's chest as well.

"Majesty," he said slowly and bowed at the waist. "My name is Gerard Pilkren. I have been sent by His Highness, Prince Jude, to collect you and your entourage, and to accompany you back to the Winter Palace. Preparations must begin." Gerard dipped his chin again and waited with his head low.

"Right, well, you had best come inside."

Clara gestured for Gerard to follow her as she walked down the hall, stopping at the dining table once more.

"Quick shift," her mother muttered, not looking up from the newspaper.

"Mother," Clara said, her voice calm and thankfully not conveying her wild emotions. Worries of betrayal and deceit, alongside fears of letting Nerrida down, swirled violently through the many layers of anxiety in her mind. The wedding preparation was what changed her proposal from *in the future* to now. Tingles spiked along the tips of Clara's fingers. "Would you please let Nerrida know I won't be able to work today?"

Felicity dropped the paper, a single brow raised. "Hello, sir," she said to Gerard. "And who might you be?"

"This is Gerard. Royal chauffeur," Clara answered for him.

Again, he dipped his chin in acknowledgement or agreement—he was certainly polite. "Apologies for the early morning intrusion, Mrs Afron, but His Highness was insistent."

"Of course," her mother muttered. Then an amused grin spread, though her chuckle was poorly veiled. "And who has Prince Jude requested exactly?"

"Her Majesty, and whomever she deems necessary for the trip."

"Her Majesty?" Clara's mother repeated. "Sir, I'm not sure you understand how titles work."

Shit.

"About that . . ." Clara muttered as she looked at her feet. With everything that had happened since the coronation, she'd not mentioned it to her mother. "I was crowned recently. You are now the Queen of Elanist's mother. Congratulations!" Clara's attempt at a jovial tone fell flat, and she scrunched her face, both from discomfort and embarrassment at not having said anything sooner.

Her mother's eyes bulged, and her brows rose high, her stiff body also betraying her anger. "Clara Renee Afron, you're going to need to repeat yourself immediately."

"I'm sorry! Ryland insisted, and it all happened very quickly. So much has happened since then it just slipped my mind. I should've told you."

"Damn right you should have!" Felicity stood abruptly, pointing a finger at Clara. But then she wrapped her thin arms around her daughter's shoulders, and Clara could feel the smile and warmth emanating from her. "Congratulations," she whispered and squeezed a little harder before she pulled away, winked, and added, "Your Majesty."

Clara chuckled lightly with her mother for a moment before Gerard ruined it by clearing his throat. Rolling her eyes, she waved him off and trudged down the hall.

So much for leaving them to sleep.

Save for a few folk starting their day early, the walk to the docks was barren. Despite having no love for mornings, Clara enjoyed the serenity and quiet of the mostly empty town. The sun rose and warmed her skin as a breeze filtered through full trees and teased the ends of her hair. It was beautiful.

She'd expected running into an associate of Fintan's would've ruined the mood, but when Reid and Hugo smiled and stopped them, Clara was pleasantly surprised to be wrong. Reid's face was bright, with an array of hoops and jewels hanging from each ear. Hugo dipped into an informal bow and then cast a casual grin their way.

"Where are you off to so early?" Reid asked, before nibbling on their oversized muffin.

Clara knew exactly where they had found such a thing and felt a pang of envy. Years ago she'd tried to convince Nerrida to make novelty-sized baked goods, though never successfully. Now, one of the cafés closer to the town centre made them, and it had been an overnight success. To be fair, the baker was good at what he did, so it was well warranted.

"Her Majesty is to begin her wedding planning, Reid." Hugo's grin turned coy and playful as he bumped against Reid's shoulder, then turned to Clara. "Will we receive an invitation?"

"What did you say your affinities were again? Your magic?" Beau prompted, though they all knew the answer, at least generally speaking.

He and Reid were both Vequil Inalis, capable of channelling all five elements.

Like Clara.

Hugo only winked at Clara, then nonchalantly said to Beau, "I didn't."

"You're all more than welcome to attend the ceremony," Clara said. "Though please be assured I do not mind either way. You're free to come and go as you please."

"You do not want us here?" Reid asked, their head cocked to the side.

"I want you to decide for yourself. I know Fintan rounded you up. Collected you and convinced you how important it was for you to be here, but frankly I wouldn't trust anything that came from his mouth, and you shouldn't either. He reminds me of a king I once killed—"

Isobel gasped behind her, while Beau tried and failed to hide his chuckle. Clara couldn't make much sense of the expressions on either Inalis' face, so she shrugged and continued.

"If you decide your time is better spent elsewhere, and Fintan throws a tantrum, send him to me. I'll deal with him."

"But I'm confused," Reid said softly, shaking their head. "I thought you *wanted* our aid in your upcoming war."

"Not by force. Now, if you'll excuse me, we have a boat to catch." Clara nodded and made to leave, but Reid's hopeful voice made her pause.

"May I come with you . . . to Morrin?"

Again, Clara nodded, not entirely sure why they would want to accompany her. Though she wasn't entirely against it either. If Reid wanted to join them in waiting for the battle and death and chaos of war, who was Clara to stand in their way? Their smile grew to twice the size of before as they fell into place beside Isobel.

Before she could say goodbye to Hugo, he spoke, his voice deep and insistent, but gentle. "I'll see you when you return, Majesty, and will do everything in my power to help." Hugo dipped into another bow, this time far more serious and formal. "You should also speak to Brontë about your nephew. She's got a soft spot for children; however, you mustn't mistake that softness for weakness. I don't think she has any weaknesses, honestly—except perhaps her brother."

"Darius," Clara mumbled.

Hugo nodded.

Clara remembered the boy and the comments Ryn had made about his powers. Not to mention the look on her face when she'd all but salivated over the magic he possessed. Perhaps he would not aid Clara directly in the war, but by keeping her heir safe . . . far, far away from the danger zone.

They were almost at Morrin's shores—the pier and sandbanks already in view—when ripples in the water pulled Clara's attention from her waiting prince. Waves built quickly, and before she could react, vicious-looking navy-and-viridian scaled mermaids with barbed elbows and weapons burst to the surface.

"Clarenna Hayes."

"Clara Afron."

"Majesty."

"Her Highness."

The voices scraped at Clara's ears, high-pitched and grating. Only two mermaids stared at her, but there felt like a thousand voices repeating the same identifying names and titles in her mind. Clara tried her best not to flinch as she nodded.

Then cold, slimy hands wrapped around each of her wrists and yanked her off the boat. From the corner of her eye, she watched Beau grab fruitlessly for her, and Isobel's face scrunched in fury as she turned on Gerard. The last face she saw before the water swallowed her was Reid's, comforting and smiling and calm.

Dozens of different shades of blue and green crashed around her. Clara couldn't tell the difference between where the water stopped and the mermaids' camouflaged bodies started. She thrashed, more than mildly concerned and unable to tell left from right, or up from down. Hardly even able to see where her hands flailed in front of her, or the barely there glint of light against her captor's spear. They soon stopped, but by then Clara's racing heart was overwhelmed, and her violently protesting lungs urged her to breathe in, uncaring of her submersion.

The water wasn't cold, but Clara's hands and feet were frozen. The numb feeling spread quickly up her arms and legs until her lungs screamed and her throat burned with fury. White dots flashed in her periphery.

"Use your magic, you foolish girl!" the mermaid hissed, her voice serpentine. Her teeth shone in the dark, somehow even more terrifying than in the light. "You need to fix this mess, and we will not tolerate an exemption by death."

For a moment, she felt rather stupid, then she centred herself and focused. Fear had always been her trigger for air magic, but the more she had channelled, the less she found truly frightened her. Being so close to drowning again had sparked her fear, but evidently not enough for her magic to take over subconsciously as it had done in the past.

So now she drew on memories of a time she was scared, for her life or another's. She recalled where in her body she felt it, the tingling and the discomfort, and focused on pulling magic from her nape and the soles of her feet.

Surprisingly quickly, Clara created a large air pocket under the waves. It wrapped fully around her head, and she could breathe again. The relief that coursed through her at her success was nearly enough to ruin the entire attempt, but thankfully the bubble only rippled and did not burst.

Due to the air surrounding her face, Clara could also see clearly again, despite being what appeared to be far under the water. Sunlight rippled above them, but in the distance. If she were a creature of the water, this might've been a spot Clara would lure her victims. The thought sent shivers down her spine.

To her left, she noticed a large metal box, almost the size of her bedroom; strangely, it was suspended by nothing but also unmoving. Covered in moss and algae, it looked like it could've been there for decades, yet she felt the distinct discomfort of iron the longer she stared or the closer she floated. Somehow, the metal had not rusted, and nothing about it felt natural. Strange energy emanated from it, like the box itself was buzzing. Almost alive.

"Fix what?" Clara asked, turning back to the mermaid pointing at her with a spear. Their slitted eyes flickered as the creatures focused on Clara.

"The stench of rot and decay pollutes our waters. A creature who does not belong to us died below the surface, and yet the water cannot claim her. Return her to the land, along with the other, or offer them to the seas."

"Who?" Clara pressed.

Familiarity washed over the corners of her mind, but the sensation did not extend far enough for her to grasp.

"See for yourself," she said, before snatching Clara's wrist and slamming it against the side of the box.

First, she saw the female lying curled on her side, her face turned away from Clara. Her bright-yellow hair was a stark contrast to the dull grey shade inside the box. With no windows or external light, it was a miracle she could see anything.

Clara didn't miss the stillness of her body, or the absence of a rising chest. This female was dead. Though she didn't know her personally, immense sadness seized Clara's heart. She knew who it was, at least by name.

A second female sat against a surprisingly dry wall. Her head tilted upwards, kohl and half-dried tears streaked her face. Even here, her eyes were milky white, but Clara knew deep in her bones they did not hold the luminous power they once did. She was tired, but it was an exhaustion that sleep would not cure.

Her arms hung limp at her sides, her legs outstretched and lifeless.

Witches did not dwell underwater for a reason. While every element played a part in their craft and was shown reverence by the witches, water was their weakest affinity. Holding them underwater was more than cruel. It would have slowly drained their life force, their essence, and their ability to channel magic. The lack of sunlight would have made it worse, and without access to fresh air and the outside world, their minds would've turned on them.

Clara didn't know how this once-bright witch had died, but she knew a lot of folk—witches and fae alike—would mourn her passing. Witches were pure souls, far more than other folk gave them credit. Clara vowed that those responsible for this crime would meet their fate, though maybe not by her hand, for there were others far more deserving of retribution. But they would meet their fate regardless, and Clara would help every damned step of the way.

"Who put them here?" Clara asked, pulling her hand away and massaging her palm as if that might ease the burning in her throat or the ache in her ribcage.

"We care not, only that you fix it." Both creatures bared their teeth. One pointed a taloned finger at Clara's chest, while the other tightened her grip on the spear. "Until you do, you shall not be permitted to pass again through these waters, by this boat or another vessel. Once the problem is resolved, you'll be free to roam as you please."

Then they torpedoed her through the water, upwards towards the surface with a speed Clara could only admire. Before she knew it, Clara was back on the boat, drenched and surrounded by worried faces, being bombarded with questions.

Without another glance her way, the mermaids scattered. They hissed nothing further, but Clara was left with

what she'd seen branding her mind, and the creatures' words
replayed over and over.

CHAPTER NINETEEN
CLARA

"You are aware of how a boat works, are you not, wife?" Jude asked with a smirk as Clara and her companions entered the front hall of the Winter Palace. The last time she'd been here, it'd been bursting with activity with all manner of fae bustling about. Now, before them stood only Jude and two others Clara did not know.

"Wife-to-be," Clara corrected with her hands on her hips, ignoring his smartass question.

"Should I send for a towel?"

"No, but what you should do is find me someone with knowledge of water manipulation. And quickly, prince. I'm already in a mood."

Clara hadn't intended to growl at him, though he laughed it off and seemed entirely unfazed.

"May I ask why you are creating puddles in my foyer?" Jude made no move to fetch anyone, only stood with his usual frustrating casualness, his arms folded loosely over his chest.

"You may ask," Clara huffed.

"Highness," Reid piped up, their tone optimistic but cautious. They dropped into a strange mix of a curtsey and a bow, one that seemed infinitely more stable than any curtsey Clara had attempted. "How gracious of you to accommodate us all. I do not mean to rush you; however, might I be informed of where I am to reside on your grounds? I have something I really must attend to."

Jude nodded and gestured for one of the staff members behind him to come forward. A female with a sharp nose and vibrant brown eyes stepped towards them, bowed to Clara, and nodded to the others. She said nothing, just curled her hand, and Reid followed. They left through a large set of double doors made almost entirely of wired glass.

"You three will share a suite. I trust that won't be an issue." Jude winked as he silently called for the other female to step forward. Again, she bowed to Clara and nodded in greeting to Isobel and Beau, sparing only a glance towards Gerard.

"Is your mood the reason you have not simply dried yourself off?" Jude pressed.

Clara heaved an annoyed sigh and rolled her eyes, but then conceded. He may as well know—after all, the prince could actually be of some help.

"I met with a few of your lake monsters," she grumbled.

"The mermaids?" Jude's gasp was entirely for show, but even knowing he was egging her on did nothing to stop the snarl that vibrated from her throat. Jude chuckled before raising his palms in surrender. "And you lived to tell the tale. I'm impressed."

"They aren't happy, prince, and frankly neither am I. Two witches, *my* witches, are locked in a giant metal box not half an hour from your shores and one of them is dead. The other won't last much longer without retrieval. Someone snatched them from *my* court and left them to die. I want to know who. I want to know why. And I want to bring them *home*. Do you hear me, Jude?"

"Loud and clear, pet. Whatever I can do to help, I will. Just say the word."

"Oh, enough with the 'pet.' It drives me mad." Clara rolled her eyes, but Jude only laughed. He most definitely was not going to stop. "I want a scholar, perhaps a group of them. I need to know how to open that box without flooding it and killing her. We'll figure out the rest later."

"Done. Patrice will take you to your rooms, and I'll meet you in my study in an hour or so." Jude nodded once, gave a flourishing bow, and then left.

"I'll catch up with you two," Beau muttered, before he pressed a hasty kiss to Clara's temple and ran after Jude.

He did not catch up with them until an hour after they had arrived at their suite, with a message from Jude on how to find him. Beau stared at Isobel, then kissed Clara's brow.

"What took you so long?" Isobel scoffed as he collapsed next to her on the large, plush mattress. Again, he stared at her silently, something warring in his amber eyes. Isobel dropped the book she'd been reading onto her stomach and gave him her full attention.

Clara wished she could've stayed, but alas, she had a prince to find and a lot of work to be done.

"Your posture leaves quite a bit to be desired." Jude clicked his tongue as he circled Clara, his arms folded and brows creased. Being assessed for public viewing and scrutiny was not something Clara had ever expected. Yet now she stood on a small platform in front of a mirror while Jude observed her and made a hundred and one comments.

They'd already discussed table etiquette, walking etiquette, and travel expectations. Clara was exhausted, and judging by the sun outside, rightfully so. It no longer stood at its peak, now moving south on its descent, which told her they'd been here for hours. She had to gather that information from the sun because she had yet to see a fucking clock anywhere in this damned castle.

"Not that I'd expect you to understand, you beanpole of a man, but these"—Clara lifted her lip in a sneer, aggressively cupping her breasts—"are heavy. I'm doing my best."

Without missing a beat, Jude snapped back with attitude of his own. Nothing sinister, as Clara truly didn't think the male capable, but more fiery than she'd seen him yet. Perhaps he was finally growing comfortable enough around her to let his walls down. "Not that I'd expect you to understand, Madam Chaos Personified, but there are expectations of royals. Your best is not currently good enough."

The sentiment fizzled some of her own attitude and irritation. Clara scoffed, despite the growing warmth in her chest.

"But never mind that," he said and waved her off. "I'll help you. What if I could have someone fashion a brassiere that provided more support? Held you up more?" Jude walked behind her, his chin lowered over her shoulder and hands splayed millimetres from her breasts. "May I?" Clara nodded, and he immediately collected the highest peak of her cups, pinched it, and tugged upward. The relief was immediate. "How's that?"

"Heavenly." Clara sighed and sagged a little. The only time anyone had ever held her breasts up was during adult activities of an intimate nature. This felt intimate, but different. "In truth, prince, if you could pull off the creation of a bra that is comfortable to wear for prolonged periods *and* supportive, I'd marry you for that alone."

"Speaking of weddings," Jude muttered, lowering Clara's bra slowly before he let it go entirely. She couldn't help the way her face scrunched disapprovingly. "My parents have settled on a date. We are to be married on the morning of the summer solstice."

An aggressive tingling shot up her spine and circled her nape. Clara was immediately on guard as her body reacted to the information she couldn't consciously capture. Her fingertips tingled, while her stomach felt full of lead and hollow simultaneously.

The summer solstice was not a good day to host a wedding.

"I do not think that is a good idea." She shook her head, trying to make sense of the reason in her mind. Nothing jumped out at her, but her insides felt jumbled and hot, as if all her organs had been removed for branding and then thrown back inside. "No, in fact, it is a very bad idea. Pick a new date."

"It's not that simple, Clara." Jude scoffed, an incredulous expression morphing his normally arrogantly confident face into one that was unsure. "It's not even up to me— my parents have decided. For a seasonal fae, the wedding must fall on a solstice or equinox. My lineage hails from the Summer and Autumn Courts, which means I must marry on the summer solstice or the autumn equinox. My parents do not wish to wait."

His voice rose the longer he explained himself, and for the first time Clara realised he was nervous about marrying someone who had been a stranger up until a handful of months ago. Who was now slightly more than an acquaintance, but someone he still barely knew.

He was taking a massive gamble by trusting her.

Clara took a deep breath and grabbed Jude's hand.

"Jude, if we get married on the summer solstice, someone is going to die." She bore her gaze into his hazel eyes and begged that her serious tone got through to him.

He sighed. "That's a tad grim, don't you think, pet?"

"You know that infuriates me," Clara ground out through a clenched jaw, her eyes narrowed on his.

"Why do you think I say it so frequently?" Jude winked and playfully poked her side. She gave him a flat smile, but only for a second.

"I'm serious, Jude. The summer solstice is not safe this year. The *Lady of Summer*," Clara said with a turned-up lip and mocking tone, already entirely done with the mysterious woman, "has plans, and no wedding is going to get in her way. Someone will die, and our nuptials will be forever tainted."

"By death?" Jude scoffed, a hint of a genuine grin pulling at the corners of his mouth. "I would've thought that excited you."

"That depends on who Death claims, I'm afraid."

The next morning, Beau was gone when Clara woke. He'd left a note on the side table saying he'd gone to explore, and not to worry. Telling her not to worry immediately set off alarm bells in Clara's mind and sent her heart racing, but the sound of Isobel's groggy voice soothed her.

"Morning, beautiful."

"And to you," Clara chuckled, the sound deep and low.

"Fancy coming back to bed and appreciating our alone time?" Isobel slowly propped up on her elbows to watch Clara hungrily as she dressed.

"Oh, I do," Clara drawled. "I fancy that very much. Unfortunately, I have a demanding prince waiting for me and witches to bring home."

Isobel's face dropped, and her eyes fell to her hands as she wrung her fingers.

"I can't believe Tindal is dead." It was barely even a whisper, but the words were loud and heavy. Clara didn't fight the pang of guilt as it worked its way up her throat.

She was guilty.

They were her folk, and she had failed them both.

"She's coming home, you hear me?" Clara knelt beside the bed and cupped Isobel's cheek with her hand. "Era too. I promise you I'll bring them home."

"You shouldn't—"

Clara shook her head and cut Isobel off. "I do not make promises I cannot keep, Isobel. I'm far too good at using linguistic loopholes. And I *will* bring them home." She enunciated every word as she stared earnestly into Isobel's crystal-and-gold eyes, waiting until she nodded and attempted a smile.

"I love you," she whispered.

"I love you too."

The following thirty-six hours in Jude's personal library consisted of a dozen dusty old books Clara could only partially read due to either terribly illegible handwriting, faded text, or the language barrier between the current and old tongue. They tediously swapped every other hour from trying to find a solution for the witches to talk of the wedding. Pointless questions like what colour scheme they ought to have, which floral arrangements should go where, what kind of fabric should be used for the tablecloths and napkins. In the end, Clara told Jude he could either choose the wedding aesthetics himself or ask his parents for their preferences.

She'd not put much thought into her wedding day, and truthfully, she had no interest now. This was a political alliance. Sure, it went deeper, and Clara now considered Jude to be a friend—perhaps one day a very close friend. However, she did not love this male, nor did he love her. This wasn't the wedding she wanted to plan, so she cared little about the details.

Besides, the seasonal fae had too many traditions to count, so who better to plan the day than a seasonal fae? Surely the queen would enjoy being included in the preparations.

"We're getting nowhere!" Clara shrieked as she pushed the palms of her hands to her eyes.

"And we won't with that attitude."

"Not helpful, prince."

Clara heard his chuckle, though she appreciated his attempt at keeping it quiet.

"Okay," he said, loudly closing a book. Clara opened her eyes to find him standing beside the desk. "Let's consider something else. Your magic—how is it activated? Or rather, channelled?"

Clara shrugged. "Most often my emotions are the trigger and I am a conduit. Fire is the only element I've really been able to control."

"And you said when you touched it you saw inside the box the mermaids took you to?"

"Yes, but I don't know if that was me or them. I cannot command my visions."

"Candor magic is some of the strongest of the Elanist fae. Surely something related to that will be helpful. Are there any patterns in your visions? Do you ever trigger them by touch?"

Clara ran her hands through her hair. "Yes, but it's random. I thought when I manifested all my elements that the visions stabilised. I finally saw complete visions instead of fragments or symbols. But that wasn't the case, and now I get random visions, but they are even more chaotic than before. I've had a few prophecies as well, I think."

"Prophecies cannot be called upon, but full and symbolic visions can be enticed." Jude paused, cocking his head to the side. "Would you like to learn how?"

Her whole body went slack, save for her eyes, which she was sure were wider than ever.

"Can you do that?" she whispered.

"Not me." Jude shrugged a shoulder, then started towards the door. "But I know someone who might be able to help." With his hand on the doorknob, he added, "Come to think of it, he might even be able to help you with your witches."

CHAPTER TWENTY
CLARA

Within an hour of Doneri's arrival, she'd brought on a nosebleed and made herself dizzy enough that she'd walked into a table. Jude had chuckled at first, but his humour had quickly turned to concern. He'd insisted they stop for lunch, and Clara had been all too eager to oblige.

After four hours of trying, begging whatever gods or deities who would listen, and internally screaming, all Clara had to show for her efforts was a pounding headache at the base of her skull. She hadn't had such a bad one since her visions became more frequent.

Now, she was so angry with herself, infuriated by her consistent failures, that her fingers ran hot. Clara drew some long, slow breaths and tried to ground herself. To remind herself there was a reason they were here and undertaking this gruelling task.

It was important.

The witches deserved to come home.

Though perhaps that was the reason Clara was being so hard on herself, despite knowing she'd never attempted such an insurmountable task before. The first time she'd called on her other magic intentionally, it'd taken her days to channel at all and then weeks to understand how she had done so. This was part of the process, as frustrating as it was in reality.

"When you have a vision, where do you feel it in your body?" Doneri asked from where he sat on the desk and jotted furiously in his notebook.

When Jude had mentioned knowing someone who might be able to help, Clara had pictured a scholar—neatly dressed, hair brushed, maybe even a bow tie. She had not expected a boy with tousled hair that reached his shoulders, dressed in clothing at least two sizes too big, which was torn all over. If these were stylistic choices, Clara didn't understand them.

"*He's an expert, trust me,*" Jude had said. Then he'd ranted and raved about Doneri, and had claimed he was the smartest fae in nearly a century with an ability to read, comprehend, and retain information perfectly every time.

She opened her mouth to answer, but for a second no words came out. Hazy images and dark, blurred movements obscured her sight. Jude and Doneri were nowhere to be seen. Clara blinked, and they came back into focus.

"Was that a vision?" Doneri pressed.

Clara shook her head. "I don't think so. I didn't actually see anything."

"But where did you feel it?"

"My eyes burned," Clara said with a shrug. "And my chest hurts."

"Now? Or as it was happening?"

"Now. I don't think I ever really feel anything during a vision. It's almost like my mind and body go numb as my subconscious takes over and plays the images."

Again, Doneri scribbled away, but Clara couldn't shake the pain or distress at such a bizarre vision. It felt the same, yet so different. Her body felt hot and heavy in its wake. A strange desire to curl into a ball and cry nearly overwhelmed her enough to succumb.

"Okay, I've got what I need for now." Doneri jumped off the desk and tucked his notebook into his pocket. He nodded to both Jude and Clara, then made for the door. "I'll come back in a few days once I've checked on some things."

"Do not dawdle," Clara warned, finger pointed at his nose. "Lives hang in the balance, you hear me?"

"Of course, Highness." Doneri bowed low this time, then left the room.

"Now," Jude said, before clearing his throat. "You are aware we're less than two weeks from the solstice, correct?"

Clara whirled on him, eyes wide and mouth open. "Shit! Seren's birthday!"

"Who is Seren? When is her birthday?" Jude paused, raising a brow. "And why is it important?"

The only acknowledgement Clara offered the prince was to smack his biceps gently. "How do you feel about hosting a ball?"

"Honestly, that's something we need to discuss. There are at least two balls required prior to the wedding. One held together, very political and public, without my parents present. We shake a lot of hands, kiss babies and whatnot. The second will be for females only. It's your farewell to society and is held the day before the wedding."

"That feels way too sexist to discuss right now. Focus." Clara clapped once, and Jude struggled to hide his smirk. "I want to host a ball for Seren's birthday. Can we do that?"

He scoffed. "You're a queen—you can do whatever you want."

"That's what I said!" Clara hissed. "But I am not the queen of this continent. Am I allowed to host a ball?"

"Technically no, but His Royal Highness, the heir to the Morrin throne, most certainly can."

A squeal burst from Clara before she could control herself. Excitement built quickly, both at being able to see Seren again and for the look on Seren's face when she realised the royal ball was in her honour. Birthdays were Seren's favourite thing, and she was not shy about letting the world know.

Water fae could be shy and timid, quiet and reserved. Seren was all those things, except on her birthday. In that case, it was the bigger the better, and Clara would make certain this ball was huge.

"Are you sure you have enough time to pull this off?" Jude asked, his arms crossed and scepticism clear on his face.

"Do you know anything about the female you're set to marry?" Clara asked. She didn't scoff out loud, but it was implied in her tone.

"I know she's determined, that's for damn sure." Jude sighed, a smile forming. "Let me know what you need, and I'll see to making it happen."

Clara squealed again and hugged her prince before she planted a sweet, appreciative peck on his cheek.

Isobel entered their suite with three large garment bags draped over her arm, her cheeks rosy and hair somewhat frizzed.

"You're lucky you didn't retrieve these yourself, *Highness*." She smirked and let out a low, quiet laugh. With a sharp exhale, she distributed the bags. "And I'm lucky Jude strolled past when he did and sent his hounds off to dress someone else. A whole pack of them were scurrying about the halls asking for you. I barely made it down the corridor before two of them caught me and confirmed for the hundredth time that you don't need any assistance."

Beau scoffed. "Do they think she's incapable?"

"No," Clara said with a sigh. "They worry about being out of a job if they have no one important to doll up."

"Regardless, you can dress yourself."

Isobel made a point of looking at Beau, who intentionally evaded her sharp blue gaze. Clara couldn't help but giggle.

"The invitations were all delivered this morning—which was an exhausting feat, by the way. I ran all over Elanist. It's a good thing I've travelled a lot of the continent already, else I'd have been shit out of luck. I also heard Seren is on her way from the docks as we speak, with no inkling the ball is in her honour."

"Good." Clara nodded while stripping off her previous dress. Jude had insisted she wear more formal, royal attire while in the palace, and she wasn't interested in arguing with him. Clara enjoyed looking pretty, and these dresses had a knack for showing her curves off well. Trousers and linen shirts were comfortable, and short day dresses were pretty enough, but the finery and luxurious garments made her feel like maybe her crown wasn't ill-placed.

Isobel cleared her throat, her gaze still directed at Beau.

He paused before he sighed heavily and rolled his eyes. "It's not like I haven't seen it all before," he grumbled, but turned around anyway.

"Not the point," Isobel replied, a subtle smugness on her face as she removed her clothing.

Oh how Clara would never tire of seeing these two naked. It almost felt too good to be true, like this was a cruel game the universe was playing with her and one day they'd both end up ripped away. But for now, she'd soak in their beauty and lap up the glory of them being hers.

Her moon and stars. They were her entire world. Bigger than anything else and far more important.

Clara fastened the ties at the back of Isobel's neck while Beau secured the buttons at Clara's lower back. Part of her wanted to forget about Seren, at least for an hour or so, and get rid of the fabric separating them.

But she was also excited to see her friend, and she couldn't deny that seeing Beau and Isobel dressed up had her core tightening, swirling and alive. Beau was in a fitted black suit, his wings, eyes, and cuffs stunning bursts of gold that stood out proudly. Isobel cut a striking image in her charcoal-grey dress, half of it sheer enough to display her tattoos, the other sparkling enough the stars might grow jealous. They looked like shadows personified, and the thought thrilled Clara. As if they were her shadows, always there at her back or her side whichever way she turned. Powerful and protective, both magical, in their own way. Clara was not shy about noticing.

Though neither were they; she felt their eyes rake over her, and she loved the burn of their attention.

The trio walked arm in arm to the foyer, to find Seren admiring the artwork hanging on the walls and the decorative moulding lining the ceiling. She looked radiant and full of joy in a pastel-yellow ball gown and sheer gloves that reached her biceps. Her bright-blue eyes bulged when she turned to see Clara, and a huge smile burst across her face.

Seren ran over and embraced her tightly. Clara hugged her back and whispered, "Welcome."

As she pulled away, Clara noticed who else was standing in the entryway.

"It's nice to see you, Mikhail," Clara said warmly, embracing him as well and noting his slightly darker-yellow bowtie. Clara raised a brow, her eyes jumping from his to the tie and back again.

Mikhail only shrugged and grinned, so Clara left it.

For now.

"Nerrida sends her well wishes," Mikhail said as the group made their way down the hall towards the ballroom, which was set up for the evening's festivities. "And also your notice of termination."

Clara whirled on him, but he cut her off with a wave of his hand.

"Regretful, but full of love and consideration. She said to tell you she hates to see you go but knows you've got bigger and better things on the horizon. Also, she insisted you were told your coin is worthless whenever you come to visit and that she'll take your visits as payment instead. Nothing more."

Clara's shoulders dropped, as did the corners of her mouth. She had never wanted to leave the bakery, nor did she want to put Nerrida in a position where she'd have to fire her. But the woman was right; there were big things coming, and a commitment to her job wasn't something she could give right now.

There was no chance Clara would trade her company for baked goods, but she didn't say as much now. Mikhail likely knew, if the almost grimace he pulled as he spoke was any indication. Such warmth and appreciation bloomed in Clara's chest at the kindness and understanding of her friends—nearly painful, but loving all the same.

As they approached the ballroom, but before the ushers could announce their arrival, Clara tugged Seren to a stop. Her friend turned, bright-eyed and eager for what awaited, with no idea it was for her.

"You know I'm terrible with gifts," Clara murmured and winced. "But after everything that's happened and before everything turns to shit—because I have no doubt it will—I wanted to do something nice for you. I will be stuck on this continent for a while, so it's the best I could do."

"Get to the point, woman." Seren laughed and her smile widened, grip softening in Clara's hand.

"Happy birthday, Seren."

Clara nodded towards the ushers, one of whom opened one of the large double doors, while the other called out into the ballroom.

"Her Highness, Clarenna Hayes, accompanied by Mr Beau Hawthorne and Miss Isobel Jeffreys. And the guest of honour, Miss Seren Archilla, accompanied by Mr Mikhail Dufort."

Seren's eyes bulged, her arm slack for a second, then she gripped Clara's hand harder than she had before. With the doors now open and Seren now aware of how many fae stood beyond them, Clara knew how hard she was trying not to squeal and bounce. But it was there, in the glitter of her eyes and the bursting smile she couldn't contain.

After a few hours filled with drinking and dancing, the finger food was served, and Clara finally managed to get Seren alone for a moment. Her friend had spent the entire night so far close to Mikhail. They danced hand in hand, drank from each other's goblets, laughed and walked and sang almost entirely on their own, as if no one else was in the room.

She learnt Seren and Mikhail had introduced themselves to Gerard upon arrival, which was lucky because Clara hadn't even thought about how the usher knew their names. There was so much for her to learn about royalty and the world she now found herself in. But for tonight, she wanted to catch up with her friend.

"Clara," Seren gushed, "this is more than I ever dreamt of! It's the biggest celebration of all. I feel like a princess!"

Clara laughed softly. "I'm glad." She paused for a moment, finding Seren's gaze had landed on a familiar winged male. "Anything you want to update me on, Seren?" Clara raised her brows, a smirk growing on her lips.

Seren blushed almost instantly, her smile softening, and yet somehow its power grew. "You know, I was so angry with your brother." Seren took a deep breath, then her smile shrunk a fraction before her eyes met Clara's. "So stars-damned hurt and betrayed. But now I think it was for the best. I'm grateful for it, honestly, with no ill will or bad feelings. He is once more the brother of my best friend. And now, I have room in my heart for someone who will truly worship the ground I walk on. But Mikhail and I are just friends."

Clara watched her lips quirk as she said *friends* and heard the unspoken *for now*.

"I don't know what's next, but right now, I'm enjoying his company. Truthfully, when he blushes, it makes my insides do flips. He's the definition of a sweetheart, and he kind of reminds me of you, just a lot more level-headed and calm. Some relationships are destined, while others are simply not meant to last. Give Evian my best, will you?"

Clara smiled and nodded, more pleased than she'd anticipated at hearing Seren's non-confession. She deserved someone devoted to her, and Clara had no doubt Mikhail was that someone. Now, or whenever they took the next steps.

As Mikhail rejoined Seren and Clara, with drinks for them both and cured-meat pastries in hand, a scream tore from the opposite corner of the room.

Clara didn't hesitate—she ran.

Jude appeared a second after she did.

A male with frosted white hair and a pale-blue shimmer to his lips stood hunched over, a wine goblet shattered at his feet. Isobel stood with wide eyes, liquid spilled down her front, while Beau dabbed at her stomach with a linen napkin. Truthfully, the napkin was doing fuck-all, but flutters warmed her belly watching him try to help. Clara did her best to remember now was not the time and tried to focus on the fae male, who looked like he was in serious pain.

He groaned and tried to straighten, his eyes clamped shut and knuckles white as he grabbed at his shirt.

Isobel took a spare napkin from Beau and muttered by Clara's ear, "I need to go outside. Fresh air." Then she kissed Clara's cheek and walked away without waiting for a response. Beau tried to follow, but she waved him off, so he stood tall by Clara's side instead. She brushed her hand along his, and the concern shadowing his face softened.

"What's going on?" Seren whispered urgently as she came up behind Clara.

No one answered, instead watching in silence as the male convulsed, gagged once, and retched up what looked to be a tree branch, full of life, with fresh pale-pink flower buds and blossoms. He gagged a second time, and the branch—which was at least the size of Clara's forearm—fell to the floor.

His grey eyes found Clara's as he wiped his mouth on his sleeve. When he pulled his arm away, the white shirt was dotted and streaked with blood.

"Please," he rasped. "Help me." The male collapsed immediately after.

"Has that happened before?" Clara hissed at Jude, who looked as confused and frightened as she felt. "Do you have a healer on site?"

"At least an infirmary or medical wing?" Seren asked calmly as she pushed past Clara and knelt next to the male. She pressed her fingers to his neck, then pulled back his eyelids gently.

Mikhail stepped forward and lifted the male at Seren's direction, while Jude called over two guards to escort them to the infirmary.

"I'm so sorry," Clara murmured to Seren as she squeezed Clara's hand in goodbye. "This was not how I wanted the evening to end."

"I've had the most wonderful time, Clara. Thank you. I love you."

Clara repeated the sentiments softly, then waited until her friend was out of earshot before she hissed at Jude, "What the fuck was that?"

"I don't know," he answered. His body was tense as he gazed off into the distance. "I think the rot is progressing."

"Has it affected folk in the past or only crops and land?"

Jude shook his head. "Only the land, but I think we just saw the first effects on the fae. That was a winter fae, and he spewed up spring blooms. Everything's upside down and wrong."

"You don't say," Beau muttered, rubbing the back of his neck with a wince.

Painful, unwelcome tingles speared up Clara's spine. Discomfort built in the dark, distant corners of her mind when she vaguely recalled a vision from months prior, where blood spilled from a male's mouth, but his body was upside down.

"That's not helpful," Clara scolded Beau, ignoring how futile her magic also liked to be, then turned her attention back to Jude. "Do you remember when I suggested your mother take over the wedding planning?"

Jude scoffed. "I thought you were joking."

"I most certainly wasn't, but I don't think we even have a choice now. Time is running out. I need to bring Era and Tindal home, and we need to save your kingdom. Planning a wedding is nowhere on my priority list right now.”

The prince nodded solemnly.

The ballroom emptied quickly after that, with Clara and Jude bidding farewell to every fae as they walked out the door. They then offered goodnight wishes to each other as they came to a stop outside their suites. Hunter stood at Jude’s door and gave Clara a slight wave before the males disappeared into their room.

Beau sighed behind Clara and wrapped his arms around her waist.

“If she’s not in there, I vote we don’t look for her just yet. This dress is doing all kinds of things to me, and I would like to rid you of it.” His low voice vibrated against her jaw, breath warm and sending goosebumps down her spine.

She considered agreeing, but when Clara had checked the courtyard for Isobel earlier, she’d seen no sign of the female, making her heart race. Even now, the air was charged, waiting for something. So Clara sighed and turned the handle, then entered their bedroom suite.

Her heart shattered when she saw Isobel lying lifeless on the floor.

Clara moved in a blur towards Isobel, while Beau raced out into the hall. His eyes darted frantically, trying to find a sign of anyone who could help. The prince's door was closed, but Beau didn't bother knocking.

"Hunter!" he bellowed as he pushed open the main doors.

Both the prince and his lover ran from the adjoining bedroom. Beau was unsure and uncaring of what time it was. "Did you see or hear anyone go into our suite tonight?"

"No," Hunter said, his brows pinching and a hint of confusion in his voice.

Beau didn't explain any further, just turned and charged back towards Isobel—Prince Jude and Hunter right on his heels. Beau's heart raced for the female, and it was slightly uncomfortable. It wasn't an emotion felt entirely for Clara's sake anymore. He'd grown fond of her, and if anything happened to Isobel, Beau would carry the grief with him forever. Not only as the tetherbond to his soulmate, but all of his own. His family.

Clara held a limp Isobel to her chest, but mumbled pleas fell from both their lips.

Relief hit Beau harder than he could have imagined. A chill ran across his body, his breath heavy but full. His heart worked double as he watched Isobel trace a sloppy hand over Clara's cheek, her chest rising and falling slowly.

"Isobel, honey, look at me." Clara pulled away slightly but held Isobel's face tightly between her palms. Her face was contorted with fear and rage.

Beau hardly noticed the swirling curtains and the frigid air that billowed the comforter, but he heard a remark behind him. Whether it was Jude or Hunter, he didn't know and frankly didn't care.

"Did you take anything?" Clara spoke slowly and clearly. Isobel tried to shake her head, but the movement was uncoordinated, as if she'd never attempted it before and didn't know how it was supposed to feel.

"No," she said, sadness filling her small voice. She sniffed and closed her eyes.

"Did you consent to someone else giving you something?"

"No!" Isobel shouted back, her eyes wide open now and her lip pulled back in a snarl.

Clara's eye twitched, but she took a deep breath and continued speaking as before. Beau didn't smile, but part of him was proud of how much she'd grown. A year ago, she would've spewed something fiery and rage-filled before considering anything else. Yet today she held her tongue, considered the situation and knew Isobel's anger wasn't intended. Clara had matured, at least a little.

"Then I need you to tell me exactly what happened tonight."

"Why?"

"Because I'm going to kill whoever was responsible, and I do not wish to murder an innocent."

Hunter inhaled sharply, but Jude waved him off as he moved past Beau to kneel beside Clara.

"I don't want her murdering half my kingdom on her warpath, Isobel dear. Do you remember leaving the ballroom earlier?"

Isobel nodded, her eyes locked on the prince.

He reached out and took her hand, then cocked his head to the side. "And after that?" he asked slowly, but Isobel only nodded again. "Can you show her?"

"Show me?" Clara asked, her head whipping round to face Jude, and Beau noticed the skin around her knuckles whiten even before Isobel winced.

Isobel took her hand from Jude's, placed it over Clara's, and the tension in Clara's body seemed to evaporate. She then jerked her chin towards Jude, who took that as an instruction to explain.

"Isobel's Candor magic allows her the ability to place images and memories into another's mind. A form of telepathy, albeit limited."

Beau hadn't realised Hunter stood so close to him until the male whispered, "Jude can read the magic a fae possesses by skin contact. It's very impressive, though he's found it to be mostly dull. Up until now, I suppose."

Beau could only nod in response, while his mind raced with every conversation he'd had with Isobel about magic and abilities or even anything he'd overheard. She'd never mentioned it before, and Beau wondered why.

Did she not care for it? Not use her Candor magic so didn't mention it? Or perhaps—and a touch of discomfort spilled down his throat at the thought—Isobel didn't trust him with the information.

But that seemed unlikely, considering Clara also seemed to have no idea, and he knew without any doubt that Isobel trusted Clara. With her life, her soul, and everything in between.

Isobel sighed, and then the room was quiet. Even the air stilled. After a few moments, the room grew hot, the air now thick and difficult to breathe. Jude watched Clara intently but said nothing.

When Clara's eyes focused again, she stood. Pointing at Hunter, she said, "You will stay here with Isobel. Send for Seren Archilla, but no one else is to enter this room." Clara turned to the prince. "Come or don't, I care little, but we are going hunting." Her bright-green eyes fell to Beau, filled with so much unfiltered emotion he struggled to meet her gaze. He nodded, and she stormed past him, stripping out of her dress on the way.

Clara dressed faster than he'd seen before, with a determination that made the room cold. Beau pulled a dagger from the nightstand and handed it to Clara, then grabbed his sword from behind the door. Hunting, indeed.

"Who are we looking for?" Jude asked, his stride casual beside Clara and Beau's fast pace, thanks to the prince's longer legs.

"A female, past maturation but scrawny. Thin and frail. Red hair, grey skin. Taller than me, but not by much." She didn't look at anyone as she spoke; instead, her eyes darted down every hallway, every corridor, and around every corner. Some doors she flung open, and others she ignored. Beau followed her lead, with no idea why she turned down particular hallways or which doors she felt needed inspection.

"Seasonal fae do not have grey skin," the prince mumbled.

"Now is not the time for you to blame particular courts, prince. Nor do I appreciate your tone," Clara snapped, and the prince's hands shot upwards in submission.

"That isn't what I meant. Narrowing the suspect field is all."

Soon they reached the alfresco area Isobel had wandered into after the ball. Every flower was in bloom, bright and delicate, though a violent wind tore through leaves and petals and branches. Clara stopped by a stone bench, spun a few times slowly, and took in the space. Looking for answers or needing a moment, Beau didn't know. She took a deep, slow breath before she planted her hands firmly on her hips.

"Running around like a headless chicken won't get me anywhere. Find me someone who can locate whoever stepped foot into this garden tonight."

"Clara, do you know how many have walked through here in the past hour?" The prince took a hesitant step towards Clara and shook his head slowly. "Staff wander through the gardens constantly for shortcuts to wherever they need to be. That'd be like trying to find a needle in a haystack, even if I knew someone with tracking abilities."

"Was there anything in what Isobel showed you that could help?" Beau asked, spearing Jude with a pointed look he hoped the male could understand. The time to discourage Clara had long passed. Now it was unhelpful, likely to be ignored, and despite any control she'd mastered, Clara might just set the male who told her "no" alight. Beau could feel the primal energy radiating from her, the fear and anger and hostility. Her sole focus was retribution, and she wasn't interested in taking no for an answer.

"Like what? An address perhaps? Maybe she told Isobel exactly where she'd be going after ruining her four years of sobriety. Something like that?"

Beau flinched reflexively, then stuffed his hands into his pockets. "If you take out all your anger on me, you won't have any left for the woman we're looking for." Clara sighed and nodded slightly, so Beau added, "We're only trying to help."

Clara narrowed her eyes at him, and he gave a subtle grin. She ignored him, instead taking slow, calculated steps over the grass and pavers. When she stopped, Clara stared intently at Beau and the prince, then closed her eyes and inhaled deeply.

Jude's eyes lit up, almost excited at whatever he thought was coming next.

"What is she doing?" Beau hissed, but Jude didn't need to respond. Clara's body turned rigid, her chin turned up slightly. Had she ever called on a vision before? He couldn't recall. A pit opened in his gut, filled with both pride and concern, and he was unsure if forcing her magic was a good idea.

His worries felt even more justified when her nose began to bleed. That had only happened occasionally that he knew of, and considering the dozens of visions she'd had since they met, he knew that was uncommon.

Clara's eyes flew open.

The air surrounding them swirled violently for a second before it once again fell still.

Then Clara whirled and ran, Beau and the prince racing after her.

"Do you recognise me?" Clara demanded as she halted in front of the ragged redhead.

The female's arms wrapped around her slight frame, and splotches of near silver were stamped all over her skin. But it wasn't the grey Beau expected, like the air fae in Elanist. These patches of her skin seemed to grey as if they had been sucked of any other colour. They were highlighted on her face by the purple veins, which spread from her eyes and nose, and tinged the outline of her lips. She shook her head, similar to how Isobel had, like it was an unfamiliar movement.

"Never mind." A sinister grin spread over Clara's face. Unlike her usual expression, this one was cold and filled with hatred. "You took something from my tether. Something you had no fucking right to, and now I'll take your life as payment."

The female stumbled backwards, her eyes wide, and mouth open.

"Please," she whispered, haggard and raspy.

"What is your name?" Clara asked with venom in her tone.

The female hesitated, surely contemplating whether to divulge this information. It didn't matter, as Clara wasn't leaving without it. She swallowed hard, then answered, "Ruby."

"You've got four seconds to tell me what happened, Ruby."

"When?" Ruby's wild and desperate eyes darted between Clara, Beau, and Jude, but both males stood in silence.

"Do not play games with me!" Clara shouted as she closed the space between them. "Why did you drug her? What on this stars-damned continent gave you the impression that was a good idea?"

"I was hired!" Ruby exclaimed as her arms moved frantically in jerky motions. "I'm not even from here—I was near the Cerulean Castle when they found me. They said they wanted me because I was from Tirenas."

"Who?" Jude asked, leaning in slightly.

"They mentioned a queen, but I don't know which one."

"How many queens are there?" Beau asked her with a scoff. He wasn't entirely sure he trusted any of what came from this female's mouth. Sure, fae couldn't lie, but he'd encountered enough who could bend the rules that bound their tongues.

"At least four."

"Focus." Clara drew Ruby's attention back to her. "What did they hire you to do?"

"To drug the one with pink hair and tattoos. They said you'd know which queen sent me, and the games would continue." Ruby shook her head, then clenched her fists a few times before she wrapped her arms around herself again. "The two who spoke to me"—her eyes flitted around before landing back on Clara—"were slow, not all there." Ruby tapped the side of her head twice.

Beau fought a chuckle. All that information did was perhaps exclude most of Morrin.

"I've been an addict for a really long time, and I hate that I took her sobriety. But I didn't have a choice." Ruby's voice was softer now, almost remorseful. Maybe she felt bad. Clara wouldn't care, though, and Beau was inclined to agree.

"You always have a choice," Clara fired back with a sneer. "Your choice was to be selfish and cowardly. Now tell me who sent you, or your death will be slow."

"They'll kill me . . ." Ruby's voice trailed off as her eyes pled with each of them.

"So will I," Clara whispered, and Beau swore a chill ran down his back.

"I swear I don't know any names! Please, they didn't say! They were tall, so tall, and kept praising summer and couldn't find the crown, and they promised Her Majesty would save me if I did what they asked! That's all I—"

Clara shoved her fingers into Ruby's mouth before she could ramble further. Her eyes bulged, while Clara's body was as still as he'd ever seen. The scene dragged up an old memory of Beau with King Urian, when he'd held Beau's tongue in much the same way.

Instead of threatening Ruby as Urian had Beau, Clara merely held her free hand out, open towards Beau. A second later his dagger lay in her palm. Her fingers tightened around it as she muttered curses and growled no doubt vicious words under her breath directed at the fae before her. In the next blink, blood sprayed over Clara's face and hands.

She dropped Ruby's tongue like she would've dropped a tissue into the bin—like waste, discarded and no longer useful. Clara didn't say anything more to Ruby, only walked back the way they'd come.

Beau and Jude shared a fleeting glance, then followed behind her.

Ruby's screams rang through the alleyway, though the sound was now garbled.

CHAPTER TWENTY-TWO
BEAU

Most of the walk back to their suites was done in silence, though Beau couldn't help but ask about Clara's earlier vision.

"Have you ever evoked a vision on command before?" he asked as he slipped his hand into Clara's.

She tightened her return grip and sighed. "No," she whispered. "We'd been trying, but so far no luck. Until tonight, I wasn't even convinced it was possible."

"I'll get Doneri back for another session today," Jude said, eyes searching the halls, likely for a staff member to contact this Doneri. "Hopefully, we can recreate it."

"Minus the bloody nose, preferably."

"You don't enjoy seeing me a little bloody?" Clara teased with a sly grin, though it was more hollow than usual. "That's not the impression I got last time."

"I don't think the prince cares about last time, sweetheart." Beau didn't really care what the prince knew of their sexual endeavours, but he also didn't want to be giving that information out willy-nilly. Especially not when it'd been too long since their last dive between the sheets.

Logically, he knew now wasn't the time, but fuck, the way her eyes glistened, he wanted to fill them with tears and lick her all over. And she was right; there was something intoxicating about seeing her bloodied. Less so when it was her own blood, but it was unsettlingly arousing when she was covered with the blood of another. She looked powerful, every bit the queen that she was, and it left Beau's cock aching for her.

After a deep breath, and ignoring the smirk from Jude, Beau cleared his throat and continued.

"How are you going on the Lady of Summer front?"

Clara let out a frustrated breath as her hand tensed slightly in his. "Not great."

"Ruby mentioned something earlier—"

"Why do you care about what she said?" Clara bit out.

"If you let me finish, you'll find out." Beau stared at her with raised brows. "May I?" She rolled her eyes but said nothing. "She mentioned there being at least four queens, but we know that isn't true. You, Eveline, and Jude's mother make only three." Beau paused in the hall just before their suites, pulling the trio to a halt and turning his attention to Jude. "Maybe the *Lady of Summer* is someone who wants the crown or expects it. Can a regular fae acquire a crown in Morrin?"

Jude shrugged. "Technically no, they must be of royal blood, but also technically yes because if there are no blood heirs, the reigning king and or queen can choose their successor. It is not an option because I am a blood heir, but it's a contingency put in place nonetheless."

"Have your parents offered anyone the throne you don't know about?" Beau asked, theories running wild in his mind.

"Fuck no," Jude said with a laugh and shook his head vigorously. "They've been threatening *me* with it since I was a child. And they're only getting worse as I get older. There is no way they would offer it to another."

"I'm not sure how to feel about this progress, but I know for damn certain I don't want to talk about it anymore right now. For the foreseeable future, I will be in bed with Isobel, and I will not be entertaining interruptions." Clara spoke to both of them, her finger tracking both Beau and Jude.

"I'll see you in the study after breakfast, Clara. I'm afraid you do not have the luxury of more time than that."

"Thank you for the support, prince." Clara nodded in acknowledgement and farewell.

The prince only smirked as he dipped into a lazy bow. "It's what husbands do, is it not?"

"Husband-to-be," Beau corrected, clearing his throat. Jude winked at him and strode ahead down the hall, not looking back as he entered his rooms.

When Beau and Clara entered theirs, Hunter bid them goodnight and dipped out quietly. Clara didn't take her eyes off Isobel as she collected a cloth from the bathing room, nor as she wet it and wiped her face. Her eyes stayed locked on her tether. After a few moments of observing them both, once Clara joined Isobel in bed, Beau decided he should also leave.

Tears sporadically spilled from Isobel's eyes, and Clara stroked her hair and held her. She made no noise, no movements, save for her steady breathing. As much as their relationship had grown and blossomed of late, Beau wasn't needed in this moment. He stayed long enough to see that she was alive and then quietly left.

CHAPTER TWENTY-THREE
BEAU

Clara hadn't pressed him any further about his secret, but it still weighed heavily on Beau's conscience. Especially in the early hours of the morning, when the stars were high and stark in the dark sky and hardly another soul wandered the palace grounds. He hadn't planned where he'd walk, just figured he'd roam the palace and work out some things along the way.

Yet now Lorelai's words echoed loudly in his mind, and Beau couldn't shake the dread pressing on his shoulders or the worry clutching his chest. What if he failed? What happened if he could not fulfil his end of the bargain and Clara suffered? If she died for it?

The question had his breath catching in his throat. What kind of creature walked between worlds? Spent time close to Death, but might answer his pleas to save Clara from its grip?

Truthfully, he wondered if his feet travelled in as many circles as his mind.

"Beau?" a familiar male voice called from behind him.

Beau spun to find Mikhail, still dressed in his finery from the evening before, though somewhat more unkempt.

"In the flesh," he replied and folded his arms across his chest as Mikhail jogged over.

"What're you doing up at this hour?"

"I could ask the same of you."

Mikhail's expression turned flat before he rolled his eyes, and his casual grin returned. "One hell of a ball—"

Beau interrupted before the male could finish. Mikhail was nice enough and had been helpful in the past, but he wasn't someone Beau wanted to engage in small talk.

"What do you know of the oracle at the Pearl 'n Lace?" he asked, observing Mikhail intently. Perhaps too much, going by the awkward scrunch of his face and shoulders.

Mikhail shrugged and stuffed his hands into his pockets.

"Specifically? Not much. Generally? Everyone who's been in Elanist long enough knows about Ora. She's scarily accurate."

Beau's lips pursed, and his shoulders tensed. He was now second-guessing whether Mikhail could help him this time, whether he'd made a mistake opening up. But considering he'd already started the conversation, he may as well get what information he could from the fae.

"I have a riddle of sorts," he said, attempting a casual tone. He tried to make it sound nonchalant, maybe even like a leisurely activity and not one of such grave importance. "I need to find someone or something, and I'm not sure if she's the one it's pointing me to."

"What kind of riddle?" Mikhail asked, his brows slightly furrowed. He pulled his hands out of his pockets. If Beau didn't know the male better, he might've assumed Mikhail was mocking him.

Beau contemplated his answer for what felt like an eternity, but Mikhail waited patiently. "It talks of a being who walks between worlds, lurks beyond Death's doors, has an eye for an eye mentality, charges for their time and brings information." He counted off the points with his fingers, and each digit snapped open with a touch more frustration.

"It'd help if I could hear the actual riddle, but your tight-ass posture leads me to believe I won't be privy to such knowledge." Mikhail raised an amused brow, then added, "Not to mention you seem visibly unsure of whether you wanted to tell me at all."

He hadn't meant to growl, but it still reverberated up his throat.

Mikhail only chuckled as Beau's eyes narrowed.

"You spend too much time with Clara," Beau muttered.

"Not for quite a while now, unfortunately." Mikhail sighed, his voice almost sad. "Let her know I miss her, would you?"

"Sure, now can you help me or not?" Beau couldn't blame him for missing Clara, but now was not the time to meander wistfully down memory lane. Not unless Mikhail wanted that activity to be the only way he saw Clara again.

He let out a soft breath before he answered. "Honestly, I don't think so, but then neither can Ora. She doesn't world walk. While she was originally from another universe, she's made it very clear she wants nothing to do with that world anymore. A few folk have asked her about it during sessions or readings, and she shuts it down. She won't even talk about it. She's permanently here and has far too much light to lurk anywhere near Death's door. Half the time her readings prevent death. You'd be better off talking to a Reaper if you can find one.

Aside from the payment part, because I don't know if they charge for their services, what you've said describes them perfectly."

Beau mumbled something noncommittal as his thoughts turned to Clara's friend Ryn. The Reaper who'd interrupted the mating haze after she and Isobel had accepted their tetherbond and who somehow remained breathing. He did not know how to get in touch with the creature, however—not without setting off alarm bells with Clara.

Perhaps he should still speak with Ora. If at least fifty percent of her readings prevented death, maybe she could still help somehow. Yet he felt like he was clutching at straws, and time was quickly running out. Summer was nearly here, which meant the Lady of Summer—whoever she turned out to be—was approaching. The universe had a thing for piling every dramatic, chaotic, and dangerous event on top of one another so there was no doubt in Beau's mind that the kidnapping Lorelai mentioned, the Lady of Summer's arrival, hell, probably even the wedding, would all coincide. The universe was cruel and sadistic that way.

In a daze, Beau took off down the hall. He wouldn't ask Clara, not yet, but he could ask Isobel. At the very least, she would know how to contact Ryn or someone who could get in touch with her. That was all he needed—a damned conversation.

"You're welcome!" Mikhail called out after him, but Beau wasn't listening anymore.

The next morning, after Clara left to meet the prince, Beau sent for Seren to sit with Isobel. She lay in bed, awake but unmoving, silent and solemn. It was a jarring comparison to her usual bubbly demeanour, and frankly, the change made Beau uncomfortable. He didn't want her to sit alone and stew for however long he and Clara needed to be elsewhere, and Clara had already approved of Seren being in the suite.

While he waited for Seren to arrive, Beau spoke to Isobel in private.

"Are you alright?" he asked her softly as he sat at the foot of the bed.

Isobel's eyes moved to his, then she blinked slowly and looked away. That was answer enough, he supposed. Of course, she wasn't okay.

"I'm sorry," he whispered. "Isobel, I need to ask you for help, though I know this is far from ideal timing. But I'm running out of options, and it's important."

Her eyes tracked back towards him, then her face turned slightly as well. Beau took that as his sign. Without explaining why, he asked how he might get in contact with Ora as someone who could not transport via magic nor traverse such a distance of land in a reasonable time.

Isobel was silent.

Beau continued, asking for help to locate Ryn. Choppy, disjointed images of the Cerulean Castle popped into his mind, causing Beau to jump. Seeing two realities simultaneously when he was entirely unprepared for it startled him. He watched as Isobel—he assumed—turned down a familiar hallway and into the library. Ryn was nowhere to be found, but he thanked Isobel all the same.

Beau knelt beside Isobel's head, then leant forward to press a gentle kiss to her forehead. When he pulled away, he whispered again, "I'm so sorry. If I can help you, I will. Even if all you need is a punching bag, okay?"

He hadn't expected a response, but when she nodded— ever so slightly—and her eyes closed, a strange sadness exploded in his chest.

As Beau made his way through the palace, eager to get into town, Gerard pulled him aside and handed over a chilled envelope. It shimmered as he turned it over to find his name scrawled in looping calligraphy on the other side. He raised his eyebrow at the fae before him.

"It's your official invitation to His and Her Highness' wedding, sir." Gerard dipped his chin and hurried off, the bag across his side bumping into his hip with every step.

He didn't know how to feel about Gerard handing him an invitation. First, why hadn't Clara mentioned anything? Why hadn't she given it to him herself? Admittedly, there was a lot going on, and he knew she was more than busy, but surely handing over a piece of paper—fuck, even just *telling* him the time and date—would've been possible?

He also knew her focus had been split. She'd been waking early and going to sleep late—which was never a good idea for Clara. Her nose had bled frequently over the past few days. Only a little, but he'd noticed, even before she swiped her hand and tried to cover it. Between the mermaids, the witches, whatever was killing Jude's lands and affecting his subjects, and the incident with Isobel to top it all off, Clara had more important things on her mind.

Beau just wanted to feel important.

Realistically, he doubted neither her nor her feelings for him. But it had been a while since they'd had any time alone and even longer since they'd last fucked. He missed her.

Hastily, Beau opened the envelope and watched as a dozen snowflakes fell to the floor and then disappeared. He scoffed, then his jaw dropped at the date listed on the invitation.

Summer solstice.

Less than a week away.

A wave of frustration rolled through Beau, but this time it was less about being out of the loop and more about the fact that he was going to lose even more time with Clara once she was wed. He had tried to tell himself she'd still make time for him, for their throuple, but he knew it ultimately wasn't up to her. The only consolation was that Jude also had a lover, someone he wasn't willing to give up, so he and Clara were in the same boat. Perhaps their unconventional dynamic would allow some leniency.

He shoved the navy card into his pocket and stormed out the door. Despite the snow continuously falling, he wasn't cold. In fact, by the time he reached the blacksmith, he'd had to roll up his sleeves and undo the top few buttons of his shirt. Sweat dampened his armpits and his lower back.

"Hello?" Beau called out as he entered the shop. A bell rang out above the door with a high-pitched jingle, and Beau would've liked to rip it from its hangar.

"Mr Hawthorne, I presume?" An older male replied, seeming to appear out of nowhere at the far end of the shop. Beau nodded, realising he'd likely stepped through a door or around a corner. "The prince told me I'd be hearing from you soon. How can I help?"

"I need to combine the magic of my feathers into tattoo ink. I was told you would be able to reduce the feathers to liquid, but I'm not sure what a blacksmith can do in the way of tattoos." Beau glanced around the shop filled with metals and weapons, pieces of armour, and even small figurines and statues. He scrunched his face with scepticism before he cleared his throat and tried to relax his facial muscles.

The male smiled, then said, "I cannot help on the tattoo front, but I'll send for my nephew. He's a tattoo artist, so between us you'll have all the help you should need."

"Convenient," Beau muttered, unsure if he trusted the male.

Yet when the blacksmith's smile stayed steady, Beau second-guessed his doubts. Maybe it was the reason Jude had sent him here—for the blacksmith and artist duo. Jude certainly wasn't stupid, nor did he seem the cunning type. Maybe it was receiving the invitation this morning that had his hackles rising.

While they waited for the nephew to arrive, Beau handed the blacksmith a feather and watched as he placed it into a small pot he called a crucible. He held it with comically large tongs and took it over to the heat. Beau's initial thought was that Clara likely could've done this part herself; it reminded Beau of their very first few weeks together. He didn't miss that time—when Urian was alive and Beau forced himself away from any romantic connection with Clara. It was absolutely fucking brutal, but he missed the simplicity when his day would consist of teaching her how to wield her magic and nothing else. Back when he was experiencing her for the first time, and despite being surrounded by power his whole life, he'd never felt someone so magical.

The male continued to explain the technicalities of melting the feather down, not burning or evaporating it, and what to avoid so it didn't explode. He spoke of different temperatures, pots, and time frames over flame and coal. Last, he explained that the timeline of the feather's magic was not infinite. Once they'd successfully melted one down and cooled it into ink, they'd only have a handful of hours before it became useless.

Their first attempt evaporated. The blacksmith swore and began removing coal from the forge, though why he did not say. He collected a new crucible and held his hand out for a new feather as well. Beau winced as he plucked another, but handed it over silently. The second attempt was also too hot, though this one didn't evaporate.

"Did you hear that sound?" the blacksmith asked, his ear far too close to the heat for Beau's comfort. "It was as if someone stuck out their tongue and blew raspberries. Chaotic and loud." He shook his head. "No, what we want is something that sounds like a thousand tiny bubbles bursting over the top of one another. Quieter and more prolonged."

"Let's hope third time's the fucking charm because I'm losing feathers at this point." Beau grumbled as he plucked a third feather.

"Sorry," the blacksmith almost squeaked out as he took the feather. "You're also going to need a test subject."

"I am not bringing some random fae in here to tattoo my feather blood into and then attempt to kill in the hopes I fail."

Just as Beau finished speaking and crossed his arms over his chest, a younger male voice called out behind him.

"I sure hope I'm in the right place. To tattoo, not to sacrifice, right?"

Beau rolled his eyes at the poor attempt at a joke, but turned to face the male. They shook hands while the blacksmith spoke.

"It doesn't have to be a fae. You could find a rodent?"

"Disgusting." Beau grimaced, then rolled out his shoulders. "Fine."

He hadn't expected such difficulty in finding a stars-damned rat, but finally Beau managed to catch one. His heart leapt into his throat as the nephew took a small portion of the liquid feather and tattooed it along the rat's stomach, then it all but stopped as the old man slit the creature's throat. Sweat built on his palms, and an uncomfortable, stiff tension rose in his shoulders and neck as they waited for the dead rat to breathe again.

It took forever, but finally its chest rose, and its tail flicked. Before Beau could truly accept what had happened, the

rodent jumped and scurried out of the shop. Maybe this ludicrous
idea of sharing lives was possible after all.

Clara didn't want to leave Isobel, but Seren offered to
stay with her after reminding Clara she was asleep. It took longer
than he'd anticipated, but Clara eventually conceded, and soon
they walked hand in hand down the paved streets, occasionally
waving at patrons who recognised Clara.

From the corner of his eye, shimmering golds and silvers
flapped across his vision. Beau turned to see the pop of colour
and found a discera. He chuckled as he pointed the futures-and-
fortunes bird out to Clara.

"They aren't local to Morrin, you know."

Beau nodded, knowing all too well that they weren't
fans of intense weather or the cold specifically. It had no reason
to be here.

"That one is obviously stalking you," Clara murmured
as she jabbed her elbow playfully into Beau's side.

"Oh?"

"It looks identical to the one we saw on the way to
Diandra's. You know the time you forced Neven to leave so you
could get me alone. Remember?"

"I remember no such turn of events, thank you. He said
he had to be elsewhere, and I, for one, believed the male." Beau
winked, then looked away. He couldn't help the grin spreading
across his face, and it only grew when Clara chuckled softly
beside him.

A small part of him worried about the reason the discera
was here, and if it was for him. Most folk believed the tales that

the bird foretold fortunes and that those successes came at a steep cost. Something good or bad was on the horizon, but everything would be okay if the tithe was paid.

Beau felt more pessimistic, and he couldn't shake the heavy feeling in his gut that whatever was coming would only bring ill.

"Listen," Beau said as he pulled Clara to a stop outside the blacksmith's shop. "You and Isobel have something undeniable; it's woven into the fabric of your beings and visible to anyone with eyes. I want to leave you with something visible too."

"No, I'm not interested in you *leaving me* with anything, Beau. What are we doing here?" Clara's voice took on a note of concern, her hand gripping his tighter as she looked around them.

"You're getting a tattoo because I need you to have something of me with you. Something more than a necklace covered in another male's shirt."

"I want the tattoo, but not as a memory, you fucking turd." Clara smacked his biceps, then asked, "Will you get one too?"

"I could get some ink," Beau said, contemplating what he might get done. As if she could read his mind, Clara offered her own suggestion with a cheeky grin and wild eyes.

"You should get my name on your ass cheek."

"On second thought, I might leave the ink to you, sweetheart."

"Pussy."

Beau winked and Clara rolled her eyes, but they walked into the blacksmith's shop with smiles on their faces and hands interlocked.

CHAPTER TWENTY-FOUR
ISOBEL

For days, the air sang loudly. Sometimes as it left her mouth on a tight breath, sometimes before then in the pit of her lungs. Every movement around her sent a small puff of air that whispered and screamed.

Her body felt numb. It was exhausting and bold and it *hurt*. Tears repeatedly stung her eyes, though only occasionally did they fall. The wet streaks ignited a fury deep in her bones, but she had no energy to wipe them. She felt like her essence was being smothered, while simultaneously being void of anything at all. It was a bitter, sorrowful double-edged sword that pierced her mind and her chest over and over again.

Two days rotting away in bed felt like an eternity. Her thoughts, emotions, and body were heavy, while guilt ate at her for her lack of productivity. She felt useless, spiralling Isobel further into herself.

Some moments consumed her. Everything she'd worked so hard for was gone. Every hour of blood and sweat and tears and vomit had been for nothing. In a second, all that effort was ripped away. Wasted. What was the point of staying sober? She did it once, but did she really want to go through all that again?

Would she be able to without Elisabeth? Her love had been tough, but it was what Isobel needed. Clara did not have the sharp heart of her sister.

Clara was her only light in the past forty-eight hours. When Clara held her, the pain and anger did not go away, but for those moments Isobel felt like maybe they didn't matter so much. That if Clara was around, Isobel could keep the desperation at bay. Her tether made her want to hold on, not only for herself but for the life they'd created together with the Phoenix she'd grown to care for as well. Isobel wanted to be better than her cravings. For all three of them, and the life that awaited them.

But stars, it was *hard*.

Not a single second went by without her thinking about finding the redhead and scoring. She thought about doing it a few times more, then weaning off.

But it didn't work the last time. Neither did seclusion, or positivity. Elisabeth had finally threatened her—get clean and stay employed under her rule, or Isobel could take her chances wandering the mountains. All manner of creatures lived in the Elanist mountains, not to mention there wasn't any access to drugs or other substances. She could either get clean with help or she'd die without.

Elisabeth gave no soft words or kind embraces. She all but handcuffed Isobel to someone new and cold and uncaring each day. They ignored her tantrums and outbursts during withdrawals, cared not when she screamed until she threw up, or yanked on the cuffs hard enough to bleed or break her own wrist.

Isobel didn't have anyone like that now.

But something about Beau's offer to be her punching bag had her hopeful that maybe, just maybe, she'd get through this without Elisabeth. Maybe Beau would let her take her frustrations out on him, with her fists or feet or something else. Then she could come back to Clara and feel light again instead of bearing such a heavy, weighted darkness.

Hope refreshed her tears, and a new one spilled down the side of her face. It pooled in the wet patch on the pillow with the others.

"Isobel?" Clara whispered. Isobel hadn't heard words exchanged between Clara and Seren, but she noted the door close, so assumed Seren had left. The water fae didn't speak to Isobel while she watched over her, and that was for the best. Isobel didn't love the idea of a babysitter, but she appreciated everyone's concern.

For the first time in two days—save for when she needed to relieve herself—Isobel sat up. Something bright glimmered in Clara's beautiful jade-green eyes, but Isobel couldn't read what.

"I have news," Clara said slowly, then she sat beside Isobel and grasped her hand gently. She took a deep breath before continuing. "There's another ball tonight, and I know what happened is still very raw for you, so if you don't want to—"

Isobel shook her head and drew in a shaky breath before she spoke. She turned her hand over in Clara's, so their fingers interlocked. "I do," she said hoarsely.

"I want you beside me every step of the way, make no mistake. But I don't want to put pressure on you to do something if you're not ready."

"Some moments I'm fine—others are brutal and harrowing. It takes every single fibre of my being to be stubborn enough not to run out and find her again."

"That'd be difficult," Clara muttered. Isobel raised a brow, and Clara sighed. "I cut out her tongue, so even if she managed to heal in the state she was in, she's likely gone far, far away by now."

A ghost of a smile tugged at Isobel's lips, and more light bloomed in her chest. Clara was the purest, most magical, violent soul Isobel had ever encountered, and by the stars, she was so overwhelmingly grateful the universe had tied them together.

"I don't know what it was about that night or that glass of wine that made me, I don't know, doubt myself, I guess. Alcohol has been spilled on me before, and alcohol was never my vice—it's a gateway, a stepping stone. But the smell hit me differently than it had in the past, so I needed to get some fresh air. Somewhere that wasn't full of liquor, where I was surrounded by intoxicated folk.

"When I got outside, she was already standing in the courtyard, looking skittish. She came right up to me and said she could tell a kindred spirit from a mile away. Offered me a wafer, but when I declined, she simply shrugged. I turned away, but she spun my shoulder back and grabbed my face. She had a wafer held between her teeth and then she smashed her face onto mine. She spat it into my mouth and pressed my tongue over it with her own. I felt violated twice. I feel dirty now." The words spilled from her mouth; Isobel couldn't stop them. Her lungs seized and her throat burned with every attempted breath, terrified with every new word what Clara would say.

She didn't strike Isobel as someone who'd have much experience with drugs. So whether she knew what wafers were, or how one might take them, Isobel didn't know. But she knew she wanted to tell Clara her story. Not only the drugs, but that she'd been forced to kiss the stranger to take them. Bile rushed up her throat, threatening to erupt at the recollection of another woman's lips on hers. Someone who wasn't Clara, and did not have her consent, who took something from her twice over. She felt tainted all over, like no matter how hard she scrubbed, the slime would never leave.

Clara was silent for a long time.

Tears filled Isobel's eyes and flowed of their own volition, but she waited in painful silence for Clara to respond. For Clara to look away or turn her nose up, to bare her teeth or to yell. Perhaps to pull her hand away or shuffle further from Isobel, so she didn't have to sit so close to her disappointment of a tether. She waited, but it did not come. Only a sad silence.

"But being with you reminds me it's bearable. Being with you is worth so much more than whatever other bullshit I'm dealing with."

Clara pulled her hand from Isobel's then, but she didn't move away. Instead, she cupped her warm palms over Isobel's cheeks and pressed their foreheads together.

"I love you more than life itself. And all that other bullshit you deal with? That's mine too. Whatever burden you bear is mine. You. Are. Mine."

Isobel closed her eyes, but the tears gushed free. Clara pressed a soft kiss to her forehead, then hugged Isobel tight. She was a shield of safety and reassurance Isobel hadn't realised she'd needed.

"You're allowed to struggle. But when you stop, I start. When you fall, I pick you up, and *we* keep going. Together. Even if it means I sit here in this room with you all fucking night, all week, or however long it takes. I'll send for snacks and get comfy, you hear me?"

Isobel nodded, the ghost of a smile more solid now.

"Might I remind you, Majesty, you cannot miss the ball tonight. It is in your honour. So if we're a team, we'll be a team in the ballroom."

"Yes, but if at any point it's too much, you will tell me and we will leave. We'll come back and take a bath or something. With smelling salts and perfumed soap."

Isobel didn't need Elisabeth. Clara was everything she needed and more. She leant forward and kissed Clara softly, feeling lighter than she had in forever.

CHAPTER TWENTY-FIVE
CLARA

Seeing Isobel livelier than she had been over the last two days eased some of the tension from Clara's body.

She'd tried relentlessly for the past week to summon a vision, with no luck whatsoever. Yet when Clara had needed a vision for Isobel, she'd managed without delay. But since that night, and now that the urgency and danger had passed, her visions remained elusive. Frustration roiled through her, hot and sharp, stretching up her arms and over her shoulders. Her neck ached, and a fierce headache ate at the base of her skull.

Doneri had mentioned that all her magic was tied to her emotions; even Candor, which she'd previously disregarded. But frustration obviously wasn't the trigger for her Candor magic, else she would've produced *something* by now. Unfortunately, like her Soil magic, it would likely take longer to master.

"The lock and key are inside you. Eventually you'll find the right combination, and then the door will open." He'd said it so nonchalantly, so sure, that even Clara believed him.

But for now, she was tired of failing, especially when she so desperately needed to succeed. Clara needed to learn to control her powers if she had any hope of finding who or what was to blame for the chaos in Jude's kingdom, of safely returning Tindal's body and Era home—not to mention saving Beau from his own stupid sense of sacrifice, and sheltering everyone from what was to come.

All day she'd tried touching Jude to pull forth a vision, yet nothing. She'd tried meditating with Jude's voice as a guide, though she knew it was a waste of time. Jude and Doneri then insisted she try meditating again while holding his crown, as if that was going to make any fucking difference. They even went outside and tried to pull magic from the ground, considering the last time she'd been successful was in the courtyard, but still no luck.

Instead, the universe gifted Clara another raging headache, the type where her spine might actually spear into her skull or perhaps explode. Thankfully, it had dulled now, as the last thing she needed while roaming the palace was a blinding migraine.

All her failed attempts somewhat reminded her of when she first started training with Beau. Except this time, she didn't have an escape like she had with Neven. Beau and Isobel were both that to Clara, but with them it was different. With them, she was still someone *important*. She buzzed with energy regardless of her status or position, because it was *them*. Her tetherbond and love match. Someone created out of the other half of her soul, and someone who fit perfectly into every crevice of her heart. They excited and terrified her and had her heart racing for a dozen reasons.

Neven was her safe space to be silent and catch her breath. Oh, how Clara missed him. Neven was exactly what she needed back then, and *stars* could she use him now. She fiddled with his ring on her thumb, rolling it back and forth, up and down the digit.

The female laughs, her long brown hair flowing on a breeze Clara can't feel. Her head moves to the side, her hand cupping her wide grin. Then Clara sees him, as happy and wide-eyed at the beauty before him. Safe and content as he takes the brunette's hand and brings it to his mouth.

When his blue eyes—so reminiscent of a winter's morning—look up and find Clara, Neven smiles. It's a genuine expression, then he waves.

In the middle of a busy hallway, Clara wiped her tears.

Some curious fae sent concerned looks her way, but most ignored her, and for that she was grateful. Her heart was bursting, so full of love it overwhelmed her—even more than after the impromptu funeral she held, and a weight lifted from her chest. She knew, even from the brief glimpse, that Neven was happy. Wherever he was, whatever plane of existence he'd landed in, her friend was okay.

Clara hadn't ever believed in an afterlife; she hadn't given it much thought really. Yet now she was sure that whatever waited on the other side of death, Neven would greet her and show her the way.

"You sure took your time." Beau chuckled as Clara entered their suite, garment bags in hand.

"I don't know why the prince won't just have them delivered," Isobel muttered.

"Because I told him not to," Clara replied before she kissed Isobel's forehead and handed her a bag. "I needed a minute to clear my head." She moved to Beau, handing him his own bag as she planted a kiss on his waiting lips. "And I took so long because I had a vision of Neven halfway down a very long and very busy corridor. I may have cried."

"You definitely cried," he said casually. "Did you call it on, or did it happen on its own?"

"I think it was on command, but I don't really know how. I was thinking of Neven and playing with his ring, then it just happened."

The trio dressed in near silence, save for the rustling of fabric and clinking of cosmetic jars and bottles. Clara was not normally a quiet individual, constantly moving or fidgeting, always buzzing with energy. But the tranquil silence between the three of them was reassuring. It was comfortable.

Though Clara couldn't deny that when Beau broke their silence, butterflies erupted in her stomach and sent tingles down her spine.

"The things I want to fucking do to you in that dress."

"You don't scrub up so badly yourself, sir." Clara winked at him in the mirror, ignoring Isobel's feigned gag.

"If you need a moment, let me know so I don't vomit on the rug."

Clara laughed, pleased to see the colour on Isobel's cheeks wasn't entirely from the rouge and that some of her light had returned behind her eyes. It was only a fraction, and she still had time ahead of her to heal from what had happened. But seeing her almost lively had Clara's heart beating faster for more than one reason.

"Maybe you should check in with the prince," Beau said as he closed the space between them with a predatory stare. His eyes never left Clara's reflection, but she knew he was not talking to her.

"No," Clara said, even while his hands wrapped around her waist and his lips found the crook of her neck. "I don't want you to go, Isobel."

"She's welcome to stay and watch . . . or join in if she fancies." Beau spoke with his lips still pressed to her skin, but his head rose and his amber eyes bore into her own hungrily. "But we will not be leaving this room until I've had a damn good taste because, woman, I've waited long enough."

"And that's my cue," Isobel mumbled as she hurried towards the door. "I'll wait with Jude. Come get me when you're ready."

"You, sir—"

Beau cut her off before she could scold him for sending Isobel away.

"I'm not very nice, I know, but you, sweetheart, are playing a dangerous game. I need to fuck you violently, and you are going to call me *sir* again before I've removed my pants? On your knees."

His demand was a low, guttural sound that made Clara's core flutter. She obeyed and watched as his eyes nearly glowed with hunger.

Beau unbuttoned his trousers, his cock already hard and begging for her touch.

So she did. Without his instruction or command, Clara spat on her hand and wrapped it around him. His moan was deep and beautiful.

Feeling him harden further set Clara's skin alight. Arousal circled them both in dizzying clouds as she kept her eyes locked on his. Beau swore as she licked her lips, and then his hand pressed so firmly around her jaw she thought the bone might shift. She hoped at the least it would bruise.

He pried open her mouth, then forced her head forward until the tip of his cock collided with the back of her throat. Clara gagged, relishing the sounds it enticed from Beau. He thrust into her mouth a few times, all the while holding her jaw open.

"Fuck," he drawled.

Clara moaned on his next thrust, and Beau released her jaw. She closed her mouth around him, pressing her tongue to the underside of his shaft and clenching the back of her mouth every time her nose grazed his pubic bone.

"*Fuck,*" Beau repeated, then pulled his cock free.

Beau reached down, and this time his fingers pressed hard along her neck. Her head swam as he guided Clara to her feet, then spun her until she was backed against the vanity. Isobel had sat here only minutes ago.

Beau let go of Clara's neck, allowing a rush of air to course back down to her lungs. He grabbed her knee to open her up for him, hiking her dress up with the movement. With so much need and aggression, she briefly worried the material might rip, though truthfully, as long as he ravaged her the way his eyes told her he would, she didn't care. She gasped as his thumb dug into her thigh and sent goosebumps across her skin.

Clara pulled his hand from her leg, brought his palm to her mouth, and spat on it again. Beau's feral groan echoed from the walls, and all she could do in response was smirk.

"Fuck me, Beau."

He growled, pumped his fist around his cock twice, then slammed it inside of her.

Clara screamed, her body on fire but savouring the heat. Pain tore up from her pelvis until she felt it in her throat. She screamed again, this time his name falling from her lips.

Beau slowed, but he didn't let up. He slammed his cock into her hard and deep. "That's it, sweetheart. Scream for me so loud the whole stars-damned castle hears you."

Fuck, how she loved it when he growled such possessively crude things, whispered violent pleas and vicious delights in her ear. His ragged breath teased her, hot on her collar. Clara's head rolled back, tears spilling down the sides of her face as her head rested upon the mirror behind her. Beau thrust into her so aggressively the vanity shook and her head tapped a rhythm against the glass.

"I'm going to come so fucking hard in that perfect little pussy." Beau's words were deep and strained, and Clara knew he was close.

The thought of him spilling inside her set her core aflame. Clara lifted her head, wrapped one hand behind Beau's neck and grabbed at his hair the way he did hers. She moaned in his ear and whispered, "Fill me, sir, please . . ."

Beau swore again, and his grip on her hair tightened. His pace sped up, and his other hand moved from wherever it was on the vanity to wrap around her throat. The light, weightless feeling from her restricted airflow and Beau's grunted sounds of pleasure had her climax hurtling towards her. It spread like wildfire, from her fingers to her toes, as it ripped another scream from her throat.

Clara moaned loudly as Beau's thrusts became faster and more jerky. She dragged her fingers along his suit jacket and wrapped her legs tighter around his hips to allow him better access.

"Yes," he drawled, so animalistic Clara considered circling her clit to draw out another climax. "Fuck yes, Clara!"

His moans turned to shouts and rough, heavy breathing. Then he growled and spilled into her. Beau's thrusts slowed as his teeth dragged along her neck, then he stilled and smirked at her.

"We need to do that more often," he said, a devilish grin on his face.

Clara kissed him. "I completely agree with you." She paused, then added, "Sir."

When Beau stepped away from her, Clara turned to check the damage. Thankfully, only the kohl around her eyes had smudged a fraction, and it looked easy enough to fix. Her hair also needed a thorough brushing, but aside from that she looked good to go.

Beau redressed with a smug grin, while Clara grimaced at every tangle. Though soon they were knocking on Jude's door to collect Isobel.

"Enjoy yourselves?" Jude asked with a wink as he followed Isobel and Hunter into the hallway.

Clara waggled her brows but admitted nothing.

She didn't have to; they'd heard everything.

CHAPTER TWENTY-SIX
CLARA

Clara enjoyed the ball, as she had liked all the events she'd attended since arriving in Morrin. Music flowed while fae laughed and danced and sang. The energy throughout the room was overwhelmingly positive.

That she and Jude were here as acting rulers—not next in line to the throne—made Clara nervous. King Taron and Queen Sylvina sent their well wishes through their son, which he passed on to Clara on their walk to the ballroom. The prince told her only seconds before the ushers swung open the doors and announced the couple. It turned out that the purpose of the night's event was to introduce the upcoming rulers to their kingdom and community without the pressure or safety net of his parents.

Resmigian fae swarmed the couple as soon as they passed the threshold, also offering wishes of luck and health and marital bliss. Many spent untold minutes profusely thanking

Clara for combining the continents, and for so graciously, selflessly, and thoughtfully offering her assistance for their dying land.

A winter fae stood towards the back of the crowd, his body language nervous but his eyes locked on Clara. She felt the cold settle over her bare shoulders whenever she looked away from him, and goosebumps erupted over her skin whenever she met his gaze. It wasn't an uncomfortable cold. Much like when a summer day felt unbearably hot, then a chill swept through the town and cooled the folk in it. The cold was welcome and gentle. Certainly appreciated in the growing crowd, which hovered so close to Clara and Jude they could hardly take a deep breath, let alone step further into the ballroom.

Isobel, Beau, and Hunter stood behind them, though soon noticed their dilemma. So the three of them spread out and ushered the crowd away, loudly announcing the royals would be present all night and there would be plenty of time for chatter.

Clara breathed a sigh of relief, and Jude squeezed her hand briefly before letting it go in favour of Hunter's. The two males made a beeline for a server carrying wide-bowled glasses filled with shimmering silver liquid.

Clara turned to check in with Isobel, but before she could speak, a familiar voice floated over her shoulder.

"I won't keep you, Highness." It was far less croaky than the last time she'd heard him, but there was no doubting the winter fae's voice. This was the one who'd thrown up a tree trunk at their last ball.

When she faced him, she confirmed it and smiled softly. "Nobility crowds are something to be reckoned with. The last thing I want is to start another. What is your name?"

"Brock Turner, Highness," he said proudly as he dipped into a low bow. Clara shushed him and flapped her hands in a very awkward attempt at stopping him. Brock only chuckled and straightened slowly. "I just wanted to thank you."

"I didn't do anything," Clara responded, shaking her head slightly. "But I can pass your thanks on to the healer."

"I've spoken with her and her partner already," Brock said. "I just keep thinking of the 'what-ifs.' If you hadn't organised the ball, I wouldn't have been in the castle. I would've been in the countryside alone. Your healer said time was on my side the other night, for had I been left in such a state I likely wouldn't have seen morning. Whatever is killing our land is now affecting our folk. Whether you can fix it, I don't know, but your willingness to try is something I have the rest of my life to be thankful for." Brock took Clara's hand in both of his and kissed her knuckles. Isobel and Beau both stiffened, the latter clearing his throat louder than necessary. With an amused, lopsided grin, Brock apologised to her companions before he turned his attention back to Clara. "If you ever need anything, Highness, please do not hesitate to reach out. I cannot offer much, but anything I have is available to you and yours."

Clara sent Isobel and Beau off in search of food while she stayed with Brock. She thanked him for such a generous offer, then continued a polite conversation with the male. He told her about his countryside residence as well as his apartment in the city. How he'd been considering leasing out one or the other but was unsure which property he wanted to part with, even temporarily. Then he mentioned he was from a family full of blacksmiths, who also extended their deepest gratitude.

They roamed the perimeter of the ballroom towards the balcony, and Clara genuinely enjoyed the male's company. Something about his deep voice and steady tone was comforting amidst the sea of unfamiliar faces. They paused at the entrance to a balcony, watching the aerialist hanging from the balcony above. Brock explained all sorts of Morrin history, starting with that of the aerialists.

The one performing in front of them had fair skin painted in a deep, contrasting blue that glittered in the flickering sconces and rising moonlight. His dark hair was slicked back, and his groin and toes were wrapped in silk, but otherwise only bare painted skin was displayed. The performer moved like a wraith, gliding and swirling around the hanging hoop. If smoke began wafting from his outstretched hands, Clara would not be surprised.

She was mesmerised.

Brock told her how the scholars believed fae also used to be winged, not only the shifters or their descendants. Some with large wings, others small and flittering, but all imbued with subtle magic. One day, an autumn fae woke to find his wings gone. Next, a spring fae's wings hung limp and useless from her back. They feared they'd angered the gods, but after a long, long time trying to figure out what heinous act they'd committed, the fae stopped searching.

"No such answers came, so the fae adapted and moved on. Magic still flowed in their veins, leaves still changed colour and dropped, and the flower buds still bloomed each morning. Eventually their wings ceased to exist, for reasons our kind still do not know. It's believed some folk who found losing their wings particularly hard took up aerial work so they could fly again. You can see it in their performances."

He was right. Even while watching this one performer, Clara could see the longing for something more that he did not have. When he threw his arms out beside him, his fingers outstretched, with only one leg keeping him secured to the ring, Clara could *feel* his need to be airborne. Fuck, it almost made her want to fly.

"Some also believe that with the right queen seated on the throne, the land will be thankful enough to reinstate the fae's wings. Some of my kin are old enough to be those very fae whose wings abandoned them." Brock murmured the words close to her ear. His body was damn near bent in half to reach, and his breath sent a shiver down her spine. When he stood and Clara's gaze met his, an emotion Clara couldn't name stared back. It pierced her—a longing, and a sliver of furious determination.

By the time they'd come full circle, Isobel was waiting with a handful of pear slices on a linen napkin. She smiled as Clara and Brock approached her, though Clara could see it wasn't as bright as normal. Her heart ached watching Isobel's sparkle dull, even slightly, but it swelled knowing Isobel was here. Clara took the fruit with one hand and interlocked the other with Isobel's.

The music slowed, so Clara dumped the fruit and napkin onto the tray of a passing server, then pulled Isobel to the middle of the dance floor. She wrapped Isobel's hand around her neck and pressed her own free hand to the small of Isobel's back. Stars, it wasn't so long ago they were dancing at another ball on another continent.

It felt like a lifetime ago.

So much had changed since the night they met, yet somehow, nothing felt different as she swayed with Isobel in her arms. Her fingers still tingled with nerves, and her lungs all but seized whenever Isobel's striking blue-and-gold eyes met her gaze. Isobel smelt the same, like summer fruits and all things sweet. Her hands felt just as soft, and her lips practically begged Clara to kiss them. And she wanted to, so fucking bad.

Unfortunately, Isobel was now Clara's consort in the eyes of the crown—at least, publicly. Just as Hunter was for Jude, Isobel was to be Clara's hidden delight. Enjoyed in private and to accompany her discreetly in public. The thought made Clara furious, but she focused on the slight upturn of Isobel's mouth whenever Clara's eyes dropped to it, and the sharp intake of breath whenever Clara pulled Isobel closer. She focused on her tether and everything else—even as Beau wandered up and stood beside the couple—faded away.

"Aren't you engaged?" An unfamiliar voice spoke over Clara's shoulder. A sickly sweet voice that promised no niceties behind the deceitful smiles.

"Yes," Clara said with a bright smile as she turned to face the female behind her. "Happily so."

"Then why are you dancing like this with the common folk?" Citrus alcohol wafted from her gaping mouth as she spoke; she was certainly intoxicated. "Surely you know how inappropriate it is to be dancing so provocatively."

Clara bristled, already wanting to slap the woman. She insulted not only Clara and her past professional experiences, but Isobel as well. She wanted to wring the female's neck, or at the very least throw the contents of her glass into the woman's face. However, this was not the place to make a scene. Tonight was about introducing Clara and Jude as the next reigning couple of the continent, not about allowing Clara's short fuse to get the better of her. So she held her smile and her tongue.

"I'm enjoying myself." Clara paused and took a breath as she tried to maintain a polite tone. "Perhaps you could do the same? Far away from me."

The female ignored Clara, as she clearly had no interest unless Clara was agreeing with her. Whether she was like this sober, Clara couldn't say, but she knew for damn sure she didn't want to find out. "I doubt the prince would approve. Don't worry, I'll have them removed for you."

In a split second, she went from looking down her nose at Clara and her lovers, to stepping closer and reaching out her open hand as if she were going to grab Isobel. Beau moved quickly, placing himself in front of Isobel and blocking the female's attempt.

Clara moved so close she could now feel the female's warm, stuffy breath on her nose. Her free hand wrapped around the female's wrist in a blur. Despite the rapid beating of her heart and energy surging through her veins, Clara's body had never been so still.

"Lay a hand on her"—her voice was effortlessly violent and barely a whisper—"and you will soon find it no longer attached to your body."

Heat radiated through her palm, undoubtedly burning into the female's skin. She had *tried* to keep calm, but when it came to Isobel and Beau, remaining peaceful was never truly an option.

The female's eyes widened as she yanked her hand back.

Clara didn't hold on; in fact, she was all too glad to be rid of contact.

"I meant no ill—"

"Frankly, I don't believe you." Clara cut her off with a dismissive wave of her hand and turned back to Isobel.

Then the female spoke again. "I only meant that as a princess, you ought to behave a certain way. I understand you were raised away from royalty, so I was merely offering advice as someone who knows better." The woman raised her chin and once again looked down her nose at the one who was going to rule the kingdom she served. Tutting, she added, "And to dance in such a way with a *female* no less."

"You need not concern yourself with me, my prince, or the company we keep—"

This time when Clara was interrupted, her resolve not to make a scene was waning.

"It's disgusting, honestly. You ought to be ashamed of yourself, girl. Of tarnishing your title and standing. What would the prince say?" Her face was aghast at the mere suggestion that stars forbid Clara display such behaviour and brand her eyesight with such vulgarity.

Clara strained not to roll her eyes, knowing damn well what the prince would say. This woman would not handle a confession like that well.

"What is your name?" she asked instead, keeping her face and tone neutral.

"Cassia."

"And are you wed?"

Cassia's gaze skittered across the room, noticing that those around her had stopped to watch their encounter. Perhaps they felt the rising heat in the ballroom or noticed the stillness of every candle's flame—not one flickered. Clara noted Jude among the onlookers, casually propped against a pillar, one foot crossed over the other in the smug way he liked to stand. He said nothing, but eagerly observed.

"Yes," Cassia answered quietly at last.

"Good. Now look at me when I say this because I need to know you're listening. Your relationship is the only one you may question or stick your nose into from this point onward. You are dismissed." Clara waved her hand, gesturing for the female to leave, but didn't bother waiting for her to move. She turned her back on Cassia, only briefly noting her narrowed eyes.

A few seconds after taking a step into the throng of patrons, Clara let out a deep breath. Though she relaxed too soon.

The grating voice called out again. Louder this time, much less sweet, and far more demanding.

"What?" Clara snapped as she spun. She hadn't expected Cassia to be so close, nor had she calculated how full her glass was as she turned.

It was only cranberry juice, so it would've come out simply enough, but Cassia didn't know that. Wine looked similar and was not removed so easily. The giant stain now dripping down Cassia's pastel gown sent her into a riot. Her face slackened at first, but before Clara could apologise, it twisted into fury.

"You fucking whore, how *dare you*!" she screeched. "I could kill you for this!"

Beau scoffed as he moved entirely in front of Isobel, now standing directly to Clara's side. "That's a tad dramatic, don't you think?"

One of Cassia's eyes twitched. Her mouth was pursed so tightly that her previously dusky-shaded lips were now white. Before Clara could register her movement, Cassia reached for the dagger at Beau's hip. He blocked her advance effortlessly, but Clara wished she'd succeeded. Then she'd have a reason to get rid of this filth of a fae.

With Beau still holding her attacker, Clara spoke loudly enough for a third of the guests to hear. Not making a scene was now entirely off the table, and Clara couldn't care less.

"If you threaten me or mine again, no one will find your body." She slowly dragged her gaze down Cassia's frame, then back up again. "At least not all of it."

As soon as Beau let go of her wrist, he turned to Isobel and said something Clara couldn't hear.

What happened next was entirely because the psychotic female could not follow instructions nor understand the severity of her threats. This time, when she lunged and yanked at Clara's hair, Clara didn't hesitate. Cassia spontaneously erupted in flames, which disappeared just as quickly. Hardly an ember remained to float behind. She was dead and gone, and Clara had never felt less following a murder.

She wasn't convinced it was a good thing, but she was glad to be rid of Cassia. What a waste of a life.

Clara's eyes flew to Jude, who was still by the pillar, though now he stood upright with a drink in hand. He raised his glass, then softly clapped against his forearm. With a subtle grin and a wink, he turned and walked away.

CHAPTER TWENTY-SEVEN
ISOBEL

"I need to find her husband," Clara muttered as she scanned the ballroom.

Isobel placed a gentle hand on her back, but Beau spoke before she could. "I'll speak to Jude. He'll deal with it."

Clara nodded, her expression now set to calm. Beau repeated the gesture before he set off towards the prince.

A small-framed fae waded through the crowd, making a beeline to the two of them, dressed in suit pants and a jacket, but with only a sheer bandeau wrapped around their torso. Isobel admired the outfit. It was something she might find in Poppy or Samara's wardrobe, and the thought filled her with a bittersweet feeling.

"Reid," Clara said, her tone more cheerful than a second ago.

"Majesty," Reid replied, dipping their chin in acknowledgement.

Isobel wasn't sure what Clara's intentions were in terms of the wider population finding out that Elanist's throne stood tall, albeit dusty.

"Do you have a moment?" Reid asked, and Clara nodded and waved subtly in encouragement for them to speak. "I know how to get the witches out of the box."

Isobel's jaw dropped, her heart skipping a beat. It felt like forever before Clara finally spoke instead of just staring at Reid with wide, slowly blinking eyes.

"How?"

"The Convergence Ceremony. I wasn't entirely sure it could be done, which is why I requested to join you. Morrin has some of the brightest scholars in the world, so I figured surely one of them must know."

Clara shook her head, her gaze averted from the peppy fae. "The Convergence Ceremony is dangerous."

"Very," Reid said, still as eager as before. "But it is also beautiful magic, and when done correctly, can boost one's magical stores, allowing both parties to amplify their abilities. We can manipulate water, and channel more elemental magic than the average Vequil can, thanks to our Inalis heritage. If there's any hope of getting those witches out of the box and onto land safely, considering one of them still breathes, this is it."

A thousand thoughts and feelings and protests ran through Isobel's body, but so did a fiery hope.

"How dangerous is it?" Isobel asked, trying to prioritise the points in her mind. Clara's safety came before Era's or Tindal's body. While Isobel wanted the witches home as much as anyone who knew, she was not prepared to put Clara in harm's way.

"If it's done correctly, the worst Clara can expect is a headache and some fatigue. It's likely to pass within twenty-four hours."

"Your brother did it," Isobel murmured as she took in every detail of Clara's face. Scrunched lines formed around her brows and inner corners of her eyes, while her gaze seemed to focus on nothing while simultaneously flickering to everything in the room. "When Elisabeth died and you . . . almost . . ." Isobel's throat burned at the thought of how close she'd come to losing Clara. Her tongue simply would not form the words. "He and Seren. It saved you."

"Do you think I should?" Clara asked, her voice barely even a whisper.

"It's not my place to say."

"No, Isobel, it's exactly your place to say. You are my tether. If the roles were reversed, I would say no. I wouldn't want you anywhere near something so dangerous."

Isobel took Clara's hand and stroked the back with her thumb. "You are my everything. I wouldn't dare let you walk into something I had worries about you walking out of, but I trust you and your abilities. Do you?"

She didn't share with Clara that the thought of her entering a power-swapping session with someone they barely knew frightened the living daylights out of her. Nor did she need to. Clara already knew, and she felt the same. She could likely see Isobel's widened, fright-filled eyes, and hear the quickened beat of her heart.

Yet Isobel had seen the incredible outcome of the ceremony before, and Clara was proof it could be used for good. Evian and Seren being alive and having experienced no adverse reactions was proof it wasn't dangerous all the time. Perhaps it came down to the artist, rather than the medium.

"Meet me at the docks at sunup tomorrow. I have morning tea scheduled with the queen, so we'll need to be fast and sure." Clara's voice held a note of apprehension, but her words came out clear and strong. She'd make an excellent queen herself, of whichever continent she intended to rule. "Oh, and please let the prince know Doneri is required. Do not let him leave tonight without confirming the scholar's attendance."

Reid nodded, then bid both females goodnight and disappeared as quickly as they had arrived.

"We need to find Beau," Clara muttered as she squeezed Isobel's hand. Flutters raced around her belly at the contact, and for once the Phoenix's name didn't ruin the moment. "It's nearing midnight, and I now have to be up very early."

Isobel laughed as she scanned the ballroom for Beau. Honestly, she'd expected to find him with Jude or perhaps stuffing his face with a myriad of snacks. Instead, her eyes landed on him chatting merrily with a tall blonde fae. Isobel could see her bright, striking blue eyes even from metres away. The mix of gold and silver jewellery adorning every part of her—from her toes to the ends of her hair, layered around her neck and wrists and earlobes—glimmered in the light of bouncing flames.

For a moment, Isobel admired the jewellery and longed to one day have such a collection herself. Until she heard Clara's huff, and Isobel turned to find her eyes narrowed and teeth bared. Then Clara stalked towards her Phoenix with Isobel hot on her heels.

The female noticed them approaching, dipped her chin in acknowledgement, and fled. Isobel couldn't blame her, though she tried to hide her smirk.

"And who was that?" Clara demanded, her eyes still narrowed on Beau.

"*That* was Kyra, a Resmigian fae who is very excited about your big day." Beau did not hide his humour, obviously chuckling at Clara's distress. She smacked him for it, but the idiot only laughed harder.

"Yes, well, she's very touchy. I don't like her."

"If it makes you feel better, she very clearly and specifically told me she wasn't trying to seduce me. Considering the fae have nasty little built-in lie detectors, I'm inclined to believe her."

"I. Don't. Like. Her." Clara enunciated each word before she physically recoiled, as if trying to shake off a bad feeling.

"Are you jealous, my love?" Beau teased.

Clara's nostrils flared as she pulled her hand from Isobel's, crossing her arms over her chest. She raised her chin defiantly, though it only turned Beau's smirk to a full grin. "Of what?" She scoffed and looked away.

Beau glanced at Isobel then, but Isobel only raised her brows and shrugged slightly.

"Of another woman having my attention," he said, and pinched her chin between his thumb and forefinger. Isobel watched her melt under his touch, as all the built-up tension left her shoulders and her face softened. "That would be rather hypocritical, you know."

His wink ruined the moment, and Clara huffed and stepped back, linking her arm through Isobel's as she flipped Beau off over her shoulder. Though Isobel would never admit it out loud, the male wasn't wrong.

"Perhaps a bath might be nice after all?" Isobel whispered, hovering so close to Clara's collar she saw the goosebumps spread across her skin.

Clara kissed her forcefully, then sauntered into their en suite.

Beau immediately removed his shoes and shirt, then threw himself onto the bed with a sigh. "Do you think she's actually upset?"

"No," she quickly replied. "Not really. I think she's easily riled and possessive, but she's also under a lot of pressure."

Beau nodded and sighed again.

Isobel smiled, appreciating his trust in her. She hadn't expected to enjoy his company, but in truth, she was glad to have him around. All day, every day, was certainly too much, but he was more observant than she'd originally given him credit for and frequently gave Isobel and Clara time to themselves.

As if she could hear Isobel's thoughts, Clara appeared beside her in nothing more than a towel. It barely wrapped around her and made Isobel feel all sorts of flustered. She wanted to rip it from Clara's hands, exposing all of her, then feast—but she wanted to do that in private. Patience was not a virtue Clara possessed, but Isobel had enough for them both.

Clara smirked and blinked slowly, then took Isobel's hand and led her silently back towards the bath.

"You didn't waste any time," Isobel said quietly, her own lips quirking upwards.

"Why would I make such a beautiful woman wait?"

Isobel's grin turned to a full, beaming smile. Quickly, she removed her own dress before slinking into the tub. The water only reached her navel, but the steam wafted much higher, warming her exposed body. When Clara sat behind her, she immediately wrapped her arms around Isobel, and a sense of safety overwhelmed her. Pure and warm and certain.

"Tell me about your tattoos," Clara whispered, trailing droplets of water along Isobel's skin.

"Which would you like to know about?"

"All of them."

Letting out a long breath, Isobel scooted forwards and spun.

"This one"—she pointed towards the crown on her chest and then held out her forearm—"and these numbers are the only ones that matter. Those dates written are in another language because I was high and thought it was cool. I don't remember how I found the language or came to know the date; I just remember feeling like they were the most important set of numbers I'd ever discovered. So I got them etched somewhere I could see them forever."

"When did you get the crown?"

"I was seventeen when I ran away from home with a friend of mine. We had hardly any coin between us, so we stayed in an alleyway in one of Breath's minor cities. I grew up in the Court of Breath, so knew my way around. After a few days, we were on rations, and I honestly contemplated stealing instead of going home, but I realised how idiotic that was and decided home was the better option." Isobel sighed again, this time with a faint smile on her lips as she remembered when she returned home.

Her mother had been so grateful to have her back safely but also furious that she'd left in the first place. Every second sentence that came out of her mouth was contradictory. One second she was praising the Mother, proud that Isobel had come home, professing her love for her daughter. The next Isobel was being scolded, reminded how reckless and foolish she'd been, how her mother didn't trust her friend and how she was a bad influence on Isobel.

But she'd never forget the strength of the hug her mother wrapped her in as she tried to hide her tears. It was the most powerful form of love she'd known until she met Clara.

"On the way back through town, I saw a tattoo artist's available designs in his window. In the middle of the sheet was a crown very similar to this. I knew it was important, but the peaks were a little off, and so I asked how much he'd charge for an amended version. A week later, I'd scrounged up enough money to pay, so I went back. It was my first tattoo, and your birthday was my last."

"What about the ones in the old language on your back?" Clara asked, her eyes trailing over Isobel's skin.

"They're a reminder of my strength and my abilities. When it all gets a bit much—overwhelming or overstimulating or whatever the case may be—they are there to remind me I've already been through hell. Pain is sometimes worth it, and pain made me stronger. It made me powerful."

Isobel didn't want to talk about her tattoos anymore. Maybe one day, when her relapse wasn't so recent and didn't sting so much. When the reminder that she'd been kissed against her will and felt tainted wasn't so fresh.

Thankfully, Clara noticed and placed a gentle kiss on Isobel's lips.

She was so grateful for her tether. Isobel was sure she could say or do almost anything and Clara would accept her. It was a feeling unlike any other.

"I love you," Clara whispered, her lips still against Isobel's.

"I love you," Isobel repeated, then kissed Clara harder. She tangled her hands in Clara's hair and pressed her mouth to Clara's so forcefully her lips stung. Clara moaned, and Isobel darted her tongue forward. Flutters erupted deep in Isobel's core.

Isobel's hands roamed Clara's body, down her neck and sides, then back up to massage her full breasts. Her nipples peaked under Isobel's palms, and for a second she was tempted to pinch them, but then Clara threw her head back and sighed.

"Stars, I love being a woman."

A soft chuckle flew from Isobel's lips as she squeezed and fondled Clara.

"Women are superior," she said, her voice low and words drawn out. A playful streak had found them, and Isobel was all too eager to give in to it. "I mean, could Beau do this?"

With a hand on each of Clara's knees, Isobel spread her lover's legs and lowered her face into the water. It took half a thought to create an air bubble so she could breathe, and then her tongue dragged gently along Clara's lower lips. Even underwater, the smell and taste of her was intoxicating. Isobel would never tire of this goddess before her, nor the option of feasting between her thighs. Especially not as she heard the moans and gasps from above the surface.

A second later, Beau's voice was in the bathroom, a place it certainly should not be.

"I heard my name and then a moan, but this sure as shit wasn't what I expected to walk in on."

Isobel broke the surface before Clara could invite the male to stay and join them.

"Feel free to walk back out again." She delivered the words with a sweet smile, while her fingers circled Clara's clit.

"Now, why would I want to do that?" Beau smirked, his eyes catching the movement underwater.

"Because if you stay—" Clara spoke before Isobel could interject, and disappointment kicked in Isobel's chest. Though Isobel had enjoyed their last encounter more than she'd expected, tonight wasn't about him. Selfishly, Isobel wanted her tether for herself. But then Clara continued, and her smile bloomed instead. "—all you get to do is watch."

"You got your turn, bird boy." Isobel couldn't help her smug expression. She also didn't wait to see Beau's reaction. Instead, she lowered herself back into the water.

With long, slow strokes of her tongue, Isobel savoured Clara's taste, who then rolled her hips in time with Isobel's movements, perfectly embodying their tetherbond. Two halves of a whole soul, made for one another. Even their magic balanced out.

Clara's hand reached under the surface and wove through Isobel's hair, sliding down it, then found purchase at the base of her jaw. She pulled gently, and though Isobel had no desire to move her face from between Clara's legs, she resurfaced. Immediately, Clara slammed her mouth to Isobel's. Her tongue dragged along her lower lip, then darted into Isobel's mouth. Rough fingers pressed into the sides of Isobel's face, the touch sending goosebumps down her naked body.

When Clara pulled away, Isobel noticed the Phoenix still staring, only now he'd found himself a stool to perch on. His eyes were fixed on Clara, his hands curled around the sides of his seat. Isobel could clearly see his bulging crotch and couldn't help but smirk.

Water splashed and lapped up the sides of the tub as Clara lowered Isobel against the porcelain, the cold jarring, but a welcome relief from the burn of her skin. It sparked a frenzy of flutters at her core, growing stronger as Clara spread her knees and slotted her thigh between Isobel's.

Isobel moaned as Clara ground against her. Clara's hands roamed hungrily, dragging down Isobel's neck, breasts, and sides. They grabbed Isobel's hips, then hoisted her upwards. Clara purred, sultry and low, causing shivers to erupt down Isobel's spine, and all she could do was gasp and mewl in response.

A deep, gravelly sound came from Beau, which only slightly pulled Isobel from her lustful haze. She turned to face the male, noting the way his eyes fogged with desire and need as he bit down on his lip. She felt for him, though not enough to share.

"You can touch yourself," Isobel whispered. "Come watching me pleasure her. She might even let you paint her with your cum."

Isobel wrapped her hand around Clara's knee and pulled it higher, then glided her palm towards Clara's plump ass. Beau groaned as Isobel squeezed, and Clara gasped at the contact.

A symphony of pleasure and breathy moans left Clara as she continued to ride Isobel, a melody she would never tire of. Isobel moaned in turn, and the pressure at her core heated and grew the more Clara moved. Isobel guided Clara back and forth, her fingers pressing into Clara's dripping skin, as the water splashed against every surface.

"I'm going to come if you keep making those sounds," Beau ground out, his fist working his erection hard and fast. His breathing quickened, eyes darting between Clara and Isobel's entwined bodies.

Clara swore as her head dropped back, her hips moving jerkily, almost entirely at Isobel's urging. Isobel sat further upright, one hand on Clara's back to hold her steady as she dragged her teeth along Clara's neck. She licked the sensitive spot beneath her jawline and, as Clara inhaled sharply, Isobel sank her teeth into Clara's skin. Clara moaned, and her fingernails dug deep into Isobel's back.

As Isobel sucked against Clara's neck, her body stiffened, and she swore. She didn't stop, and though Clara's movements slowed, she continued rocking against Isobel, her fingers digging into Isobel's spine as she whispered close to Isobel's ear. "You're so fucking beautiful," she said, her voice as tender and tantalising as her warm breath on Isobel's skin. "Show me what you look like when you come on my hand."

Then her fingers were tracing circles around Isobel's clit, drawing her climax so close to the surface she couldn't do anything but let the wave crash over her.

"Yes, honey, just like that. Come for me."

Isobel cried out as her release tore through her. Energy pulsed out from her core in dizzying waves. Her body was overrun with pleasure and power, and she hardly registered when Beau cursed again.

The next thing she knew, he grunted, and warmth splattered her cheek. When she opened her eyes, she saw Clara's chin in his hand while he held his cock with the other. Cum saturated Clara's face, which beamed as she looked between Isobel and Beau.

"I don't remember saying you could paint *me*." Isobel scrunched up her nose. "Gross."

Beau chuckled, but Clara swiped her thumb over Isobel's cheek, removing Beau's seed before she sucked her thumb clean.

"I got it," she said, her jade eyes full of playful lust.

"Fuck," was all Beau muttered, staring at Clara with desperation.

Isobel couldn't blame him—she looked at Clara the same way.

CHAPTER TWENTY-EIGHT
EVELINE

After a little over a week without an advisory council, Eveline almost believed she didn't need one. Though perhaps she was merely convincing herself so she didn't have to worry about filling the empty seats.

Thankfully, the only matters that needed to be attended to over the past few days were grounds maintenance and the financial accounts. She personally ensured her staff and soldiers were paid monthly, and yet even with how long she'd spent on the throne, the task had grown no less tedious. So many to pay and only so much in the coffers. However, by this time next month, the yearly tithe would have been paid, and the finances would surely feel less burdensome.

As she flicked through the ledgers, Eveline's head spun with numbers. She saw them bounce on the pages and float behind her eyes every time she closed them. With a grumbled sigh, she slammed a pile of papers onto the desk and looked up to find Evian staring at her.

Not that she was surprised, he'd been staring at her an awful lot lately. Almost as if he could see into the layers she kept hidden. Though it wasn't uncomfortable. It felt like the first sunny morning after a dull and grey winter, of opening the window and finally seeing the horizon instead of thick fog. As if he noticed every part of her soul and simply enjoyed looking.

Eveline felt truly seen.

In his hands was a plate of fruit, with the strawberries pre-sliced and the orange pre-peeled. She'd mentioned once how she hated when the strawberry seeds got stuck between her teeth, and in the same breath how she despised the feel of orange peel or pith on her tongue. The next time he'd brought her a plate, those inconveniences had been fixed. Eveline smiled, but Evian's expression didn't change.

It almost looked like he wanted to say something, maybe shout at her, but he kept his lips firmly pressed together. Maintaining eye contact, Evian handed her a salad fork. When she thanked him and averted her gaze, Eveline heard him sigh.

Before she could take her first bite, Evian snatched the silverware back.

"Fuck it," he muttered, as his palms cupped the sides of her face.

Then his warm lips were on hers. He tasted so decadent, so rich. A moan slid free as he pressed his mouth firmly to Eveline's, and for a second, she lost all rational thought. Everything faded away, leaving only the two of them. Their kiss, his taste, the velvety texture of his lips and the warmth of his tongue as it glided over her bottom lip.

All she felt was bliss and weightlessness. It was perfection.

But reality hit her as she ran her hands down his chest and felt his breastplate. The reminder of his rank all but snuffed out the fire he'd ignited in Eveline's chest. She should not be kissing a soldier. Stars, she shouldn't even be *alone* with him.

"Evian!" Eveline screeched as she pulled back, her hands pressed firmly on his chest to prevent any further advancement.

"Eveline," he replied coolly, a coy grin spreading across half his mouth.

"That was against protocol." Her voice carried absolutely no authority. It was breathy, and he knew it.

"Fuck protocol," he whispered, his hands still against her cheeks, his thumbs gently rubbing back and forth. Tingles shot through her body at such a small, yet monumentally intimate, movement.

Despite herself, Eveline laughed. This time when Evian leant in, he moved slower. Perhaps he was apprehensive about her pulling away, or maybe he was giving her time to prepare. Either way, Eveline let him kiss her. She knew technically it was wrong, that politically it wasn't proper. But when his lips were on hers, and their bodies so close, it felt right.

Heat passed between their bodies, through roaming hands and fast, hard kisses. Their passion built far quicker than Eveline had expected. As if kissing her was something Evian had dreamt of his whole life but never dared to hope would come to fruition. Her body melded with his, anticipating where he might place his hand, and it rose to meet him. Or she instinctively knew when he was going to dip his tongue into her mouth and opened it for him.

For a moment, Eveline wondered if maybe she'd been dreaming of him her whole life as well. Her body and mind and heart felt unanimously content as he brushed his fingers through her hair and the smell of him washed over her. Eveline felt calm in her soul, yet simultaneously the most alive she had ever been. All while he was less than a breath away, entwined with her.

She hadn't noticed her dress had slipped from her shoulders and now pooled at her waist. Only when Evian broke their kiss to remove his breastplate and shirt did she realise he'd unclipped it at all. Metal clanged as he discarded it hastily, then pulled Eveline close to his bare chest. Her breasts pushed into his abdomen, nipples peaking from contact with his cool skin. Eveline gasped at the movement, but soon smirked at the feel of the solid bulge at her pelvis.

Evian pushed her gown to the floor, then dragged Eveline towards the bed. It was frivolously large, and two-thirds of it went unused. Even when Solaris had spent the night, they'd only ever taken up half its generous space.

When Evian sat at the foot, several cushions tumbled towards his still-clothed legs, so Eveline hastily threw them to the carpet. Slowly, she untied and unbuttoned his trousers, sharing a subtle chuckle as he shimmied slightly so she might pull the fabric away.

And then they were both fully nude.

It seemed as if the world paused.

Tales of soldiers and queens never ventured into states of undress, but this queen was all too eager to write one of her and her soldier. Something deep in her chest entwined between them and pulled Eveline onto her soldier's lap.

She straddled him, and Evian groaned as she rocked back and forth, then he grabbed at her hips and thighs as his lashes fluttered closed. The coiling in her chest ran hotter and then far lower into her core.

Evian's hands wandered over her body, his nails dragging along her skin until Eveline wrapped her long fingers around his wrists. Evian's brow rose, but he said nothing.

"Hands off," Eveline purred.

A hint of shock ran through Evian's grey-blue eyes, but he said nothing. He didn't protest. Instead, he let her guide his arms above his head until they were lying down, and she held him pinned. Tight, hot flutters flew through Eveline's body, tingling her fingertips and toes. Her heart raced as Evian's cheeks flushed, and his eyes bore straight through to her soul.

When she released his hands, Evian kept still, wrists staying exactly where she'd pinned them. Eveline's arousal grew.

She knelt over Evian silently, wrapped her fingers around his large cock, and positioned his erection directly at her slick opening. Eveline then lowered herself slowly all the way to the base as she moaned, with her eyes closed and head tipped back.

Evian's sounds of pleasure were lower, much deeper, and far more coarse. Stars, the things this male did to her.

As she rolled her hips over him, Eveline leant back and propped a hand on Evian's thigh for balance. She slid her fingers of her free hand between her legs, circling the most sensitive part of her as her orgasm grew closer. Tension wound her whole body tight, though nowhere so fierce as below her navel and deep within her chest. It felt almost divine, *bigger* than sex or lust or even love.

Evian continued to groan and grunt beneath her, his eyes bouncing between her eyes, her fast-circling fingers, and then he squeezed them closed in ecstasy as his head tipped back into the mattress.

"Evian . . ." Eveline purred as she dragged her nails down his naked torso. Rosy lines formed immediately and sent whirls of lust through her body. He moaned in response, which only heightened her growing emotions. "Have you ever been taken from behind?"

"No," he said breathily. "I have not."

"Would you like to?" Eveline smirked, excitement building.

"For you, I'd do almost anything." Evian's eyes flew to hers, and again, drilled into her soul.

"That's not something you want to admit out loud, soldier," Eveline scolded as she ran her nails over his skin again, a fraction harder this time. His grin was almost intoxicated, as if he were high off her touch. "It makes you vulnerable."

"But I *am* vulnerable with you."

Realisation struck Eveline like a barbed whip. She wasn't sure she hadn't physically recoiled. Such things were from bedtime stories and fables with no merit. At least that was what she'd been led to believe.

If such bonds were real, and not figments of a hopeless romantic's imagination, vulnerability was the worst thing ever. It was more than being caught off-guard or exposed and raw with someone. This vulnerability would get her killed. Or worse, Evian.

She did her best to push those thoughts from her mind, to focus on sex and nothing more. Anything more would be a problem for another day.

"Would you like me to peg you, Evian?"

"Yes," the male confirmed without so much as a blink.

Eveline raised herself off him—much to their mutual disappointment—and padded to her dressing room. A moment later, she emerged with her glass strap-on and a vial of lubricant.

"May I lick you?" Eveline asked after instructing Evian to position himself on all fours.

He did not hesitate to answer, all but begging her to feast.

Hearing him plead, so desperate for her touch, did scandalous things to her insides. Her core tightened, her pussy already dripping. Eveline stood at the end of the bed and spread Evian's cheeks, then caressed his hole with the tip of her tongue. Softly at first, slowly to ease him in. Then she sped up, licking further and harder, all while squeezing his thighs and butt cheeks.

Evian groaned and cursed, arched his back and pressed his rear further into Eveline's face. He gasped when she pushed her tongue inside him and hardly breathed as she moaned onto his skin. Stars—she loved the sounds he made.

When he was ready, Eveline secured the straps around her pelvis and poured on the lubricant. For his first time, she'd expect him to be a little hesitant, but she'd do everything in her power to minimise any pain.

She warned him before she penetrated him, and told him every time she was about to thrust a little deeper, preparing his hole for the entirety of her strap-on. He welcomed her every time.

As she pulled back, readying to thrust all the way in, Evian gasped again. "Please," he begged.

It set off a desperate frenzy inside Eveline. Gliding inside him slowly was the last thing she wanted to do. She wanted to slam into him, hard and fast, over and over, until he spilled on her sheets. But she held a steady pace until he spoke again.

"More," Evian begged between moans and clenched fists.

Eveline was eager to indulge him. As she bucked more wildly into him, Evian's breathing quickened. He grunted through each wave, and when he swore, Eveline's core sparked. Arousal surged between her thighs the closer he grew to his climax.

She reached around him until her hand found his erection. Wrapping her fingers around him, Eveline stroked until he was howling in pleasure.

"Are you close?" she drawled, barely more than a whisper.

"Yes, fucking stars, yes . . ."

"Then come for me, darling."

After only a few more thrusts, Evian growled through his release. Some of it warmed her fingers, and the rest splattered over the linen.

"Good boy."

Eveline removed her strap-on from his body, and Evian immediately turned. He looked up at her with such adoration and lust-filled devotion that she found it hard to look away. Then she noticed his hand was wrapped around his still fully erect length.

"Want some more?" she asked with a smirk. To her surprise, and pure excitement, Evian nodded.

"Please," he repeated.

Eveline did not bother putting her strap-on away. Instead, she left it lying beside them on the mattress and climbed atop her soldier again. Though she had not yet reached her own completion, bringing Evian to release had skyrocketed her arousal. Wetness pooled between her legs, allowing Eveline to seat herself fully over his erection. Evian's growl of pleasure was so deep and raw, Eveline could only moan in kind before she began rolling her hips.

"Tell me, soldier, which part of you is the most sensitive? Is it here?" Eveline murmured, tracing sharp fingertips up Evian's sides. Evian moaned softly, though it was not the response Eveline was looking for. "Or here?" She then circled his nipples with the pads of her fingers, and Evian sucked in a sharp breath. Eveline let out a sultry chuckle, then pinched the soldier's nipples.

His jaw dropped, eyebrows rose for a second and then slackened, and a guttural moan slipped from his tongue.

"Beautiful." She hadn't meant to have whispered the last part. Not that it wasn't true—Evian was the most beautiful male she'd ever laid eyes upon. Sandy blonde hair that shimmered silver under the moon and was near pearlescent under the sun. Icy blue-grey eyes that held more depth and soul than she'd ever seen on anyone, so full of love and kindness and ferocity. A strong jaw and high cheekbones, with lips that seemed to be dusted by rose petals and were even softer. He was also the most accomplished sexual partner she'd had the honour of bedding, but she hadn't meant to admit it out loud. Thankfully, with her thumbs and forefingers clamped on his nipples, and her hips gyrating over him, Evian didn't seem to notice. If he did, stars bless him, he did not acknowledge it.

Soon, Evian swore again. His hands curled and balled, arms jerking as if he might grab her again, though he kept them to himself. His obedience was thrilling and heady. She smiled down at Evian, then leant forward and ran her tongue over his abdomen. Along every firm muscle, deep ridge, and line of definition she could reach while remaining impaled on his cock. All the way to his peaked nipples, where she removed one of her hands and replaced her fingers with her tongue. Then her lips. And when he was begging for more, Eveline gently took his nipple between her teeth.

Evian roared and cursed again, more desperate now.

"Are you getting close again, dear?" she drawled, her mouth still pressed to his skin. Evian shuddered and moaned, then nodded fervently. "Would you like to fill me?"

"Yes," he whispered as his eyes fluttered closed and his head tipped back. Eveline slowed her rhythm, letting his anticipation build a little longer.

With one hand, Eveline continued to circle Evian's nipple. The other reached upwards until she found purchase on his jaw. Eveline grabbed him and jostled him a fraction before she lowered her voice and demanded, "Beg."

"Please," Evian croaked. "Please let me . . ." He was hardly able to form a sentence between his moans and rapid breathing.

Lust and need tore through Eveline's body. She leant back again and began circling her fingers between her legs. Evian watched her, cursed, then continued to beg.

Just as she'd asked.

She did not answer straightaway. Instead, she tortured him for a few moments longer, until her own climax was close enough to reach out and grab. Then she smirked. "Fill me, Evian. Come inside me."

Evian panted a few times before he grunted and stilled as spasms overtook his body. He cursed and clutched the sheets between tightened knuckles. When his body relaxed again, his breathing now even, all that was left in his stunning icy eyes was devotion and a hint of obsession. His cheeks were flushed, and his cocky grin was plastered on his face.

Eveline continued to ride him and rub herself, her climax so close.

Evian's eyelids fluttered before he murmured, "Fuck, Eveline, if you keep going, I'm going to come again."

All she could do was laugh—a low, sultry sound, but a laugh nonetheless. She felt lighter with him, even coated in sweat and surrounded by the thick smell of sex and seed. As she continued, moving faster with both fingers and hips, the coiling heat at her core built and overflowed. Warmth radiated down her arms and legs, leaving her head swimming and her breath fast.

Then her climax hit her like a tidal wave—more powerful than any she'd experienced before. A thousand pricks of energy coursed through her skin, zapping and sparking and leaving a trail of tingles in their wake. Her body felt as if she were floating while simultaneously so heavy she could not move.

Wave after wave of power surged through Eveline. Although she had not felt true power in years, it wasn't something she'd ever forget. Pure magic.

"Fuck!" Evian roared as his body jerked, and the soldier exploded for the third time. "Eveline!"

CHAPTER TWENTY-NINE
CLARA

The sun had yet to rise when Clara trudged along the Morrin shoreline by the docks. The boat she'd arrived on still bobbed on the calm waters, moored alongside three other vessels by the pier. Reid and Doneri already stood ankle deep in the water, the former noticing Clara and smiling brightly. Doneri seemed less pleased, though Clara could not fault him. With only a handful of hours' sleep, she wasn't exactly pleased either.

Clara struggled to rein in her yawns as she wrapped her arms tightly around her midsection, hoping to ward off the early morning chill. But being in the Winter Palace and by the sea at such an hour, there was only so much she could do. Even though they did not pile, snowflakes continued to fall, and they sprinkled the sand along the Winter Court's shore.

"Morning!" Reid said, with a far too chipper note in their voice. Clara only grumbled a response, a sentiment which Doneri repeated.

"Might I ask why I'm here? Reid knows what to do." Doneri folded his arms as he spoke, expectant gaze turned on Clara.

"Because I was told you're an expert. Heavens forbid I request a professional be present when I'm performing dangerous magic I have no experience wielding." Clara couldn't keep the bite out of her tone.

Doneri rolled his eyes but sighed and nodded.

"Doneri is the one I have been meeting with," Reid said with a casual grin. "Are you ready?"

"No." Clara shook her head as she looked out over the horizon, still purple and full of shadows. "Not even a little. What am I supposed to do?"

"It's all about intention. You merge blood, as little or as much as you feel is necessary for the task, with the clear intent to share the power at the forefront of your mind. You do not want to take, only strengthen each other to achieve your mutual goal." Doneri gestured over the water, then pulled a small blade from his chest pocket and a handful of crystals from the satchel at his hips. "These will be placed in a circle around you both. One strengthens your unit, and another is for your individual strengths, so you can recognise where you start and end when your magic converges. The third is for mental clarity, so you can focus and hone your intention, and the last stone is for protection. It wards off any negative energy or beings who are waiting to pounce."

"Is that something I should be concerned about?" Clara asked, her brows knitted tightly together.

Doneri shook his head. "No," he said flippantly. "That's what the crystal is for."

This time Clara rolled her eyes.

Reid took the blade from Doneri and sliced down their forefinger. Initially, Clara raised a brow and questioned the placement, then Reid's smile softened almost sadly as they handed Clara the blade. "I have a tether too," they whispered. "I sliced my palm when we accepted our bond. It's my dominant hand, so for any rituals requiring blood, it makes no sense to use the other one, but that space is sacred now. I don't like to share it."

The rope forever burning around Clara's heart and lungs tugged more fiercely at the comment. She nodded and took the blade, slicing her own index finger as Reid had.

Once Doneri had placed the crystals in position, Clara and Reid linked fingers and smeared their blood together. Neither cut was deep, only enough to bead and drip.

"The ceremony to take one's power involved incantations and verses, but you won't need any today. Simply focus your minds on retrieving the witches, feel each other's power and work together."

Clara nodded and Reid squeezed her hand, then they both closed their eyes. Within a few deep breaths, Clara managed to forget all about the frosty seaside wind as her body warmed. She didn't know how to visualise her power, but as she tried to focus on finding Reid's, splashes of powder blue and the lightest shade of green darted behind her eyelids. It swirled and danced, captivating Clara for a moment.

Then Reid's voice chimed through her mind.

Focus, Majesty. They may be pretty, but they're distracting for a reason.

Clara nodded once, then tried to move past the glowing ribbons of Reid's power. It truly was beautiful.

The witches. They need air.

Considering one of them was already dead, they didn't both need air, but Clara didn't press. Instead, she thought back to the day she'd arrived in Morrin. To her conversation with the mermaids and her vision of Era and Tindal. There wasn't anything particularly identifiable about their location, save for the metal box.

Trying to find that in the vastness of the sea would have them stuck on the shore all day. So Clara changed tactics slightly. She didn't know how to communicate with Reid, so she spoke aloud and hoped for the best.

"I'm going to create an air bubble around Era and Tindal, while you manoeuvre the water to bring them to the surface."

You can just direct your thoughts at me, you know. Speaking aloud will split your focus and physically pull you back.

Oh, Clara thought in Reid's vague direction. It was strange, and Clara wasn't entirely comfortable with this method of communication.

What about opening the box itself? Any ideas?

Not a single one . . .

She really should've thought this through a little more before now. Was this even going to work? Unfortunately, they'd run out of options.

How well do you wield flame, Majesty?

Clara scoffed aloud, her grin undeniable. *You have no idea.*

Burn the hinges. Melt them down. Then we proceed with your plan.

Clara nodded and took another deep breath. She'd yet to light something on fire without seeing it, but there was a first time for everything. Every fibre of rage she tried so hard to keep a lid on boiled to the surface. The crude, homophobic assholes dressed up as nobility. The expectations of less time with her tether and her Phoenix, now that she was to be wed and a royal twice over. All the secrecy from Beau, the violation Isobel had to endure. Neven's death, and Elisabeth's, and even Solaris', not to mention those deaths she could feel so deep in her bones that were still to come. The ones she knew she wouldn't be able to stop.

Everything fuelled her, and she didn't need Reid's comments to know she'd struck her target. Instinctively, Clara knew the walls of the box had melted away. She could almost hear Era's fear, despite her severely incapacitated body being unable to move.

Water burst in, and Era instinctively curled her body in on itself, not able to brace any better than ducking her head and raising a single arm. Clara didn't know how she was seeing this happen, but right there in her mind's eye, she saw everything.

Then Era lowered her arm, her eyes wide and uncertain, but her chest still rising and falling as it should, if not slightly haggard. Clara couldn't help but smile as the first half of their challenge was met.

Holding the power of two elements simultaneously took more effort than Clara had expected. Sweat beaded on her forehead, and chills swept down her spine. A sharp throb started at the base of her neck, sparked up her jaw, and ran towards her ears. Then Reid's coloured tendrils wrapped themselves around Clara's arms and breathed air into her lungs. They glowed golden along Clara's skin, and she felt like she could run a marathon.

Thank you, she thought towards Reid.

Teamwork. My turn now.

And exactly as they said they would, Reid manipulated the water until the waves burst upwards. Bubbles and jets shot towards the surface until water sprayed their faces. Clara opened her eyes, as did Reid. Before them sat a malnourished and pale Era, with Tindal laid out by her side. Her once-vibrant yellow hair was now dull and clung to her grey skin as tightly as Era held onto her lifeless hand. Tears ran down Era's face, her shoulders racking as she sobbed.

Clara squeezed Reid's hand gratefully, and they nodded in acknowledgement. No further words passed between them, nor from Doneri as he handed them both bottles of water. Not until Clara insisted that both witches be taken to the infirmary and for Isobel to be notified.

Era refused to let go of her friend but grabbed Clara's wrist like a lifeline. She didn't say anything, but as she stared up at Clara with so many emotions burning in her tear-filled eyes, she didn't have to. Clara crouched before her and circled the witch in a tight embrace. She did not pull away until Era shuffled back. The witch then nodded and brought Clara's hand to her lips before she placed a hard, desperate kiss on Clara's knuckles. Clara realised then that Era hadn't expected to make it home. She hadn't ever expected to make it to land.

Somehow the news of Era's return to the Winter Palace had beaten Clara back, and her rooms were empty as she dragged her feet towards the ensuite. Neither Beau nor Isobel was here, though it was entirely for the best. Clara was in no position to get sidetracked or waste time.

As was tradition in Morrin, in the days leading up to a wedding—particularly a royal wedding—Clara was scheduled to meet with her future mother-in-law and spend the morning in the queen's company. Clara had no clue as to the reason, and only a small part of her was intrigued about what the hours ahead might hold. Mostly, Clara was terrified.

She'd received her formal invitation a few days prior, but it gave nothing away. The ribbon-wrapped parchment detailed how it was customary for the in-law of higher standing to organise a breakfast, luncheon, or tea party with the newest member of the family and, in not so many words, told Clara she had no choice but to attend.

So she washed and dressed quickly, then set off for the carriage she'd been informed would wait at the rear exit of the palace. Clara understood why the carriage did not wait in the front courtyard—for such a historical event, the wedding would be broadcast and shown round the continent, maybe even across them all. There would be many eyes on the day, and likely just as many in the lead-up. Though the courtyard was vast and separated the palace from the town, the rear provided a much-appreciated privacy.

It was a miracle, however, that Clara didn't get lost, though she did second-guess a handful of turns before she spotted the horses. Queen Sylvina was already waiting in the carriage, a powder-blue teacup and matching saucer in hand. Clara dipped her chin and lowered her gaze out of respect as she entered the carriage.

"I hear you've been quite busy these past twenty-four hours," Queen Sylvina muttered before taking a sip.

"I have." Clara didn't know if it was an accusation or merely an observation, as the queen's tone gave nothing away.

"My condolences," she said at last. "Regarding your witch."

Clara only nodded. She sounded sincere enough, though always so poised and stoic that it was hard to tell what the queen truly felt. Clara assumed it was how royalty ought to behave, at least in the presence of others.

"Now tell me about the ball." Queen Sylvina's harsh green eyes bore directly into Clara, as if she could see any half-truth Clara was preparing to spin. Not that she would, as it would not bode well for Clara, not with the queen.

The carriage shifted into movement, though the queen seemed not to notice. Her back stayed perfectly upright, with no bobble of her head or splash from her teacup. She looked every bit the royal she was, exuding power and intimidation.

Clara swallowed as she considered how to deliver the news that she had murdered a subject of Morrin.

"Might I ask what you already know?" Clara decided it would be best to gather more information on the queen's position and emotions before she answered the question.

To her surprise, Queen Sylvina smiled. A frightening grin that proved there was a healthy amount of malice beneath the ruby-encrusted crown of Morrin. She set her cup and saucer down on the bench beside her and clasped her hands in her lap.

"Well played," she said casually. "Always gather *all* the information before you spread any of your own. Truthfully, I know exactly what happened. I watched it play out. You were brazen, and not exactly mild-tempered, but the dreadful woman had it coming. You gave her fair warning, and it was ignored. I am rather impressed with your skills, I must say. For someone who only manifested their power . . . two years ago?"

"Something like that," Clara mumbled as Queen Sylvina waited expectantly, brows high.

She nodded again before she added, "It was her own fault, really."

"You aren't mad?"

"Gods no. Truthfully, that woman had become quite the inconvenience. Always drinking more than she should and pissing in my flowerbeds. A right nuisance."

Queen Sylvina clicked her tongue as she shook her head. She then turned her gaze out the window, and the rest of the carriage ride was silent. Clara wasn't sure if it was a good thing or not, but having the queen's approval—at least regarding Cassia—was definitely a positive. Her nerves settled a fraction.

After an hour of uncomfortable silence that had Clara aggressively picking at her nails, the carriage drew to a stop. Queen Sylvina's shoulders softened, and her thin lips spread into a relaxed smile. She looked like she'd finally come home.

"Once upon a time," the queen began as Clara exited the carriage behind her. Then she stood tall, with her face pointed towards the sky, and inhaled deeply. "I used to hunt. Mostly arrogant fae males who believed they had a chance at convincing me they were better for me than my husband. They were wrong." A feral gleam shone in her eyes as she looked at Clara.

Excitement emanated from the queen so strongly that Clara's own heartbeat increased. Energy rose throughout her body and left her wanting to bounce on her toes. Though that could have just as easily been nerves.

"I enjoyed hunting males very much." Queen Sylvina sighed, then gestured for Clara to follow her.

She continued to speak as they walked over a stone-paved road towards a cottage-styled building made of red bricks and wood panels. Ivy and moss clung to every corner and there were flowerbeds under every sill. It looked almost quaint, except for its sheer size. Easily four times Clara's home, and almost two-thirds the size of the Winter Palace.

"I moved on to birds later, once the throng of idiot males ran out. As I aged, and as Jude grew older, it became the easier option. To hunt the wildlife for relaxation and recreation, without the exertion of a full hunt. It's not as satisfying, but enjoyable regardless."

"I'm a vegetarian," Clara said, quickly understanding why their morning tea had brought them all the way out to the middle of nowhere.

A uniformed staff member stood at the opening of what Clara assumed to be royal land, with a satchel strapped to each of his shoulders and a pair of bows in his hands.

"I do not understand why your dietary requirements are pertinent to this conversation." Queen Sylvina glared at Clara, her brows drawn slightly before she shook her head and turned towards the male.

"I do not condone hunting animals, Majesty, not for fun. If you've brought me out here to bond over a hunt, I'm afraid I will have to disappoint you."

Queen Sylvina huffed and rolled her shoulders. Clara couldn't see her face, but she was sure frustration was plastered over her regal features. Though when she turned back to Clara, with the smaller of the two bows in her outstretched hand, Clara did not find any annoyance on her face.

"Fine," she said with a sigh. "I'll use a tree. Surely that is an acceptable alternative, or do you believe they, too, have souls needing protection from fae?"

Clara attempted to hide her smile, though she truthfully did not try very hard. She hadn't expected the queen's acceptance, much less a willingness to accommodate. "I think that's a much larger conversation we don't need to have today. The trees will survive a few arrows, I am sure."

The queen beamed, ferocity and hunger glinting off every exposed tooth. "Excellent. Take it and follow me." She thrust the bow towards Clara's chest, then clicked her fingers and prowled through the forest.

CHAPTER THIRTY
EVELINE

"Are we going to talk about the bond now, or later?" Evian finished drying and wrapped the towel around his waist. Water dripped from his hair, painting his naked chest. The sun snuck through the cracks in the drapes and caught on his wet skin. The soldier simply glistened.

Eveline wanted nothing more than to stare at him all day, or perhaps remove the towel and continue what they'd started. But she took a deep breath and forced herself to look away.

She sat at her dressing table and focused on fastening the cuffs of her simple, long-sleeved gown, something Evian could not rid her of so easily. While she wanted him to, she knew they could not continue to engage in such activities while she was the ruler of this continent. It was yet another reason Eveline wished she could abandon her crown.

Her father oozed selfishness, but the strain of his inflated ego, his belief he was the ultimate king, did not extend to his daughter. No, Eveline was weighed down by the burden of her title. There was no one else to fill it, to offer her reprieve, or to save her from the position entirely. So she stayed and ruled her kingdom to the best of her ability. It was the least selfish thing she would ever do.

Perhaps the second least, as the first would be to ignore Evian's questions for as long as she could, and to avoid the possibility of their bond altogether.

"You cannot ignore it and hope it goes away, Majesty." Evian folded his arms, though his tone did not suggest he was angry. More that he understood, better than Eveline gave him credit for.

"I certainly cannot acknowledge it, *soldier*." The bite of his title burned Eveline's tongue.

"Do not take that tone with me," Evian said, his voice stern and firm. "Not when mere hours ago you used that title endearingly." He shook his head and locked eyes with her in the mirror. "I do not know whether you knew before, or whether you're only realising now, but let me be perfectly clear. A tetherbond is more powerful than any other bond. It is more than a crush or a summer fling. You are the other half of my tetherbond, Eveline Thelst. You are the reason I've spent my entire life—multiple centuries—feeling out of place within my home court. It is why I felt like my life in Wave was missing something, as you were not there. My sister nearly died at your hands, yet I ran towards you, because you hold half of my soul. In those beautiful, delicate, powerful hands. Hands I will spend the rest of my life, however many more centuries I have to come, hoping I may hold. Do you understand? It isn't simply love or lust. This is everything."

Tears welled in Eveline's eyes. Hearing her full name on his lips was the first time it did not repulse her or remind her of her father. It made her feel seen, as a being entirely her own. Evian did that, he saw her.

She shook her head and looked down at her lap. "I thought they were nothing more than old faerietales."

"Oh, they are so much more." Evian crouched by the side of her stool and reached to grab her chin. His gentle hold forced her face towards him, and she felt his gaze boring into her. Into her soul. Maybe pulling it towards his. She did not know what to do, only that he was right, and that frightened her more than anything else.

"I cannot accept it," Eveline whispered, not able to look at the male before her. "Not while I bear the crown. Certainly not while there are attempts on my life. I am vulnerable, with no solid information on who is targeting me, or why." She looked at him then, with no room for argument in her eyes. "I will not give them leverage. They will not use you to get to me, or against me. I will not make you vulnerable." Evian's face softened into a lopsided grin. His mouth opened, poised to interrupt her, but she held up a firm hand. "No, don't bother. I heard you before, and I won't hear those words from your tongue again, do you hear me? This is serious. Clara would eviscerate me if anything happened to you. I may not want my crown, Evian, but I'm rather attached to my life."

The soldier laughed, so genuine and light, Eveline almost laughed with him. But her heart was heavy and surrounded by barbs, as if it was angry with her for not accepting the bond she could no longer deny. She could ignore it, but she knew it was there. It wrapped spindly fingers around her heart and lungs and filled her feet with cement whenever she walked away from him. It sent lightning through her arms whenever she reached to touch another.

So violently present, Eveline wondered how she might ignore such a bond. But more than that, she reminded herself she must. Even if she wanted to, she could not accept it. Not now.

The next morning, Eveline walked into the northern sitting room to have breakfast alone. For the past few days, Evian had joined her, though after their revelation yesterday she suggested he send someone else to guard her. At least for the next twenty-four hours, to give them both time to take a breath and decide how to proceed.

An unfamiliar doorman swung open the door to the sitting room upon her arrival. He dipped his chin low and avoided eye contact, the same as the others, the way they were all taught under her father's rule. Eveline nodded in acknowledgement and took her seat at the head of the small oval table. A spread of at least a dozen fruits and half as many pastries was laid out, along with carafes of juice and wine. No plates or cutlery sat before her, however, only a short tumbler and a wineglass.

She took a deep breath as she tried to ignore the feeling of a thousand bugs crawling along her spine without Evian close by and poured herself some juice.

"Heard you rid yourself of an advisory council, Majesty." A male voice rang out from the staff entrance to the sitting room as another unfamiliar employee entered. He carried a tray of silverware and a selection of plates and bowls. "Have you also abandoned your guard?"

"Excuse you?" Eveline asked, her lip pulled back, and brows drawn.

The male chuckled, an utterly disgusting sound—far too wet and nasally. Truthfully, he sounded as if he needed a healer. He flung the tray towards her, but his movements were slow and jerky.

Eveline ducked as the door behind her swung open. She whirled to find a female soldier with pale-grey wings and short black hair already wielding a sword.

"Wait!" Eveline cried. "Keep him alive."

The soldier looked confused for a moment but did not hesitate. She brought her weapon down quickly, removing the stranger's hand as he reached towards Eveline with a blade of his own.

He howled a gut-wrenching wail as he cupped his bleeding stump to his chest. Tears streamed down his face as the doorman stormed in behind the soldier.

Her defender hardly broke a sweat, spinning as if combat was second nature. She did not remove any limbs; rather, her blade pierced the doorman's chest, and he crumpled quickly. Blood pooled under his spasming body. He coughed twice, then his body stilled. Eveline knew he was dead.

"Oh my days," Eveline breathed, her hand at her chest as if it might calm her racing heart.

"Why were you here alone, Majesty?" the soldier questioned. At any other time, she might've scolded a soldier for taking such an accusatory tone, but today, Eveline was simply grateful to be alive.

"I sent Afron to see about a replacement. He's been working around the clock, and I felt he needed a break. I assume you are his replacement?"

"Dalia Rion, ma'am." Dalia bowed low as she sheathed her sword, then sneered at the whimpering male on the tiled floor. "I understand you have a need for more constant security, Majesty. Typically, one sends for relief before the current security officer departs." She spoke so gently, someone might miss the underlying annoyance.

"Tell me, Rion." Eveline stood and folded her arms. "Why did Afron send you?"

Dalia's eyes widened a fraction, and she opened her mouth twice before answering. "I assume it was because I trained him, and perhaps because I passed him on his way to his dorm. If he had another reason, I am not privy to it."

Eveline nodded. "Has he mentioned anything to you regarding my security detail? Or current advisory council?"

The soldier shook her head quickly, her lips firmly pressed together. Eveline nodded again, then looked at the absolute mess of a male leaning against her table.

"Any experience with interrogations, Rion?"

She shook her head, though her eyes lightened and her hand flew to the pommel of her sword.

Eveline smiled at the soldier.

"In-interrogation . . .?" The stranger stuttered. He clutched his still furiously bleeding limb to his chest, though his shoulders sagged, and his face had turned a pallid shade.

"Indeed. Or perhaps blackmail. I need information, and you most certainly need a healer." Eveline clicked her tongue as she dragged her gaze over the male.

"I won't tell you anything." He spat at Eveline's feet, though the glob of saliva did not reach that far. A truly pathetic attempt that left him looking even more idiotic than before.

Eveline shrugged, then nodded to the soldier, who pulled her sword from its sheath. Another whimper left the male, and Eveline's grin spread. Perhaps she had inherited more than she liked from her father, but her love of violence came in handy. Especially for those who deserved it.

"Nothing at all?" Eveline drawled, her voice taking on a singsong tone, and the stranger's eyes flickered between her and Dalia's sword.

"No!" he cried. "I'll hold my tongue, so my rightful queen knows she can trust me when her crown is returned!"

Idiot.

"You can hold it in your hand if you'd like," Eveline spoke calmly, gesturing for Dalia to crouch before the male, and she did so without question. Eveline quite liked this soldier. "We'll cut it out for you, and your *queen* can have it as a gift. A token of your allegiance. When does she intend to take back her crown?"

"I will tell you nothing about the Lady of Summer!"

Eveline rolled her eyes and shook her head.

"Don't bother cutting out his tongue, soldier. Cut off his head instead. He's given up everything he knows."

The stranger's eyes widened further as he balked and stuttered briefly, but the silence that followed was welcome. His head rolled to the tiles with a soft thud, then Dalia wiped her blade clean on the back of the male's shirt and sheathed it once more. Eveline gestured for Dalia to follow as she exited the sitting room.

"You struck as soon as you entered the sitting room. Why?"

Dalia shrugged a shoulder before quietly but firmly announcing, "It's my job to know who is and who is not an employee of the crown. I did not recognise him."

Eveline nodded and hummed, appreciative of this soldier's assistance and commitment to her job. Though she also felt uneasy—she hadn't recognised the male either but hadn't given that a second thought. Perhaps she ought to pay more attention.

"As soon as we get to the library, you will find Afron. If he's asleep, wake him. If he's eating, tell him to bring me something. Do not stop to speak to anyone on your way there or back. Understand?"

"Yes, Majesty."

The library was quiet, as was normally the case. Dalia left immediately, as requested. Most of her staff stayed clear of the dusty aisles. Her father never cared for the space, and she couldn't remember if her mother ever visited. Solaris, however, loved sitting among the piles of books. Her sister loved to read. Everything from legends and myths to histories and war tactics, children's books and erotic love stories. A sad smile spread over Eveline's face as she wandered the aisles to find Ryn.

The Reaper frequently came and went from the library, and from the castle grounds in general. Mostly, she was holed up researching, and today that worked in Eveline's favour. She found Ryn in an alcove towards the back, hidden between two stacks as high as her hips and just as wide.

"Reaper," she called as she approached.

"Queen," Ryn replied, not looking up from the tome she was immersed in.

"I need to ask a favour."

"I'm not the favour-granting type."

"Please," Eveline pressed, and Ryn finally looked up. Annoyance washed over her thin face, but she raised her brows and waved a hand for Eveline to continue.

"I need to get a message to Clara. She agreed to help with my assassin problem, and I now have information."

"You are aware she gets married in a handful of days, correct? To a prince, no less." Ryn scoffed and looked back towards her research.

"I am, yes, but this is important. The Lady of Summer, whoever she is, has a collection of idiots under her command. Though perhaps she herself is a few coins shy of a money box. She believes she is the rightful heir to the throne and deserves her crown back. I am unsure why I've been targeted, but I'm willing to bet so has Clara, or maybe those she's close with, as I can only assume she wishes to sit upon the Morrin throne." Eveline couldn't help rolling her eyes, as who would even want to be queen? Though Clara would certainly fill a throne well.

"I have what I want. So why do I need to help you? Queen or otherwise, I have no reason to do as you ask." There was a playfulness to Ryn's tone and a chaotic sparkle in her dark eyes.

Eveline couldn't tell if she was truly speaking in jest. Perhaps this was merely her neutral tone. Either way, Eveline was eager to finish the conversation.

"Please," she repeated.

Ryn sighed and nodded, then pushed to a stand.

"Very well. Though remember, Majesty, favours need to be returned. Do not think I won't come for what is owed."

This time Eveline nodded, and the Reaper disappeared in a whirlpool of black smoke and deep shadows. She shivered once Ryn was gone but didn't have time to dwell as footsteps approached.

Evian and Dalia halted as Eveline turned around. The former held out a plate of grapes and red apple slices, which Eveline took eagerly.

"Give us a moment," she said to Dalia, who bowed at the waist and took a few steps away. In a hushed tone, Eveline asked, "Do you trust her?"

"Trust is relative, Majesty," Evian said with a wink. "I trust her enough professionally. Why?"

"I need a list of everyone you trust completely."

"That list is rather small, I hate to say."

"Why?" Eveline scoffed and took a grape. "Who's on it?"

"You. Clara. My mother."

"We are not roping your mother into this, stars above. I need a personal guard and at least one adviser. An idiot assailant and his useless accomplice made it onto the castle grounds this morning. Somehow they knew I was without a council and alone for breakfast and were going to attack me. Dalia arrived in the nick of time." Eveline paused and sighed, realising their change of plans. "Pack an overnight bag and find two soldiers you trust enough. We're going to your sister's wedding."

CHAPTER THIRTY-ONE
CLARA

By the time Queen Sylvina had decided on a tree to target, Clara had stumbled over two exposed roots and damn near rolled her ankle on a large, loose stone. The queen certainly noticed, though was kind enough to ignore her clumsiness. Clara managed to stay upright at least.

With another click of her fingers, Queen Sylvina's assistant dropped the satchels he was carrying and scurried over to the grand oak tree. He pulled a small knife from his pocket and carved a series of circles and crosses in a pattern.

"It is so incredibly important that a female knows how to defend herself, Clara. Not only politically, but physically." The queen spoke without looking at Clara, her palm open and outstretched, waiting for something. The male quickly dove into one satchel and retrieved a quiver filled with feathered arrows.

"I agree," Clara said while nodding. "I've recently taken up self-defence training with my guard. I've also put a lot of work into channelling my magic, which has been interesting, to say the least."

"Strong with magic, but your power is unpredictable."

"Yes, actually." Clara turned away, so Queen Sylvina might not see Clara's widened eyes and surprise at her understanding. The queen only nocked an arrow and positioned herself to aim.

"Do you feel more equipped to assist those you've called to aid you in your war? Since you've started these training classes, that is." Her tone suggested something Clara couldn't quite put her finger on. Incredulity? Derision? It almost sounded like a mockery, though Clara chose to ignore the rage flickering in her belly and answered calmly.

"I do, thank you."

"You've changed since you first visited us." She looked to Clara then, a single brow raised as she gave Clara a once-over. Then the queen hummed and fired her arrow, all while staring at Clara. It hit the centremost point of the markings etched in the oak tree. "You've grown, or at the very least your attitude has improved. The trip to my dungeons did you well, I suppose."

"Is that why you locked us up? For my attitude?" Clara couldn't keep the incredulity from her voice. Nor did she miss the slight uptick of Queen Sylvina's lips.

"You'll also be able to do that one day, you know. Lock folk up on a whim." She waved her hand lazily before moving her attention to nocking another arrow.

"Why would I want to?"

The queen shrugged. "I thrive on a little chaos and desperation." She fired again, this time hitting the top left point of the same cross.

"Elisabeth said you sent her a scathing letter. That you were positively fuming with my behaviour."

She shrugged again and sent a third arrow flying. It soared before piercing the lower left point. And then another, this time the lower right.

"I may have exaggerated a tad." Queen Sylvina sighed before releasing a fifth arrow, which landed in the final point of the cross. Every arrow hit its mark with lethal precision, despite the queen only paying a fraction of the attention Clara knew was necessary. "You'll get bored eventually, Clara—all royals do. There are only so many laws, so many nobles, so much *whatever* to deal with before you've done it all. The life of a queen is dull after some time. I crave retirement like you wouldn't believe."

"What will that look like for you?"

"Certainly more hunting, perhaps larger beasts. No more uncomfortable meetings with kiss-ass politicians and nobles. I cannot wait to stop wearing that awful fucking crown. I've left blood on the damned thing, it's so sharp—so do be careful. Perhaps I'll cook for my husband again, like when we were on our honeymoon. That was the last time I prepared us a meal."

She paused and sighed, then turned her longing and wistful expression towards the sky. Her eyes closed for a moment before she looked back at Clara, with no trace of the soft emotions of a moment prior visible. Now all the lines on the queen's face were hard, and her eyes stern.

"The question you ought to be asking, however, is what my retirement will look like for *you*. After all, you have your own kingdom, and soon you will inherit a second. Where will you spend your time?"

"Are you asking me now?" Clara should've expected such a conversation, though truthfully, she hadn't.

"Are you stupid?" the queen countered, a single brow raised, concern etched deep in the lines around her eyes and mouth.

"No, sorry." Clara answered quickly, shaking her head. "I haven't thought about it, to be truthful."

"Well, you'd best start. You'll be wed in a matter of days, and by year's end, you'll be coronated. How many heirs will you produce?"

"As many as your son requests of me," she answered honestly. Clara did not particularly *want* to become a baby-making factory, but she was aware of what her role as Jude's queen would entail. He required heirs, and so she would provide them.

"And what of your own? How will you decide which child inherits which throne?"

"We have an heir to my throne." Clara ignored the fact that Queen Sylvina apparently knew she was already a queen. As did her groom-to-be, though it had not been mentioned to him either. Perhaps it was part of their Resmigian makeup, to know things not yet told. Regardless, the inability to keep anything private made Clara uncomfortable.

"Not yet, you do not. That boy has displayed no magic, so he cannot be counted. Regardless, why do you think royals try so hard to have multiple children? You need a spare."

"That's a terrible way to describe a child." Clara scoffed and scrunched her face.

"And yet, it is what it is." Queen Sylvina lowered her bow as she continued. "The eldest, at least in Morrin, will take the throne when his or her predecessors die or retire. In Elanist, a royal must not only be of golden blood but also must bear Inalis magic. Not one or the other, but both. In Tirenas, he or she who wears the crown decides who wears it next, provided they are a blood relation. Without a named heir, it goes to the eldest living blood relative. You must ensure your line and your crown continue past you, or whatever you achieve is worth nothing."

"What would you have me do?" Clara asked quietly.

"I do not care, provided you produce one child of each sex for my son's throne. A son and a daughter. The rest you can do with what you wish."

"Anyone ever mentioned how cold you can be, Majesty?"

The queen chuckled, low and short-lived. "You are aware I am a winter fae, are you not?"

"Actually, no. Jude said his lineage was of the Summer and Autumn Courts."

"Yes, our lineage is, but I was born in the Winter Court. It was unintentional—my parents were passing through, and the weather decided it should not be as brief a journey as my parents had planned. They were snowed in, and I was born in front of a roaring fire. The gods commemorated the occasion by gifting me winter magic, and if you were to test my blood, a percentage of it would hail from Snow. Our gods like tricks; they're like foxes. As are the winter fae—cunning, sly, tricky, and hard to read. You should never trust one at face value."

"Do you possess only winter magic?" Clara asked, genuinely intrigued.

Magic was divided amongst fae differently depending on where in the world they hailed from. Yet the one constant was that higher beings—the Mother, Helmos or Nyrene in Tirenas, or the numerous gods worshipped in Morrin—decided their fates. Here stood a queen of summer and autumn heritage, who spoke and acted as if she were winter fae.

"I do," the queen confirmed, only furthering Clara's interest.

She realised, however, that Queen Sylvina was no longer interested in discussing her heritage or power, as she handed her bow off to her member of staff and closed the space between them. The queen trailed long, thin fingers over Clara's arms and shoulders, then positioned her to wield the bow.

She tutted more than Clara appreciated, but her tone was always gentle as she corrected Clara's form. The first arrow narrowly avoided their male companion, though to his credit he did not balk or flinch. He merely turned and ran to collect the arrow, then handed it back to Clara silently. She tried to apologise, but he held up his hand and shook his head. Perhaps he had no tongue, for he certainly didn't use it.

Over the course of what looked to be an excruciatingly long fifteen minutes for the queen, Clara managed to hit two targets. With every miss, Queen Sylvina grew more and more distressed, as if it physically pained her. Maybe she took Clara's archery failures personally.

When the queen shifted Clara out of the way and collected her own bow, her shoulders relaxed again. The lines around her eyes softened, and her mouth pulled into a small but genuine smile. She took a deep breath, then nocked and fired her arrow—all with her eyes still closed—and hit directly below her first shot.

Clara's jaw dropped a fraction. She enjoyed seeing this comfortable, at-ease version of the queen. Without the weight of a crown or an uncomfortable high-backed throne, and no responsibility for thousands of folk on her shoulders.

With barely a thought, Clara called to the wind and brought it towards them. No leaves fell from branches in the Winter Court, but the trees were not barren. Instead, the luscious evergreen foliage held piles of fresh snow, which also floated along the breeze. She plucked different-sized leaves from the surrounding trees and held them in an array at a distance before them.

Queen Sylvina looked at Clara with her head cocked and with a quiet excitement lighting her striking green eyes. The first arrow hit its mark easily, as did the second, but on the third, Clara sent the leaves spiralling instead of holding them still.

Queen Sylvina whirled, and for a second, Clara expected her to be angry. But all she saw was a barely containable grin.

So Clara kept the leaves spinning as the queen continued to fire. By the time all the leaves had been pierced, Queen

Sylvina laughed, and Clara felt a welcome pride and acceptance from her mother-in-law.

The next morning, the halls of the Winter Palace buzzed with fae. The usual faces bustled past, paying no heed to the newcomers as they carried plant pots and vases, trays of plates and silverware, rolls of fabric, and all sorts of other décor. Many were arriving for the wedding, and for the first time it sank in that Clara was to be married.

Tomorrow.

She'd been so wrapped up in finding the witches, keeping folk alive, while also trying to remember her head whenever she had to race out the door, and she hadn't had time to really think about it.

This time tomorrow, she would be bound to another. To a male whom she did not love—not as a bride should—and would spend the rest of her days as his wife and queen.

Stars, becoming the queen of her own continent had barely sunk in, let alone a near future in which she ruled two. The realisation was enough to make her dizzy.

"Sister!" Evian's familiar voice boomed from behind her, and Clara spun to greet him. She was pleased to see him, both as the brother she missed and as a welcome distraction.

Clara hugged Evian tightly. To her surprise, once she pulled away from her brother, his queen leant forward to embrace her as well. Her eyes widened and brows rose, but Evian only grinned, and so Clara awkwardly patted the queen's shoulder.

"I did not think you'd be in attendance," Clara murmured as the queen pulled away.

A slight quirk of her lips suggested she had not intended to bear witness to Clara's impending nuptials. "Yes, well, we're here now. Your brother hounded me like a child in a sweets store, one conversation turned into another, and the rest is a matter for another time. Did Ryn speak with you?" Eveline asked as she leant closer into Evian's side.

Clara did not miss the earth-toned jewels hanging from her wrist, casting an array of light prisms over the white hallway as the sun caught them. Evian had done rather well, Clara had to admit.

"No, why?" Clara asked quickly. "What's going on?"

Eveline shook her head calmly and waved her concern off. She'd never seen the queen so at ease. "I have information about my assailants, but you need not worry about that before your wedding. Come and find me afterward, and we'll speak then."

"I dislike it when you're vague," Clara said with narrowed eyes and firm hands on her hips, but Eveline only smiled, took Evian's hand, and walked away.

After being waylaid by what felt like a dozen random folk, a heartbreakingly overwhelming face appeared in the crowd. As soon as Felicity noticed Clara, the confused lines around her eyes and mouth settled. She waded through the throng of guests, Jacob's hand grasped tightly in hers.

Clara wrapped her arms around her mother for the first time in too long. She hadn't disliked being stuck in Morrin, but she'd certainly missed home. Her mother most of all.

"Oh, how I missed you," her mother whispered into her hair, as she pressed a soft kiss to the top of Clara's head. She'd always been good at reading Clara.

"What kind of cake will there be tomorrow?" Jacob asked, before he bothered with any greeting. Clara couldn't help but cackle as she bent over to hug her brother. "Did you make it?"

"I don't know, I'm afraid," Clara answered with a shrug as she took her mother's free hand in hers. "I don't even know if there will be a cake. I'm not sure what the customs here are. But if they do not serve any, I'll whip something up just for you."

Jacob's eyes lit up, and his face burst into a smile. Clara's heart cracked a fraction at seeing one of his canines missing. He'd lost two of his baby teeth already, but he'd been slow to lose the others. The first two Clara had pinched while he slept and thrown into the water as offerings, as was the custom in Wave. She'd not long since read a tale of a fae mother exchanging her son's teeth for gifts, so she did the same for Jacob.

His first tooth had earned him a carved wooden cinnamon scroll, which he fell in love with, so Clara had an almond croissant made for the second tooth. She'd wanted to make it a ritual.

Seeing his third gone made her feel like she'd missed something big, and her stomach bottomed out a little. Then the realisation that it likely wasn't the third, considering how long she'd been away and how much time had passed, had her tearing up on the spot.

Clara cleared her aching throat and turned to her mother. "Thank you for coming."

Her mother scoffed and rolled her eyes, bringing Clara's knuckles to her lips for another gentle kiss. "You foolish girl. What could've possibly kept me away?"

Another throat cleared beside her. Clara turned to find Keyne with a duffle bag held in front of him. He was accompanied by Oren and Aleska, with Finch trailing in behind.

"Do you intend to make a habit of offering folk jobs and then disappearing before you pay them, Majesty?" Keyne asked, a single brow raised. Clara winced and turned to her mother, who only chuckled and shook her head.

"I'll leave you to deal with that, love. We'll catch up with you in a bit." Both her mother and brother gave Clara another brief hug before they wandered off down a busy hallway, likely in search of their accommodation.

"I'm sorry!" Clara rubbed her fingers over her brows. "There was a whole incident with the mermaids, and I couldn't leave the continent. I managed to find the witches, which was bittersweet if I'm truthful. I'll make sure Ryland includes a sign-up bonus and distress compensation on the account."

Keyne laughed, echoed by Oren, whose laughter boomed throughout the foyer. Aleska rolled her eyes and elbowed her brother, while Finch tried—and failed—to hide his smirk.

"You will do no such thing," Keyne said, his grin wide as he pulled Clara in for a hug.

It was the first embrace they'd shared that Clara didn't want to pretend he was his brother. Having him here for her wedding was a comfort, but not because he reminded her of Neven. Clara wasn't sure whether it was her own growth, and her grief had become more manageable, but the alternative left her heart aching. She refused to believe it was because she didn't miss Neven as much.

She would always miss him, though perhaps since her last vision of him, Clara knew Neven was well, and that eased the pain of losing him.

"Thank you for coming," she said, looking at all her guards. They were her protectors, and in a way, a new branch of her family tree.

"We wouldn't miss it for the world!" Oren bellowed as he barrelled past Keyne and embraced Clara tightly. He almost lifted her from the ground until Aleska poked him in the ribs and growled at him to move over. As he whirled to face her, his ponytail whipped Clara's cheek.

"I trust you'll keep this out of the way." Clara muttered, her fist now tight around his dark, mildly wet hair.

"We'll see," Oren replied smugly, shrugging a shoulder. "Salt water does wonders for it when it isn't tightly bound. And I prefer it down. I get more attention that way too." He waggled his brows at Finch, who pinched the bridge of his nose and shook his head.

Clara tightened her fist in his hair and pulled, so his face was almost level with hers. "I'll give you ample attention if it gets in my way."

"Duly noted," Oren said, still grinning but less smug.

"I'm more than happy to chop it off, if Her Majesty requires it." Aleska's smile was devious and almost sinister.

Clara couldn't help but smile with her. "Oh I've always liked you."

Aleska beamed as she wrapped her arm around Clara's waist for a side hug.

"Do you know when Ryland is arriving by chance?" Clara asked as she welcomed Finch with a quick embrace and a muttered comment on how well his ear was growing back.

He rolled his eyes but failed to hide his chuckle.

"No," Keyne said, hoisting his bag over his shoulder. "I haven't seen him since your last training session."

"I'm sure he'll be here sooner or later," Aleska offered as she took Clara's hand and insisted she show them to their rooms personally. Clara was more than happy to comply, especially considering the number of fae had almost doubled since she'd arrived at the palace. She had absolutely no capacity for entertaining dozens of folk she didn't know, and frankly didn't care to.

"He wouldn't miss it," Oren called from behind Clara. "I think he fancies you."

Finch pinched the bridge of his nose again as he walked beside Clara, then shot back over his shoulder, "Oren, are you blind or stupid?"

CHAPTER THIRTY-TWO
BEAU

Clara's wave was brief, just a sweet flutter of her fingers over her shoulder as she passed Beau in the hall. He hadn't seen her much since the ball, and the early hours following. She'd raced out of their room before the sun rose yesterday and had fallen into a deep sleep almost as soon as she returned from her outing with the queen.

Beau loved watching her flit down hallways and laugh with her friends, but, fuck, he missed her. He was in two minds whether to follow her and steal her for himself. Then Beau heard Ryland clear his throat, drawing his attention.

"Morning." The commander almost seemed excited, as if he held a secret he wanted desperately to share. Beau grunted in response, not at all interested in the male's company.

Isobel, however, seemed her cheery self as she greeted Maja and the twins. Her smile was bright, which eased some of the tension in Beau's shoulders. He relaxed further as he watched her embrace Samara, while unable to control her grin at Poppy.

In a heartbeat, his tension built again when Beau noticed a familiar, black-clad being leaning against a pillar at the opposite end of the corridor.

"Excuse me," he muttered to Ryland, who only clapped Beau on the shoulder in acknowledgement before they parted ways. Beau made a beeline for the Reaper.

"Phoenix," she said dryly. "Where is Clara?"

"I need your help," Beau snapped, unintentionally ignoring her question but not really caring either way.

"You need to learn some manners." Ryn pulled back her top lip and narrowed her eyes at Beau.

"So I've been told." Beau refrained from rolling his eyes and sighed. "Please," he said more quietly, though no less urgent. "I'm looking for the one who 'walks between worlds' and 'works with Death.'"

A sinister grin spread across the Reaper's face. "You're looking at her," she drawled, gesturing to herself dramatically.

Confusion and relief punched Beau in the gut. A chill settled over his shoulders and down his spine, though he couldn't tell where it originated. He wasn't afraid, nor was he cold, but the chill lingered.

"How do I kill Death's Daughters?" He figured that beating around the bush would do him no good.

"Not easily," Ryn said with a shrug. Her gaze absentmindedly scanned the palace hallway.

"Are you going to help me, or shall we run in circles?"

Ryn's attention was noticeably elsewhere, and Beau's patience was running thin. The Reaper narrowed her eyes once more and flared her nostrils. "For a price."

"My life is already given. I have nothing else."

"I'm not here for your life, Beau." Ryn scoffed. "Not today."

"Then what?"

"Names. Your fallen king—"

"He was not my king," Beau spat. "Merely my employer."

"I do not care. He had an advisory council that his daughter has since dismissed. I need to find them. You will give me their names, and I will pass on the information you seek to Clara. Does she know what you plan?" She raised a thin, pointed eyebrow as she continued to stare down her nose at him.

Beau rolled his shoulders—an attempt to dispel some of the scrutiny and discomfort from her gaze—as he shook his head silently.

"Then I shall also keep your secret. Clara learns how to defeat her opponents, and your involvement stays hidden."

After another sigh, Beau answered. "Reuben Da, Mertyl Kallechna, Antoni Shesza, and Augusto Lairn. I know where Reuben and Antoni live, but for the others, I can only provide names."

Ryn waited with her brow raised and arms crossed as Beau recounted what he knew of Reuben and Antoni's whereabouts. She didn't write anything down, though he wondered if it was necessary. Beau didn't know what sort of power a Reaper possessed, but perhaps it included a superior memory.

Regardless, she listened intently, then sauntered off following the path Clara had taken earlier.

Beau was left with a thumping heart and clammy palms. Now he just had to wait and hope that the Reaper stayed true to her word.

"Sometime in the three days leading up to a wedding, the bride will meet with her mother-in-law for a private gathering." Jude spoke casually as he led Beau down an unknown hallway.

They walked alone at slightly less than a brisk pace as he maintained the prince's speed. When they'd first met, Beau had thought Jude to be freakishly long and lanky; now, the only time he considered Jude's height was when he was trying to keep up with the male.

"Clara did that yesterday," the prince continued, with a hint of a smirk. "She actually managed to make my mother laugh, from what I've heard. Tonight, the night before I become a married man, I celebrate with my friends. I do not have many of those—thanks to my crown—but you and I are about to become a lot closer, so I figured we could share a drink and get to know one another better."

Heat built in the back of Beau's throat and tightened his chest at the mention of the future. Truthfully, while he hoped something drastic changed over the course of the next few weeks, perhaps even dissuaded Death's Daughters altogether, Beau was not foolish or naïve enough to hold his breath. So far, the only beings who knew he was scheduled to die permanently were the deity, the Reaper, and Beau. He wouldn't burden anyone else with the knowledge, and certainly not Clara's betrothed. Especially not tonight, on an occasion he got the feeling was meant to be fun. Instead, Beau cleared his throat and put on a smile. "I do love a drink."

"Excellent!" Jude clapped as he paused outside a small, navy-blue door with cubes etched into the centre.

Beyond was a dimly lit den that smelt of leather and whisky. There were no windows, but the room was lit by blue-tinged orbs, which hung or floated near the ceiling. The room was easily twenty-five metres long and lined with various-sized tables and chairs. The furniture was luxurious—heavy, rich wood that was oiled or glossed or upholstered with fine fabrics.

Towards the middle of the room, against the left-hand wall, stood a bar, with stemmed glasses hanging above the bench and dozens upon dozens of liquor bottles stacked behind. It was currently unmanned, though Beau had the suspicion that if he wanted a drink, he needed to help himself.

Soft music flowed throughout the space. Quiet enough he couldn't pinpoint the instruments or where it was coming from, but loud enough he could hear the tune. Honestly, it was the perfect volume for relaxing; casual background noise so a conversation need not be shouted.

Hunter stood from a bucket-shaped loveseat placed not too far from the doorway. Next to him stood a dog, who reached halfway up the male's thigh, which for a Resmigian fae, was *high*. Hell, the canine's nose would almost be in line with Clara's navel.

"This is my puppy, Allira!" the prince all but squealed. Beau didn't know whether to chuckle or run. "Isn't she beautiful?" Jude immediately dropped to his knees and began petting her, and in return she nuzzled her long snout into Jude's neck. His face beamed as his hands ran speedily up and down her sleek, mostly black coat.

Her ears stayed high, their peaked tips impressively pointed. Large, dark eyes darted back and forth between the prince, his lover, and Beau. Then the dog fixed him with a glare that said he was an outsider and that she did not know him. Her body remained poised, despite her clearly enjoying being rubbed. A collar made of pearl and silver almost glowed in the luminous blue haze of the den, and clanked every time Jude brought his arm up to her head.

"She looks like she might maul my face if I stick it too close to her," Beau muttered, not taking his eyes off the truly majestic creature. Pretty beings could be as dangerous as ugly ones, sometimes even more so. He was cautious, just as she was.

"She absolutely would, but only on command." Jude beamed with pride at his four-legged friend. "She's very well trained."

"I don't think I want to put that to the test."

The prince laughed, a booming sound that left Beau feeling slightly more at ease.

Hunter smiled as he came up behind Allira and handed Beau a glass. The liquid inside shimmered almost green, and Beau couldn't tell if it was from the light or if the liquor was intentionally that colour. "She is also an excellent judge of character. If she trusts you, then I trust you."

"Here's to keeping my face, then . . ." Beau raised his glass first, and the others joined him. They nodded in unison before taking a sip, then Jude ushered Beau towards one of the shorter oak tables lined with velvet.

Jude sat on the same loveseat Hunter had risen from earlier and shuffled a deck of cards as he explained the rules of the game. Despite him speaking slowly and providing examples and generally communicating with Beau as if he were a juvenile, Beau still struggled to keep up.

"Makers" was played with numerically valued cards, split into four suits—coins, scrolls, swords, and cups. They each represented one of the four gods the Resmigian fae worshipped: Tharia, the goddess of artistry; Auronis, the god of knowledge; Seone, the goddess of warriors; and Herin, the god of healers. Beau had no issue following that much.

But when Jude explained how to collect cards, which would be most beneficial, and how many Beau could hold or place at a time, that was when his confusion set in. Understanding how to win was something Beau hoped would become clearer the more they played.

In the first round, Beau managed to score zero and collected only seven cards. Jude's stack was almost a centimetre high, and still he hadn't won. Hunter merely smirked as he shuffled the deck.

"The aim is to earn the values of the gods," Jude reminded Beau, with a subtle grin and a wink. Beau only narrowed his eyes. "I don't understand where the numbers come from, in all honesty. They seem entirely arbitrary."

Next round, Hunter won again, by his winning hand in one sweep, though Beau did not lose so poorly. Jude had helped him, but Beau wasn't prepared to acknowledge the prince's involvement.

Soon, Beau caught on to the game enough to collect cards on his own and even managed to secure decent numbers. "Making the gods" was the term for collecting cards of the gods' values. It was an almost sure-fire way to win, but not the only possibility. As it turned out, if no gods were made, then having the highest value collection of suits at the end was triumph enough.

Isobel had been right to call him out on being a sore loser. She'd never seen him compete to win a game, though, and Beau was self-aware enough to know that was far worse. He hooted and startled Allira, and gave Jude and Hunter something to laugh about, though he apologised and eagerly downed his drink.

As Hunter sauntered away to refill their glasses, Jude stared after him longingly.

Beau wondered if that was how he looked when Clara walked away from him. And knew it was almost certain. After the next round, thoughts of Clara weighed heavily on Beau, more so than normal. He couldn't help asking the questions that burned on his tongue. Beau stacked his pile and handed it to Hunter to shuffle before clearing his throat. "I have to ask, prince—"

The prince scrunched his nose as he shook his head and interrupted Beau. "Just Jude. We've seen each other naked and balls deep, I think we've earned first-name status."

"Jude," Beau corrected, poorly veiling his smirk. "What is expected of your relationship with Clara? After the wedding, I mean. You have Hunter, and she has Isobel. Are you all to spend the rest of your lives as housemates? Are Hunter and Isobel to be only guests in your marriage? What is the dynamic to be?"

"Whatever she wants, provided Hunter *never* feels like a *guest*." Jude turned up his nose at the remark, and Beau raised his palms apologetically. "He is the holder of my heart, and I will not accept him feeling anything less. The same goes for you and Isobel, of course."

Hunter smiled, his cheeks blushing and lashes fluttering as he looked down at the deck of cards. He leant in a little closer to the prince.

"Okay, so let's bring it back to the basics for a moment. Where will you reside? She has a kingdom in Elanist, and a palace of her own, as you do here."

The prince shrugged and cocked his head before he answered. "I do not know. Perhaps we will take six months of each year in Morrin, and the remainder in Elanist. I'll have to pose the question to Clara."

"And in that time," Beau pushed, "will you share a room? . . . A bed?"

"A room perhaps, though that is up to her. We have plenty to go around. But my bed is for Hunter. Unless we're all involved in some debauchery or attempting to produce an heir, that is how it shall remain." Jude took Hunter's hand, his thumb brushing over his lover's knuckles. Quickly at first, but as Hunter squeezed the prince's hand, his thumb slowed and their bodies somehow relaxed even further into each other. Soon they'd be in each other's laps. Though Beau wasn't mad—truthfully, he was happy for the prince. For one thing, he looked as happy with

Hunter as Beau was with Clara. And second, he knew there wouldn't be a moment where his intentions with Clara were unclear or untrustworthy.

Jealousy was a violent, ugly creature, but its claws dug deep into Beau's lungs and heart whenever Clara was involved. Fuck, it was a miracle their relationship had successfully expanded to include Isobel. A year ago, Beau might've murdered anyone who suggested such an arrangement. Guilt washed over him as he recalled the last time he was jealous of a male who held Clara's attention.

"And what of her time? How will she spend it? What will her role be?" He couldn't hold back the questions that flew from his tongue.

All Beau wanted was to set Clara up for success. As he would not be present to ensure it, Beau had to question these things now. His heart beat a mile a minute, though he managed to keep his breathing steady. Hopefully, he did not outwardly let on just how much he worried.

Thankfully, Jude's face relaxed into a reassuring grin. He leant forward on his knees and looked at Beau earnestly.

"I'll support her, Beau. Here"—Jude waved both arms as he gestured around at his palace—"she will be my support and my friend. She will have a voice in anything she wishes, but she need not worry about my continent. If Clara does not want to, she does not need to be burdened by it. I enlisted her help to clear the rot, and once that is done, if she wishes to only use this land as a holiday destination, she is free to do so."

"And what do you expect your role will be in Elanist?"

"Whatever she asks of me. I fear you are too concerned about this arrangement, Beau. This is not something I've concocted to increase her stress. It is a mutual agreement for the betterment of our kingdoms and to allow love to remain in our lives. I love Clara dearly, but not as I love Hunter, and not as you and Isobel love her. She is a close friend and someone I will forever be indebted to, someone I hold very dear to my heart. All I want for her is happiness. I need you to trust me when I say I will do everything in my power to give that to her."

Beau nodded stiffly, his throat raw and aching again. Allira stretched and stood, then padded over beside him. He held his breath, unsure of what the dog intended to do. But then she yawned and sat by Beau's foot, resting her enormous head on Beau's lap. His sigh of relief was audible. Jude cheered and raised his glass to Beau, while Hunter laughed quietly beside him. The tension lessened in Beau's shoulders, though the stress of not being around much longer lingered.

After another dozen drinks and a few more rounds of Makers, Beau decided it was time to call it a night. It was nearing midnight, and he wanted to get back to Clara before she was too deeply asleep to be roused, and he was growing tired. He finished the rest of his drink and stood, clearing his throat and offering his farewells.

Jude walked Beau to the door while Hunter took their empty glasses to the bar and packed away the cards.

"I'm not sure if I'm really in any position to be asking favours, but with the storm brewing, I have to."

Jude gestured for Beau to continue. "Of course."

"There is an isle far up north and relatively void of citizens—"

"Helshire?"

"Yes." Beau hadn't expected the prince to know of his home continent, though perhaps he should've given the scholar fae more credit. "My mother lives in an eastern village. She moved there after she married my father, though she is a Resmigian fae. I need to ask you, if anything were to happen to me, can I trust you to ensure she's taken care of? I do not want to burden Clara with such things. Not that she would hesitate, but—"

"Beau." Jude cut him off for the second time this evening. "I hope you do not consider me emotional for suggesting such a thing, but I consider us now family. Even more so after tomorrow. If ever you cannot, I will personally see to the care and wellbeing of your mother." The prince laid a large, warm hand on Beau's shoulder.

"She isn't entirely *well*, I must admit. Not since my father died, and then my sister. I'm all she has left." Rubbing his hand against the back of his neck, Beau tried to sound blasé. To not to let the discomfort of the topic show too much.

"My deepest condolences," Jude said softly.

"Thank you, truly." Beau offered his hand to the prince, who shook it firmly.

"No need. I cannot call you brother after the activities we've engaged in, but you know how the saying goes." Jude's lips parted in a feline grin.

"I'm glad you're the male she's marrying, Jude. If not me, you're the next best option."

CHAPTER THIRTY-THREE
CLARA

Clara fluttered her fingers as she passed Beau, wishing they were already wrapped up in their sheets instead of roaming the palace preparing for the wedding. She led her guard towards the guest wing of the palace, which in truth had better views than her own suite. Mid-morning sun filtered through the stained-glass windows, creating bursts of colour and rainbows that danced along the walls and floors. It was a view she could find at any corner of the palace, any location with windows, and she adored it.

Maids wove between passing guests, sprinting from one room to the next to ensure the accommodations were ready. Clara did not envy them. Not for their uniform that looked scratchy and stiff, nor their tightly bound hair that seemed to pull back the outer corners of their eyes. And certainly not for how most of them seemed to be out of breath as they raced around stressed, without a second to pause.

She wondered briefly whether she ought to be more worried, maybe do something, or be involved in tomorrow's planning. But it was only for a fleeting moment, as Clara quickly realised she did not care. While she wanted tomorrow to go smoothly, without a blip or hiccup, exactly *how* that came to be was beyond her. This wedding wasn't for her. It was for Jude, for their kingdoms, and for love, just not one between Jude and Clara.

"Clara!"

She whirled to find Jacob running down the hallway towards her. She'd barely left the child, yet he acted as if he hadn't seen her for decades. A calloused hand wrapped around her heart and squeezed tightly as Clara considered how rarely he had seen her over the last year. Stars, how long had it been since Beau and Neven first arrived on their doorstep? She didn't even know, couldn't remember except for the fact that so much had happened since then. It felt like a lifetime.

"Yes?" Clara asked, as an apprehensive smile spread over her lips. Her guards stiffened around her, though only slightly.

As Jacob came to a stop in front of her, he bent forward to brace his hands on his knees to catch his breath. The concern left her as Clara watched him take comically large inhales and hold his finger up.

With a slow exhale, Jacob stood and planted his hands on his hips. "Cake," was all he wheezed out, and Clara burst into laughter.

Her guards relaxed, and Keyne entered the room directly beside him. The others turned and found their own rooms, all labelled with their names in both the common tongue and the old language. Clara couldn't read it all that well, but she recognised some differences among letters. She assumed it was a local dialect and admired the cursive font regardless.

"Cake?" Clara repeated once she and her brother were alone. She took his hand as he nodded, and they strolled back down the way he'd come.

"Will you make one . . . for tomorrow?"

"No, Jacob. Tomorrow I'm getting married, so I have no time for baking wedding cakes." Clara chuckled at the heartbreak in her brother's eyes. "Perhaps I could make you some muffins instead?"

Jacob's eyes lit up, such a fierce and striking blue that they rivalled a summer's day. "I have something for you," he muttered, then swung his crossbody satchel around. Clara hadn't noticed it before, but it was rather small. Out of it he pulled an apron, lace lining the hem, intricate swirls embroidered along the ties, and *Afron* embroidered into the neck. A single tear welled in Clara's eyes, but she blinked it away and smiled at her brother. "Just a little reminder of your family."

"I could never forget you, baby brother." Clara took the apron from Jacob, then wrapped her arms around his small shoulders and squeezed.

He quickly escaped her hug and shook himself off with a grumble. "I'm not a baby."

"Your Phoenix misses you, Clara. Surely you are not hiding in kitchens the day before your wedding. He's rather attached, you know."

Clara sighed as she poured the batter into a baking tin and set it on the counter. But at the voice, Jacob jumped and stumbled backwards into the open fridge door, knocking butter to the floor and rattling the jugs of milk, juice, and water. He let out a small screech and clutched at his throat, then quickly moved to Clara's side.

"I had noticed," Clara murmured, before she quickly added, "and I'm not hiding."

Ryn stared at Jacob for an uncomfortably long moment before Clara cleared her throat, regaining the Reaper's attention. "Eveline said you were looking for me."

Ryn nodded slowly. "She wanted me to pass on information. Should we speak privately?"

Clara's heart skipped a beat as she looked to her brother. He stood close, yet a fraction in front of her, as if he might block Clara from any harm. "Jacob, go find the prince and demand the sweets you want at the ceremony tomorrow. If that includes cake, don't take no for an answer."

Jacob turned to look at Clara, then whispered, "Will you be okay by yourself?"

"Of course." Clara laughed, and thankfully Jacob noted the sincerity of the sound. "Ryn is a friend."

He nodded, then squeezed Clara's hand briefly before jogging towards the door. The entire time, Jacob kept his slightly narrowed eyes on Ryn, who did well to keep her face neutral until he'd left.

"Oh, Jacob!" Clara called after him. When he stuck his head through the doorframe, Clara smiled and added, "Would you also ask him to send someone to watch these? I don't have time to sit in front of the oven all day."

Jacob nodded again and disappeared.

"That boy will give your mother a heart attack one day," Ryn drawled as she stepped closer to Clara. She ran her finger along the flour dusting the countertop, sniffed it, and grimaced before wiping her hand on a cloth.

"I hope that isn't a warning, Ryn." Clara folded her arms and raised her chin.

"Merely conversation," she said, shrugging a shoulder far more casually than Clara had seen before.

"I thought you didn't chitchat."

"I also don't take children."

"What did Eveline want me to know so badly she sent a Reaper?"

"Truthfully, I think I was the fastest creature she could send." Ryn pursed her lips. Was that a hint of emotion tucked beneath her vague expression? Clara tried not to smile as her imagination ran wild with the thought of Ryn feeling used. Oh, the irony. The Reaper sighed, then continued. "She said, and I quote, '*The Lady of Summer, whoever she is, has a collection of idiots under her command. Though perhaps she herself is a few coins shy of a money box. She believes she is the rightful heir to the throne and deserves her crown back. I am unsure why I've been targeted, but I'm willing to bet so has Clara, or maybe those she's close with, as I can only assume she wishes to sit upon the Morrin throne.*'"

"She said 'Lady of Summer'?" Clara repeated, unable to stop her eyes from bulging.

"I quoted verbatim." Ryn's expression hardened. She appeared almost annoyed that Clara had questioned her in the first place.

"Why would she be targeting Eveline?"

"I do not know. Have you been attacked of late?"

"No, but Beau was shot a few weeks ago in Wave. The townsfolk ran about in an altered state, full of rage and wrath for him specifically. Could they have been manipulated?"

"I can't see why not. Though a Resmigian fae is not capable of mind play—only the Darsmun are."

"Perhaps she has one working for her? A Darsmun fae also attacked Isobel only a few nights past. She said she was at the Cerulean Castle when two males picked her up and gave her orders. She told me they said I would know which queen sent her. The witches were also taken in Soil, on my land, under my sister's rule." Clara paused, her mind spinning a mile a minute.

The answer was *right there,* but she just couldn't grab it.

Then it hit her like a pile of bricks.

"We've been pitted against each other. Elisabeth, Eveline, and I." Memories played in her mind, things that had felt unimportant at the time now connected to form a much bigger picture. "Whoever the Lady of Summer is, she has been plotting for months to turn us against one another in the hope we'd separate. We'd be alone. Maybe even so no one would be here to fix the land. I guarantee she's behind the rot as well. Fuck."

Ryn seemed unfazed by Clara's revelation, moving on past it. "Well, that's all I have from Eveline, but I also wanted to leave you a wedding gift. Something small I think you'll find rather helpful in the coming weeks."

"I love presents," Clara murmured, still trying to recall the events of the past few months, but slightly less so since Ryn mentioned a gift.

"You have a battle on the horizon, Clara. War is coming. You need to remember there are no winners, not really."

Clara winced, her whole body uncomfortable. Her brows drew closer together, and she folded her arms once again.

"This is not a very nice gift so far, Ryn."

"Death's Daughters are powerful, but they are not infallible. Their power, magic, and their very life force is held within their markings. Morana's brow, Cassandra's arm, Lorelai's chin. Remove the mark and they'll die a mortal death. You must cleave the fatal blow, but I trust it will not be difficult."

"You want me to skin deities? That's disgusting."

"There are far worse ways to be rid of a deity, Clara. Be grateful this is all you need to do."

"All?" Clara scoffed.

Ryn stared at Clara for a moment before closing the space between them. The Reaper took Clara's hand firmly, then something that looked a lot like compassion softened her face.

"And remember, you cannot save them all."

Unfortunately, Clara had no time to contemplate Ryn's parting words because Darius knocked on the doorframe to the kitchen. She hadn't expected the sound and jumped as he walked over the threshold.

"You scared the shit out of me, kid." She clutched at her chest, similar to how her brother had when Ryn arrived earlier.

"Apologies, Majesty," he replied quietly, then bowed.

"Oh, don't bother with that." Clara waved him off. "Is everything alright?"

Darius nodded and looked up at Clara. "I just arrived. Hugo and Brontë too."

"How was your journey?"

Clara knew there was a reason Darius had found her, and it was not to talk about his travels. But as she didn't want to push or pry, she stood calmly, with her hands clasped in front of her and a soft smile on her face. Very queen-like, if she said so herself.

"Fine," Darius answered quickly. He inspected the kitchen, running his fingers over the countertops as Ryn had done. When he noticed his hands were now dirty, he wiped them on his pants. Finally, without looking at Clara, he asked quietly, "Is Fintan your father?"

"Technically . . ." Clara wasn't sure how to answer. Fintan was her father. He'd sired her, and she shared his blood. But he hadn't raised her. Nor cared for her, not really. He wasn't anything like Tasman. If someone asked who Clara's *father* was, she'd answer Tasman without a second's hesitation.

"Why did he round us up?" Darius asked, glancing at Clara again. His face slowly filled with confusion and frustration. Between his slightly furrowed brows, lines a child should not possess yet had formed. "He keeps saying big things are coming and we can do something special, something great. But Fintan won't tell us what it is, and my sister is not far off throwing punches."

Clara scoffed. "She won't hear any reprimand from me."

"Why are we here?" Darius pressed, his voice barely a whisper.

"In the palace? I'm assuming for the wedding. In Fintan's little band of special fae? Because he's selfish and delusional. Please listen to me, Darius." Clara took a step towards the boy. "You do not owe Fintan anything. If you and your sister want to leave, you are free to go at any point. If you want to stay in a palace," Clara said with a genuine smile as she gestured around her, "then you are more than welcome to do that too. I will not hold you here, nor will I turn you away. However, I would like to speak to your sister first if you decide to leave."

"She won't say no," he replied, seeming to ignore everything else Clara had said.

"I'm sorry?" She regarded him with her head slightly cocked.

"If you ask her to take your nephew. She'll huff about how we do not have the coin to raise a child, but she will not refuse. Being a mother is all she's ever wanted, and she'll take any opportunity to make it a reality." A small but genuine smile crept over Darius' face.

"She will be heavily compensated—I'm not asking for charity," Clara said quickly. "If she agrees, you all will be taken care of. I will see to that."

Brontë crept silently around the doorway, so sly Clara didn't notice her at first. It was only seconds before she spoke that Clara saw the wild-haired fae staring at her with apprehension.

"May we stay for the ceremony?" she asked, more timidly than Clara had expected. Brontë was not normally a shy individual, but today she almost seemed vulnerable.

"Were you eavesdropping?" Clara raised a brow, poorly veiling a smirk.

"Technically," Brontë muttered, rubbing her hand over her elbow as she held it close to her body.

Clara couldn't help the laugh that burst from her throat. She didn't miss the repetition of Clara's earlier statement. "As I told your brother, you're welcome to come and go as you please. Stay, eat, drink, dance. I don't mind."

"Would you like updates on your nephew once he leaves with us?" Brontë asked quietly, the violent light in her green eyes softening as she looked at Clara.

Clara shook her head slowly, a sad smile spreading across her face. Pain danced around her ribs as she whispered, "No, but thank you." She shook her head and cleared her throat. "I do not know what threat comes for him, so the less I know of him, the better. You can reach me if you need to, and I will find a way to contact you if the need arises."

Brontë nodded, then took her brother's arm and turned to leave. Before they made it through the door, Brontë turned to Clara. "You're nothing like your father, you know?"

Clara scoffed again, then planted her hands firmly on her hips. "I pride myself on being nothing like Fintan."

CHAPTER THIRTY-FOUR
CLARA

Isobel's footsteps slapped on the tiled floor as she emerged from the en suite. Water dripped slowly down her petite, naked body, pooling at her feet when she paused in the middle of the room. Clara stood by the window, her fingers red and tingling, her attention divided.

As Isobel ran her towel over her scalp and dried her hair, she stared at Clara. They were both silent until Isobel asked her what was wrong. A small part of Clara warmed at Isobel knowing, without words and hardly even a glance, that something was off. But it was only a small part of her heart.

"Beau should've been back by now," Clara muttered.

"It's only midnight," Isobel said with a shrug. "I'm sure he'll be along soon. They're probably still drinking." She chuckled, but it was hesitant, as if she didn't fully believe it, or maybe saw how Clara certainly didn't.

"No." Clara shook her head. "Something is wrong." Their eyes locked for a moment, gazes intense before Isobel nodded once.

"Would you like to go find him?"

Clara nodded quickly, her eyes searching out the window as if the stars could provide a map straight to him. Closing the space between them, Isobel placed a gentle hand on the side of Clara's face, and her fingers wove through Clara's hair. With a quick kiss to her tether's cheek, Isobel turned and threw on an outfit, then took Clara's hand. Fingers interlocked, they left their suite.

She wasn't normally one for a brisk pace, but tonight her feet maintained a hurried speed alongside her racing heartbeat. It thudded inside her chest, almost loud enough to hear it echoing through the eerily quiet halls. Her gaze swivelled at every turn and through every open door on the way to Jude's den.

Clara hadn't been to his little man cave yet, but Jude had been kind enough to provide directions just in case she needed him. Whether he'd intended it for this evening, or just generally, Clara didn't know. She struggled to keep her mind focused on their route instead of the millions of reasons Beau hadn't yet come to bed. Isobel offered her own reasons, gave a handful of feasible, simple explanations for where he could be, but truthfully Clara wasn't listening. Cold air tickled her nape and the backs of her arms. Her hands tingled as violently as the soles of her feet.

Her hand hovered above the door handle as Clara paused and took a deep breath. Her eyes travelled over the cubes engraved in the near-midnight-coloured door, and her heart sank.

She knew he wasn't inside.

Opening the door anyway, Clara found the room as empty as her chest.

No light, no sound.

No Beau.

Her breathing came faster, as did the circling wind. It settled a fraction when Isobel took Clara's tense and shaking hand, but only a fraction. She stormed from the den, dragging Isobel along beside her, but saw nothing until they stood outside Jude's suite. Clara could barely remember how she got there.

Not interested in knocking or waiting for a response, Clara threw open the doors. The swelling air pushed the heavy wood panels until they slammed into the walls on either side of the doorway. Clara stepped into the suite, moving towards the prince's bedroom. Jude sat bolt upright first, though Hunter quickly followed. Both males rubbed at their eyes and tried to rid their bodies of sleep.

"Where is he?" Clara demanded, still in the doorway. Her feet wouldn't take her any further.

"Where is who?" Jude croaked as he stood.

"Beau!"

"He left us an hour ago," he answered as he continued rubbing at his eyes. "Gods, Clara, you are aware we have an early morning, are you not?"

"Not until he has been located," Clara spat. "I want anyone who could be even remotely helpful brought here now. This wedding will not go ahead until I know he is safe."

"How do you know he isn't?" Hunter asked, his voice husky and quiet.

"Because he didn't come back! Do you know how much that male loves me? Enough that he'd not wander the halls the night before I marry someone else instead of spending the night with me." Clara ran her hands through her hair, only barely registering Isobel's hand at her lower back. She turned to the prince and pointed fiercely. "Something is wrong, and you will assist me to fix it. So fucking help me, Jude—"

"Okay," he said with force. "I hear you. I'm up. What do you need from me?"

"Wake your mother."

Confusion laced his hazel eyes, and his brows furrowed, but he sighed as he retrieved a pair of trousers. Hunter dressed quickly and silently, then the quartet walked to the king and queen's quarters. Clara remembered little of that walk, save for the burning determination and cold calm that settled over her body. She didn't feel the least bit calm on the inside. All her organs tightened, her heart beating twice as fast as it ought. Yet outwardly her hands held steady, her chin sat high, and her eyes focused firmly ahead. Even the air stilled around her, enough that Isobel gave her more than one side-eye on their way.

The guard stationed outside the king and queen's suite did not hesitate to let Jude through, and after a reminder of Clara's position, she was granted entry as well, with a hasty and nervous apology.

Isobel and Hunter were required to stay outside, so Clara demanded the doors remain open. She was not interested in losing anyone else this evening.

Once the queen had donned her robe, Clara asked, "Fancy going hunting, Majesty?"

A crooked smile gleamed on her face. It would have been terrifying if Clara had any reason to fear this female, and in the dim light of the small candle King Taron held, anyone else might've cowered. Clara met her sinister stare and appreciated the grin, for it meant the queen would help. Eagerly and willingly.

"Taron," Queen Sylvina said over her shoulder, her cold eyes still locked on Clara. "Call the hounds."

"Tell me you keep familial records," Clara blurted, ignoring who—or what—the hounds were.

"Of course." Queen Sylvina scoffed. She looked at Clara and raised her brows, almost as if she were offended. "Why?"

"I need them," Clara stated plainly.

"Excuse you?"

"How badly do you want your retirement, Majesty?"

The queen called in her guard and sent for the records immediately. A small sigh of relief escaped Clara, and she explained her theory of who the Lady of Summer might be. She recounted the time Beau died in Wave, and Isobel's forced relapse. Her conversations with Ryn and Ryland, her visions, and everything she and Jude had learnt of the rot in the land. The quickly strung sentences spilled from her tongue at record pace, but the king and queen both focused on her intently—even in the excruciatingly long silence that captured the room the moment she had finished.

"Impossible." King Taron stepped closer to his wife and placed a large hand on her shoulder. "We would know if we had spare royals running around." Queen Sylvina nodded as she covered his hand with her own, though their son was uncharacteristically quiet. Jude's hands were stuffed deep in his pockets, while his eyes traced over his bare toes.

The guard raced back into the room with two scrolls in hand. One was tied with a navy ribbon, and the other with powder-blue twine. The king took the scroll wrapped in twine, while the queen unbound the one rolled in ribbon.

"What is this blotch here?" Clara asked, reading over the queen's arm and pointing to a later submission on the family tree. It looked as if someone had written something, then spilled ink over it, and no one had bothered to fix it.

"A cousin of mine had twins," Queen Sylvina answered with a shrug. "Last I heard, they died."

"No, actually they didn't," Jude said quietly. He sighed and rubbed the back of his neck before he continued. "Aunt Corril sent them away like changelings. She didn't want them in line for the throne."

"Jude Tobias Lorson!" the queen shrieked. "That is not information you ought to keep private!"

"Where are they?" Clara demanded.

"They have multiple properties throughout Morrin. I have little contact with Conner, so I'm unsure where he is now."

"Find him." Clara spoke clearly, with no room for argument or excuses. "Now."

The hounds—who were a breed of fae of Resmigian and Soliqe heritage, created when their bloodlines had joined—found Conner far sooner than Clara had expected. A bubble of hope rose in her chest. They brought him to the palace still in his nightwear, though he didn't seem all that fazed.

He looked familiar, but Clara couldn't place from where exactly. His golden blonde hair, peppered with chestnut and almond-coloured strands, fell in loose waves to his shoulders. His eyes were as blue as Jacob's, ringed in green and surrounded by long lashes. A single gold chain hung from his neck, and a matching ring sat on his index finger.

His voice was deep and calm, like waves on the shore at low tide, as he explained how he was raised in Bloom with his sister. Conner hadn't seen his parents in centuries and wasn't even sure if they were alive. Clara's throat stung, as she couldn't bear not knowing if her own mother lived. It would've been daily torture for her. Stars, it was one of the few reasons she ever obeyed Urian's ridiculous demands—to ensure her mother and family's safety.

Conner continued to tell them how he and his sister had grown apart over the years but had maintained contact until a few months ago. "We spoke rarely once I left home to study abroad," he said with a shrug. "But when I got back—I don't know, two years later, maybe?—she started ranting about how much we deserved, that we were owed a better life. She started shit-talking our birth mother, and I wasn't interested. I understood why Corril did what she did, and I don't blame her.

"My sister wasn't so forgiving. When the news of your engagement surfaced"—he turned to Jude and dipped his forehead to the prince—"she spiralled. She became a total recluse, and I haven't heard from her since. I can give you the addresses of each of our properties, plus the private land I know she owns herself. She's most likely to be in Snow—always spoke of how it was where she felt most at home. I don't know why, since we're summer fae." He shook his head, confusion etched deep on his face.

Clara couldn't focus. Couldn't listen to any of the details he listed, nor his expectations of where his sister might be found. All she heard was that they were summer fae, and Clara's suspicions were all but confirmed.

Then her conversation with Jude echoed in her mind.

"If we get married on the summer solstice, someone is going to die."

Summer solstice had officially begun, which meant the Lady of Summer wasn't far behind.

If she wasn't already here.

CHAPTER THIRTY-FIVE
CLARA

Word travelled fast among the soldiers and guards, so when Clara pounded on Keyne's door, she was met immediately with a fully dressed entourage of fae.

Her fae. Her guard.

The speed with which they'd organised themselves warmed Clara's heart and her cold, tingling fingertips.

Finch nodded as Clara entered the room, while he continued to strap various daggers to his chest and thigh. Oren and Aleska greeted her with the same nod of acknowledgement, their normally goofy expressions replaced by far more serious ones. Ryland paced by a small table in the centre of the room, his fingers pinching the bridge of his nose.

"What are your orders?" he asked as soon as he noticed Clara. He looked at her with tired eyes and with concern etched into every line of his face.

"We're to depart in a moment. You'll be split into groups, each with a palace guard and a hound. Oren, Aleska." Clara turned to them as she spoke, and handed the former a small piece of paper scrawled with their address to investigate. "You'll be paired with two hounds and one of the queen's guards. They will meet you at the stables—you're going to the border." Then she turned to Finch and Keyne, handing the latter their destination. "You two will be paired with two hounds and two guards. They are waiting for you at the eastern entrance of the palace."

Each of her guards nodded and filed out of the room. Isobel stayed silent beside her, though her hand remained wrapped in Clara's, keeping her grounded and able to maintain some semblance of calm. Clara took a deep breath before she continued speaking to Ryland.

"You are to remain here," she murmured. "Just in case."

"*Just in case* of what, exactly? You have a kingdom to consider!" Ryland retorted. His tone was hushed, but the disapproval rang loud. She grimaced and took another calming breath.

"Not over him, I don't."

Ryland sighed forcefully, his hand back on the bridge of his nose. But before he could speak further, to disagree with Clara some more, she added, "You are to hold down the fort, keep the prince company. Make sure my mother does not worry when she wakes and cannot find me."

"As you wish." Ryland's reply was resigned, his expression drained and his shoulders limp.

If Clara made it out of the next twenty-four hours alive, and the next week, or month, or however long it took for war to pass, she'd make sure Ryland got a sleep in at the very least. Maybe she'd send him on a holiday; perhaps he could spend some time in the Court of Breath, amongst the fae known for liveliness and carefree fun. He could visit the beauty of Florence Hills in person.

Isobel and Clara walked hand in hand to the main foyer of the palace, where Queen Sylvina waited for them.

King Taron stood behind his wife, his hands on her shoulders and chin resting on the back of her head. He pressed a quick kiss to her hair before nodding to Clara and wishing them all luck. Jude was nowhere to be seen, though Clara didn't mind. There were other matters for the prince to attend.

"I understand you've sent parties to the border and the property along the western shore, but I must ask, where are we going? Conner provided two other addresses, and we cannot be in two places at once. I'm good, but not that good." The queen gave a half-assed chuckle, perhaps to lighten the solemn and heavy air.

Clara did not answer.

Instead, she closed her eyes and focused her breathing. Deep, in through her nose and then out, slowly, through her mouth. Over and over. Until her feet felt as one with the polished floor, and her arms felt like an extension of the air circling her. She was heavy and weightless all at once. With her heartbeat echoing in her ears, she reached into every corner of her mind.

She opened every dark and dusty box she'd mentally packed away to think about another time, and searched them for the answer. Twiddling the pendant that Beau gave her with one hand, the other hovered over her recent feather tattoo until it seemed to come alive and burn under her fingertips.

Various buildings flash through Clara's mind. A redbrick house with an orange-tiled roof. Then a cottage with snow-filled gutters and the blinds drawn. Another redbrick home, this time with an overgrown yard and cobblestone path to the door. They fly before Clara's mind's eye, there for only a second before they disappear.

All except for one building.

Grey and tall, with as many windows as expected from its three storeys. The image floats through the carousel multiple times, each time lasting a second longer than the last.

Clara knows where it is, though she cannot say how.

Just as she knows that's where Beau waits.

"The warehouse. Where is it?" she asked the queen, who held a list of properties and their descriptions. Clara's grip on Isobel's hand tightened as a wave of dizziness washed over her. She ignored it and focused on Queen Sylvina, anxiously awaiting her response.

Blood dripped from her nose and quickly coated her tongue. She absently wiped her face with the back of her sleeve while trying her best to ignore the spearing headache at the base of her skull. It was a pain so violent all she could do was use it, turn it into fuel to find Beau.

She hadn't had such a blinding headache in a long time, and that it coincided with her forcing a vision left a niggling realisation in the back of Clara's mind. Such an insight would have to wait, though, as now was not the time.

"Also near the border," the queen replied quickly. "Further north."

"That's where we're going."

Tian and Malik dismounted their horses first. The two hounds inhaled deeply, then continued with short, sharp sniffs as they circled the perimeter. At another time, Clara would've laughed. Today, she was grateful for the faes' infinitely superior sense of smell and sound.

Blood tinged Clara's tongue, as she could hardly stop biting her cheek in frustration. She couldn't find any humour, not until she set eyes on Beau and he was safe and breathing.

The queen's guards—Anton and Sabir—collected the horses once everyone's feet were firmly on the lightly snowcapped ground. Anton tied them to a nearby street post, then spoke quietly with his female counterpart. Perhaps about strategy. Clara didn't care; she was itching to get inside.

"We'll scan the external perimeter of the warehouse and locate an entry point. You three stay put until we get back." Sabir spoke with so much authority, and to a queen no less, but Queen Sylvina only nodded and settled her bow in front of her. She reached for an arrow, though she held it loosely in her hand instead of nocking it.

It felt like an eternity until they returned. The air was still and silent. Isobel tapped the pads of her fingers to her thumb on one hand, while the other hovered over the mid-sized blade at her hip. Clara had brought no weapons—truthfully, she didn't need them. She trained well enough and knew her way around a sword, but her magic was stronger. Today was not a day for fumbling with blades when fire was at her disposal.

Anton recounted the layout of the building. There was only one viable entry or exit—which was the front door—and none of the windows were practical for entry, as none of them had wings. Tian confirmed there were at least half a dozen fae inside, plus Beau, if his scent coming from the building was anything to go by.

Clara didn't need the hound's confirmation, but appreciated it nonetheless.

"There was a guard by the door, but he's been neutralised." Tian smirked as she announced it, and Clara couldn't tell what emotion it stirred. But with such a cruel half-smile, she was glad not to be on the opposing side to Tian.

"Is he dead?" Isobel asked, with caution clear in her voice.

"No," Tian replied with a shrug. "Not unless you want him to be."

Ignoring Tian, Isobel walked towards where Anton said the entryway was located. Clara followed closely, as did the queen. The guards walked on either side of the trio, while the hounds covered the rear. Isobel took a deep breath and moved into a more balanced stance, preparing to raise her leg.

Before she could land a kick to the door, the queen tutted and grabbed Isobel's knee. Then she pushed past Isobel and turned the door handle effortlessly.

Clara had assumed it would be locked, and evidently, so had Isobel.

"Perhaps some common sense next time? No need to waste energy. Go."

The guards pushed in first and immediately took the stairs. Clara scanned the hallway, unsure of how best to locate Beau. Her gut told her he was here—her magic and the hound had confirmed as much. But was it hope that now told her which way to go? Did it matter? Would the handful of moments between checking this level and the one below make any difference?

Once they were all inside, the hounds split up. Tian moved through the hallway, peeking in each door she passed. Malik took the stairs two at a time, and soon Clara couldn't see either of them.

"I'm going downstairs," Clara told Isobel, deciding to trust whatever nudged her towards the basement. Hope or magic or intuition—it didn't matter. She trusted it.

"How do you even know there's a basement?" Isobel asked, also scanning the hallway. There were no other staircases. Only a bend in the corridor and the doors on the opposite wall.

Clara barely noticed the queen nock her arrow before it soared through the air, her loose strands of hair flying out after it. Clara whirled just in time to watch it land between the wide eyes of a fae male. He was not tall enough to be Resmigian, but otherwise Clara couldn't tell where he was from. He stood in the doorway of one room, a mug in one hand and a biscuit in the other.

He stayed upright for a second before he crumpled in a heap on the floor. Whatever he'd intended to drink spilled over his face and neck, the steam rising lazily.

The trio walked silently over him, towards another door, which indeed led to a lower level. Clara shrugged as she turned to Isobel, who only gave her a small, admiring smile before tugging Clara's hand backwards. She stepped around Clara and began the descent first.

The staircase curved halfway down, and with no light source, Clara relied heavily on the thin railing to keep her upright. At the base of the stairs was another door, slightly illuminated around the edges. Dulled voices filtered through, but Clara couldn't make out the quiet words. Isobel tugged on the handle, slowly and only a touch, before she peered through the tiny gap.

Isobel's hand clenched into a fist, her magic surging. The ground rumbled beneath them, and the voices beyond the door grew worried, becoming louder, then fell silent. Isobel pulled the door back. She waited for Clara to pass through, then the queen. Finally she, too, entered the basement and let the heavy door slam behind them.

Just as Tian had predicted, there were six fae standing before them. Isobel had five restrained by roots in various shades of dark green and brown, which bulged from the cement floor.

The final one had their back turned to the females and was slightly hunched over something Clara couldn't see. Of those restrained, two were large enough to be Resmigian fae, and one had the markings of a water fae. Clara didn't recognise, nor could she discern the heritage of the others, though the queen was visibly disappointed by a Resmigian—let alone two—being involved. She sped past Clara and Isobel, muttering furiously as she slapped the first and spat at his feet. Only as his head swivelled did Clara recognise his frosted white hair and the distinctive blue shimmer to his lips.

"You!" she screeched. His eyes whipped to hers, though he only smirked. Clara narrowed her eyes and held out her hand, palm up. In seconds, a blade rested there, and she curled her fingers around it until her knuckles turned white. "I helped you!"

"Indeed, you did, *Majesty*." Brock spat the word like an insult.

Queen Sylvina turned to Clara. "What did I tell you about the winter fae, queen?"

She had never called Clara queen before, and the title, meant as an endearment, felt unfamiliar to Clara's ears. For a moment, she froze.

"Well?" Queen Sylvina pressed.

Clara flung the blade and called on the air that normally howled in fear, yet today it danced to Clara's violent melody. The blade embedded itself in Brock's neck.

The second Resmigian fae opened their mouth, but Queen Sylvina did not wait for the words to fall from their lips. She pulled an arrow from her quiver and slammed it through the opening, lodging it firmly in the back of their throat. Blood splattered, then their head fell backwards. The queen spat at the second fae's feet as well.

Clara scanned the room, a cold sweat forming along her spine when she couldn't immediately see Beau. The second she found him, her heart settled. Then a quiet rage took over as she stormed forward.

"Don't you ever do this shit again. Do you hear me?! I almost bled out trying to pull a vision to locate you. And I've got guards and hounds spread all over the damned continent. I'm supposed to be getting married today!"

Beau only smiled up at her, entirely smitten, and it threatened to melt her resolve.

Until the fae she couldn't see stood and turned to snarl at Clara.

A familiar tall blonde female stared back. Her eyes a bright, striking blue even in such terrible light. Mixed gold and silver jewellery adorned every finger, reaching halfway up her forearms, and dangled from her neck and ears.

Kyra.

The Lady of *fucking* Summer.

"I *knew* you were no good," she muttered, before turning her attention back to Beau. "Did I not fucking tell you?"

"Sweetheart," he drawled, far too casually for someone bound to a chair. "Now is not the time for I told you so."

"I think now is the perfect time. You're not going anywhere."

"I took him so you would know what it felt like to lose something you care deeply about." Kyra folded her arms lazily, distaste clear across her face.

Clara saw red.

"Something? Some*thing*?! That man is my heart. You could not possibly know what it feels like to have one. Not someone as wretched as you."

"You were thrown in our dungeons and now you're to sit on our throne? How does someone of such insignificance climb the social ladder so quickly? Did you fuck your way to the top? Do you even know what you're taking when you wear the crown?"

"I am the top," Clara drawled with a smirk, and a soft blush crept over Isobel's cheeks. "Enlighten me—what might I be taking when I am crowned queen? Aside from your freedom at the very least."

"That crown does not belong to you. It belongs to *me!*" Kyra continued. The intensity of her words did not lower, though her volume did. "To *my* foremothers and fathers. We ruled once, and there was no blight on the land. The earth was well, and now you tarnish the name of royalty and sully the ground you walk on by your presence."

"You do not deserve *my crown*," Queen Sylvina snarled.

Clara hadn't seen the royal so riled before. Though the queen did not raise her voice, the impact was resounding. Shivers erupted over Clara's shoulders and down her arms.

Kyra was an idiot or entirely too brazen.

"Oh, and she does? An outsider? She is a nobody, and you would have her take your place? Royal Resmigian blood flows through *my* veins, not hers! My stupid mother thought a peasant life would be best for us. She was useless, and your family has been selfish, taking the entire continent for yourselves!"

"It was you," the queen whispered, as she took a menacing step towards the fae. "You've been poisoning my land."

"Yes," Kyra said, her voice barely louder than the queen's. She smirked boldly. "It was me. The bloody spell grew out of control and became a bigger problem than I intended, but I'll save us all and find my way back to *my* throne."

Clara couldn't hold back her laughter. "You delusional fucking fool."

"Wrong!" Kyra shouted, pointing a finger at Clara's chest. "Do you know how many parts there are in my plan? Do you have any idea what I've done? No, your tiny little Vequil brain couldn't possibly fathom. I've led attacks on every continent—manipulated and toyed and taken what I needed, what I wanted. The last step is to get rid of you so I can have my crown."

"Wrong," Clara repeated, no more than a whisper.

Kyra's eyes widened as her shoulders tensed and her arms fell lax at her sides.

Fae blood was made up of a significant amount of water. Clara hadn't ever paid enough attention in school to know exactly how much, but she knew it was enough to boil. Drawing on both her water and fire magic, Clara's limbs tingled as the blood inside Kyra's body heated.

This was for Jude and his land.

For the powerful queen Clara had befriended. And the queen's tether, who shouldn't have been anywhere near death but had come too close on more than one occasion.

For Isobel, who had something precious stolen from her.

For Beau, who'd died for fuck's sake and then been kidnapped at this vile woman's hands.

Mostly, though, it was for Clara.

She would no longer be a pawn in anyone's games, let alone one so selfish and dangerous.

Kyra exploded.

Ribbons of blood and chunks of her body scattered around the room. Thankfully, the smell was tolerable, though less so for the hounds, who both grimaced and gagged, then pinched their noses.

"That was rather dramatic, even for you," the queen muttered with a casual grin.

Clara shrugged. "I felt she deserved a dramatic end, what with all her theatrics."

CHAPTER THIRTY-SIX
CLARA

"Thank the gods!" Jude exclaimed loudly as Clara and Beau entered the foyer, which he'd apparently been pacing before her arrival. Isobel and the queen followed on their heels.

"They had very little to do with it, prince," Clara replied with a sardonic grin.

"Were you injured?" Jude asked Beau, giving the Phoenix a hasty once-over. "I have the healers on standby. Where were you?"

Beau shook his head. "I'm fine. A few bruises, but no need to worry. In truth, it was rather humorous towards the end." He turned to Isobel and Clara before he added, "The ground shuddered right before you burst in, and they all shared the same confused and mildly frightened look. I was the only one who knew what was coming."

Isobel smirked, though she remained silent, while Clara patted Beau's cheek. The queen handed her cloak, gloves, and bow off to a nearby staff member, then joined their discussion.

"I have to say," she began, with an approving expression at both Clara and Isobel, "I was rather impressed with you both."

"And I you, Your Majesty," Isobel said softly, dipping her chin to the queen.

"Have fun did you, Mother?" Jude raised his brows expectantly at his mother, who smirked back at him. Mischief and delight swirled in her emerald eyes, and Clara could only smile.

"I'll say," Beau muttered. "One fae secured an arrow to the back of their throat, *through* their gaping mouth. That was incredible. Then she let two of them go so she could 'hunt them properly.' It was an absolute honour to watch. One received an arrow to the throat, the other to the chest and—if I recall correctly, Your Majesty, because he didn't die immediately—another was sent to his crotch."

Queen Sylvina smiled proudly and nodded with all the regalness of a royal. Every time she encountered the queen, Clara was more sure that this was the type of ruler she aspired to be. One day, she'd make Queen Sylvina proud to have passed her throne to Clara.

"Not to mention the speed at which she fired her arrow. We hadn't even seen the fae yet, but she fired and clocked him between the eyes," Isobel added, her own lighting up at the recount. Then she whispered, mostly to herself, "Breathtaking."

She did a wonderful job hiding it, but Clara knew violence sang to Isobel. It danced along her skin and swam within her veins. Isobel was cheery and fun, bubbly and boldly expressive. But she had a wild streak, where she turned into a murderously dangerous weapon that Clara was proud to call her own.

Jude shuddered and sighed again, while Clara did her best to hide the amusement from her face.

"Well," he said. "It's still summer solstice, and Death has claimed her souls for today. May we get married now? I do not wish to anger the gods any further or tarnish my marriage before it has even begun."

"Oh, I don't know, son," Queen Sylvina drawled, sparing a wink for Clara. "I think today's begun splendidly."

The prince only groaned and dragged a hand down his face. He then looked to Clara, a sliver of hope on his face, and she couldn't argue.

"We can marry today, prince. Now that my prophecy has been fulfilled."

"Right." Jude nodded slowly. "Well, here's to weddings, deaths, and magic, I suppose."

The halls felt unnaturally empty as Clara wandered towards her mother's guest room. Normally, fae were coming and going at almost all hours, but today it was quiet. She did not pass anyone, nor hear any commotion from another hallway or beyond the thin doors.

Everyone was busy readying the grand hall and adjoining ballroom. Clara was getting married in a matter of hours, to a prince, no less! Fear danced past her fingertips and tingled a hair's breadth from her spine. Close enough that she felt it, but far enough away that it did not stir her emotions in a way she had no time for. There was no use worrying now, not when by this time tomorrow she'd be wed. Both a princess and a queen.

For now, all Clara wanted was her mother.

She hesitated for a moment before knocking on the door. Perhaps her fear wasn't so far away after all. Clara shook her head and rolled her shoulders, then tapped gently.

Felicity embraced her quickly, without hesitation or question. Clara melted into her mother until Jacob interrupted them, shouting about boredom and scratchy waistcoats. Their mother rolled her eyes, rubbing at her brows and shooing the boy off down the corridor to annoy his brother.

"You get that suit dirty before the ceremony and I will skin you!" she called after her son, who brushed her off before turning a corner, his chuckles echoing along the walls. "Who am I kidding? We all know it's an empty threat."

Clara giggled as she took her mother's hand. "Will you help me get ready?" she asked, her voice quiet.

"That isn't royal custom, is it?"

"No," Clara said, shaking her head subtly. "But it's what I want. Your mother dressed you for your wedding, did she not?"

Felicity's eyes welled. Her lips pressed together, and Clara didn't miss the twitch of her chin as she tried to mask her quivering lip. She nodded eagerly and pressed a warm hand to Clara's cheek.

"I'd be honoured, my sweet girl."

A strange pang of sadness hit Clara's chest. Words that fell so frequently from Elisabeth's lips, but never sounded right, rolled from her mother's tongue naturally, nice and warm. Never did the statement sound anything but possessive when it came from her sister.

Clara would be lying if she said it didn't spark a hint of grief, and perhaps guilt, hearing those words. At the reminder of Elisabeth. Clara believed she would've loved to have witnessed a royal wedding—even more so, that of her little sister.

When they arrived at Clara's empty suite, she found a bright-ivory gown waiting for her. It was draped over the edge of the bed, the intricately designed hem only an inch off the ground.

Beaded appliques dotted the hemline, as well as trailed down the sides where she assumed her hips would sit. The bodice was structured with boning and covered in pearls and beaded lace. Sunlight glinted through the window and reflected off it magically. Thin, draped sleeves connected to the highest points of the V-shaped bodice before trailing down and cuffing at the wrist.

It was a stunning gown. The queen had done well.

But it wasn't Clara's dress, not the one she wanted to wear.

The one she wanted, and had gone out of her way to secure, was bold and sexy. Cherry red and covered from top to bottom in glitter. Clara strolled past the ivory gown and instead pulled the figure-hugging, backless gown from her wardrobe. The neckline cowled so low, her cleavage would certainly be a problem for some, and the back fell in much the same way.

This was the one.

Stars, she was excited to put it on. Just to wear it, regardless of the event.

"Do your in-laws know you intend to wear this to marry their son in front of their entire kingdom? I doubt Her Majesty had something chosen at random for you." Felicity raised a single brow at Clara.

Clara shrugged a shoulder, her eyes raking over the ivory gown quickly before darting to the red. It was stunning, truly, but it wasn't *her*. The queen knew who her son was marrying, and it certainly wasn't someone who fit into any mould.

"They'll find out soon enough. Red is a powerful colour, you know."

"Not in Morrin, it isn't."

Clara couldn't help the peal of laughter that burst from her throat.

Her mother chuckled quietly while shaking her head. It was a very motherly thing to do, and something she'd done Clara's whole life. Especially when Clara would do or say something Felicity didn't agree with but didn't necessarily find wrong. So she would lightly scold her and usually laugh. Looking back on her childhood, Clara had been truly blessed. The only hardship she'd ever known was when her father died. She was so grateful to have been raised by such incredible parents. Clara only hoped her mother knew it.

"Stop it," she whispered. "Tell me more about your wedding day."

"As if you haven't begged me to tell you a thousand times before," Felicity whispered back, shaking the comb at Clara's reflection. While she detangled the wild mess atop Clara's head, her mother relayed stories she had indeed heard many times before, but she never tired of listening to them.

"The day started uneventfully. My closest friends and I ate and drank and danced at my mother's house. She brought a continuous stream of snacks upstairs. When it came time to dress, we all sat before the one tiny mirror and tried to apply our cosmetics and fix our hair. There was so much shoving!" Felicity shook her head, her eyes distant as her mind recalled the fond memories. "Then my mother kicked everyone out so she could dress me. One of the eyelets on my corset wasn't attached properly, and half the bodice ripped. Oh, how my mother shrieked!"

Clara winced as her mother tugged at a knot, and her head jerked backwards. Her mother grunted, then continued.

"Thankfully, one of my friends was married to a seamstress' brother. I'd never seen her run so quickly, nor has she since, if I'm honest. But she came through for me that day, as did the seamstress. No one could even tell once she was done."

"I'm glad my dress doesn't have a corset or eyelets to worry about," Clara muttered, before she inhaled sharply and tried her best not to swear as her mother attacked the tangle.

"Clara," her mother said plainly, hands paused. "Your dress is barely a dress. It's more like a skintight stocking with three holes."

"Mother!" Clara shrieked, unable to control her grin.

Felicity only shrugged and turned her attention back to Clara's hair.

"Your father got so intoxicated, he kept screaming into everyone's face about how he'd stolen the prettiest woman and that no one else would ever compare." She blushed as she spoke. A sad combination of love and pride bloomed in Clara's chest. She wished her father were here today, if only so he could see what had become of her.

Growing up, Clara had been difficult. Far more than Evian. She put it down to what she now knew was her Flame heritage, but as a child, no one knew. Her parents had believed her to be a water fae, though her temperament had not reflected that fact. Tasman had never punished Clara, only tried to teach her about her emotions and reminded her to be calm, compassionate, and kind. Some days he'd looked so exhausted with her, and Clara felt bad simply recalling the memory.

She wanted him to know how far she'd come since her outbursts as a child. Since she'd thrown things and shouted when she didn't get her way, far more often than any other child in their town ever did. Oh, how she wished he could see who she'd grown into.

"It was such a wholesome shout," her mother continued, now putting the comb down and moving to select pins to secure Clara's hair. "No one reprimanded him. They all simply clapped him on the back and gave him more ale. Truthfully, that only made things worse. I danced on a table! Oh, it was thrilling."

Felicity paused and sighed. "My hem got so muddy because it was an outdoor ceremony, and naturally it poured with rain."

"That is an issue I might actually run into," Clara said. "Being the Winter Court, and all."

"Well, you know what they say about traditions," her mother muttered, pins poking out from between her teeth.

"What traditions did you start?"

"At the end of the night, your father and I ran off the pier. He almost drowned, and I had to drag us both back to shore. I lost my wedding dress to the sea, but it felt like a fitting sacrifice for a life full of love." Felicity smiled so brightly at her reflection, then placed a hand on Clara's shoulder. "I don't recommend you almost drown the prince, but there isn't much need to keep your wedding dress if you only plan to marry once, is there?"

"I might burn mine," Clara murmured as she rested her own hand atop her mother's.

"That is *not* what I meant," Felicity muttered. "Oh, my—"

"I said *might* . . ."

CHAPTER THIRTY-SEVEN
ISOBEL

Felicity walked out of the room first. She took both Isobel and Beau's hands in hers and gave them such a pride-filled smile—with light bursting from her crinkled eyes—then hustled along the hallway. Even without words, Isobel knew the woman would not last long before tears spilled, if they hadn't already.

Isobel and Beau had stood outside their suite for quite some time. Only a handful of months ago, Isobel would've dreaded the thought of spending alone time with the Phoenix, but today she found she didn't want to wait with anyone else. He'd proven to be so much more than Isobel had originally anticipated, and she was genuinely pleased. Beau was still arrogant, smug, and entirely too sure of himself, but also kind and gentle, and more patient than Isobel suspected he even knew. He had a good heart, and though she would never admit it in fear of his already overgrown ego inflating some more, Isobel enjoyed his company. She truly had grown to love the bird boy. If she had to spend her days sharing Clara with anyone, Beau was a fine and appealing choice. Provided there were no games involved because the male was a terribly sore loser and an even more boastful winner.

When Clara finally exited, Isobel's heart stopped. Her breath caught, and time stood still. She'd always likened Clara to the sun—warm and radiant, stunning and bold and bright. A comfort and driving force. But today, Clara outshone any sun, any moon or star. Words disappeared from Isobel's mind, and her tongue sat paralysed in her mouth. All she could do was exhale, as Clara stole the last breath from her lungs.

There was no word strong enough to convey Clara's beauty. On any normal day, she rivalled the goddesses. Hair tousled and clothes half on, sweaty or covered in grass stains, it didn't matter. She was the epitome of beauty, and Isobel fell in love with her more and more every day.

But today she sparkled like a thousand rubies under firelight. As if the remainder of the Farlannen shed their wings and dust for Clara alone. She bloomed as though she were the first rose of the season, and every bud to blossom after her could only dream of meeting her standard. Clara rivalled the muses as the inspiration of every artist, every classical painting, or half-concocted idea for a sketch. She was no longer merely the epitome of elegance, but the definition of divinity.

"Fuck," Beau murmured, then whistled long and low as he raked his eyes over Clara.

Despite all her earlier thoughts of the male, in this moment as he dragged his hungry gaze over her tether, Isobel could only deem him partly worthy. A lot of her wanted to cover his eyes, so she might keep Clara all to herself.

"Red has never looked so good," Isobel whispered, finally able to use her voice again. Clara winked at her, then her jade-green eyes travelled down Isobel's body, and suddenly she felt bare. But oh, how she wished they were both entirely bare, and most certainly not off to a wedding where Clara was to marry another male.

Beau cleared his throat. "In my culture, on their wedding day, the bride and groom will share a moment right before the ceremony and offer a few things to each other. The saying goes, 'something of mine, something of yours, something combined and something born.'"

Clara's brows drew together, and her head tilted as she looked between Beau and Isobel.

"He obviously isn't the groom, and I am certainly not the bride, but we wanted to remind you we're not going anywhere." Isobel smiled and reached out for Clara's hand. "We're together for good, prince or no."

"That isn't exactly something I plan to forget," Clara whispered.

"Regardless, Isobel has gifted me an earring on a chain—" Beau moved to lift the necklace he referred to, but Clara interrupted.

"What, no piercing?" she teased with a smirk. Isobel didn't understand the reference, but watching Clara toy with the male was infectious, so she smiled too.

"Shush, you," Beau whispered, but Clara only chuckled. He reached into the inside pocket of his coat and pulled out a small oval box. "I've been waiting for the right moment to give you this, and honestly I can't think of a better time." Beau lifted the lid of the box to reveal a stunning ring. The hexagonal-cut emerald stone had gold coils wrapped around it to secure it in place. It almost looked like the Inalis markings on Clara's skin. "It was my grandmother's."

"Beau . . ." Clara breathed, her eyes flicking between him and the ring he held.

"Something of mine," he whispered.

"And something of yours."

"We were thinking perhaps . . ." Isobel started, her voice picking up in pace as it did whenever she got nervous, or flustered, or excited. Any emotion that wasn't rage or rage-adjacent, in all honesty. "I know you got your tattoo recently, but your back is bare aside from your Soil markings. I have some beautiful new paints"—she spared an appreciative look at Beau—"and happen to be a decent artist. Your gown is backless. How do you feel about some new artwork?"

"I think if I'm late for this ceremony, Jude is going to have a conniption," Clara said, her eyes and mouth scrunching. "So be quick."

Isobel beamed as Beau pulled the few brushes and tubes of paint he'd stashed in the other inside pocket of his coat and handed them to Isobel with a soft smile.

Clara spun and swept the half of her hair Felicity had loosely braided over her shoulder, and Isobel began.

Using short strokes at first—as they were more of a guide—with the bone-coloured paint that was a shade or two lighter than Clara's skin tone, Isobel roughly applied the outline of two hands to Clara's back. One to the left of her soil marks reaching down towards her lower back, and one slightly to the right reaching up towards her shoulder blades.

With the citrine and aubergine paints, Isobel created depth. Shadows and light, dimension and tension, along each finger. Then above Clara's golden markings, Isobel painted a crown. A simple piece really, though it seemed to glow as she added a halo-like highlight around it. Much like Clara, with or without her royal title.

Beau nodded approvingly as he watched Isobel paint. Whether he knew what it symbolised, or even that one hand was more masculine than the other, Isobel couldn't be sure. Though her chest swelled at his admiration.

Darting back into their room as soon as she was done, Isobel quickly threw the brushes into their bathroom sink and gave herself a once-over in the mirror. She prayed she hadn't smeared paint onto her dress—at least nothing noticeable.

"And something born?" Clara asked as Isobel re-entered the hall.

Isobel and Beau shared a look and mirrored a shrug.

"We hadn't got that far, but I suppose considering there are three of us and this isn't a typical arrangement anyway, we could forego the last one."

"No." Clara shook her head vehemently. "It is a wedding, which I will take part in, so we do this properly. I think instead of presenting myself to the prince, you two can do it. We will birth a new tradition."

"And how exactly might one present you to the prince?"

As it turned out, presenting Clara was quite simple. Isobel knew of various cultures where a member of the bride's family would offer her to her groom, walking her up to her soon-to-be husband's side before shaking the male's hand and congratulating them in advance. This ceremony was rather similar.

Isobel now stood beside Jude before an altar set up on the dais, in front of the king and queen's thrones. It was barren aside from a pale-blue rope, a wide navy ribbon, a blade, and an empty jewelled chalice. Jude's eyes darted to where his lover waited for him in the throng of guests and witnesses. Hunter's eyes never strayed, nor did his soft smile falter. Isobel took warm comfort in knowing Jude shared with Clara the reality of another love. Someone who was not and would never be hers, as he would never be for Clara.

The grand hall was full of nobility and commoners alike. Chatter resounded, everyone light-hearted and excited to bear witness not only to a royal wedding, but to the joining of two royal lines. It was without question a historic day. A Resmigian fae stood in each corner of the room atop a podium, smoky pearl spheres in hand. Isobel didn't know what they were for, but they certainly were pretty. The spheres almost seemed to glow in the gentle sunlight peeking through the windows beyond the thrones.

Isobel did her best to find the folk she recognised amongst the crowd, but only managed to find a handful of their friends and family before the heavy doors swung open and the king and queen were announced. They walked slowly, with such confidence and presence, before nodding to their son and taking their places on their respective thrones.

Then Clara entered.

Gasps echoed throughout the hall, and though Isobel could not see behind her, she had no doubt the queen's eyes were narrowed. As divine as Clara looked, she was not dressed as the queen had intended.

Jude's shoulders instantly relaxed, as did his face before it fell into a loose smile. He took a deep breath before he faced Isobel and waggled his brows. She managed to stop her eyes from rolling, though couldn't maintain a neutral expression.

Beau offered his elbow to Clara, which she took eagerly before they made their way to the altar. Isobel stepped forward, off the dais as she was instructed to do, and waited what felt like either seconds or hours or aeons. Coins lined the floor to encourage a prosperous alliance, while carnation petals and patchouli leaves covered the central runner, for protection and fertility. Cinnamon dusted the entire grand hall in the hopes of success. Together they created a spiced-wood aroma, laced with just enough floral notes that it left folk calm and eager.

By the time Beau reached Isobel, her hands were shaking. Beau took her hand in his and squeezed reassuringly before he bowed low to her, then offered the same greeting to the prince. Clara smiled at Isobel as they, too, joined hands, if only for a moment, before Isobel curtsied to Jude and placed Clara's hands in his. It was bittersweet, holding her for mere seconds before handing her to another.

She quickly took her seat beside Beau and Hunter as the celebrant moved out from behind the dais. Isobel had never seen such a fae, much less a Resmigian. He was tall, though none of him was lanky. Despite the flowing robes, much of his form stretched the material and contrasted with the sharp features across his face.

He did not introduce himself, which Isobel thought might've been appropriate, or at the very least, polite. Instead, he boomed, "We begin with the binding," in a voice far deeper than Isobel had expected.

Clara held out her left hand, which Jude took with his right, and the celebrant wrapped their wrists with the coarse rope from the altar. Once the knot was tied, and tied again, Clara and Jude extended their other hands and were bound the same way but with the satin ribbon. The bindings looked much the same as the queen's used on the familial records.

"In comfort and in pain, you support one another," the celebrant boomed again. "You are bound. Today you join in matrimony, in power and in presence. You are bound as one. Once these burn to ash, it cannot be undone. While the rope and ribbon burn, you will each state your promise to each other, and to the gods who watch over your union."

The celebrant struck a match and held it to both ribbon and rope, then he bowed quickly and hobbled off the dais. He stood to the side and watched the soon-to-be married couple far too intensely for Isobel's liking. Or perhaps it was simply the celebrant she didn't like.

Jude spoke first, his voice calm and practiced. "I promise to teach you kindly, for Auronis, in exchange for you allowing me to learn too. Without judgement or ridicule. Teach me your ways, your customs, and preferences, so that we might share them."

Next, it was Clara's turn. Isobel didn't know if they'd rehearsed these verses ahead of time, or if they were standard among weddings in Morrin, but every word from Clara's lips felt like magic. If she closed her eyes, Isobel could almost pretend Clara was whispering them to her, and her alone.

"I promise to care for you and yours, for Herin, in exchange for good health of our own. I will share with you my practices, and of those who came before me, so we might heal our land and our kin together. So that we might grow old together, raising a new generation full of love, light, health, and harmony."

"I promise to admire you, for Tharia," Jude said, with a subtle wink. "In exchange for every peaceful sunset and glorious sunrise. I will appreciate your beauty, which is justly deserved, and be sure you never feel less than the goddess you embody so the artists are inspired by your smile and the musicians lured by your laugh."

"I promise to protect you, for Seone, in exchange for safe travels and returns. I will guard your sides when you cannot reach and watch your back when you cannot see, for that is true partnership. So you always feel safe, and you know trust with a fury so powerful it will not be tempered."

As soon as Clara finished speaking, the celebrant was in front of them again. He was truly getting on Isobel's nerves.

"May the gods take your offerings and return to you your exchanges. May your marriage be prosperous and full of love. May our kingdoms know serenity and connection, as you two have found within each other."

He bowed once more to Clara and Jude before he disappeared the way he came. The rope continued to burn, albeit incredibly slowly, and Clara did not seem interested in waiting. She had never been one for patience, or standing still. After a few long and silent moments, Isobel noticed Clara's knee jolt inside her dress, then she rolled her shoulders and stretched out her fingers.

Jude gave her an almost imperceptible nod, and suddenly the flickers of flame were larger and brighter, and both the rope and ribbon burned twice as fast. Cheers erupted as the last embers flickered out, but Isobel knew it wasn't a sign of the gods accepting their marriage as the folk might believe. It was Clara's growing impatience.

Isobel tried not to laugh and had to cover her slight chuckle with a cough.

"What's so funny?" Beau whispered as he joined in the applause for the newlywed couple.

"I'll tell you later—the ceremony is almost done. Keep clapping."

The king and queen both stood, applauding their son and new daughter-in-law. King Taron took Queen Sylvina's hand before they walked around the dais and stood beside Clara and Jude.

"Your binding is complete," the king said with a bright grin. "To conclude your wedding ceremony, you will each prick your finger and bleed into this goblet. Clarenna Hayes, Queen of Elanist. You will take the first sip, as your title holds seniority." He nodded towards Clara as he handed her the blade.

Her nose crinkled, but she did not argue, simply pricked her finger and squeezed her blood into the goblet.

The king then turned to the prince. "Now you, son, Jude Lorson, Crown Prince of Morrin."

Jude pricked his finger, bled into the cup, and then sucked his finger clean.

The queen shot him a look only a mother could summon, though Jude ignored her as he drank from the goblet. His father spoke again as Jude handed the cup to his bride. "And now we bid you all farewell, so the couple may enjoy their marital bliss and embark on their future together!"

CHAPTER THIRTY-EIGHT
CLARA

"Congratulations." Queen Sylvina's expression showed genuine joy.

"You make a beautiful bride indeed, Clara," King Taron added as he dipped his head slightly in acknowledgement.

"Thank you, Your Majesties." Clara dipped into a small curtsy, and the king smiled approvingly.

Queen Sylvina took in a slow breath and clasped her hands at her navel before she spoke again. "Now, we know where your hearts lie, and we do not expect an heir immediate—"

"No, we do not expect you to try right away," King Taron interjected with a not-so-subtle glance at his wife.

"Right." She didn't even attempt to hide the rolling of her eyes. "However, tradition requires that you spend the next twenty-four hours alone."

The prince only sighed, but Clara's nose and mouth scrunched of their own accord. Without being able to stop it, she looked away. Thankfully, neither royal commented on her reaction.

"Do remember," the queen continued, "four weeks from today, you will be crowned."

"Four weeks!" Jude shrieked. Clara's gaze flew to his unexpected outburst, finding his brows furrowed so closely they'd almost joined. His jaw hung open, though the muscles running along it and down his neck were tensed.

"It's not so bad, son. Having a kingdom to rule over."

"You say that now," Jude all but hissed, then turned to Clara. "But how will you feel when there are two kingdoms instead of only one?"

"Double trouble," Clara mumbled as she shrugged.

Surprisingly, now that the wedding was over, Kyra had been stopped, and everyone she cared about was alive and well, Clara was rather relaxed. Interested almost, in what the coming weeks would bring. Though not eager for the war she knew was still on the horizon, for the moment, she pushed all thoughts of that aside.

"Or twice the fun." The queen winked at Clara before again addressing both her and the prince. "It depends on your perspective. We will begin the arrangements shortly. Tonight, enjoy your peace and quiet." Then she linked arms with her husband and glided away.

The walk back to Jude's suite was not a long one, though the pair travelled in virtual silence. Their footsteps and breathing were the only noises, which was unsettling. Jude hadn't been so quiet the entire time Clara had known him. But now he seemed nervous or uncomfortable, and his demeanour was so unlike anything Clara had seen from him yet.

"Would you like to spend the night with Hunter?" Clara asked softly. "I'm happy to leave you—"

He cut her off with a wave of his hand and exhaled a heavy sigh. Jude shook his head. "The next twenty-four hours, we will be '*watched by the gods.*' We must spend it together so they may judge our union." He sounded thoroughly exhausted.

"Are you okay?" Clara pulled him gently to a stop.

"Of course," he answered, and plastered the falsest smile across his face. "I have a beautiful bride, and a wonderful companion to my throne. Why would I not be?"

"Because you do not love me the way a groom should love his bride," Clara said, stabbing entirely in the dark but sure she was close to the mark. It made sense for Jude to be hesitant. He did not want a bride, and his heart was pledged to another— of that, she was intimately aware. Clara tilted her head towards the prince, a hopeful smile on her face as she whispered, "I'm not offended."

"No?" His eyebrows raised, almost hopefully, as if he'd forgotten fae could not lie.

Clara's smile grew. "No," she repeated and shook her head slowly.

Jude moved so quickly he blurred, his arms wrapping around Clara's shoulders. Even on tiptoes, she did not reach a comfortable height to hug him back, but the prince bent down to meet her halfway. With firm hands and a slightly shaky rise and fall of his chest against hers, Jude's body released some of its tension. Their embrace was comforting, one full of vulnerability and fear, but also gratitude and hope.

Once they'd separated and reached the top of the stairs that led to their private quarters, Clara cleared her throat. The rest of their journey had been quiet, but of a much nicer kind.

"Can we send for something to eat?" she asked. "I haven't eaten since yesterday, and I am fucking famished."

Jude's laugh bounced off the walls. "I'm so hungry I could eat a small child, honestly."

As they arrived at Jude's suite, the prince pulled the guard aside to discuss their preferences for food, while Clara took a moment to stare longingly at her own door. She was so close she could almost smell Beau and Isobel, tucked in their room where she desperately wished she could be. Not that spending the night with Jude would be bad. She simply had her own preference, much like he did.

They entered the bedroom together to find Hunter tucked on the floor with his head between his knees. Beau knelt beside him with a hand on his shoulder, and Isobel was spread across the bed. Clara didn't miss how much larger it was than her own, nor how many butterflies erupted low in her core at seeing Isobel lying across it. She had one leg bent, her hand in her hair, and an incredibly smug look on her face.

"How did you get past the guards?" Jude asked, his eyes wide. Hunter's head shot up at the sound of Jude's voice, though he immediately winced and lowered it again. His face seemed a shade or two greener than the last time she'd seen him.

"Magic," Isobel sang, as she twirled her pendant between her thumb and forefinger.

Clara broke into a grin.

No wonder Hunter looked so ill—he'd been transported. Uncomfortable memories of the first time Clara had travelled using Isobel's pendant circled her mind. They were vivid enough that she almost felt the wave of nausea rise again in her throat.

Clara joined Isobel on the bed, and Beau took a seat at the end, close by. Jude walked straight to Hunter, ran a gentle hand over his face, then brought the sickly fae towards a nearby chaise lounge. He veiled his small chuckle quite poorly as Hunter climbed onto the seat beside the prince, curling close into Jude's side. Their food was soon delivered—which Clara collected through a slightly open door—and the group ate together.

"I noticed you sped up the rope burning, by the way," Isobel commented, before stuffing a whole potato in her mouth.

"I am not a patient female, and it was taking an awfully long time." She shrugged, then turned to Jude. "Hopefully, your parents missed it."

"I have never been so grateful to know a fire wielder," the prince replied between mouthfuls of his own.

"You don't strike me as the impatient type," Beau said casually, tipping his head towards Jude.

The prince finished his bite and dabbed at his mouth before he answered, despite not having made any mess. "I'm not," he said at last, his eyes flickering to Hunter before moving back to Beau. "But if I'm being truthful, I wasn't entirely comfortable with such a public wedding."

Hunter took Jude's hand and began tracing subtle lines over the prince's knuckles with his thumb. Clara couldn't help but smile.

"Surely you do not suffer from stage fright," Beau said with a scoff. He clearly did not know Jude's hesitations, and Clara couldn't blame him, though he frequently stuck his foot in his mouth. Clara had a sense that tonight would be no different.

"I do not."

"Then what—"

Clara pinched his shoulder and hissed, "Would you shut up! Leave the male be."

"She was not his preferred fae to stand beside and pledge himself to, you idiot," Isobel whispered to Beau, whose eyes immediately widened.

He clamped his mouth shut, cleared his throat, and looked away. After a quiet moment, Beau murmured to the females, "Should we leave them be?"

Clara shook her head. "No, Jude and I must spend the next twenty-four hours together. Something about solidifying the promises made to each other and being watched by the gods. I don't know, but we stay together."

"And if I wanted to fuck you in that scandalous wedding dress, where might I do that?"

"Wherever you like, Phoenix," Jude said casually with a wink. "I am not heartbroken to be married to Clara. In fact, I couldn't think of anyone else I would rather be my queen. I have alternative gender preferences, but that doesn't mean I don't enjoy a good show."

"As does she, if I remember correctly," Hunter added. It was perhaps one of the most playful things he'd said, at least in Clara's company. She liked this mischievous side of him, but all she could think to do in response was wink, to which Hunter waggled his brows.

"So is this what it's to be like from now on?" Isobel asked, her crystal-like eyes flittering between the others, her voice hesitant. "Group activities?"

"No, not at all. It doesn't have to be," Jude said calmly as he leant closer to Hunter. "I will require an heir at some point, but we have time. Tonight, I was merely suggesting we get to know one another a little more intimately."

Isobel nodded, though Clara couldn't gauge how comfortable she truly was with the idea. "We don't have to if you don't want to."

"No, I don't mind," Isobel said, her eyes earnest as they locked with Clara's. "Perhaps, however, we could ease into having so many penises out, and so many eyes on you? One at a time is manageable, but right now we females are outnumbered."

Laughter resounded from all, genuine and understanding. Clara only nodded and cupped Isobel's cheek before she leant in to kiss her. The taste of salted potatoes erupted on Clara's tongue first, but soon eased to the summer fruits she preferred. The taste of Isobel.

Beau's hands roamed Clara's body, soft at first but quickly growing firm. Starting at her feet and ankles, they then moved up her legs to explore her thighs. Next, her ass and hips, all the way to her breasts and throat. She could faintly hear his heavy breathing behind her, and oh, how it turned her on.

"Let us know when we're welcome to join in, won't you, Isobel?" Jude asked casually, though he sounded entirely distracted. When Clara turned towards Beau, she noticed why, as Hunter's hands now roamed his body, paying extra close attention to the bulge at his crotch.

Isobel murmured something agreeable from where her mouth was pressed against Clara's neck.

Clara hardly even registered the removal of her dress, her own hands wandering and mind focused elsewhere. It was only as Isobel guided Clara back down to the mattress that she realised she'd stood at all. Isobel knelt at the end of the bed, her hands reaching towards Clara's thighs. She splayed her fingers near Clara's hips, and with barely a touch, spread Clara's legs and pressed her face between them, inhaling the scent of Clara as if her life depended on it. Isobel moaned, then the warmth of her tongue glided upwards, starting at Clara's wet and desperate hole and sliding to her sensitive and begging clit. Clara sucked in a breath as her eyelids fluttered and neck arched. Isobel's tongue swirled in glorious patterns around Clara's clit, sending wave after wave of heat directly to her core. She exhaled sharply through her nose every time her tongue lowered, and the heat from her breath only ruined Clara further.

Beau palmed his crotch as he stood next to the bed by Clara's head, his gaze flitting between Clara's face and where Isobel's was buried. As soon as he undid his trousers, his erection sprang free. He gripped Clara's chin tightly, his stare demanding she open her mouth. Clara did so without hesitation, not only because she loved the sound of his gravelly, desperate voice when his cock was in her mouth, but because she wanted to taste him. She craved the noises he made, and they did torturous things to her mind and body.

As soon as Clara's tongue met his cock, Beau groaned beautifully and closed his eyes. Only for a second, though, then his grip on her face tightened and his eyes locked with hers. Clara struggled to maintain eye contact with him as Isobel licked and sucked on her clit, and as her tongue darted in and out of Clara's cunt. Such agonising bliss, especially when her teeth ever so gently grazed over Clara's sensitive skin.

Both Isobel and Beau gave Clara divine torment and near unbearable pleasure.

Unable to help herself, Clara darted her eyes towards the chaise where Jude and Hunter still sat. She could faintly hear their heavy breathing and subdued moans as their lips pressed together. It was as heated and wild a kiss as any she'd seen.

"I prefer it when her eyes are on me, but I'm afraid Clara enjoys watching others." Beau gritted through a tight jaw, though his gaze was on Isobel when Clara looked back at him.

Clara pulled off his cock, still pumping him firmly with her hand, as Isobel looked up at her. With a shrug, Clara stayed silent, though the corner of her mouth kicked up into a smirk.

Isobel circled her thumb slowly over Clara's clit as she turned to face the prince, who was currently too occupied to notice her. "How easy is it to remove semen from clothing, prince?"

"Not very," he replied, his lips only off Hunter's for a second. Then he murmured, "But there are worse stains."

"Perhaps you might consider your laundry staff and remove your clothes. Out of consideration, of course."

"I do like to be considerate."

Clara's core tightened further. Her excitement and anticipation built quickly, along with love and pride. Isobel had invited the prince and his lover to join them so freely and casually, and it warmed Clara to know she was comfortable. That she felt safe and secure. Not to mention how neither Jude nor Hunter rushed to rid themselves of their clothing, instead taking their time despite being given permission. There was so much acceptance and respect within their group, and Clara couldn't have been prouder of the family she'd created.

The prince and his lover undressed each other slowly, before Hunter lowered to his knees and took Jude's considerable length into his mouth. Jude moaned long and low, and flutters erupted in Clara's core. They soared lower and lower as Isobel toyed with her clit, her tongue warm and languid over Clara's sensitive skin.

She was so close to falling over the cliff of ecstasy, but Clara maintained her firm grip and steadily stroked Beau's cock. She was too close to take him back into her mouth, though he didn't complain. He continued to groan and growl, and as Isobel moaned over her pussy, Clara came undone. She spiralled and screamed, revelling in each wave of pleasure. Almost floating, Clara smiled in a daze and sighed contentedly before she rose to her elbows. She smirked at Isobel, who hadn't moved but was licking Clara's wetness from her fingers.

"My turn," Clara purred as she invited Isobel up onto the mattress.

"But how will you watch the prince and his lover if your face is between my legs?" Isobel asked with a soft chuckle.

"Fret not," Jude piped up. "We'll join you." His grin was wide, but he stilled until Isobel nodded. Only then did he and Jude take their places on the bed.

Isobel scooted towards the head of the bed and lowered onto her back, a pillow placed underneath her hips to prop her up. Clara raked her eyes over Isobel as she knelt, then lowered face first to her beautiful cunt, her own ass up and presented to Beau. He wandered behind and cursed as the mattress dipped at her right foot, no doubt from him resting his knee there for stability. Then his fingers dug into Clara's hips, and she moaned over Isobel's pussy, her tether moaning in kind. Clara paused as Beau entered her, despite him doing so slowly. His warning to

Isobel the last time they shared such an intimate moment was still valid. Her jaw opened briefly, then Clara bit down on her lip so hard she felt blood bead.

Beau entered her slowly, but he quickly built in speed and intensity. After only a few strokes, he was slamming into her so hard she swore she could feel him in her throat. It was the most pleasurable kind of pain.

Hunter lay beside Clara and Isobel, while Jude held the backs of his lover's knees and pressed them into his chest. The prince smirked as he spat onto Hunter's asshole before gliding his shaft inside. Hunter's eyes rolled as he groaned, his hands curling into fists in the sheets.

Isobel's hips rode against Clara's face, and she couldn't help but smile. Fuck, she could do this all stars-damned day. Such intimacy in its rawest form, shared by those she trusted and loved. Not to mention how insanely arousing it was to be surrounded by folk pleasuring and being pleasured. It was intoxicating.

Clara slid two fingers inside Isobel, curled them, and stroked her inner walls. She roiled and bucked, her sounds of pleasure intensifying. They grew louder, as did the grunts and curses coming from Beau. So, too, did Hunter's moans, and Jude's ragged breathing.

Then Isobel gasped sharply, cried out Clara's name, and unravelled on her tongue. Clara grinned again at the absolute divinity.

"Fuck, Clara," Beau groaned out, still thrusting into her. "You tighten every time he moans. *Fuck—*"

Hunter howled as he found completion. Cum shot from him, splattering over his bare abdomen, and Clara couldn't help but mewl as she watched. Jude swore, his pace quickening and his movements becoming jerky. Beau grabbed Clara's braid and yanked her head backwards, murmuring his approval. He tilted her head so she could watch Jude follow his partner over the edge. Jude grunted as he slammed into Hunter a few more times before he stilled. Then the prince winked at Clara while he caught his breath.

"Your turn," Isobel purred, now sitting and trailing her fingers over Clara's collarbone. She reached forward to cup Clara's breasts, then a cold, rogue wind flew directly towards her clit. Clara gasped again, and Beau swore. His movements grew rapid, while his fingers dug so forcefully into her thighs, she thought they might bruise. The fist he had tightened around her hair loosened, though only so his hand could snake around to her throat.

"I can't hold out much longer," he whispered huskily beside her ear. "Come, sweetheart."

And she did. Clara fell headfirst and dizzyingly fast into her climax. It was so strong her fingers tingled, and heat soared through her body. Beau followed her after only a handful of erratic movements, growling as he spilled into her.

They both breathed heavily while Isobel continued massaging her breasts and Hunter wiped himself off with a towel. The room smelt of sex and sweat, and Clara imagined it would continue to do so for quite some time.

CHAPTER THIRTY-NINE
EVELINE

Eveline hustled towards Jude's suite again, and this time her nerves were near unbearable. Her hands shook so much she had to clamp them together, knuckles white and fingertips aching. She'd come the day before as well, but the guard stationed outside his door was quick to deny her entry.

Truthfully, he'd been brazenly rude, and Eveline had been close to reprimanding him. She quickly remembered that while she was a queen, she was no one here in Morrin. Hopefully, she'd grow used to being insignificant.

The guard informed her that the prince and princess were to receive no visitors for twenty-four hours. The title of princess felt strange when referring to Clara, considering Clara was, in fact, a queen. Eveline did not know if that was public knowledge. Obviously, the king had not been aware, or maybe Clara had intended to announce it in such a way. Regardless, there were several gasps and shocked expressions on the guests' faces at the ceremony. No doubt even more so when it was broadcast Morrin-wide. Evian certainly hadn't known, though his mother did not seem as shocked.

After she'd been turned away, Eveline wandered the palace, noticing how different it was from her own. How lively and colourful and personal, instead of sterile and cold and distant. It made her homesick, being in such an unfamiliar environment, with only a handful of folk she knew. It made her vulnerable, especially with the threats as of late.

But more than that, she was hopeful for all the colour and enrichment she might get to see the more she strayed from home. A strong sense of wanderlust indeed.

As she approached the prince's door again, she found the entryway void of any guards. Her heart skipped a beat. A repeat might've just sent her over the edge. She knocked—three precise raps—then stepped back and waited.

Clara answered the door, wearing a feral smile and wild, untamed hair. Cosmetics were smeared across her nose and jaw. As she stepped into the hall, she secured the waist tie of a dull-brown trench coat that almost reached her ankles.

"Am I interrupting?" Eveline asked with a smirk.

"Not at all," Clara answered, mirroring her expression. "We've just stopped for snacks."

So that must've been where the guard had gone. Either way, it worked to Eveline's advantage.

"And the coat?"

"It's so that you don't have to stare at my naked body while we discuss whatever is important enough that you've come past twice in as many days. It was the first thing I grabbed." Clara gave her a pointed look. One that said she knew more than Eveline gave her credit for. Eveline sighed before she spoke.

"I do not know how to beat around the bush, so let me be frank. I've discovered who I believe to be responsible for the attacks, though I have not unmasked her yet. The Lady of Summer. Ryn told me she would pass that information on. But more importantly, I would like to gift you my throne.”

Clara’s jaw dropped, and she blinked twice slowly before her head tilted to the side. “Excuse you?”

“You heard me perfectly well, Clara. I don’t want it. I don’t want the kingdom or the crown. I am tired and so very done. My continent needs someone trustworthy to rule it. Someone fair and powerful.”

Oh, how wonderful it finally felt to say those words aloud. Eveline could suddenly breathe more easily, as if the words had blocked her lungs, and now that she’d finally spilled them the air could flow freely. Even her shoulders relaxed, and the tension in her spine lessened.

She still had to wait for a response, after all.

“Are you complimenting me sincerely, Eveline, or are you kissing my ass?” Clara asked, confusion knitting her brows.

“At this point, Clara, I’m begging. Please.”

“This is a much bigger discussion than I can have with you in a trench coat and without my husband.”

“I understand,” Eveline said quickly. “And I’m sure there would be a transition period in which I would be required to remain on the grounds and in a leadership position. I am fully prepared to do so—”

“How much thought have you put into this?” Clara chuckled after she cut Eveline off.

“Truthfully, not much.” Eveline shrugged a shoulder and looked away. “I had been contemplating it loosely until I watched you marry Jude. That night I scoured every inch of his library for something that proved this was possible.”

“We would need to have a proper meeting with him and his parents before any decision was made.”

“I understand,” she repeated, more slowly this time.

"Do not get your hopes up, Eveline. I cannot guarantee anything."

"I understand," she said for the third time and bowed with a small, far-too-hopeful smile.

Excitement at finally being rid of her burden, of all the expectations piled onto her too young, built rapidly. Regardless of what Clara said, for the first time in a very long time, Eveline hoped.

She dipped her chin in acknowledgement of her fellow queen and made to turn away. Eveline was only a handful of paces down the hall when Clara called out.

"Oh, also . . ." Eveline turned to find Clara halfway behind her door already, wearing another wicked smile. This one was far deadlier than the last. "The Lady of Summer won't be bothering you anymore."

"No?" Eveline asked, her brows knitted.

"She's dead," Clara chirped with a shrug.

Eveline's brows rose to her hairline as she pointed towards Clara in a silent question.

Clara waggled her brows and maintained her devilish grin.

Eveline couldn't help but let a small grin of her own loose. "Why am I not surprised?"

The females shared a chuckle before Clara waved and disappeared behind the bedroom door.

Eveline did her best but couldn't control the bounce in her step as she hurried to find Evian. Perhaps they might not have to wait all that long to accept their bond after all.

CHAPTER FORTY
BEAU

Beau stirred from sleep to find soft fingers trailing along his chest. Then harder fingernails dragged down his abdomen. Slowly, he opened his eyes, though they were still heavy with sleep.

Fiery red hair and mischievous green eyes stared down at him. Beau grinned lazily and let his eyes close. When he opened them again, Clara's hands were no longer wandering his torso; instead, her mouth was already wrapped around his dick.

"I told you that one day you'd wake up with your cock in my mouth," she murmured, kissing his tip and stroking his shaft.

Fuck, what a way to wake up.

Truthfully, he'd never expected it to happen. Dreamt of it, sure. He even believed Clara was as keen as she said. But logistically, sharing a room with a third party made mornings like this difficult.

"Where's Isobel?" he asked, his voice husky.

"With Era," Clara said cheerily, before she ran her tongue torturously slow up and down his length.

"Thank the fucking stars," Beau growled, propping up on one elbow and reaching to cup Clara's cheek with his free hand. "There is absolutely no part of me that wants to share you right now."

Clara smirked before she took his cock into her mouth again, pressing her tongue along the underside as she bobbed. *Fuck.*

She rose, sucking hard until she reached the tip, then let go. Her tongue swirled around him, teasing every part of his throbbing erection. With each flick of her tongue, her hand spun, rotating around him as she pumped. This fucking woman, she was an absolute gift from the gods. From the stars. Or from whomever or whatever was looking over the universe and in charge of all good things.

"Fuck yes, sweetheart," Beau drawled, his hand moving to the back of her neck, his fingers splayed over her head. He pushed her lower, further onto him until she gagged. As she came back up, she moaned onto his cock. Beau couldn't help the growled curse that flew from his lips.

Oh, how he loved filling her pretty little mouth with his dick. Loved hearing her gag and cry and scream over him. She'd done it plenty of times in the last few days. After their twenty-four hours were up, Clara and the prince separated to their own suites, but Clara kept fucking Isobel and Beau. From what he could tell, so did Hunter and Jude.

If he could, Beau would fuck Clara senseless for the rest of his existence. He was not one to dream, nor did he remember anything from the night past, but a bad feeling crept up his spine and stung at the back of his eyes. It told him that the rest of his existence was not to be long at all. So today, he would fuck her hard, exactly the way he knew she craved.

"Lie down," he demanded.

She toyed with him only a moment longer before releasing her vice grip around his cock and obeying.

Beau climbed over her immediately and lifted one of her legs to rest on his shoulder.

Clara grinned at him eagerly, then spat onto her hand and rubbed it over her cunt. A sweet pussy he fully intended to ruin. She slid her fingers from her hole to her clit so fucking slowly it drove Beau mad.

He so desperately wanted to fill her, but watching her was so erotic all he could do was lean back for a moment and stare. Then he realised she was teasing him.

Beau clicked his tongue as he leant over Clara, as he grabbed her jaw between his fingers and squeezed. She gasped, her mouth dropping open wide enough for Beau to spit into—and he did. Desire swirled in her vibrant-green irises as she maintained eye contact with him the whole time.

"I'm going to fuck you now, sweetheart." Beau lowered his hand, sliding it under her jaw, his thumb pressed just firmly enough to restrict her airflow.

She took another soft breath in as her eyes widened, then gave the quietest moan as she breathed out.

"And you're going to let me."

Clara's slight smirk and desperate eyes told him everything he needed to know.

Beau didn't have the willpower to go slow, not with how impatient he was to fill her tight cunt. He slammed into her, revelling in the scream he tore from her. Over and over, Beau filled her hard and fast. Her cries were music to his ears. The scratches she left along his forearms sent tingles to every part of his body, even along the muscles of his wings.

As he groaned, Clara's eyes fluttered closed, but not from lack of oxygen. He wasn't squeezing hard enough for that, but still she disobeyed his standing orders–she knew he wanted her eyes on his. His hand met her face, the slap echoing in their empty room.

Clara gasped, her fair skin already turning rosy.

And then she smiled, a divine expression bordering on the brink of insanity. Stars, he fucking loved her. She grabbed his wrist, forcing his free hand to wrap around her throat as well. His cock twitched inside her, and her pussy walls tightened in response. Fuck, he would not last long if she kept looking at him like that and clenching around his length.

Beau maintained his speed and rhythm until Clara's nails drew blood. Then he slowed. It was only a fraction, but still enough to elicit her whine. He chuckled deep and low.

"I'm so close, Beau," Clara whimpered. "Please . . ."

How could he say no?

Clara reached between her legs as Beau picked up the pace once more, sending himself as close to completion as she claimed to be. For a moment, he watched her. Watched her fingers circle her clit, slide between her lips, and then graze his cock as he pumped in and out of her tight little pussy.

"*Fuck,*" he growled, unable to look away. "Keep rubbing yourself, you pretty little slut, and I'm going to fucking explode."

"Please, sir," Clara begged.

Beau erupted. He swore as his hands tightened around Clara's neck, and he spilled into her twitching cunt.

"Fuck, Beau!" she screamed, a few tears sliding free from her shuttered eyes.

He looked up at her face for only a second before her spasming cunt pulled his attention away.

Clara came hard, her back arching and legs straightening. Her nails dug into his forearms, forming gashes in his skin. "Fuck," Clara breathed out, a giddy expression covering her face.

She grinned at Beau so easily, he thanked every fucking star in the sky he got to look at such a beautiful, heavenly face. Much less got to fuck her like *that*.

Beau excused himself to run the bath. It was a generously sized porcelain tub, though if they both sat in it together, his wings would be cramped. The walls were too high for him to sit comfortably and have his wings hang over the sides, but it was a price he would pay so he might steal a few more intimate moments with her before Isobel came back. They'd have forever together, but Beau's forever would soon expire.

Once he'd gathered what he hoped were the right products and sprinkled whatever smelling salts Clara had left beside the sink, Beau called for her to join him. She did so lazily, simply strolling through the doorway and sinking into the water.

"How charming of you," she murmured as Beau slipped in as well.

"I try," he whispered against the velvet skin at her collarbone, sweeping her hair to the side.

She hummed in response and leant her head further to the side, granting him better access to her neck.

"That chain of yours is freezing." Clara turned slightly, reaching up to take the small black ring between her fingers, and inspected it closely.

Beau did not miss the emerald stone on her finger.

"Green suits you." He nodded towards the ring, and a small grin tugged at her lips.

"Gold, however, does not mix so well with silver." Clara dropped his necklace, the token Isobel had shared with him before Clara's wedding. He hadn't taken it off since she'd placed it around his neck.

Clara held up her hand to inspect her ring, along with Neven's, which she wore on her thumb.

He smiled softly, took Clara's hand, and brought it to his lips before reaching for a comb he'd left beside the tub.

As he began the process of ridding Clara's wild hair of tangles, he murmured, "I love you, Clara. With my whole heart."

Still inspecting her jewellery, Clara didn't respond straight away. Then she replied, "The bride and groom share three rings on their wedding day in Elanist. The first to symbolise the beginning of their love, the second to symbolise their devotion to one another and the wedding itself. Then the third represents their everlasting love and faith in each other. Past, present, and future. They don't do that in Morrin, and though I will only have one wedding, I like that I have honoured it a little with this ring. It's a nice blend of mine and yours. What was it you said? Something made, something born." She rotated her head, and Beau paused combing as their eyes locked. "I love you, Beau. With my whole heart."

With only the stars and a half-moon illuminating the trio as they lay in bed, Beau smiled sadly to himself. Isobel and Clara were already asleep, but Beau's mind raced. After the intoxicating morning he'd shared with Clara, and the intimate bath where they mostly sat in silence, they'd wandered the palace hand in hand. It was such a small gesture, he hadn't realised he'd missed it so badly until her fingers locked with his again. He remembered the way her cackling had filled the entire kitchen as he spilled eggs and milk down his front, and how it had somehow grown louder when he undressed and could only find a dusty, threadbare apron to wear. Her laughter made the embarrassment of wandering back through the castle damn near naked entirely worth it. There was a spark of joy and mischief in her eyes every time she pinched his ass.

Beau knew his time was running out. All he'd wanted was to spend as much quality time with Clara as he could before he died. She slept cuddled to him, with her face snuggled into his chest, one hand reaching behind her to hold on to Isobel. A rush of pride bloomed in his chest at being hers, at knowing that somehow, he'd done something worthy of keeping her. But guilt ate at the corners of that feeling, and at him, for knowing he was going to leave. At actively waiting for Death to take him.

Tonight, though, he didn't care for Death. If this was his last night with Clara, all his thoughts were reserved for her.

CHAPTER FORTY-ONE

CLARA

The bitter air burst through the open palace doors, and a foreign wind circled Clara. It caused goosebumps to erupt all over her body where it warred with the fire in her blood. Armed fae poured from every direction, storming outside. They blurred with the staff scrambling to get back into the palace.

Clara took Beau and Isobel by the hand and pulled them hastily towards a nearby cupboard. It was filled with random supplies used to clean the palace. It was exactly what she needed—somewhere closed, nondescript, and easily ignorable. Clara flicked her wrist, and the candle braced against the wall inside the door came alight.

Beau smirked seductively, and Clara's heart lurched into her throat. "A quickie before battle?" he said with a wink.

"I love you both so much. I need you to know that."

"Of course." His expression was no longer playful, but now serious, as he should be.

Clara continued, "And I would do anything to ensure your safety. Absolutely anything."

"We know," Isobel said, taking a half step closer to Clara.

"Clara . . ." The way Beau whispered her name, almost a plea and full of distress, made the lump in her throat she'd thought was her heart turn to stone. It was lodged so hard she could barely breathe, let alone say everything she wanted to.

She kissed Beau, her words unable to form, and then Isobel, the taste of them both so different. One was citrusy and tart, rough and rich, while the other was warm and sweet, gentle and soft.

With tears filling her eyes, Clara let go of their hands and stepped away. She couldn't look at their faces, knowing at any moment they would protest. But she had no choice, not if she was going to keep them safe and alive.

Clara slipped out the door and locked it quickly behind her.

Their screams and shouts from the other side started immediately. The door rattled as they banged against it, kicked and pounded. As she walked away, she did her best to ignore their wild and frantic pleas, reminding herself that her actions were to ensure they lived to see the day through and could watch tomorrow's sunrise.

Doing her best to calm herself, Clara returned to the main entrance of the Winter Palace. She took a deep breath, vaguely noticing others now stood by her. When they'd fallen into step, she didn't know—she had not been paying attention.

The cold threatened to freeze her lungs and render her lips useless as she entered the castle bailey. The Winter Court was always cold, in its eternal state of frost and snowflakes, though never to this extent. Almost as if terror flew in on the unnatural wind.

The weather did not stop the fae soldiers, however, as they spread throughout the large open space. Statues and fountains and other pretty but impractical items filled the outermost court of the castle, though today they made mediocre cover. The soldiers did not know who—or what—they were facing, and yet they readied as best they could. Their armour reflected the moonlight, and uniforms camouflaged with the shadows granted by the midnight sky. Some were outfitted with breast and shoulder plates, shields or spiked helms. Maces and swords clanged as soldiers moved, the sounds echoing within the stone walls.

A small collection of snow along the ground, still fresh and soft, was trampled underfoot as soldiers rode on horseback, lining near the forward perimeter and scanning beyond the gates. Hot air flew from the animals' nostrils in small puffs outlined by the moonlight, their whinnies as discontented as Clara's soul. Soldiers hid among the fruit trees and on the battlement walls, bows at the ready, using height to their advantage.

Silence reigned.

No warnings or words of advice. No encouragement.

She could barely even hear the wind, though its icy chill was as silent as it was deadly. It carried something terrible tonight, and this time it was not only Clara who could feel its foreboding nature.

She didn't know whether she preferred the silence or hated how it left space for fear and the thousands of what-ifs to fester. Clara stared up at the sky, which promised bloodshed soon enough, and admired the few stars she could see. It wasn't the time for stargazing, but truthfully, she wasn't sure if she'd be around for tomorrow night's display.

Suddenly three horns blared in the distance, one after another.

The sound pulled at Clara, and as far as she could see, crows shot into the sky. They circled above the castle like a tornado of black-feathered bad omens. They blurred and morphed into a depthless grey cloud of smoke, floating closer and closer to the ground. As it settled in the middle of the bailey, among them all, the smoke transformed again.

A horde of bone soldiers now stood snarling at the fae soldiers around them.

Then they attacked.

At first, their movements were jerky, as if they'd only just been pulled from their graves. But they quickly remembered how to swing the tarnished clubs and swords gripped in their bony hands. How to duck or block the incoming hits, as the fae soldiers attacked. Though they were not alive, they moved too fast for the dead.

Clara's breathing quickened, and panic set in as the first of her soldiers stumbled—and worse, fell.

Jude appeared beside her, and her guard sprang into action, shielding her from battle. "Where are Beau and Isobel?"

"Safe. Would you like to join them?"

"I will not leave you here to fend for yourself, wife." Jude's hazel eyes bored into Clara's.

She nodded once, unsure, before she turned her attention upwards to where a new cloud formed.

This one swirled like oil—slimy and iridescent under the moon. The smell of death and decay coming from the bone soldiers was heightened, and some of the fae gagged. It sloshed and whirled until three figures emerged. Thick and oozing liquid pooled at their feet, and though the slime spilled over, none fell to the battle below, and the figures did not dry in the raging wind.

Death's Daughters had arrived.

The deities, the sisters, or whatever Clara ought to call them.

War was here.

The females' hair stuck to their faces and was pasted over their gaunt shoulders. They peered out over the rapidly increasing carnage, remaining unnervingly still and imposing. Moonlight reflected silver and blue on their wet skin, rebounding off their bony frames.

"Where is the Phoenix?" the female with the tattoo over her chin finally called out.

She was the youngest sister. Clara didn't know how she knew, but she was certain she was not wrong.

"Not here!" Clara shouted back, her teeth bared.

"Then we will take you instead," another sister replied. This one wielded a sword and had a tattoo over her forearm—the middle sister.

"I think the fuck not." Oren and Aleska spoke in unison.

Though her guard had spread out, the twins stayed close to Clara. Their grunts echoed each other, their movements in sync. As she watched, the twins took down another three bone soldiers together, the once again useless skeletons crumpling into the snow.

In her periphery, Clara noticed the archers coming down from the trees and battlements, their bowed weapons futile against soldiers made entirely of bones. Soldiers had raced to the armoury to gather additional weapons to ensure their brothers and sisters in arms were not totally defenceless, then together they began a brute-force attack on the skeletal army. Bones crushed and flew from sockets. Some feet, some abdomens, some arms. Fae blood spilled just as quickly, and soon there was more bloodshed than bones broken.

Clara looked up from the carnage, to where the sisters remained safe in their cloud of superiority, cloaked in a promise of death, to find the eldest with her palm open and arm outstretched. She watched in dismay as the fallen bone soldiers rose again.

"Come now!" Clara shouted as she threw a shield of air around a fae soldier who stood too close to a rising skeleton. The shield formed with only a second to spare before a club reverberated so hard Clara stumbled. "I thought we might discuss this, you know, like civilised folk!"

"We are not folk, Clarenna Hayes. We are gods, and you will bow accordingly!"

"That's a shame," she replied as she pulled a dagger from its sheath at her waist. "I don't believe in gods."

A skeletal soldier raced towards her, but Clara saw it coming. Though a blade was not the best weapon against a skeleton, it was not entirely useless. Clara swung and decapitated it cleanly, its skull falling with a thump at her feet. Its body twitched, but it did not stand. Clara burned the remains anyway, so the sisters could not raise it again. Ash would not rise; it could not fight against her.

The bone soldiers advanced. They weren't multiplying, but their numbers didn't seem to dwindle either. Clara supposed it was a cruel benefit Death's Daughters had—they simply started again. They kept raising their army and murdering the fae. Their horde was limitless.

The sisters floated above in a chariot of rotten clouds and did nothing.

Torrents of violent rage swirled inside Clara. It filled her body to the brim, heating her from the inside, so much that she was sweating. These so-called gods came all this way, and for what—to sit there and watch?

With a guttural shriek, Clara threw her blade into the skull of a bone soldier. Partly to kill it, but the larger part to let go of some of the burning fury raging inside her. Thankfully, it was a successful strike, and the bone soldier stumbled. Clara followed up with her flames and moved on.

Clara watched on helplessly as more fae soldiers lined the ground than bones, frozen in place while a blonde Resmigian female was decapitated. Then another female with bold brown eyes was stabbed with her own blade. Three other Resmigian fae fell, then a Vequil. Too many bodies without heartbeats. All in the space of a single moment.

"We need a higher vantage point," Finch called as he ran back to Clara. "Somewhere we can assess who and what is coming. Somewhere our soldiers can make a stand."

Reid took Clara's hand silently, pulling her behind the line of soldiers and up the staircase towards the palace. She hadn't noticed the small fae approach, hadn't seen them among the chaos.

After a few steps, she heard Aleska shout out her name over the noise of the battlefield. Clara spun just in time to notice the bone soldier Aleska warned her about racing after them. With a thought, Clara incinerated the soldier. As Clara's gaze turned back to Aleska, she saw her jaw slacken.

A sword pierced through Aleska's neck. Blood splattered forwards, saturating her clothes and spilling forcefully from her mouth. Her eyes widened for a second and then the light left them. She fell limp. Doused in crimson, sword jutting from her neck.

Clara's heart froze. She didn't have the courage to look for Oren.

Another friend gone.

The bone creatures tore down fae effortlessly, somehow now moving in a blur.

Clara tried to process what she'd seen—who she had lost. Air and water fae dropped like flies, the Resmigian following quickly behind. Their corpses lay in bloody piles, and with every heart that stopped beating, more and more blood stained Clara's hands.

"Clara," Reid said urgently, pointing towards the outer castle gates. "Is that Darius? I thought he'd left?"

"He is not supposed to be here," Clara hissed back. "*Shit!*"

They were so focused on the young fae they did not notice the bone soldier that had slipped through their defences, nor the blade it embedded in Reid's side.

Clara shrieked with rage. Reaching forward, she pulled off its skull with her hands, fuelling her strength with nothing more than fury and determination. Her eyes were no longer on Darius but on Reid, who was quickly bleeding out.

"No . . ." Clara whispered, her tears landing on Reid's cheek. "I'm so sorry—I wasn't watching . . ."

But Reid only smiled, blood already staining their teeth. "It's okay," they whispered, croaky and wet. "I can finally be with my tether again. I miss him so much." Tears spilled from Reid's eyes as they closed, and their chest fell for the last time.

Another death on Clara's hands. Except Clara wore this blood on her skin and felt their final breath with her own palm. She could hardly breathe. Her heartbeat swelled in her ears, murderous and loud. Rapid and wild.

Clara sprinted into the midst of the soldiers, joining them in their battle for life and death. She pulled bones from the undead, taking up a weapon from a lifeless fae at her feet. The sword was heavy, but still she raced forwards, furiously removing the heads of her foes. She turned their skulls into nothing more than embers and ashes.

Soon she was by Darius' side, where he stood by the battlements, eyes darting across the bloody scene. Brontë would sever Clara's head if she knew her brother was here.

"I want to help," he insisted.

"Darius, you're a child," Clara cried as she fended off another bone soldier, taking out its legs before she removed its skull. Whether the skull had to be removed, Clara didn't know. But she saw a solution and would not question it now.

"Let me help!"

"No," Clara said firmly, much to the boy's disapproval. "Leave now, please."

Clara scanned the battlefield, searching for a safe exit for Darius, but what she saw made her heart seize.

Beau and Isobel had escaped their supply cupboard and stood silhouetted in the palace doorway, above the chaos.

Her mind raced so fast the ground spun beneath her feet as she watched them both sprint down the front steps and into the bailey. Clara screamed and willed them to go back, but still they came. Time seemed to warp. Everything moved differently, in a blur, somehow in slow motion and rapid succession all at once.

Beau's brilliant-amber eyes found hers, but he glanced away towards the deities floating above. He nodded in their direction, almost imperceptibly as she took a step towards him, but her legs were heavy. Every attempt was sluggish. She was barely able to lift her foot from the snow-covered grass.

She watched on, powerless, as a bone soldier severed Beau's wings.

His face and shoulders scrunched, but he made no sound. No cry or plea. He did not fight them off or protect himself.

Then they took his head, and Clara fell to her knees, gasping for breath.

Isobel screamed beside him, his blood splattered across her fair skin. Her eyes landed on Clara's, but Clara couldn't look away from the male who'd stolen her heart and healed it, only to tear it away again. Though she knew the female who completed her soul should not stay where she was. She had to move, or else she would be next.

Darius called her name from behind, but by the time she turned, he was already slumped on the ground. Blood pooled beneath him. The snow absorbed the offering quickly, as though its life depended on his blood as sustenance.

Clara hadn't been paying attention. She'd been focused on Beau, and now he and Darius were both dead.

This wasn't how it was supposed to go. Clara couldn't focus; she couldn't think.

She just froze.

The sister with the tattooed chin—the youngest—moved forward, waiting for something. Though Clara didn't know what.

Isobel screamed again as her body contorted and spasmed.

"No . . ." Clara whispered. Her throat burned, and tears filled her eyes, so she could no longer see. She knew what was about to happen but could do nothing to stop it. Her body would not respond.

One skeletal soldier stood on either side and raised their swords, then drove them straight through her torso. Their points bloodied and dripping, breached her other side.

Everyone was dying—or already dead.

Then, in a single moment, Clara's world shattered— Isobel died.

It was the exact moment all the pain stopped. Clara had felt everything—the adrenaline of battle, the fear as she watched Beau's head roll from his body, the piercing of the swords through Isobel's body—all so vividly.

And then it stopped. Her mind was deathly quiet, her body so violently still.

Isobel was dead.

Clara watched the light leave her eyes. Eyes that remained locked on Clara. The only light glinting off her now was the sun that caught on her pendant.

In the distance, Clara heard someone scream, "Shield! Now!"

But Clara paid him no mind. She had no emotions left, no feelings at all. Not a single care for anyone still breathing on the battlefield. Nothing.

So she pulled all her power—every raw and rattling inch of it, every soft caress, and every brutally violent flicker. She screamed and let it tear through her as it gathered, uncaring of the aftermath.

Clara was done.

And once she had collected it all, she exploded.

CHAPTER FORTY-TWO

CLARA

Clara jolted awake. Blood dripped from her nose down to her mouth and onto her pillow. Her throat was scratched raw, sore from screaming.

Beau and Isobel both loomed over her, fear etched into their faces.

Taking a deep, painful breath, she pulled them both into a tight embrace. Hysterical sobs bubbled in her chest, but she silenced them before they could escape her mouth.

It felt so real.

Yet already her nightmare slipped away.

Clouds of smoke.

Screams and blood.

The ominous silence and the lack of beating hearts.

And the memory of Isobel's pendant glinting in the early morning sunlight was all that remained.

Along with a deep, visceral feeling she couldn't quite name.

"What did you see?" Beau asked as he pulled away to inspect Clara's face.

She couldn't explain how, but Clara was certain he already knew what she'd seen. There was a fear in his eyes that wasn't for Clara's safety, or sanity, or wellbeing. It was the fear of his secret being discovered.

She shook her head. No answer she gave would ease their worry, and she couldn't recall much anyway. All she knew for certain was she needed to get her hands on Isobel's pendant.

A furious pounding on their door took their attention. Isobel gasped and turned towards the door. Clara quickly jumped out of the bed, her ears ringing slightly from how fast she'd moved. The banging did not let up until Clara swung the door open to reveal Mikhail breathing heavily, his eyes frantic. He briefly questioned the blood staining Clara's upper lip, but she ignored his query and asked one of her own.

"What is it?"

"They're coming," he said urgently. "The birds are tense. They can feel it."

Death's Daughters.

Another flash of Clara's vision hit her. This time of the trio of deities as they stood upon their dark cloud. Each marked with a tattoo—one above her brow, one along her forearm, and one over her chin.

"How much time do we have?" Clara asked.

"A day, maybe? I don't know, but not long."

Clara nodded, her mind racing. "Take Seren home. If on your way to her you see my brothers, mother, or Queen Eveline, send them straight to me. But you and Seren are to leave immediately, do you understand?"

Mikhail nodded and ran back down the hall. Clara turned to Isobel and Beau, hands on her hips and a flighty feeling soaring through her gut.

"Alert my guard, then my husband," she said to Beau. Then she turned to Isobel. "Take Era back to the Golden Palace. If her body is ready to be moved, take Tindal as well. You may stay in Elanist." Though her last comment was quieter than the rest, Isobel heard her clearly.

"Excuse you?" she all but snarled.

"I won't force you," Clara said quickly, moving to place her hands on Isobel's cheeks. "But please hear me when I say I would be far less afraid if you two were far, far away from here when battle strikes."

"Fear is an excellent motivator, sweetheart." Beau's voice was far too nonchalant considering the news they'd been given. He winked, slipping into trousers.

Clara narrowed her eyes and flung a pointed finger in his direction. "You are not helping."

Isobel's face softened a fraction before she kissed Clara firmly and dressed in silence.

A moment after she left, Beau grabbed Clara's wrist and pulled her into an emotional kiss. It felt rushed and fearful, but so full of love Clara's heart hurt. Tears filled his eyes as he pulled away. "I love you, Clara."

Clara cupped his cheek, nodded softly, and whispered, "I love you, too, with all my heart."

As he jogged out the door, his back turned to her, Clara had a terrible feeling it might be one of the last times she got to see him. She did her best to push that thought to the back of her mind, but it persisted. Every step in the opposite direction felt like she was drowning, and this time, he wouldn't be able to pull her out.

She found Ryland first, who was in the process of dressing Christopher for the day. Clara chuckled quietly at the boy's adamant refusal to wear socks under his shoes. She was pleased that even amidst the chaos already spreading, something so normal was taking place. She snuck up close to Christopher before crouching in front of him and guiltlessly bribing him to put his socks on.

"How would you like to go on an adventure?" she asked, her face in as wide a smile as she could produce.

His own face lit up so quickly, and then he was gone—racing to find his socks.

While he was distracted, Clara gave Ryland his instructions: find Brontë and bring her to Clara, then gather the other Inalises.

Clara told Christopher about Brontë briefly, explaining that he would travel to a new home. A new, exciting home she couldn't wait to hear all about one day. Brontë entered the room quietly as Clara tied Christopher's laces.

Ryland left quickly, off to find the other Inalises as Clara had requested.

"Brontë might seem a little grumpy, but she probably just hasn't had enough sleep." Clara squeezed the boy's shoulder before pulling him close to her chest. "She'll take care of you, I promise."

"Will I see you again soon?"

His eyes were so filled with hope, it was all Clara could do not to let her voice crack as she answered. To not show the tears she felt welling behind her eyes.

"I hope so, little prince."

Christopher beamed at the nickname, and Clara's face melted into a smile. She watched as he took Brontë's hand, and the volatile fae softened and welcomed the boy into her space. Brontë offered him a biscuit and took the time to introduce herself, the fae she was to travel with, and where they were going. That their home might not feel like home straight away, but that she promised to always take care of him and keep him safe.

Promised that she would do whatever she could to make sure he was happy.

Christopher waved at Clara with a genuinely excited grin, then he took Brontë's hand, and she led him away. She nodded to Clara, and Clara mouthed her appreciation back. For this role at least, Clara trusted Brontë. Trusted her nephew would be okay, and far, far away when the carnage unfolded.

Suddenly very alone, Clara made her way to the docks, where Evian, Jacob, their mother, and the Queen of Tirenas were waiting, bags at their feet. A sailor began to unwind the rope securing a boat to the pier, and their mother's eyes grew frantic, her lips pursed and fingers wringing.

"Clara Renee, you tell me what's going on this instant!" Felicity demanded, fear present in her voice.

"You and Jacob are going home, Mother. Evian and the queen will travel with you. You're all going to be safe." Clara hoped that if she spoke calmly and matter-of-factly, if she hid the quiver in her own voice, or the deep need she felt to pick at her nails, it might help settle her mother.

"And you?" Felicity pressed. "Are you going to be safe?"

"Would you like me to tell you the truth or be quiet?"

"Clara!" her mother shrieked, smacking Clara's biceps. Her lips shook now, and Clara took another deep breath so she might stay outwardly steady.

"I love you, Mother." Clara pulled Felicity into a tight hug, then whispered, "This is not up for discussion. Do you trust me?"

"Of course, my strong girl. More than you'll ever know." Her mother pulled away to plant a kiss on Clara's cheek—a drop of sunlight on an otherwise cold morning.

"Then get on the boat and wait for me to send word."

"My army can be here in a day, maybe two," Eveline said, before handing her own bag to the deckhand loading the boat.

"I don't know if we have that long." Clara shook her head but offered the queen an appreciative smile.

"Let me send for them anyway," she insisted, her hazel eyes boring into Clara intensely.

Clara nodded. "I'll take all the help I can get. Your other guards, the ones who came with you. Where are they?"

"Awaiting your orders at the palace."

"Thank you, Eveline."

"You're welcome, Majesty."

"I do not want to leave you, sister," Evian said as Clara hugged an already crying Jacob.

Between trying to calm him and insisting their mother board the boat, she now had to deal with Evian. She knew without a shred of doubt all Evian wanted was to help. That he loved his sister and would do anything for her. Clara knew that.

But today was not the day to be obstinate.

"You do not have a choice, Evian." Clara looked up at him with a stern expression that left no room for arguments. Evidently, she failed.

"I've trained for this—"

"No, you haven't," Clara said quickly, cutting him off as she ushered their younger brother onto the boat. "You've trained to be the queen's guard in Tirenas with hundreds of other soldiers. You have not trained for a battle in which there will be more dead than survivors. I will not have you anywhere near here."

"You cannot force me away."

Always so stubborn, the damned male never listened. But this time, Clara would not budge.

"I am the queen, brother. I can do what I want."

"Only of Elanist, and last I recall, we're on Morrin soil. Not to mention my allegiance to another crown." His eyes flicked over to Eveline, who Clara was genuinely glad he had found. Despite their past, Clara knew the queen had a good heart. Perhaps held deep inside her chest, but Clara knew it was there.

"The crown I was all but thrust a few nights ago? Or this soil I am set to reign over in a matter of mere weeks? Which queen would you prefer to deny your request, Evian? Now get on the damned boat."

Evian sighed—he knew when he was beat. His shoulders sagged, and his hands fell loosely to Clara's sides.

"I love you," he whispered.

"I love you, Evian. Which is why you must leave. I cannot lose everyone."

As their boat left the dock, each of Clara's loved ones stood by the railing and stared back at her. Her mother held up a hand, too frightened to wave but unwilling to leave her daughter without some expression of love. Eveline nodded earnestly as she held Evian's hand, who stared back with a well of anger and concern on his face. Jacob sniffled, wiping away stray tears, but didn't let his eyes wander from Clara. She was proud to call them her family.

The waves swelled quickly, propelling their boat further out to sea. Then the same mermaid who pulled Clara underwater prior to her arrival on Morrin soil emerged from the water. Her expressionless face stared, unblinking, but at least her spear pointed to the sky this time instead of towards Clara.

"Clarenna Hayes, Clara Afron. Her Majesty, the Helenican Queen." The mermaid didn't open her mouth, though her voice echoed around them. One voice, or perhaps many, Clara couldn't tell. It was as unnerving as the last time.

"Hello again," Clara said politely.

"Aid is on the way. The waters turned frigid, and we knew something was coming. A call was sent, and it has been answered." The mermaid nodded, then the water began to rise and thrash again.

"Why?" Clara asked, before the mermaid could disappear.

"Because you did as we asked. Consider this our thanks."

"Mermaids are not known for gratitude or altruism."

"No, we are not. We are self-serving. The water fae will offer themselves to the sea after death, and we happily accept their sacrifice." A deadly smile crept over the creature's face, her razor-sharp teeth instantly on display.

"Conscription is illegal, you know."

"Not in the water." The mermaid shrugged a shoulder, then continued. "Regardless, the call put out was not done by the sirens. Mermaids are not all that different in truth, except our call can be ignored. Sirens may not call to land dwellers, but we have had no such restrictions. They had a choice, and fifty-nine Vequil fae past maturation and with no offspring answered." She floated closer, far too quickly for someone whose torso didn't sway or move at all. "I expect all deceased to be delivered within forty-eight hours of their passing. They taste so much sweeter when they're fresh. You are welcome."

Then she disappeared below the waves, and the waters calmed. There was no trace that she had ever been there at all.

CHAPTER FORTY-THREE

ISOBEL

Isobel stormed through the palace, forcing herself not to run. The staff were not yet alarmed, so there was no need for her to worry anyone. But her heart raced as quickly as her feet.

You may stay in Elanist.

The nerve of that stars-damned woman, expecting Isobel to stay away? To be on an entirely different continent while Death loomed over the shoulder of her tether. Threatening the other half of her soul. Either Clara had gone completely insane, or she was more frightened than she let on. Either way, Isobel would return Era to the Golden Palace, and she would return to Morrin. There was no question. No argument or conversation to be had.

In a blur, hardly noticing which hall she turned down, Isobel arrived at the infirmary where Era waited. Tindal's body lay in the farthest bed from the door, closest to the window. She was wrapped entirely in red cloth and guarded by Era, who sat on the floor at the foot of her bed, her face turned out to watch the still-dark sky.

Red was a powerful colour in Elanist. Not so much where the witches came from, but Isobel hadn't encountered many who fought the traditions of their adopted home. The witches still completed their own rituals, maintaining their own beliefs, but they'd merged with that of Isobel's continent. The red symbolised strength and magic, the continuity of life after death, and the magic that rolled throughout the cycles. It was eternal.

"We have to go," Isobel said as she came to a stop by Era.

"I know," the witch replied, not yet looking away from the view.

"How?"

"The wind changed." Era shrugged, then finally turned to face Isobel. She stood slowly, then said, "But she cannot be moved yet."

"How long?"

"Not until tomorrow, which is honestly almost funny."

Yet no one was laughing.

Body wrapping was a tradition witches held for the dead. It was said to protect the body as the soul crossed over. The body could not be moved, not even touched for seven days and seven nights once wrapped, in honour of the seven original covens the witches continued to worship for guidance.

Era's eyes were bright and frightening. It eased a small fraction of the stress building in Isobel's shoulders, threatening to spill through her body. It was a reassuring touch of terrifying normalcy.

"I'll come back for her," Isobel promised.

"I know."

With nothing to pack and no one else to say goodbye to, Era blew a kiss to her friend and held her hand out for Isobel. Then they transported to the Golden Palace.

Era took a deep breath as they appeared in a small alcove on an upper level of the palace. It was an alcove Isobel knew she frequented regularly, one Isobel sat in with her often. Era sat immediately, smiling slightly and turning to face out the window once again. Her legs curled into her chest as her chin rested on her knees. Isobel didn't say anything as she wandered off in search of Poppy and Samara.

She found them quickly, although a niggling feeling told Isobel the twins had found her. Perhaps they'd been waiting. Unable to form any polite introductory conversation, Isobel blurted out Clara's plans for Christopher. She explained he was to leave with Brontë—one of the Inalises Fintan had conscripted—upon Clara's request. Isobel had been assured he would be safe, but they were foregoing any information on the boy's whereabouts, another failsafe of Clara's. Samara's voice, stiff with concern and no doubt a dozen thoughts and strategies, popped into Isobel's mind.

Shall I track them anyway?

"Yes," she answered quickly. "But don't tell me or Clara. Keep that to yourselves until she is ready to find him."

Copy. Samara nodded sharply.

"Are we needed back in Morrin?" Poppy asked, her eyes full of worry.

"I don't think so, not yet. Stay here, but be prepared just in case."

Back in Morrin, Isobel found Beau with Clara's guard and the prince. They were surrounded by several soldiers she did not know. Some had arms folded across their chests, and none looked anything close to pleased.

Beau nodded in acknowledgement as Isobel joined their group. Ryland appeared an instant later, joined by an imposing Resmigian soldier with a large blade sheathed across his back. He introduced himself as Harold, the king and queen's head of security, which sparked a round of introductions. Isobel learnt that the original soldiers belonged to the prince.

"The king and queen have been moved to an alternative location for their safety," Ryland announced, and the royals' head of security nodded.

"Can we move Clara to an alternative location for safety?" Isobel muttered.

"Yeah, good luck with that." Beau scoffed, and had the gall to grin at Isobel.

She narrowed her eyes at the Phoenix.

"Where is she?" Prince Jude asked, his eyes scanning their surroundings.

"She's here," Clara called out from somewhere behind Isobel. She spun to find Clara marching up to them, lips slightly pursed before she continued. "And I'm slightly more hopeful than any of you seem to be. The mermaids appreciate the witches being removed from the sea and have called in reinforcements."

"I didn't think they were the kind to think of others?" Keyne's brows furrowed, his gaze flickering between his companions for confirmation.

"Or to give thanks," Finch grumbled, stuffing his hands into his pockets.

"They aren't. Also, they've requested the dead water fae within forty-eight hours of passing."

"What is the plan here, Clara?" Ryland asked, his dark eyes boring into her.

Isobel was pleased, if for nothing else, that Ryland didn't stare at her that way. The intensity made her skin crawl.

"I don't know?" Clara let out an exasperated sigh. "I'm a little new to this, Ryland. What's *your* plan?"

"First, you and the prince need to reconsider being relocated. Second, I've spoken with Harold about the layout and vantage points of the grounds. We do not know where they'll hit, but preparation is key. Dalia Rion is acting superior from Queen Eveline's army and has informed us more of her soldiers are en route. But they won't arrive for at least another twelve hours."

"Do we have twelve hours?" Isobel fought not to bite her lip, and to keep her breathing steady.

"Unsure, but they're coming anyway."

"This is good, right? Strength in numbers?" One of the prince's guards piped up, his expression naively hopeful. Bless him. He'd probably not had this job for long, and now was preparing for a battle that was never expected to land here.

"Not necessarily." Ryland didn't sugarcoat his response. "Deities are not known for their willingness to roll over. They're hard to kill, and we're up against three of them." Then his attention turned back to Clara. "Do you even know why? What do they want?"

"My head, I'm guessing? Maybe his." Clara gestured to Beau. "He's an asshole at the best of times." Isobel assumed it was supposed to be a joke, but no one laughed, nor did they meet her awkward smile. Beau's normally dark and sun-kissed skin turned a shade paler.

Ryland levelled a flat stare at Clara, then shut his eyes briefly, and when he opened them again, he said, "We'll have archers in most trees, some soldiers on horseback towards the perimeter of the grounds, and the majority of soldiers on foot. Every entrance to the palace will be watched and covered."

"Archers won't do much, truthfully." Clara shook her head slowly as she looked at her feet. "You must remove the tattoos on their skin that are marked by magic, then kill them. Archers cannot do that."

"How do you even know that?" Isobel hissed, only a second shy of the prince, who looked like he was ready to throttle his bride as well.

Clara brushed them off. "What if they bring an army of their own? Do we know what to expect?"

"We do not," Ryland said grimly.

"Some of the winter and spring fae are on standby for barrier and protective magics—shields and whatnot," Frances, Jude's guard announced.

Ryland nodded, then spoke directly to Clara and the prince. "At least one of them is with both of you at all times." Then he turned back and spoke more generally. "The rest will be split into various parties. They cannot all be together. Finch, Oren, Aleska, and Keyne will be split between you"—he pointed to Clara, then Beau and Isobel—"and you two. Jude, your guards have their protocols, but I must stress that they do not leave your side. Assign one or two to Hunter, but do not leave yourself undefended. Your parents had the sense to leave, now you need to have the sense to listen and follow orders."

"Understood." The prince nodded, then practically sprinted down the hallway. No doubt in search of his love.

Ryland continued discussions with Keyne and all but one of the prince's guards, the others quick to run after Jude the second he turned and left. Clara took Beau's and Isobel's hands and made to pull them aside but sighed when Oren, Aleska, and Finch followed. They walked in silence as Finch moved to the front of their group, with Clara giving directions. Oren and Aleska trailed behind, still close enough for Isobel to hear their footsteps.

Soon they found themselves on the southernmost turret of the castle, overlooking the ocean and sunrise. It'd only just begun, the navy-blue sky lightening along the water and clouds forming far into the horizon.

"Please. Just a moment," Clara pleaded with her guard. They shared a look but finally conceded, and then Isobel, Beau, and Clara were alone.

"It's such a beautiful view," Clara whispered, looking out over the gently rolling waves.

"Indeed," Beau said softly, looking directly at Clara. Isobel said nothing, a bad feeling growing in the pit of her stomach, her eyes unable to pull away from her tether.

"If this is our last sunrise, at least it will be bold and bright and beautiful."

"Last sunrise . . . Clara—" Beau began, but Clara cut him off.

"No, let me speak. Please." She paused as he nodded. The pit in Isobel's gut turned to a block of cement, heavy and painful. "Beau, you turned my entire life upside down. Nothing's been the same since I met you. You brought chaos my way, which is saying something, but I'm so grateful to have met you. Even knowing everything I do now, I'd do it all again in a heartbeat. Giving you my heart was worth it."

Then she turned to Isobel, who thought her heart might freeze with the way Clara looked at her. With love and awe, so furiously appreciative, yet almost apologetic all at once. She looked frightened, and Isobel knew she couldn't stop what was coming.

"Isobel, I didn't know what it meant to feel complete before I met you. You are everything my soul was missing, and for someone who I'm terrified of losing every day, you brought me so much peace. You're two sides of the same coin, and I'm honoured to have both of you in my life. I cannot express the amount of love I have for each of you." Clara's adoring smile turned hard, and her expression became far less welcoming. "Nor the intensity of my need and desperation to keep you safe."

"Clara—" Beau tried again, but once more Clara interrupted.

She placed a hand on his chest and whispered, "No. I'm not done." Her free hand gently cupped Isobel's cheek. Energy radiated from her—nervous and flickering. She kissed Beau first, and whispered against his lips, "I love you with my whole heart." Clara kissed Isobel next, the subtle taste of tears mixed in with the cinnamon Isobel adored. "And the entirety of my soul."

Then she rested her forehead on Isobel's before her hand lowered to the middle of Isobel's chest. To her heart.

"And I am not sorry."

Clara tore Isobel's pendant from her neck and silently backed out the door.

"Fuck!" Beau growled for what had to be the hundredth time since they'd been locked away. Prompted by his many failed flying attempts and genuinely painful falls.

"Have you ever done this before?" Isobel asked, her arms crossed and brow raised.

"A little less criticism in your tone would be appreciated, Isobel." Beau spat the words at her.

"I'm sorry. Do continue flapping a fraction off the ground and then falling on your ass. It's getting us so far."

"What do you want me to do?" he shouted. "I can't think of any other option."

"Again, I have to ask, have you done this before?"

"No, Isobel, I have not. If I had, perhaps we'd already be on the ground instead of locked in a fucking tower." Beau forced himself to his feet and rolled out his shoulders before bouncing on his toes and gearing up to try again.

"Stop." Isobel couldn't help her eye roll. "Let me try to help. I had to learn magic the hard way, on my own. I grew up with air fae, then found myself surrounded by witches and Candor fae. So while I may not be the strongest with flame or earth or water, I can wield. But I need to know what you can and cannot do so far."

Beau sighed. "You've seen what I can do, so I'm sure you can gather what I cannot. How long did it take you to master?"

"Too long." Isobel shook her head, then relaxed her arms at her sides. Calm body language made for easier conversation, and she could use all the help she could get. "You don't need to master flying—you only need to be able to take flight. I can guide us down."

"Us?!" Beau all but screeched the question, his brows at his hairline, and his arms folded as he shook his head. "No, you're staying here."

"The fuck I am," Isobel spat. She didn't swear often, but today had been too insane to censor her vocabulary. "You want my help? You take me with you."

He contemplated it for a while—so long Isobel lost some of her gumption and began to fidget—but then he caved. "Fine, but I need your word on something."

"Spit it out."

"When I give you the signal, and I promise that you'll know when I mean, you will run to Clara with every ounce of speed you have. Do not deviate and do not look back." His amber eyes stared daggers straight through Isobel.

Never had she seen him so insistent. That terrible gut feeling from earlier sent out another wave of nausea through her, tightening the tension in her shoulders and squeezing at her lungs.

"You hear me, Isobel? I know you can take orders." Beau winked, but it held none of his usual charisma.

"Don't make this weird, you perv. What's going on?" Isobel whispered.

"I'm trying to keep her alive. Both of you. Please, just trust me."

"I do, Beau. Do you trust me?"

"Of course," he answered quickly.

"Then fill me in. Let me help you. If you've got some self-sacrifice bullshit planned, she won't survive that, so you're helping no one."

"I'm not trying to help her," Beau mumbled, his eyes distant and body deflated. His voice was barely even audible. "I'm trying to keep her alive."

Isobel's heart dropped. Her shoulders sagged, and her fingers fell lax. Entirely out of fear.

"But she won't really be living, only breathing. And those aren't the same thing."

CHAPTER FORTY-FOUR
CLARA

Shouts blasted through the door. Followed by banging that reverberated all the way through Clara's bones. A single tear slid free, stinging her eye as she welded the hinges and lock shut. It was a grim hope that locking the love of her life and the eternal holder of her soul away would keep them safe, but it was all she had.

It was all she wanted—what she craved and needed more than anything else. And they could scream and shout and beg and plead; they could break their fingers and toes and whatever other bones as they futilely pounded, but Clara didn't care. Not so long as they were alive.

She tucked Isobel's pendant between her breasts and hoped it stayed put. Though truthfully, if it were lost in what was ahead, Clara wouldn't lose any sleep.

Her guards each gave her a wary look as they followed her, though no one mentioned what she'd done. They shared covert glances with each other, but Clara ignored them and kept her intermittently blurring vision focused ahead. Breathing slowly did nothing to soothe the pain in her chest, nor the rapid beat of her heart as she came to a stop in the main bailey of the Winter Palace.

Soldiers were everywhere. Dozens gathered along the battlements or behind the cover provided by the trees, scattered buildings, and the kitchen garden. Squadrons prepared on foot, while others readied on horseback near the castle gates.

Clara had no time to consider where she and her guard might stand when three blaring horns sounded. Almost like foghorns, but darker. A warning or an announcement.

Jude jogged to Clara's side, taking her hand quickly and squeezing it tight. Perhaps it was meant as reassurance, but all Clara could think was whether he'd get the chance to do it again once the day was through.

"Where are Beau and Isobel?" He searched the throng of fae surrounding them. Mostly Resmigian, but Vequil fae dotted the crowd, just as the mermaid had promised.

"Safe. Would you like to join them?" Clara spilled the words without thought.

"I will not leave you here to fend for yourself, wife," Jude said. His voice had become so familiar; she hoped today would not be the last time she would hear it.

Clara's attention was drawn to a dark cloud forming above the castle bailey, positively reeking of threat and decay. She gasped as it quickly lowered and swelled to swallow the thin layer of snow at their feet. It extended in every direction, roiling like a miasma but faster and far more deadly. Then once it stilled, a chill ran down Clara's spine and lanced painfully through her jaw as claws of unease dug deep.

The fog morphed once more, and in its place stood hundreds of skeletal soldiers.

They bore no shields or armour, though Clara supposed the undead did not need those. No skin, nor muscle or sinew, only bones bound by thick fog. Their skulls were empty, without eyes or teeth, but menacing regardless. The stench of death spread through the courtyard, and Clara heard multiple gags from the fae.

Immediately, the bone soldiers struck.

Their movements were jerky, almost clumsy at first, but too soon they found their footing. Their clubs struck flesh, and tarnished swords skated against those of the fae. Boned frames moved far too quickly for the dead, striking without thought, aiming only to damage and destroy. Clara noticed with fear and her breath warring for her lungs that the fae soldiers were already stumbling.

Death's Daughters appeared above, astride an iridescent cloud reeking of corruption. Oil coated their pallid skin and saturated their hair, which stuck to their faces. The slimy, iridescent liquid clung to their protruding bones, welling in the hollow of their collarbones, then dripped, thick and oozing, down their thin and frail-looking bodies. Yet Clara was not so easily convinced of their frailty. These deities were more than harbingers of Death. They were puppet masters of destruction, disguised as gods. Powerful enough to convince the world.

As her gaze flew around the castle bailey, searching for any sign, or perhaps somewhere she might help, Clara noticed the archers racing down from the battlements. Now that they knew their opponents, they could adjust their tactics. Arrows were of no use against soldiers made of bones. Soldiers had raced to the armoury to gather additional weapons, so their fellow comrades were defended. The soldiers atop horses rallied to stampede the flank of the undead army. The sound of crushing bones against stone, as the horses reared and stomped the skeletons, grated inside Clara's ears, but the alternative left her heart stalling, so she ignored the discomfort. Blood spilled everywhere, and soon there was more squelching than crushing.

Clara looked up from the carnage, to where the sisters lingered in their cloud of superiority, to find the eldest with her palm open and arm extended.

"Where is the Phoenix?" the youngest sister called. Her tattoo moved as she spoke, contorting and writhing over her chin like a snake.

"Not coming!" Clara snarled back.

"Then we will take you instead," said the sister wielding a sword, her tattoo on her forearm. Her sinister grin radiated dark promise, and though she did not shout, her voice boomed in Clara's skull as if she'd screamed directly in her ear.

"I think the fuck not," Oren and Aleska yelled in unison, their swords raised in sync. It sparked a memory Clara couldn't quite reach, as it flashed in her mind's eye.

The eldest sister said nothing; her silence weighed ominously. She narrowed her eyes, and the tattooed crown of thorns flickered at her brows. At the twist of her outstretched fingers, every fallen skeletal soldier rose. Pulled back together by invisible fingers after being trampled and dismembered.

It was then that Clara realised they were not prepared at all. The aid she'd gone in search of, the research she'd done, or how they'd prepared—none of it had mattered.

She was not ready, and neither was anyone else.

Clara threw up a wall of air, shielding a fae mere seconds before a bone soldier's club could collide with his neck. Her quick thinking saved him, but Clara did not let her hopes rise. The battle had only just begun.

She pulled a blade from the hand of a dead soldier at her feet. Clara raced forward and swung, cleaving the skull of a bone soldier from its spine. The rest of its skeleton twitched, but finally it fell still.

Use your strengths. Aleska's words from all those months ago rang in her mind. *Surprise your assailant. It isn't foolproof, but survival isn't about that.*

Clara paused, taking a moment to consider her strengths and her weaknesses. At best, she was acceptable in weapon-based combat—it would not keep her safe. It might barely keep her alive.

But Clara was one hell of a fire wielder.

The bone soldiers advanced too quickly for Clara to gauge. She canvassed the battlefield and found her guard engaged in melee combat with the undead, her prince protecting a water fae, and dozens of fae soldiers sprawled lifeless on the bloodstained snow.

All the while, the bone soldiers' numbers did not dwindle, and Death's Daughters watched with disdain from above on their throne of despair.

All they did was *watch* impassively as more fae fell.

Clara heard the silence of their deaths.

She didn't know how, but the absence of their heartbeats echoed in her soul until her ears ached.

All the while she pulled at her magic. Forced bone soldiers' skulls from their spines. Threw fire at their twisted frames until the bone soldiers were only ashes. Erected as many shields as she could, trying not to shatter as half of them rose too late. She pulled roots from deep within the ground, twining them around bones, tugging them apart.

Clara swore she heard Aleska's voice, but it was too quiet amidst the clang of swords and grunts of soldiers. She spun, searching for her friend. Between two bone soldiers, she saw Aleska swipe the head off one before ducking and cutting off the other at its kneecaps. The bone soldiers crumbled. Clara reduced them to floating embers before the skeletons hit the ground.

Aleska smirked and winked at Clara—such a casual, familiar gesture, cut forever short by a blade from behind. Her eyes widened and then the light left them. She fell limp while Clara's heart froze. She didn't have the courage to look for Oren. Searching for him was unnecessary, as his scream tore through the bailey and rattled the windows. The sound cut through Clara's already seizing, aching heart.

Another friend gone.

His sister—Oren's twin.

This was her fault. Again.

Clara screamed, violent and murderous, as she bludgeoned through the bone soldiers. She tore them limb from limb. Their remains were burned regardless of how they fell, as she forced her way through the battlefield, towards where Death's Daughters floated high above the action.

Still they stood on their miasma of smoke and death, overseeing the carnage but doing *nothing*.

Beside her, Reid avoided the club swinging at them. They ducked swiftly, yanked the club from an undead soldier, and slammed it into the attacker's neck. The bone soldier's skull popped off at the force of Reid's swing.

But Reid did not notice the second undead soldier, nor the blade it embedded in their side.

Clara shrieked with rage. Reaching forward, she pulled off its skull with her hands, fuelling her strength with nothing more than fury and determination. But too late.

"No—I'm so sorry—I wasn't watching," Clara choked out as she pressed her hands into Reid's small and injured body.

"It's okay," they whispered, their voice now croaky and wet. Blood stained their teeth when they smiled. "I miss him so much." Tears leaked down their cheeks as their eyes closed and their chest fell for the last time.

Devastation rocked Clara, and a small sob broke free of her throat. Though a tiny bubble of peace warmed the underside of her hand over Reid's heart. She didn't know who *he* was that Reid spoke of, but in that split second, Clara wasn't afraid. She knew Reid was at peace and being welcomed by whomever was waiting for them.

Another death. Except this time the blood stained Clara's skin, and the final breath was exhaled with Clara's hand on their chest.

As she looked towards the deities, her eyes snagged on Darius. Nerves shadowed his face. The teen looked so out of place amidst such death and violence.

"He's not supposed to be here," Clara muttered to herself.

And then she remembered.

She realised why everything felt so familiar.

Why she thought she'd heard Aleska say something. How she knew Reid would be okay after Death took them.

She'd seen this scene play out already.

For months, snippets of this vision had flashed in her sleeping mind, disappearing as the sun replaced the moon. Nightmares she couldn't remember. Finally, last night she woke with a bloody nose and raw throat because she had finally seen it play out in its entirety.

To its devastating conclusion.

Clara knew what she would see before she turned around.

Beau and Isobel.

But they didn't emerge from the palace this time. Instead, they raced towards her from the south—running over the snow-speckled grass—fear and determination in their eyes.

Beau grabbed Isobel's wrist, then muttered something to her before he shoved her into the crowd.

She bolted for Clara, tears spilling down her face, but she didn't look back.

Clara knew she had a decision to make.

Beau or Darius.

If she didn't turn back for Darius now, he would be dead.

In the vision, she couldn't save Beau—he was too far away—and he was even further now. Darius was only a few paces away from her, and Isobel had changed the course of her vision by sprinting towards Clara and away from the deities.

Beau stood still at the top of the stairs. He knew what was coming.

Stars, she'd locked them away to keep this from happening.

Isobel's pendant sat heavy between her breasts. She'd subconsciously taken precautions to keep them away from the battlefield, but the fucking bastard was going to thwart her twice. How he had even managed to get down from the tower while still breathing was beyond Clara. He wouldn't take many more, though; they both knew that.

Ora had known.

She knew when Clara had visited the Pearl 'n Lace all those months ago. She had told Clara about Beau's conversation with Lorelai, and of his plans. Clara didn't tell Beau that she knew, as she'd expected him to come clean on his own.

Fucking prick.

Now she was going to watch him die—for good this time. Her heart fractured in her chest.

It broke as she turned away and ran to Darius, choosing the boy that Ryn said would sway the tide.

Clara reached Darius before the bone soldier, covering him with her body and turning the bones above them to ash. All the while, her heart shattered in her chest. She knew what was coming. Could feel it happening already. "Do not leave my side, do you hear me?"

Darius nodded, and Clara took his hand. She could feel his erratic pulse race and raw magic swell.

Isobel crashed into her seconds later, but Clara couldn't move. Her body, her eyes, and her broken heart were frozen.

Yet, by some sadistic turn of fate, Clara was forced to watch as Beau's wings were severed from his body. She didn't want to, didn't want to see it again, knowing this time his death would be permanent. She was rooted in place, unable to breathe or think or feel anything other than fear and pain. It was only as Isobel pulled Clara's head to her chest and blocked her view that Clara found the ability to inhale. One long, sharp, devastated breath. Clara heard Isobel's cries echoing her own as her chest was racked with grief.

She didn't need to see it again, when the same moments from her vision would not leave her mind.

Beau launches his dagger at Lorelai's chest. His eyes lock with Clara's, then within moments his head rolls across the stones.

A silent sob claws its way up Clara's throat.

The ground rattles violently, almost as if it might open and swallow them all.

Clara hopes and prays to any of the gods still listening that it does.

CHAPTER FORTY-FIVE
BEAU

True to her word, Lorelai spared Beau any discomfort. He felt no physical suffering, but she couldn't take the pain that broke his heart as he watched Clara turn away. He didn't want her to watch him die, but he was selfish enough to hope her eyes were the last thing he saw.

Instead, she curled tight into her tether, who he knew would ensure she was alright.

Clara knew what was coming.

He didn't need her words to confirm it. He knew her vision the other night was of the battle. Deep in his bones, he had felt it.

The fear on her face, replaced by relief and swirled with uncertainty as she opened her eyes to find him and Isobel. She'd never looked so frightened despite everything she'd been through since they'd met. Since Beau had the privilege of learning her name, and the honour of getting to know who Clara was.

As his wings fell to the ground behind him, he knew he only had a handful of seconds left. He'd made a deal, and now he needed to honour it. Beau lifted his sword and threw it straight at Lorelai.

She did not balk or shift or flinch. The youngest of Death's Daughters welcomed his blade with quiet, subtle gratitude. Then he looked back at Clara and recalled the first night they'd met. She'd changed so much since then. Grown.

Still as fiery and stubborn, still as magical and strong. Even more beautiful with every passing moment.

She would be an excellent queen. He only wished he'd be by her side throughout her reign. Perhaps under her, for a time, and before her on his knees.

Beau regretted only a handful of choices. Overreacting and getting her friend murdered, taking so long to admit his feelings for her, and not being able to spend an eternity with this woman who deserved the world. She deserved every sun-kissed morning and soft, shimmering moonlit midnight. Endless peaceful minutes, and even more furious, rage-filled moments in her honour. She deserved to dance under the stars and float on warm waves, and he wished he could have been one of the special souls who got to share those experiences with her.

But for her to experience them all, he would sacrifice himself a million times over. Sure, she wasn't going to be okay right away. She was going to be positively livid at first. Then maybe she'd be sad for a while longer. Eventually, though, with folk around her who cared, she was going to be okay. She had her tether, and her prince, and their families for support.

Besides, Clara was never Beau's anyway. Not really, and certainly not fully. She had a tether, the ultimate bond for a fae. So much more than a love match of the heart, Isobel was the other half of her soul.

Clara was never Beau's to keep, but fuck, if he wasn't the luckiest bastard in the world to get to pretend for a while.

He didn't feel it when he died. Perhaps he should've trusted Lorelai more than he had.

Some of his deaths were excruciating, while others simply happened. This time, all Beau did was blink, and he was no longer in his body. His head rolled away in slow motion, his body slumped in a pool of crimson where he'd fallen.

Before him stood Ryn, with a sad, almost disappointed smile on her face. He hadn't known the Reaper could express emotion.

She held out her hand, and instinctively Beau took it. It was colder than Clara's, gangly and uncomfortable in comparison. But still, he held on as if his life depended on it, almost chuckling at the irony.

"Ready, Phoenix?"

"No," Beau whispered, looking back at Clara. He took in as much of her as he could, knowing this was the last time. Beau wasn't anywhere near ready to leave, but Ryn squeezed his hand, and he knew it was time to go. Perhaps one day, in another life, in another timeline, he'd meet her again. Maybe next time it'd end differently.

For now, at least his Reaper was a familiar face.

CHAPTER FORTY-SIX

CLARA

"Did she just choose me over him?" Darius whispered from somewhere close.

Clara's eyes were squeezed shut, as if perhaps by closing them—being unable to see the surrounding carnage—she could ignore what had happened. Pretend that dozens of fae weren't dead, including her friends.

Pretend Beau was still alive.

"Yes," Isobel answered, her own voice hushed. "But now probably isn't the best time to bring that up."

Clara ignored them, but when she finally opened her eyes, the sight before her pulled a wounded gasp from her throat. Oren hunched over his twin sister's lifeless body, his broad shoulders shaking as he cried. The sound chilled Clara's bones.

"Where are they?" Clara asked, dread racing up her throat. "The bone soldiers?"

"The ground opened, and they fell in," Isobel said softly. Her eyes searched Clara's for something, but Clara didn't have the energy to figure out what.

"Did anyone else *fall in*?" Clara asked, suddenly fearful of the answer.

"No," Darius answered quickly. "But the deities seem unfazed, except the small one—she's pissed."

"How can you tell?" Isobel asked, her thumb stroking Clara's knuckles.

Half of her wanted Isobel to smother her entirely, to hold her and never let go. The other half of Clara wanted to remove her own skin—it felt restrictive and painful, and Isobel's strokes somewhat enhanced that sensation.

She voiced none of this to her tetherbond; there was no point. Clara knew the gesture had good intentions. Best to leave it at that.

"I can read her emotions. Candor magic at its most useless, I'm afraid."

"It's because Beau didn't hold up his end of the deal," Clara muttered.

"You knew?" Isobel asked, her sad eyes wide.

"Ora told me," Clara replied numbly. Even providing the bare minimum of answers felt like an impossible task.

"Clara," Darius breathed, his voice quiet and delicate, hardly more than a whisper. "You saved my life."

Clara could only nod.

"I don't know how to ask this without sounding incredibly insensitive or childish and stupid," Darius began, more certain this time. "So I'm just going to ask. Would you mind if I get rid of the daughters?"

"How?"

"I'm very powerful," he answered with a shrug. Far too casually for what had transpired.

"*How?*" she pressed, her eyes narrowed.

"I can conjure elements out of nothing. Most can do it a little, play with raindrops that weren't there a second ago, or roast fruits over their fingertips. I create tsunamis without a thought and am very precise with jet-fast water. Remind me to show you my wood carvings."

"I want their marks," Clara ordered, not caring about her tone. Her eyes locked with Lorelai for a fraction longer than the other two, and the deity almost seemed appreciative.

Darius smiled menacingly, almost eagerly, and nodded. With a single flick of his wrist, the sisters were screaming. Sticky black tar dripped from the eldest's brow, her crown gone. The middle sister's forearm had hardly any skin left in sight, let alone her vine-like tattoo. Missing from Lorelai's chin was her tattoo, just below a barely perceptible smile. Darius floated the patches of the deities' skin down to Clara on a phantom wind.

They fell into her hand and felt colder than she'd expected. Her heart was much the same way, never to be as warm as it once was. She'd expected to be pleased, but truthfully Clara felt very little.

"Thank you, Darius."

Clara incinerated the contents of her palm. Flames engulfed her hand, though she kept her gaze trained on the sisters.

"You think you win?!" the eldest shouted, more tarry liquid oozing down her face.

Then Clara lit all three of Death's Daughters on fire. They burned slowly, but Clara watched every second. She made sure no part of them was missed. The smell was absolutely horrid, though that seemed fitting.

"No," Clara said quietly, a hint of violence still on her tongue. "There are no winners in war."

CHAPTER FORTY-SEVEN

ISOBEL

Art had always been therapeutic for Isobel, and since before she could remember, she'd had chalk or coal in her pockets, or paint stuck under her fingernails. Whenever the noise grew too loud, or her skin felt too tight, or whenever reality was simply too much, it was art she turned to. The drugs came later, but even then, the magic of art was never far.

Yet now it felt fruitless.

A hopeless endeavour to bring life back to her limbs as they moved heavy and numb. She'd sat before her canvas for an hour, with her paints on the table and brush in hand, but nothing came. No image that wasn't gruesome, no memory that didn't hurt. Nothing helpful—only painful reminders of a loss she didn't wish to recreate.

Beau was dead.

Permanently and irreversibly gone.

And it was Isobel's fault.

Yesterday's events coursed through her mind in a vicious, repetitive cycle. A dozen different choices could've been made, and he might've lived. Yet now they would never know, and Clara would have to grieve his loss forever. Not like Isobel, or the many others who knew Beau was an arrogant prick but loved him anyway.

Clara would have to grieve the loss of her heart, while one still beat in her chest. Isobel couldn't even imagine, and neither did she want to. She never wanted to know what it felt like. Though if she could trade places with Clara, and spare her the pain, Isobel would do it in an instant.

Maybe if she'd fought Beau harder, pushed him to reconsider his deal. If they'd come up with any sort of plan instead of Isobel eventually conceding. It was Isobel's manipulation of air that softened their fall. The wind cradled them as fiercely as Beau had held Isobel to his chest as he flew.

For a second, she'd been so proud of him for finally learning to do what his body had been made for. Something he'd given up on happening. His smile, for the briefest second, was as wide and fulfilled as she'd ever seen. And Isobel had shared that with him.

Ultimately, it was her decision to guide them to the ground that got Beau to the battle. That decision cost him his life, but it cost Clara more. Guilt racked her bones until her frozen, outstretched hand shook.

A knock at the door pulled Isobel from her remorseful haze, and she spun to find Clara standing in the entryway. Her eyes were distant, hair still plastered to her face with the sweat and blood and tears. Soot covered her fingers from the bone soldiers she'd incinerated. Isobel's pendant hung at her side, glinting in the sunlight as Clara offered it back.

"I thought you were going to clean up," Isobel said softly, standing and crossing the study she'd borrowed. Clara blinked slowly, then shook her head and looked away. "Let me help you."

"How?" Clara asked, her voice so quiet and broken Isobel barely heard it.

"First, I'll turn on the water, and then—"

"I feel like something is missing." Clara's tear-filled eyes shot back to Isobel's.

Her heart ached and her lungs restricted, watching Clara in so much pain.

"Something I know I can never get back. I don't know how to move on from having my heart ripped from my chest. I don't even know how to breathe anymore. My chest is empty, and my mind is numb."

"You've been through so much. Too much," Isobel whispered as she wrapped her arms around Clara tightly. Clara did not hug her back, only stood limply in Isobel's arms. She stroked the back of Clara's head, trying to smooth some of her hair, then Isobel whispered, "I can take it from you, if you want."

She wasn't sure if it was a wise idea, but she had to at least offer. Perhaps selfishly, for if Clara said yes and her pain was gone, Isobel wouldn't have to stand by and watch her grieve anymore. She'd give anything to see Clara live again. Happy and free. Even in such a short time, Isobel knew Clara would never fully heal. How could she?

Would Isobel choose to forget Clara, just so she didn't have to feel the heartbreak of losing her? Was it worth giving her up entirely so there was no pain?

Pain was her only reminder now. If Clara wanted someone to take it, she would find a witch who would. But was asking her to give it up the right thing? Isobel didn't know. Pain and memories were all she had left of Beau. All anyone had left of the Phoenix.

"The witches have many talents, Clara. They can take your senses, your pain, your memories. If that's what you want."

Clara shook her head, then murmured, "Pain will strengthen me, eventually. Right?"

"Right."

She sobbed then, as Isobel held her, and they both sank to the floor. Clara's body shook uncontrollably, as it hit her for possibly the first time since Beau died. There would be more to come, but for now, Isobel would hold Clara until her world didn't feel so broken and her lungs didn't feel so frightfully, horribly empty.

Three days later, Clara announced she was ready for Beau's funeral. Jude had sent for Beau's mother, Nina, as soon as the dead were tallied. She was apprehensive when she'd first arrived, and Isobel sat with Jude as he told the woman her son was dead. Nina looked a lot like Beau, though she wasn't identical, and truthfully, Isobel was pleased. Clara had not met her yet, and would do so for the first time at the service. If Nina and Beau had looked any more alike, Isobel feared how Clara might react. She'd only just started eating more than a bite or two and got out of bed when Isobel did that morning.

Seeing someone who looked akin to the dead man who held Clara's heart? Who took it wherever he went—no, Clara would not take that well. Isobel didn't want her to suffer any more than she already was.

The funeral for Beau was private. Only Clara, Nina, Jude, and Isobel were present. Nina had requested they hold it by the water, though she did not disclose any details and no one pressed her. Clara and Isobel waited with Beau's body, which had been wrapped and tied with rope painted gold. One of his feathers was secured beneath the bindings.

When Nina and Jude arrived, the group was silent for a long, uncomfortable moment before a choked cry escaped Nina's lips and her hand flew to her mouth. Clara clamped her eyes closed, her lip already quivering and her grip strong on Isobel's hand. Then she opened her eyes, let go of Isobel's hand and closed the gap between herself and Beau's mother.

"I'm so sorry," Clara whispered, her voice broken. Nina nodded, unable to speak, but pulled Clara close to her chest. They stood there, sobbing and swaying together for a while before the funeral began. Isobel and Jude turned to watch the waves roll, in an attempt, at least, at some privacy.

"We do not believe in an immediate afterlife in Morrin," Jude said softly, turning as Clara and Nina separated and turned to face Beau's body. "Resmigian fae prefer to believe our lost loved ones are not in fact lost at all, and instead linger. They stay close—to guide and protect—until we are ready to join them. Beau was a good male. Strong and kind and fiercely protective. There were no two females he cared for more than his mother and his love. I had the honour of knowing Beau Hawthorne in many capacities, though none greater than that of his friend and chosen family. I do not expect his soul will wait for mine, but I take comfort in knowing one day we'll meet again. Mrs Hawthorne, I extend my deepest, sincerest condolences. You raised a man you ought to be very proud of."

Nina nodded quickly, her eyes filling and overflowing as Jude addressed her. Clara clasped her hand tightly, her jade eyes not straying from Beau's body. Then Jude turned to Clara.

"Clara, my wife, I have no words for the loss you face. My shoulder is always warm and dry, and yours if you find you need one."

Her tears spilled rapidly; her free hand shot to cover her open mouth. No sound came out, but Isobel could imagine the gut-wrenching wail. It was not a sound Isobel ever wanted to hear come from her tether's lips.

"In Elanist," Isobel said quietly, gently. "Each court celebrates the life and mourns the death of loved ones differently. In Wave, the deceased are sent out to sea. In Soil, they are buried. In Flame, their bodies are burned, and the ashes marked onto the skin of the loved ones left behind. If you have no objections, Clara has requested we burn Beau's body."

Nina's mouth turned down as her eyes closed. She nodded once, then squeezed Clara's hand.

"Are you ready?" Isobel asked. Clara shook her head, eyes now pleading with Isobel's. Tears ran in furious streaks down her face.

Isobel cupped her cheeks and wiped away some of her tears, despite new drops falling immediately.

"You will never be," she whispered. "There will never be a time when you're prepared to say goodbye. It's not something you should ever have to say to the one you love. It's not fair, and it's going to hurt for a long time to come. If you don't want to do this now, we don't have to, but he deserves a chance for his soul to rest."

"I can't—"

"Clara," Nina said, pulling Clara's attention. "There is nothing any of us can say to you that will prepare you for walking away. For going on about your day, your life, without him." Her voice broke, as any mother's would do at the mention of their dead child.

The sound sent a cold jab to Isobel's heart, and she briefly squeezed her eyes shut so her own tears did not well or spill.

Nina shook her head, then continued. "In Helshire, we do not mourn the dead—we celebrate the life they had before. Today is not about saying goodbye." She shook her head with a small, sad smile pressed to her lips. And again, her voice faltered.

"It's only for a little while. Death will claim you, too, one day, and he'll be there when she does. Today is for you to remember him as he was last week, last month, last year. Do it for yourself so that you can heal. Or at least try to."

Clara didn't say anything, but Beau's body burst into flames behind Isobel. She nodded, kissed Clara's forehead, and then crouched over the flames with her hand pressed to Beau's chest. A moment later, her hand emerged covered in ash.

Isobel marked Nina first. One vertical line, from the middle of her lip to just below her chin. The mother's mark. Then Isobel turned to Clara. First, she drew a horizontal line across Clara's cheek—as Beau's spouse—and then over her pounding heart. Isobel finally allowed her tears to fall as her thumb swiped over Clara's skin.

Beau's consciously chosen love. Not a stars-determined soulmate, but every bit as important.

CHAPTER FORTY-EIGHT
EVELINE

Eveline did not particularly care for the Phoenix. She'd enjoyed toying with him in the past—and there was no denying he was nice to look at—but their relationship had been very minor. Beau was an employee of her father's, and she had been his prized daughter. Most of her amusement had come from a small place of rebellion, in truth, as her father did not like her speaking with him, and on some subconscious level Eveline enjoyed that.

Today, as she packed up the last of her belongings, her most important possessions she could not part with, Eveline carried a heavy blanket of grief on her shoulders.

Her soldiers had not made it to the Winter Palace in time. Not to truly help. Only to clear the dead and alert their families. They'd reported the losses, and Eveline had returned immediately. She cared even less for many of the dead, most of whom she did not know, but Beau's death hit her in a way she hadn't expected. There was nothing she could say to Clara, who barely acknowledged Eveline's existence. Not that Eveline could blame her.

So while Eveline gathered her things in preparation to leave the Cerulean Castle and royal life behind, her excitement was tainted. In part with grief, but also guilt. By some stars-forsaken miracle, Clara had granted Eveline her greatest wish: to be free of the crown and in turn pursue her tetherbond. But Clara had to suffer through the loss of her greatest love and gained a new crown in the process. It felt a lot like she was getting everything she wanted while Clara suffered. It wasn't fair.

And so her joy was clouded, far darker and heavier than it was supposed to be.

Now, Eveline stared at her single packed bag and sighed. Solaris' hairbrush sat unused since the morning before she died, still full of hair Eveline could not push herself to discard. Her notebooks, filled with song lyrics and stray musical sheets. A handful of simple dresses, silk and with no beading or structure past the bust, with no lace frills or trims, and no bodices designed to restrict her airflow or force her breasts to her chin. Her mother's tiara she'd found hidden away in a dark and dusty portion of her father's old rooms. But it wasn't the crown, only a reminder of who Eveline came from, and like her sister, their mother was not a part of her family she wished to forget.

Leaving the castle did, in truth, feel like leaving her mother and sister behind. Her mother had died within these very walls. A lot of Solaris had died here too, regardless of where her heart had stopped beating. Yet in her heart, Eveline knew they'd be with her wherever she went—always and everywhere.

In anticipation of Clara's coronation, Eveline had taken on a few last tasks as queen of this continent. First, she'd laid off ninety percent of the staff. With help from Evian and Dalia Rion, Eveline created a list of trusted employees, ones who did their jobs well with clean records and no suspicion. Almost all the castle's employees had been hired while under her father's rule, so Eveline took an educated guess and decided Clara would not be interested in any of those. Most who stayed were selected by Eveline's mother or had even been around when her grandparents sat upon the throne nearly a millennium ago.

As Eveline was sealing her written recommendation for Rion, Evian strolled through the open door. He did not possess his usual cocky swagger; instead, his shoulders curved in slightly. He simply leant against the doorframe, staring at her until she looked up and offered a small smile.

"I suppose you weren't meant to be a soldier after all," Eveline murmured and stood, moving around the desk and gliding over to him.

"I was supposed to be with you, in whatever form that required." Evian placed warm, firm hands on her hips, and pulled Eveline closer still. His grey-blue eyes swirled with ferocity, determination, and intensity.

"Stars, you're sappy," she said, rolling her eyes and looking away in a poor attempt to hide how his sentiments made her feel. Though perhaps his ego would not inflate any further to know his words left her cheeks flushed and her knees weak.

"I love you, Eveline. When can we make it official?"

"Needy too," Eveline muttered with a smirk. Then she finally looked back up at him. At the eyes that always saw her, truly and deeply saw her, to her very core. The face that only ever showed her love, devotion, and a little mischief. To the male she fully intended on sharing the rest of her existence with. "Once this transfer is finalised and when your sister is coronated. It is only a matter of days now until I sign the kingdom over to her and Jude. Then we're free."

Those last few words felt illegal to utter, and Eveline could only manage them in a whisper. They felt too good to be true, and her heart sped up as they fell from her lips.

"And then you'll accept the bond?"

"Gladly, soldier."

CHAPTER FORTY-NINE

CLARA

Clara sat in the bathtub until her fingers pruned and the water went cold. She didn't have the energy or care to reheat it.

She lay awake in bed at night, with the stars half blinding her through the open curtains until the sun rose and took over. Everything was too bright.

She was frightened to sleep, for she knew the disorienting moments would come right after. When she woke, and couldn't remember. When he was still there somewhere, and she did not yet remember that he was gone.

That he had left her.

Fear was the only emotion she had left.

She was terrified—more than she ever thought someone could be. Terrified that the universe would take Isobel from her as well.

Clara's heart still beat, but it was foreign now. It no longer beat for a purpose, only pumped blood throughout her body to make sure the other organs did their job—to keep her breathing.

She wasn't alive, not really. She was merely breathing. Yet numb and petrified of sleeping, and of every cruel moment she stayed awake. She felt hollow and heavy and so alone. Isobel stayed with her. Every second of every day, Isobel was there. Clara wasn't physically alone, but she was missing someone vital, and her body knew. It had no choice but to carry on, though it all felt different now. This new normal, where Beau didn't exist, was wrong.

Thousands of fae flocked to the Winter Palace, lining the hallways towards the open throne room and along every inch of pathway and ground leading up to the front doors.

The gates were wide open, though surrounded by guards and soldiers from every continent. Their wings held taut, helmeted heads peaking over the tops of everyone else's, while witches hid in plain sight. All there to protect the new king and queen.

Jude Lorson and Clarenna Hayes—King and Queen of Morrin and Elanist, and by the day's end Tirenas as well.

The Helenican Queen—that's what the mermaid had called her. Clara couldn't tell if it was a title to be celebrated or feared. All she knew was that folk who should have been present today were missing. Her adoptive father and biological mother. Elisabeth and Solaris. Tindal. Reid, and their charming aura. They were gone.

Aleska, and her confident grin which always lit up the room. How she teased and was such an immediate friend. But she, too, was gone.

Neven, and his fierce protection of her right until his last breath. He had taken Clara from her home, unknowingly handing her straight to an enemy. Though he didn't question her when Clara told him she was in danger; instead, he kept her alive far longer than she was supposed to live. He died to keep her alive.

And Beau. His kind heart and gentle soul, wrapped in a traumatic past. Clara understood—she took too long, but she accepted. As he did her. Clara and Isobel shared a soul, and while it wasn't quite how the legend worked, Clara had no doubt she shared her heart with Beau. He held it so tenderly, so viciously, and with so much love that it overwhelmed her. Beau gave his heart so she could keep hers. And now he was dead too.

Maybe he wouldn't be if Clara had been smarter. If she'd pushed him to talk sooner, or if she'd listened to Ryn's advice. Clara repeated countless conversations and moments in time, replayed over in her mind every possible choice that might've altered the outcome of the battle. All it served was to extend her devastation, which truthfully seemed limitless. There was no benefit in questioning herself or her choices. Beau was dead, and there was no changing that, no matter how deeply she prayed or solemnly she begged.

Many soldiers had died that day. Clara spoke to every family member—every spouse and parent and child, every sibling and loved one. Isobel was right when she said there would never come a time when someone was ready to say goodbye to the one they loved. So, too, was Nina, who told her there was nothing anyone could say that would make their loss more bearable. Every conversation Clara had showed her how right they were. With every tear, Clara shed her own, as if they were unending. Maybe they were.

Today felt wrong, incomplete, without her loved ones. Even Elisabeth, who hadn't quite earned her way into Clara's life when her own was taken. But Death claimed her sister before Clara ever had time to find out.

As Clara and Jude exited the throne room, crowns atop their heads and royal capes trailing far behind them, Clara remembered everyone she'd lost to get here. To the point where she hoped, above all else, she might be able to make a difference. Allow more love, and less loss throughout her kingdoms.

She attempted to look everyone in the eye, which made for a very slow exit procession, but she refused the alternative. Everyone stood before her, welcoming her to the throne and allowing her a place of leadership, so they deserved to be acknowledged. They deserved peace and unity and protection.

So that was what she vowed to give them.

"Congratulations, son." Jude's father came to a stop beside his son at the top of the main castle stairs. They'd stopped outside the doors, still waving and nodding to those who approached with congratulations and well wishes. Jude shook his father's hand before the previous king turned to his daughter-in-law. "Clara," he said with a small bow. "You will do well—I know it."

"She's a little too much like me, husband. She cannot *not* do well." Jude's mother winked as she took Clara's hand. "Take care of my son, won't you? And yourself. My deepest condolences on your Phoenix."

"Thank you, Majesty," Clara said quietly, dipping her chin and lowering her gaze.

"No, no. It's just Sylvina now." Sylvina placed her thumb and forefinger on Clara's chin, bringing her face upwards. It was a distinction Clara would need to get used to, though perhaps it would become second nature once she was actually ruling the kingdom. "You're the queen, remember?"

Clara smiled, but it felt forced.

Sylvina pinched her chin like only a mother could, then she proceeded down the staircase towards a carriage waiting by the gates. Jude squeezed Clara's hand as his parents rode off towards their retirement.

Ryland hobbled up the stairs quickly after, relying heavily on crutches. Clara tried not to gasp or react, but it was hard to see. From just above the knee, Ryland's left leg was gone. Yet another thing missing.

Clara squeezed her eyes shut, trying to forget where she was standing, and how close her feet were to where Beau last stood. To where his head rolled and wings fell.

"I think you might give me a run for my money now, you know," Ryland said with a chuckle, pulling Clara from her spiralling thoughts.

"I wouldn't bet on it." She scoffed, though it was a quiet sound.

"Your sister would be proud of you." Ryland's voice turned serious as his dark eyes bored into Clara.

"Maybe for the crown, but not who I share it with."

Clara took a deep breath, wishing Isobel were with her. Instead, she stood with Hunter, somewhere in the crowd or within the palace. Not by the queen's side, as ruled however many centuries ago. *Consorts* had no place at coronations. Oh, how Clara despised such a word for her tether, and for Jude's.

"She didn't hate all queers, you know."

She scoffed again, louder this time. "Just cunt- loving females?"

"Stars, you're crass." Ryland sighed and shook his head.

"But you wouldn't have me any other way now, would you?" Clara said, though her words lacked their usual charm.

"No, no, I would not." Ryland offered a sad smile, and paused briefly before he asked, "Do you want to know why?"

"I don't know. Do I?"

Ryland ignored her question. "She thought she had fallen in love with a female once. She was very young and, believe it or not, less interested in the crown than you are. Her magic had only just manifested, so it was entirely possible she'd be heir to the throne, and your grandfather, King Vaughn, started grooming her for the role. She rebelled as all youths do and developed what she believed to be feelings for her friend, Malan."

Ryland's sad smile returned, though it was heavier now. As his eyes turned back to the crowd, and Clara followed suit, they both watched as Jude spoke to a fae at the bottom of the steps.

"They were inseparable, and soon enough, Malan developed feelings for Elisabeth as well. She fell much harder for your sister than your sister did for her, and Elisabeth realised she didn't love Malan, only what she represented. She was fun and buoyant and loud and free. With no responsibilities or cares in the world, but full of love for your sister. When Elisabeth realised, she spoke with Malan and told her the truth of how she felt, but Malan became angry. Cold and bitter. King Vaughn tried to console your sister by telling her all the ways romantic female relationships could crumble and fail, but he sowed too many seeds of doubt in Elisabeth's mind."

He shook his head then, and Clara did not fail to notice the slight rise of Ryland's upper lip. "He was many things, a lot of them good, may his soul rest well, but manipulation was high on his list of talents. Eventually, Elisabeth moved on, found a man named Yul and finally knew how true love felt. And well before Christopher was born, she had another child. His name was Hedley. When Malan found out, despite not having heard from the woman in years, she went crazy. She murdered Hedley in cold blood. Elisabeth couldn't forgive her. Malan was hanged for her crime, and all those doubts your grandfather planted solidified."

Their conversation paused as a young spring female wandered up the steps, her hair a vibrant shade of red, and freckles covered her sweet face. Clara smiled genuinely as the tiny fae wrapped her arms around Clara's knees and looked up at her with nothing but excitement.

The girl's mother rushed up and apologised profusely, but Clara only waved away her concern. She told the young girl that princesses needed to stick together, and the little one's eyes lit up. Her smile beamed and warmed a small part of Clara's cold chest. The mother thanked Clara and bowed, then took her child back into the crowd.

Clara cleared her throat and gestured for Ryland to continue.

"We later learnt Malan had married. Her wife stormed the palace, burning everyone in her path to Yul. Including your grandfather, who burned while he slept and never saw her coming. She vowed to take Elisabeth's love, as Elisabeth had done hers. Yul was burned alive for hours while Elisabeth was made to watch, and from that point forward, Elisabeth gave no time to the community. In her mind, everything your grandfather said was true, and she couldn't look past it. She wasn't always that way—rather, she was made and manipulated. Trauma changes folk, and while I'm not condoning her prejudice, it would be a lie to say I do not understand why she snapped."

Clara couldn't find any words at first; her mouth hung open like a fish. She blinked several times, silent until she blurted, "Ryland, that is horrifying."

"Indeed, it is."

"Who is Christopher's father?" Clara asked softly, her eyes still tracking the small redheaded fae and her mother as they danced and twirled out of the palace gates.

"We do not know," Ryland said with a shrug. "Elisabeth slept with dozens of men to continue your lineage before she located you. Once she did, the attempts were called off. Two months after Elisabeth found out where you were, she realised she was pregnant. And now here we are."

"Now here we are," Clara repeated, in only a whisper. She thought of her own mother, her brothers, and how her life had changed because of them. Clara had been raised well and loved dearly, and she had no doubt Christopher would be well taken care of with Brontë, but . . . "I want him back."

"Beau?" Ryland asked gingerly, his face softened.

"Of course," Clara answered quickly. Not that she needed to stress that with Ryland. He knew the lengths she would go to if she could have Beau back. Ryland was the one, after all, who'd been there the first time Beau died. "With every fibre of my being. But I was referring to my nephew. I want him home with me."

"Are you ready to raise a child?" Ryland asked sceptically.

"No, but he deserves to be raised by family."

"Very well," Ryland said, nodding and turning back to the crowd. "I'll let Samara know you're ready."

"Was she keeping tabs on his whereabouts?"

Ryland smirked but said nothing more. Clara laughed then for the first time in what felt like a century. She knew it didn't really sound like her laugh, but it was lighter than she'd felt in weeks. Title aside, that was a reason to celebrate and be grateful.

CHAPTER FIFTY
CLARA EPILOGUE

Clara made her way down the pristine corridor swiftly, a bounce in her step and excitement running down her arms. One hand was wrapped tightly around a small, dainty pendant, while the other kept her skirts from becoming trapped beneath her feet.

Mildred would surely be ready by now, though certainly nervous. She'd been a confident enough child—fearing next to nothing, from small spaces and absurd heights, to running across banisters with swords, and facing ridiculously large social gatherings. Then she grew. Her wants and needs changed, along with her perception of the world around her. All of a sudden, Millie was frightened of her own reflection, let alone what others saw, or thought. She always worried they'd still see her as the boy she used to be, before she found herself. It was a fear that hung over her head, and one Clara could not shoulder for her.

Today would be huge. A step into the adult world, just slightly dipping her toes into a different society. Clara was so proud of how she'd grown and changed over the years. To finally see her step into the light and welcome the attention—oh, how her heart swelled. Elisabeth would be so proud, Clara was sure.

The pendant was a small token of the unfiltered, unconditional love Clara had for that beautiful woman. A gift of appreciation for having been allowed a front-row seat to her journey. A reminder of Clara's eternal respect and support, no matter where she went or what business she found herself in. No matter who she decided to be today, tomorrow, or ten years from now. She told Mildred every chance she got, so Clara wasn't sure she needed a reminder, but she got the sense the pendant belonged to Millie now.

Truthfully, it had never felt like Clara's, though she'd had it for almost two decades. She had stored it in her nightstand at her family home in Iloura, then in a jewellery box in the Winter Palace in Morrin. For the past few years, it'd been wrapped and safely hidden in the Golden Palace throne room. Clara wasn't sure why she kept it there, but no one disturbed it since no one knew it was there.

Crimson fractals bounced off the walls as light dove in through windows, and the pendant swayed in Clara's grasp. She knocked on Millie's door, polite but incessant until the youth swung it back with a sigh and nervous eyes.

"Already?" she asked, her green eyes—even brighter than Clara's—skittish as they searched Clara's face.

Clara nodded eagerly, her beaming smile spreading. "I have something for you first. A congratulatory gift, with a dozen other reasons for giving it to you."

"I didn't think gifts were necessary for New Moon festivals?" Millie asked, eyes now narrowed and a hand on her hip.

"No," Clara said, and gestured for Millie to turn. She swept her dark hair over her shoulder, exposing her fair skin and golden-marked back. "I didn't think you wanted to wear such a revealing dress?" she mentioned casually, then immediately continued, leaving no room for an answer. "It's beautiful, regardless. Now, no, technically there are no gifts at the festival, but this is a little different from most. I've brought it forward by a day to allow for your introduction to society as the Crown Princess of Elanist. I thought you deserved something nice on such a stressful day."

Clara hung the pendant over Millie's collar, clasping it and then spinning her so Clara could appreciate it properly. In a dark-blue dress, with Millie's near-black hair and porcelain skin, the touch of red shone. The simple necklace turned into a statement piece, and for a second Clara wondered whether she was perhaps only inviting more attention towards Millie than intended.

Oh well. As crown princess, she'd be getting more attention than she bargained for.

"I got that years ago," Clara said wistfully, thinking back to the night it was handed to her.

Keep it close. Pass it on when the time comes. You'll know what to do and when to do it.

"The love of my life gave it to me, though it was just a daemdrana scale back then. He told me I'd know what to do with it eventually, and then he left the next morning before I'd even woken. Stars, he was a prick." Clara smiled softly, remembering her Phoenix and everything she missed. "There isn't a day that goes by that I don't think of him."

"Then why are you giving this to me?" Millie asked, twirling the scale between her fingers.

"Because I know exactly what to do with it now. It's yours, my sweet girl. Revel in its beauty and commandeer its strength." Clara pulled her niece into a tight embrace and planted a kiss on the crown of her head.

Millie's arms flew around Clara instantly, gripping her tight. In all the years she'd raised Millie, her most fiercely followed rule was to never end a hug first. That was for the child to decide. Even now, despite Millie being a few months shy of twenty-two years, and old enough to attend her first New Moon festival—Clara would never pull away first.

So they stood in the doorway for a long time, as Mildred mentally prepared herself to step out into the world as the new crown princess, and while Clara emotionally prepared herself to watch. For Millie to leave the nest and learn to spread her wings.

When they finally split, Jude was standing across the hall waiting patiently. His smile lit up as he saw his wife and the woman they'd raised together.

"Are we ready, ladies?" he asked, offering both Millie and Clara an elbow. Millie smiled and blushed, as she always did when Jude was overly formal. He flourished his hands and dipped far too low into a bow, but it always made her smile. "Gods, the last seventeen years have flown," he mused as they walked, then sighed and shook his head.

Clara could hardly believe how long it had been since she'd taken Millie into her home. She certainly couldn't even begin to imagine what adventures awaited her. The daughter of an incredibly powerful fae and niece of a queen who somehow managed to connect three continents that split centuries before either of them were born. "You've grown beautifully, pet."

"Oh, you know how much I hate that nickname," Millie groaned out, but Clara and Jude only laughed. "Aunty Isobel!"

Mildred squealed as Isobel held out her hand at the door to the palace.

Not only had Clara brought the festival forward a day, but she'd also announced it would be held in Candor for the first time since the continents merged and the folk of Elanist learnt they indeed had a queen, and now a king and succession of the royal line. Isobel winked at Clara after raking her eyes slowly over the queen and pausing intently at her exposed cleavage.

Clara could only smirk as Jude slowed their pace and whispered, "We need to start reproducing. Having Mildred to raise has been wonderful, but now I want a child of my own. A niece cannot take my throne, I'm afraid."

"If you want to fuck me, king, you need only ask." Clara turned her smirk on Jude, who gave her a roguish grin in return. "We can start trying for an heir, if you'd like."

"I would," Jude said and nodded. He squeezed Clara's hand slightly, then let go of her altogether and bowed. "Shall I see you tonight, queen?"

Clara curtseyed back. "It's a date."

THE END

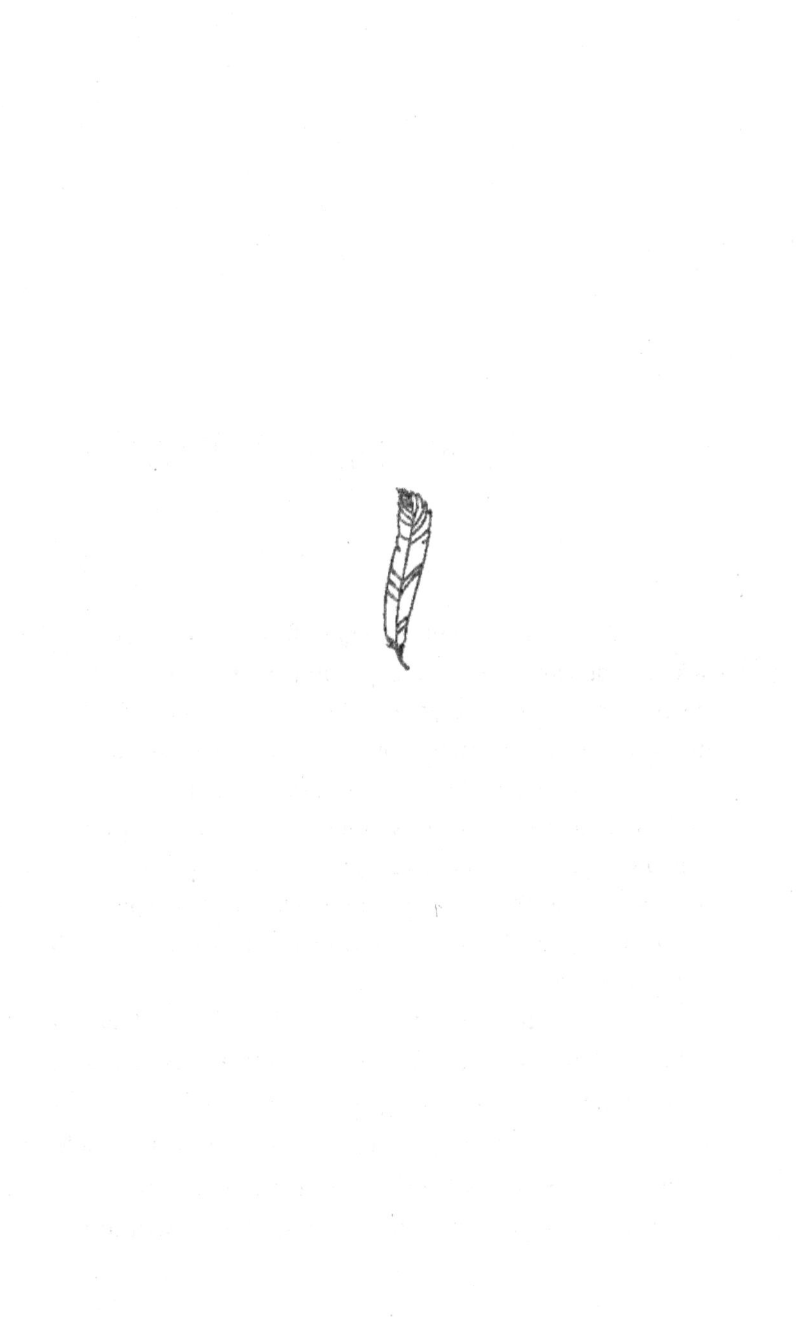

ACKNOWLEDGEMENTS

By this point, very few care about the acknowledgements and honestly, half the time I'm the same–but if you're here, at the end of my debut trilogy, thank you. I had so many big dreams and high hopes for this series, so many plans and thoughts and possibilities–only a handful of those have come to fruition, and instead I'm surrounded by a world of love and support larger than I could've imagined. I've found readers who love my characters as much as I do, who fall as deeply into the worlds I've created as I do, who read to immerse themselves and I am honoured.

To Cat & Kelly, my wonderfully patient and incredibly helpful editor from Cat Jay PA & Author Services, and exceptionally thorough proofreader, at Messenger's Memos - Fiction Editing Service. I started writing at a level I thought was pretty decent, and its gone through quite a few stages to get to this final product, which would not be possible without your fine tooth combing and supportive, constructive criticism. You've turned my writing into something I can only be proud of, something greater than I thought I could create.

My betas, my street team and arc readers, to my incredible community who keep coming back for more of the torture I put out and love it just as much as I do. The community I've found, collected, curated, its absolutely magical and I couldn't imagine a better bookish family. With a special mention to Bree and Devon, who are forever hyping me up and helping me in ways you probably don't even realise. And an even more special mention to Anne, for without whom I'd be a permanent resident on struggle street, not knowing my way up from down, my beautiful PA and friend. I don't know where I'd be without your help and constant, unwavering support. My appreciation for you and everything you've done and continue to do for me is endless, thank you doesn't quite cover it.

To every bookstore that stocks my books, every social media page that mentioned me at all, any individual who helped at some point to get me to where I am today–sharing my love of words and heartbreak with you all–thank you. With a special mention to Faith at Woodland Collection, my local bookstore and the first to stock my books. It's been an honour and a privilege– and one I am very excited to continue into the future.

My husband, who encouraged every second of my hard work and incomprehensible ramblings. Who stayed up later than he should have to help me work through plot holes he never understood, who answered very specific questions with zero context. Who has supported me endlessly and has made writing loveable, kind hearted, gentle souled males effortless. No one is perfect, and you aren't going to find a perfect character in my books, but they are *good*.

To you, who's made it through the end of this heart wrenching book. I cried while I wrote it, so if you cried while you read it, we sob in solidarity. Thank you for taking a chance on little ol' me, and sticking around to the end of my debut trilogy.

I can't believe Clara's journey is over–at least for now… It's been an incredible journey so far and I hope you've enjoyed the ride–at least a little–and will join me for whatever comes next. Maybe it'll be something cosy–a palette cleanser, if you will. Maybe not…

Stay tuned my loves, and as always, happy reading xo